Gluttony

Love is Cure, Vol. 1 - Vices & Virtues Series

Book Five

Brookelyn Mosley

85 MEDIA

Gluttony
Love is Cure Series, Vol. 1 - Vices & Virtues Series
Book Five
© 2023 Brookelyn Mosley. All rights reserved.

This is a work of fiction. Names, characters, places, and incidents are either the product of the author's imagination or used fictitiously. Any resemblance to actual persons, living or dead, or actual events is purely coincidental.

ISBN (eBook): 978-1-965507-02-5

ISBN (Paperback): 978-1-965507-11-7

First Edition: January 2023

Cover Design by Brookelyn Mosley

Published by 85 Media LLC

BrookelynMosley.com

Printed in the United States of America

MORE BY BROOKELYN MOSLEY

Novels/Novellas/Novelettes/Series

No Fraternizing, Pt. 1
No Fraternizing, Pt 2
No Fraternizing, Pt. 3
First Came Love: The Love, Hate & Revenge Prequel
Love, Hate & Revenge, Pt. 1
Love, Hate & Revenge, Pt. 2
Love, Hate, & Revenge, Pt. 3
Girl Code
Mr. & Mrs. Jones
Forbidden: An Anthology
They Call Me Mello
A Love Deferred
Indecent Arrangement
Last Comes Love
Ebb & Flow
PRIDE
Meant To Be
LUST

Loveless
GREED
Rekindled
My First, My Last
ENVY
Ready or Not
So This is Love
Home Before Midnight

Short Stories

Just Friends
Chateau Luxure
Lena's Ex-File
Dream Boss
Unsilent Knight
Twice In Love
Home For Christmas

Message From The Author

Thank you for your purchase of *Gluttony*. *Gluttony* is book 5 in the *Love is Cure, Vol. 1 – Vices & Virtues series*. This series consists of seven books. Although *Gluttony* is a part of a series, *Gluttony* is a standalone, like the other stories in the series. This means you can read it first if *Gluttony* is the first book that's introducing you to the series. You have permission to dive in :-).

Trigger Warnings: While this story is an easy read, there is a flashback scene that details adolescent death. The scene is brief, but it is of a sensitive nature. *Gluttony* also has instances of binge eating in earlier chapters of the book.

Gluttony contains profanity and sexually explicit content. If you are not a fan of foul language appearing in dialogue or sex being described in explicit details in books, *Gluttony* may not be the reading experience for you. *Gluttony* is, however, a book best enjoyed with an open mind.

That's it, that's all!

Enjoy and thank you again for choosing *Gluttony* as your latest read.

Love,

Brookelyn.

Acknowledgments

A loving thank you to my amazing husband who is without a doubt one of my biggest supporters. Your support is worth its weight in gold. A huge thank you to my beta readers, beta editors, and my ARC reader community. Y'all saw this book at its rawest, filled with all its flaws. Whew! I cringe at the pre-published writings lol but I thank you so much for seeing through it all.

A special thank you to my reading family and early supporters of my work. I'm sure you've noticed the changes; you've even commented on it. I thank you for sticking beside me and growing with me. You all have embraced my brand of writing and I'm beyond appreciative of it. Shout out to the readers who have reached out to me to share your thoughts regarding my books. I thank you for keeping me motivated and excited to create new projects for you. When I write, I keep you in mind. Thank you for your support. It's my soul food.

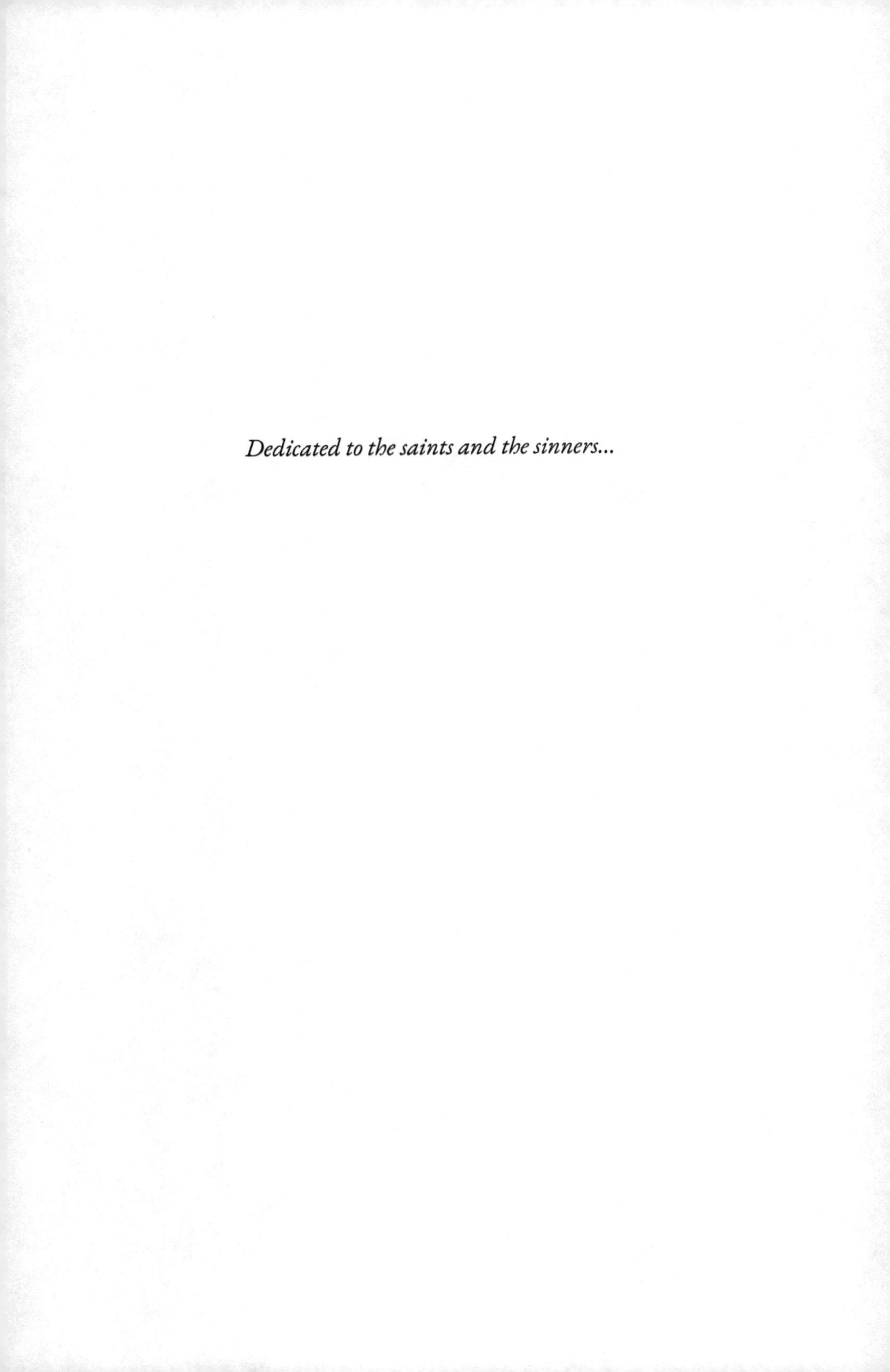

Dedicated to the saints and the sinners...

ONE

Never in my 38-years of living have I ever thought to gouge my eyes out of their sockets with my bare hands... until today.

Her moans echoed out of the mounted flatscreen speakers and bounced off the ceiling and walls. And each time she cried out in pleasure, those walls seemed to close in on me.

I hadn't blinked since pressing play on the DVD player. Hadn't moved an inch either. All I could do was swallow courage to keep watching, which was worthless because why the *hell* was I still watching?

"Harder. Yes," she shouted on the screen. "Just like that. Just like that!"

That screen was like a mirror to me.

The scene was identical to where I sat.

Same bed, same sheets. Same hand-painted boudoir portrait of her nailed to the wall over the bed, a thumb's height from the headboard that was banging on the wall behind it on screen. The only thing that wasn't identical on the screen was my presence.

"Fuck!" she hollered, closing her eyes and holding them tight as she braced herself.

Her body shook and convulsed uncontrollably next.

I held the breath I inhaled, my jaw slowly hinging opened. Because I knew that reaction. I knew that face. I know this woman. Or at least I thought I knew her.

Brielle Chadwick.

My girlfriend.

The love of my life... or who I thought was the love of my life? Because if she were *the love of my life*, should I be watching a video of her being double penetrated by two men.... not one of them me?

Brielle's moans in chorus with their groans made me sick to my stomach. But it couldn't compete with how loud their skins slapping against hers were or the wet macaroni noises her body made as she took a pounding like I've never seen before.

Her warm beige skin reddened from the contact it made with theirs. And soon her eyes were rolling like she was in a trance.

My heart felt like it would explode in my chest.

I was so wrapped up in what I was watching, I didn't hear when Brielle returned home.

She approached the threshold of her bedroom door in real time, but I didn't see that either.

I heard her though.

It was hard to miss the frantic gasp she expelled when she found me seated at the foot of her bed with my eyes glued to the mounted flatscreen, watching her get fucked by two strangers. Well, two strangers *to me*. The way they worked her over, though, she was very familiar with them.

Brielle looked at me, then up at the screen. She'd arrived at her door right on time to watch herself climax from the relentless drilling she endured from both men... at the same time.

They looked nothing like me. Not one of them even resembled me slightly. They both looked identical, though. Narrowed waists, model height and physique. As if they'd walked right off a billboard advertising a men's clothing sale for Bloomingdale's.

"Everett!" she shrilled. "What the hell are you doing?"

Somehow, I feel that should've been my line.

But I said nothing in return. My tongue felt too heavy and stuck to the roof of my mouth. My head was light, likely because of lack of oxygen. I felt like I'd been holding my breath for as long as it took for the woman who I was ready to make my wife, to climax with the most violent orgasm I'd ever seen her have and with a man, excuse me, *men...* who were *not* me.

I clutched the ring box I held in my tatted hand and pointed at the screen with the other.

She took enormous steps toward the flatscreen, kicking up the trail of red rose petals I'd sprinkled on her floor minutes prior.

With my sense of reality fading in, I could hear Major.'s "Why I Love You" playing from my phone that I'd hooked up to her Bluetooth speakers. I set the song up to play on repeat as I decorated Brielle's co-op with the purpose of asking her, my girlfriend of officially five years, to marry me on Valentine's Day... and our fifth-year anniversary.

The flatscreen went black, and she turned to look at me with tears in her eyes.

I'd been planning this for weeks. Even got my sister, Eryn, to help, even though she fussed the entire time. Eryn hated Brielle, always has. And I would always take Brielle's side, insisting Eryn had no reason not to like my girlfriend.

I won't hear the end of it when Eryn finds out what Brielle did.

"Everett," Brielle whispered. She glanced to her left and out her room door, focus returning to the rose petals again.

There was no doubt she'd seen the small dinner table, too. The one with the two chairs positioned opposite each other with the empty white plates that would've held our anniversary dinner for two. She definitely couldn't have missed the cinema light box that read *"Brielle. Will you marry me?"* that sat on that small table between those plates, prematurely lit up. She probably giddily followed the trail of red rose petals to her bedroom, as I'd planned. That was the only reason I was in her room to begin with. To hide her ring. I was doing a trial run of everything before she arrived home. The words on the light box, the spot where I'd hide her ring. I was supposed to hide the ring and return to the living room in time for her arrival. The ring was a ring I had her pick out without her even knowing. A trip to the Diamond District in New York, I insisted, was only a coincidence when we visited just so I could get her to pick out her dream ring and try it on. I promised it was just for fun.

I planned to hide the ring in a place that was significant – in the pair of red velvet stilettos she wore the night we met for the first time. The plan was to hide the ring box inside the shoes in her closet and, while we ate, casually ask her to slip on the heels, for nostalgia's sake, since it was our anniversary. She was to reach for the shoes, see the ring box, walk the ring box back to the table in shock, only to find me down on one knee waiting for her to return. The light box would have been lit with my proposal for her to see. It would've been the perfect anniversary proposal on Valentine's Day.

But then I found the box of DVDs labeled with dates that went as far back as four years ago, along with labels as recent as last month. So my curious ass singled out a random disc from the box, slid that disc into her flatscreen's built-in DVD player to find the woman I had intentions of making my wife, being double penetrated by two men... both fucking her at the same time.

I wanted to make tonight a night to remember.

And now it would be.

"Bri...?" I started, my voice unrecognizable to me. "What did I just watch?

She stood before me, motionless. Only her chest moved as she inhaled and exhaled with visible tension.

"Well, that's a dumb question, right?" I scoffed while scratching the roundest part of my nose. "Because *I know* what I watched. My girlfriend having sex with two men."

I squeezed the box in my hand, feeling the edges of it press into my palm.

"Everett, I... I can explain."

"Great." I widened my legs in my seat at the foot of her bed. "Because I would *really* love that right now, Bri. Along with a teleportation device so I could teleport the fuck up out of this moment."

"Okay, okay." Brielle released a shaky breath. "This will sound crazy—"

"Oh, I'm sure." I took a breath to remain conscious. "But, please, let's hear it, anyway."

She pointed at her flatscreen. "I did all of that for you, for... for us."

I arched both brows. "Oh, word?" I pointed at the screen, too. "Because that looked like it was very much *only* for Brielle."

"I was practicing for you."

"Is *this* the crazy part?"

"Everett, you *love* sex, and you can't deny that. It's everything to you. And my father has always told me how valuable sex is to men like you."

"Men like me?"

"Successful black men. Men in the limelight. I didn't want you to get bored with me, so, I—"

"Let two men run a train on you?"

"I had a threesome," she corrected through her teeth.

"Uh-huh." I nodded. "*Right*. My fault." I ran my fingers down my low-trimmed beard. "How disrespectful of me to mislabel the fucked up shit you did. That you recorded yourself doing, in fact. My bad. *I'm* the one wrong here."

"Everett—"

I bayed a laugh, which made her stop speaking.

"Karma is something else, huh?"

Had to be. This had to be what this was.

I jumped up out of my seat on the bed, prepared to storm out when she flinched at my sudden move, stumbling back before regaining her footing.

I scoffed. "What the hell are you jumping back for?"

She pressed her hand to her chest.

"I'm not gonna do anything to you." I shrugged. "I've done nothing to you. Not for you to jump back like that. Not for you to have even done this wack shit." I jabbed the air with my finger, gesturing at the box of DVDs sitting on the floor near where I sat. "A whole fucking box, Bri? Are you fucking other dudes on all these DVDs in this box? While you were in a relationship with *me*? Is this for real right now?"

"They're not all threesomes," she admitted slowly.

"Oh." I slapped my hand to my chest and exhaled exaggeratively, feigning reassurance. "Thankfully, they're *not* all threesomes. *That's* a relief."

She stuttered an inhale.

"Shit." I ran my hand down my mouth slowly. "I can't believe this is happening right now."

"Everett—"

"Damn Brielle." I stood there, genuinely stunned. With no proper words to say, without an idea to hold on to, to make sense of what was happening. This was not what I had planned. "I loved you."

"Baby." She sniffled. "I love you too—"

"I have never lied to you."

I lied to other women, though.

"Never cheated."

I cheated on other women. Many times.

"I saw a future with you."

And I never saw one with them.

That's why this hurt *so* much.

When Brielle and I met at a private nightclub in early January 2016 and clicked as soon as we met, I consciously told myself I wouldn't fuck this up. We hooked up that same night at my condo, but she turned out to be more than just another hook up for me when I found out she was the daughter of Julian Chadwick, billionaire founder of a media and sports conglomerate that owned The Sports Report - an international sports channel on basic cable. TSR is the biggest sports channel in the world and Brielle was the heir to it all.

She was sports media royalty. I had no choice but to step my game up. So, I suggested we make things official a month after our hookup, on Valentine's Day, and she agreed with conditions. We both had conditions. And I decided when we got together I wouldn't promise this woman the world only to turn it upside down by being disloyal. Promising high and delivering low like I used to with the others. Those days of being selfish were done. I was wild in my 20s, but my 30s was going to be when I would get my shit together. I had my fun. Plus, I'd gotten it out of my system. My finances were finally back in order, credit perfect. Lifestyle secured. My heart was the last frontier. I was ready.

And I did everything I could to make Brielle see that. I did everything to make her comfortable in our relationship.

"Yes," Brielle professed through her tears, disrupting my thoughts. "I'll marry you. Let's do it."

I folded my arms over my chest.

"I saw the setup outside." She pointed before lowering her eyes to her hardwood floor. "The rose petals. The dinner table. Your effort." Brielle approached me. Her nose was red and her eyes were red-rimmed and brimming with tears.

I lowered my view to meet hers so not to lose focus. Sincerely, I couldn't believe the same loving eyes looking back at me, that I fell in love with, the innocent smile she tried to give me as her peace offering. This petite love of my life who I would've sworn on my last breath would be the mother of my children.

I couldn't believe she, of all people, would do *this* to me.

"They meant nothing," she promised, pressing each of her hands to either side of my cheeks. "I didn't love any of them. You are who I love."

Oh. Shit.

She's pulling an Everett on me.

I've spoken this line to women, after doing the very thing Brielle was apologizing for doing... although I wasn't dumb enough to record it.

"I wanted to be perfect for you. To please you in every way. You love sex—"

"I *loved* you," I interjected. "I didn't care about how good or bad you were in bed. Shit was good between us. Why'd you do this?"

"Loved?" she questioned, her eyes telling me she already knew the answer to what she was questioning. "What do you mean by loved?"

"You were perfect, Bri, just as you were. To me, you were perfect. And if you wanted to be better, you should've told me. Having sex with other men? That was not the way. You had to know that shit."

"Okay, okay." She cleaned the tears from her face quickly. "The DVDs were a bad idea. It was stupid of me to make them. It was a little kink. Sex with models. I thought I could also use them as practice... for you... which I did. I swear to God, Everett, I'm done with all that now. Promise."

I stared without blinking. "So, *this* is the crazy part."

"They meant nothing."

"Yo," I exhaled into my fist, stepping back from her. "This is wild right now."

"Everett, just hear me out—"

"I've heard enough." I shook my head. "And to be honest, I think it's best I don't hear anymore. Let me leave here with a shred of dignity. Damn."

Brielle combed her fingers through her black curls.

"Well, shit." I shrugged. "At least you waited a year before you cheated. More patient than I ever was."

"Single until married, remember?"

I blinked hard in response.

"That's what we agreed on at the beginning: single until married. Do you remember that?"

When we started dating and she told me about the guys she'd been with and the cheating she'd had to endure with them all, I told her we could just hang out. I admitted to my many infidelities in my past relationships and that made her uncomfortable... made me uncomfortable just thinking about being faithful. But she liked me, and I liked her, so we agreed we were single until we were married to give ourselves wiggle room, just in case.

My idea.

But that was five years ago. Things change. Things actually changed.

I suggested that condition so we wouldn't feel the pressure of being in a relationship. She didn't want to have her heart broken, and I didn't want to break it either, so to avoid that, she needed a reason not to be all in and I needed a way not to feel under pressure although I was pretty sure I could do it this time—commit in my relationship. But she insisted on needing a lane to expect the worse.

So, I gave it.

Single until married, was that lane.

Me? In my heart of hearts, I knew I was done with lying and cheating, but I wanted her to be comfortable, so we agreed we were single until we were married.

I didn't keep my word.

For me, she was the one. I knew by our second date she'd be my wife. And every move, every decision, until when I retired from professional boxing, had been in anticipation of making Brielle what I've always wanted her to be since our second date. My wife.

So while I told her we were single until we were married, I never acted like that with her. And I didn't think we had to announce that single until married was off the table the moment we exchanged 'I love you.' In my head, she was already Mrs. Peters. I just needed to ask at the right time. And since I'd retired from professional boxing the month prior, now was the time.

Until I found the box of DVDs.

I shook my head as I made my way to the bedroom door.

"Everett, please don't go," she cried behind me.

I ignored her, taking gigantic steps toward her co-op's door. Major.'s voice filled my listening space, taunting me with the reasons he loved the love of his life. It seemed like a great idea to have the song play on repeat. Now I wanted to rip the lyrics from my ears.

"Everett, please," she begged, as I snatched my phone and disconnected my device from her Bluetooth speakers.

The rubber bottoms of my Nikes crushed the petals as I turned and followed the red trail to the front door.

"Whatever you want me to do, I'll do it."

Brielle once told me she wanted to be my everything, and I thought that was sweet. Never did I imagine she'd be my pain, too.

"You'll do anything?" I asked, turning to face her.

"Anything you want." She nodded, her head movement forcing the tears brimming from her eyes to slide down her cheeks.

"Good." I nodded too. "Then don't call me after I leave here tonight. You hear me? Do *that* for me."

I was out her door before she could agree.

Two

EVERETT

It was four days after what should've been the day I proposed, and I was still waking up from sleep thinking about Brielle.

The foam bottoms of my slides squished against the dewy titles as the insides of the slippers slapped against my heels. Day hadn't broken yet, so it was still dark outside. I've done well with sticking with daily routine after my last fight a month prior. Up at 5am working out an hour later. Since retirement, I'd attempted to stay active. Hence my morning starts.

The hollowness of the space gave life to the body of water housed inside it. I could hear the pool's presence in the dimly lit room.

The pool was inside my high rise, a few floors down from my condo. My private elevator brought me straight to it. The amenity was one of the selling points for me making a home here.

I dropped my towel on the plastic table and left my gym bag there, too. Quickly pulled at the hem of my white tee and stepped out of my gray joggers next. My goggles were in my grip before I left all my belongings on the table and turned to the pool.

Brielle honored her word. She hadn't called.

Her father did, though.

"Everett," Julian Chadwick, who I always referred to as Mr. Chadwick, said into the phone the day after I walked out of Brielle's co-op. "How are you?"

It shocked me to see his name flash on my phone's screen. I'd saved his number under his name after she invited me over to his estate for dinner a month after she and I made things official. He'd pulled me to the side, gave me his phone number, telling me to call him anytime. In the five years Brielle and I have been together, I never did. So his call was a surprise.

"Mr. Chadwick?" I sat up from my recline on the lounge chair out on my balcony.

"I'm sure it's odd to see me calling you, and I apologize for the surprise, but I wanted to reach out. Brielle told me what happened."

I jerked my head back. "Sir?"

"She also told me your plans to propose." He sighed into the phone. "That child of mine can be a handful. I did my best with her, but there's so much you can pour into your children before their own free will gets the best of them. Something you'll learn when you're a father yourself, I'm sure."

I wrinkled my brows.

"Brielle's happiness is paramount to me. She loves you, Everett."

"Sir, I don't know if this is something I want to discuss with you."

"I completely understand. It's just that she's getting up there in age and she's been so excited at the prospect of settling down with you, you know, before everything happened between you two the other night. Which is why I'm calling you."

"Okay...?"

"I was waiting to offer this to you over the summer once our host's contract was up, but since you've got plans to join the family—"

"Mr. Chadwick," I interjected. "With all due respect, all that changed when—"

"I want you to host Neutral Corner."

I took a breath and held it for a moment.

Neutral Corner was the biggest boxing commentary show in the country, the planet, if you let boxing enthusiasts tell it. In every sports market, the award-winning show was the leader. The host, Kyle Leigh, was a household name because of Neutral Corner. It was the CNN for boxing.

"$200,000 an episode to start," Mr. Chadwick offered. "With an option to renegotiate your contract and request a salary increase in one year."

"Shit," I whispered, impressed.

"Take as much time as you need to let me know if you're interested... and to give Brielle a call so you two can work this thing out."

It was a wild phone call to receive and sit through. Though my financial situation was stable, I was retired. Those big fight checks would not be rolling in every year anymore. I had to find something stable, and a cushy hosting job with consistent pay on a major cable network would offer the security to help me sleep like a baby at night. And the two hundred thousand dollar per episode offer would make life really sweet.

For the past few days, I grappled with the idea and the situation with Brielle. Finding those DVDs was still fresh in my memory, so in that instance, getting back with her, considering getting married to her, seemed impossible after what she did, although I've always wanted to be forgiven for my indiscretions.

Maybe that's what's got me conflicted. Feeling this emptiness of her not being around but also this disdain for what she's done.

When I arrived at the pool's ledge, I gripped the goggles mounted over my forehead and lowered them over my eyes. I walked to the edge of the pool, leaned forward, and dove in face first.

The water greeted me and parted for me to enter. It covered me completely and silenced all the inner chatter and the unwanted mental replays of days passed.

It was just me and the water... just how I liked it.

Its presence is cool, calm, and still, even when I've interrupted its stillness. Unyielding but forever flexible. It holds me down, but still makes me feel weightless and unrestricted. The one element on this earth I feel has the power to ground me.

The love I have for water wasn't something I was born with. I didn't even like it at first. I feared it. My chest would ache at the thought of touching it. The love I developed for swimming was like an acquired taste. In fact, life imposed my love for it on me.

I closed my eyes behind my goggles and sunk lower into its depths, only stopping when my feet touched the pool's floor.

"Hey, Everett, wanna do something fun?"

It was the summer of 1992. My father had missed the deadline to pay for camp that year, despite my mother constantly reminding him to do so months before. So my summer was free with nothing to do. My father was traveling for business that day and my mother had a full book of clients, so my parents hired help who hadn't helped at all. Heather Moore. The most popular girl in her high school and in the neighborhood. So popular she spent every moment of her babysitting gig watching my baby sister and me, while running her mouth on our phone, running up our bill. While my baby sister could spend her entire day dressing and undressing her Barbie dolls, my mind, at 10-years-old, was far too active for single play.

"Sure," I replied to Chase, using my hand as a visor to shield my eyes from the sun. "Fun like what?"

Chase was my friend from elementary school. We'd known each other since kindergarten. We sat next to each other in fourth grade. He was the adventurous type. Very energetic. I often found it impossible to keep up, but I never shied away from trying to. But above all, Chase was fearless. He was his namesake, constantly chasing a good time.

"I'll show you." He grinned. "Come on."

Looking back at things, he wasn't a focused child. He'd hop from one activity to the next without spending more than a few minutes on each task.

For instance, that day, he'd stopped by to visit our brownstone after his mother left for work. He lived on the first floor in the apartment building two blocks down from me. When he arrived that afternoon to hang out at my brownstone, we went from playing video games, to playing Uno, to pushing our socked feet into sneakers to shoot my basketball outside, and eventually to this new fun mysterious thing he had planned for us to do.

He'd only been at the brownstone for all of one hour.

Kids packed the block. Girls jumped Double Dutch on the sidewalk or played hopscotch while the boys rode their bikes or shot their basketballs through bottomless crates wired to rusted fences.

It wasn't unusual for kids to be left on their own in Bed-Stuy in the 90s. During the summer, if there was no place to ship us off to during summer break, outside is where we spent the time if we weren't inside in front of the TV. The neighbors all shared the takes-a-village mindset, so it was usually all good, making it safe enough for most. The adults who didn't work 9-5s, mostly elderly, would sit out on their stoops, people-watching, and would monitor us kids.

"It's this way," Chase promised, pulling my hand to follow him.

Classic reggae played from a passing car's speakers as we pounded the pavement, running toward a place I knew would be worth the trek. Chase knew all the cool spots and how to get there.

"Look." He pointed ahead. "Over there."

I squinted through the sunshine and honed my focus forward. Over the slides and past the monkey bars was the pool. Brand new. The pool had been the center of conversation in the neighborhood since the winter prior when construction of the space started.

It was late July and although there was water in the pool now; the space had yet to open. Through conversations overheard between the elders in the neighborhood, we learned community organizers couldn't afford to pay a lifeguard to work during park hours.

So, the pool served as a seasonal tease. Neighborhood kids would walk past the gated pool, staring in wonderment, wanting so badly to cool off in it instead of settling for the park's sprinklers.

The gate was normally closed with combination padlocks to keep people out.

I heard the rattling of Chase climbing the side of the short metal link gate closest to us before I saw him in action. If I'd seen him first, I probably would've had time to talk him out of what he planned to do.

"What are you doing?" I asked, reaching for one of his legs.

The kid was fast and strong though, and remember, fearless.

He kicked his leg free of my hold and climbed the short gate to the top, straddling, then climbing down on the other side. I peeked behind me, hoping someone would see us and stop him, because deep down I knew this was wrong. It felt wrong. But my 10-year-old mind figured it was uncool to voice that.

Surrounded by paved concrete, the pool's water reflected blue from my view.

"Do you even know how to swim?"

I knew the answer to that. No one in the neighborhood knew how to, at least to my knowledge. When the job listing for a local lifeguard got pinned to every pole at every crosswalk within walking distance of the pool, all the older teenagers were interested because of the pay, but no one applied because no one knew how to swim. At least not well enough to lifeguard. And because of the neighborhood, very few people from other areas of Brooklyn cared to spend a single moment of their summer there.

He jumped down off the gate. His landing on his feet made a light thud on the concrete.

Chase shrugged. "How hard could it be?"

He stood on the other side of the gate.

I gripped the metal link gate, biting at my bottom lip. "I don't know about this, Chase. The water might be cold."

He tittered cockily as he closed the distance between himself and the pool. "Oh, come on!" Chase squatted in front of the still water and leaned in while throwing a glance at me over his shoulder. "How would the water be cold in the sum—"

It happened so fast.

Chase losing his balance in his squat and falling into the water face first. Splashing about while garbling through the water as his head and body bobbed in and out at the top.

My heart sank.

"Chase!"

His voice carried around us. He frantically tried to grab at the water for stability but could find nothing firm enough to hold on to.

I was too scared to climb the fence. Too scared to jump in the pool even if I made it over. So, I took off in search of help.

I screamed for help, hoping someone would hear us and some did, but by the time we made it back, Chase was as still as the water.

I pushed myself up through resistance; the water parted for me effortlessly. I inhaled the surrounding air, chest heaving in as much of the oxygen in the room that my lungs could take.

The summer my friend Chase drowned became a turning point for me. I never really recovered from his death. It stuck with me into adulthood. His name was one of my first tattoos. I got his name tatted on my forearm when I was eighteen, right beside my tattoo of Bed-Stuy, as a remembrance. That little thing helped me cope a little better with the loss.

The same year I lost Chase, my parents went from separated to divorced. I started the fifth grade without my best friend, and I developed a short fuse and an explosive temper.

My mother signed me up for swimming lessons to help with my budding phobia of water and my father signed me up for boxing classes when the school threatened expulsion after I'd gotten into my sixth fight only two months after school started. And that's when my love of swimming and boxing began. Birthed from tragedy. Two loves I've felt guilt for loving because of how it came to be.

———

"Uh, yeah," I shouted into the drive-thru speaker. "Let me get a triple cheese two patty burger with Baja sauce, extra large fries, an extra large cola, and spicy cheese dipping sauce."

Day had broken, and it was two hours before noon.

"Will that be all?" The voice boomed from the same speaker.

I moved my eyes up to my Range Rover's roof, thinking.

"Nah. Let me get an order of hush puppies, too."

A line of cars was forming behind me.

"Will *that* be all?"

I nodded. "Yeah."

"Please drive up to the second window for your food."

"Thanks," I replied, shifting my gear from park to drive to do as told.

The California sun was high and bright now, lighting up the area and giving it the shine the state was famous for.

Baja Burger was a new burger joint out here in Los Angeles, but it fit right into my routine.

This was my cheat day. The day I allowed myself to have whatever I wanted to eat. It was also the day I worked out the hardest at the gym. My trainer used to hate this about me and couldn't wait for me to book my next fight, so I'd start training camp. Because at training camp, I couldn't touch this shit.

Which was why I hated training camp.

Most boxers maintained very strict diets to match their strict workout regimens. To them, investing the time in the gym and undoing it by consuming junk seemed counterproductive. I believed in balance. My cheat day offered that. I was about to have the most fattening meal with the sloppiest ingredients and planned to burn it all off for three hours. My mouth was already watering.

I pulled up to the service window and lowered my window.

The second the drive-thru worker got a good look at who was behind the steering wheel, her face lit up.

"EP?"

I nodded my answer, handing her the exact cash for my food. "What's up?"

"Oh my God!" she squealed and smiled big, accepting the cash, confirming the total with a quick count. "My boyfriend is a huge fan. He recorded your last fight with Kevin Claymore and has been watching it on repeat. He's not gonna *believe* you pulled up today." She handed me my food. "You eat this?" She turned away from the window briefly to pick up the drink that was nearby. "You shouldn't be eating this."

I smiled as she handed the drink to me. "I shouldn't, so let's keep this our secret, aight?"

She giggled.

"Tell your man I said what's up and to watch the fight I had with Romeo Terrain on repeat instead. It was way better and lasted longer."

"Ha!" She nodded. "I will."

"You take care."

"You too!"

In a parking spot in the lot outside the burger joint, I dove in. Every so often, I dropped my head back against my seat's headrest as the burger landed on a tastebud that detected the flavor, helping the meal to hit the spot. Momentary heaven is what I liked to call it while eating high-calorie foods. Flavor rolling around my tongue with each bite I took.

Food has always been my escape. A mood lifter. I got excited at the thought of eating something good. Eating was an amplifier at every moment. I coped with it, celebrated with it, sometimes included it when making love.

Just the thought of making love reminded me of Brielle. And that thought of her brought me back to four days ago. My delight quickly turned to a slow build of rage.

I chewed harder.

As hard as I tried to forget what happened, to move past it, I couldn't get myself to do it.

Brielle cheated. This should feel like nothing. I loved her, true. But she was just a woman. There's plenty of them. Most of them I could have now. I should be over Brielle by now.

That's what I'd hoped.

Instead, I was eating my food with thoughts of her on my mind now. Mindlessly shoving fries in my mouth between bites of my burger. A meal that just minutes ago was hitting was now losing its taste.

I turned to food during many blows in my life. When I lost my friend Chase, after attending his funeral, when my parents got a divorce that same year only months after I started the fifth grade.

I'd turned to food so much my father kept me busy. Signing me up for boxing, despite my mother's disapproval, and forcing me to work out after every meal I binged... something my mother was so against, she filed for divorce when he refused to stop encouraging me to eat then work out right after. Their divorce was in the making before that, though. His insisting I eat then work out was just the feather that tipped my mother's scale.

His advice helped me practice balance, though. Like now. I was eating this food, but in an hour or two I planned to spend at least three hours at the gym burning it off without fail.

See, balance.

But when I arrived at the gym an hour later, I still had Brielle on my mind. So much so, I tapped over to her page on social media to find photos of her, new ones, living her life as usual. Out to brunch with her girls, a slideshow of photos of her new manicure she posted just for likes. There was even a video of her singing her favorite song off key with joy in her eyes.

All this only four days after I ended things.

Because she cheated.

The fuck?

This couldn't have been the same woman damn near slapping tears off her face, begging me not to end things so we could get married, as I planned.

It was a Monday afternoon, so people didn't crowd the gym like on the weekends. Things would change in an hour. The Hollywood strip types would be here shortly, so I had to make it quick. I was in no mood to shake hands, confirm I was who I was to excited fans, socialize or flash an all-white smile for any cameras. Not with my mind so caught up on Brielle not being caught up with me.

I adjusted the weight stack pin beneath the plates on the chest fly machine and positioned myself on the bench. Gripped the chest fly with each forearm and pushed, gritting my teeth as the pads closed in front of me.

My work on the machine activated all my muscles. And my anger. Images of Brielle sandwiched between those two guys, the sound of her headboard colliding with the wall behind it, echoing their *sexercise*.

My teeth were bared as I pushed harder. The weight plates, each time I released pressure, slammed against each other, sending a crashing sound around the gym.

I grunted and released and stood from my seat at the chest fly machine, pacing the floor in front of me. Balled my hand into a fist and slammed it into my open hand, feeling my knuckles against my inner palm. I took giant steps toward the treadmill and pressed a few buttons to turn it on. The belt was rolling before I got on it. I inhaled a deep breath and ran on, adapting to the speed and promptly finding my rhythm. The impact of my feet on the already rolling belt sent another wave of crashing sounds throughout the gym. I increased the speed more. My heart rate increased so much, my heart beat pulsed in my palms. I grunted with each foot that slammed on the belt beneath me. Yelled when the tension got too much. The tension in my legs swallowed the impact of my high-speed running. Tension was in my heart as the muscle tried to keep up with it all. The images of Brielle shutting her eyes tightly blinded me. Her limbs covered in rivulets from her own sweat. Her body shaking, the wave like pulsing her skin did whenever the taller guy slammed into her from behind and the other model guy pumped his hips up. I punched the air a few times, which quickly developed into my shadow boxing while running at high speed. I wished it were his face, any of those guys faces. What I wouldn't give to split their bottom lips or feel the bones in their nose crack against my knuckles.

I jumped off the treadmill, almost losing my balance and toppling over, but I regained my footing quickly.

Pacing again, my mind was in shambles. I couldn't decide where to put myself next. Rage coursed through my veins, amping up my desire to hit something. I *needed* to hit someone.

"Uh, Mr. EP... sir?"

"What?!" I approached with clenched fists. My face was so wet with sweat. Beads of it were dripping down my eyelids, gathering on my lashes, the salt in my sweat stinging my eyes.

The young man stumbled back but regained his balance. He was usually the guy who greeted me at the front counter whenever I entered. A fan. I've signed a shirt for him. He's congratulated me on at least three of the fights I've won when I returned to the gym, including my last bout in Vegas.

The blood drained from his face immediately. He was shaking like it was cold, but it was at least 80 degrees outside, making it 65 or 70 degrees in the gym thanks to central air.

"Umm..." He cleared his throat nervously while looking around.

I looked around too. All eyes were on me. Most of them looked away the moment my eyes slammed into theirs, but it was quite clear who the center of attention was during their time at the gym.

"Some... umm... members are concerned for their, uh... safety, because of your routine," he stuttered.

I glanced around the space again to see them diverting their eyes away once more.

"I mean, *I* get it," he offered.

I turned to focus on him again.

"All a part of the winning process, right? He smiled with trembling lips.

Wrong.

I never worked out like this. When I said I'd go hard in the gym on cheat days, I didn't mean like this. Heavy cardio and strength training, true. But this shit was excessive today. My trainer would be so disappointed. So would my physician. Putting all this wear and tear on my joints unnecessarily and at my age. I could hear them chastising me as I stood there looking like a meat head.

"But..." the kid continued, "do... do you think you can—"

"No problem," I growled.

My stomach growled too, but it didn't feel empty. I had enough from earlier. I ate everything I ordered from Baja Burger, including the extra hush puppies, too. I wasn't hungry. It was impossible to be. But somehow... I wanted more. Just the thought of having my favorite, a margherita pizza, was already lifting my mood and giving me something to look forward to after all that. The pizza was more appealing than being at the gym.

As innocent of a craving as it was, this should've been the first sign of destruction. But I ignored it.

"I'm about to bounce anyway," I told him. "I'm going to get something to eat."

THREE

APRYL

I've officially lost my appetite. At least, the little appetite I had.

The buzz of chatter around me was the only thing reminding me to keep things cute.

I was on a date. Possibly one from hell. And what's worse? It was the first date I'd been on in two years.

What a welcome back this was.

This is something I do not miss.

"I believe in a woman's independence," my date, Darryl, claimed as he chewed an item off his $50 surf and turf plate with his mouth opened. "I love what y'all single ladies have been on lately. It's right up my alley."

I had to inhale deeply to keep from rolling my eyes. Not only at what he said, but at how pompous and uncouth he'd been since I took my seat at the table.

It was a Friday night in New York City, which meant half the city was out and about. The ice chill outside was standard for February. The recent snowfall did nothing to keep everyone indoors. I was regretting my decision to be there that night. I'm one of the select few New Yorkers who prefer a Friday night in and alone with a bowl of popcorn and a movie I've watched at least twenty times streaming on my TV for the twenty-first time.

"I like you, Apryl." He cheesed like cameras were around. "You make your own money, very good money at that."

I cringed.

"You have your own house," he added. "A woman with her own won't ever want a thing from me. I love this for us."

Darryl Rockwell, the clown.

Every time I thought he couldn't say anything worse than what he said before, he proved me wrong.

According to our match on HeartMates, he and I were compatible.

And I could see why.

He checked all the boxes I had on my list. Didn't have any kids, didn't work a dead end 9-5, didn't have rotten teeth.

He was perfect... for someone else.

I should delete the app.

"So..." He forked another piece of grilled lobster tail into his already full mouth. "Tell me about your last relationship. How'd that end?"

The app is definitely getting deleted.

I gritted my teeth. "I'd rather not." I looked away as I lifted my glass of spring water to my lips to sip.

What am I even doing here?

Trying to get my feet wet in the dating pool again after wringing myself dry from a nasty breakup that had me crying myself to sleep for one entire year was what.

I focused my attention on my Cobb salad, pushing around the hard-boiled egg bits with the prongs of my fork.

My sister begged me to go on this date. It was my first in two years and, according to her; I needed to get out.

"Aren't you tired of working every hour of every day and not having time to go on dates?" she asked one afternoon in her kitchen when it was only us two. "Don't you miss the company of men?"

No.

No, I don't miss it.

Especially not going out on dates with the Darryl Rockwells of the world.

"Bad breakup, huh?" He mocked. "His loss. You are a catch."

I forced a smile.

My previous relationship lasted an entire eleven years. When we met and fell in love, I was sure I wouldn't be back here, on a date, playing nice with a man I would've never entertained on any other night. I pictured a life unlike this one with my ex. One where we were living out a black romance film even after the credits rolled. We made so many promises to each other and I ended up being the only one keeping them.

Now I was sitting in a business casual restaurant wanting to be anywhere but there because my date reminded me why I didn't want to end a relationship that had ended itself.

"Did he try to stifle your independence?" Darryl queried.

"No." One-word answers were the only thing keeping me from being rude.

"You should really taste this wine."

"Darryl." I took a breath to remain levelheaded. "I've told you several times already I don't drink."

Despite that, he insisted on ordering an entire bottle of Merlot. He was on his third glass and getting on my last nerve.

"Is that like an *Alcoholics Anonymous* thing?"

"It's a choice *thing*."

"I don't think I've ever met anyone who had the space and opportunity *to drink* casually but *chose* not to."

"I can say I've never met a person like you, either." I forced another smile. "There's always a first time for everything."

"Can I get you two anything else?"

A life vest, please.

Our leggy server honed her focus on me. She'd been very attentive through the night, addressing me more than Darryl, who was extremely dumb or completely oblivious to how disinterested I was in him.

I peeked down at my salad and my almost empty glass of spring water, then smiled up at her. "No, I think we're all good—"

"Actually." Darryl lifted a finger. "I think I'm going to test out your crème brûlée."

The server and I shared a glance.

"How is it, anyway?" He asked her. "Any good?"

I had to tighten my lips to keep my jaw from dropping. I watched this man devour a twelve-ounce filet mignon, a two-ounce lobster - claws and tail included - two ounces of shrimp, and a one ounce crab. He swallowed over half a bottle of red wine and still he had room for dessert.

How?!

The server was less discreet with her reaction. "You have *quite* the appetite."

"Oh, of course." He grinned and winked at me. "Especially when I'm being treated."

I narrowed my eyes at him.

"Oh... kay." She tucked a lock of her black bob behind her ear, then slid her notepad into her apron's pocket. "I will be right back with your dessert, sir." She looked at me. "And the check."

Did I miss something? Why did she look at me when she said that?

"Treated?" I questioned once we were alone at our table again.

"Well yeah." He shrugged. "I figured you got this."

I blinked hard. "Got *what*, exactly?"

"Our meal," he replied matter-of-factly. "The bill."

"And how'd you figure that?!" My voice climbed an octave.

"You're a celebrity fitness trainer," he stated, gesturing at me. "I Googled you and got hit with hundreds of web articles about you and the celebrities you've trained. I can't believe you trained Chloe Rae. She's *fione*."

I almost bit my tongue, clenching my jaw.

"Aside from that, you've modeled for Nike, endorsed brands like Gatorade and Vitamin Water. You're paid, paid."

"*I'm paid, paid*." I mocked. "Wow."

"That's why I left my wallet at home," he informed.

What the fuck did he just say?!

"Excuse me?"

"It's like I explained," he continued, leaning back in his seat to get more comfortable, I presume, "I fully support a woman's desire to be independent. Women want to be equal? Cool. I believe we, as a collective, should expect women to do everything a man is supposed to do, too."

I scoffed again.

"That's the reason I didn't bother planning this date and why I have no intention of covering the bill."

I inhaled the surrounding air, wanting to punch it.

"You ladies want to earn more? Do it. Be the breadwinner? I insist. I'll accept for my meal to be paid for. I can be a stay-at-home boyfriend and even a dad."

"So, a kept man?"

"Yeah." Darryl adjusted his black leather belt around his waist. "That sounds like a glorious life."

"Oh, my God," I whispered, pinching the bridge of my nose.

Throw the whole man away.

The buzz of chatter in the restaurant grew in volume as silence settled between us. On an exhale, I felt like saying something I'd regret. So, I did the next best thing.

"I'm going to run to the bathroom." I pushed my chair back. "I'll be *right* back."

"And I'll be *right* here." He smiled.

The moment I stood to my feet and turned away from him at the table, my fake smile was no more. I scanned the room quickly, searching for the leggy server. I spotted her standing a few feet away near a dip in the wall in one corner of the room.

"Hey, excuse me," I called when I neared her.

She peeked up from pecking at the computer touchscreen with her finger long enough to see me headed her way. "I was just about to make my way over to you with the check."

"Let me save you the trip." I wedged my clutch between my arm and rib. "We're going to need to alter this bill a little."

Her threaded brows wrinkled.

"See that brother you've seen me with all night? He's lost his damn mind and I'm gonna help him find it."

She snorted.

"He thinks I'm going to cover his expensive ass meal, but he's about to have humble pie with his crème brûlée. Here's what's gonna happen."

"Oh, I'm listening."

I giggled while peeling apart my clutch to retrieve my platinum Amex. "I'm going to cover the cost of my salad, my spring water, and your tip. Then you're going to send him the bill for his meal with his crème brûlée, of course, and he's gonna cover that himself because I've had more than enough of his shit and I'm leaving."

———

My heels were the first things to go, the second I got on the other side of my townhouse's door.

With each room I entered, I flipped the light switch, gradually illuminating the space. The tension throughout my body was clear. I could feel it on my shoulders, my back, and my neck. Keeping a lot of things in usually did that to me. I was mindful of my words most times the same way I was with what I consumed and tension was the result. The only way I knew how to relieve the tension was by doing what I always did.

Work up a sweat.

I rolled my head around my neck and closed in on the staircase to head straight to my bedroom upstairs.

I saved up for this townhouse and bought it cash for my 32nd birthday. My sister begged me to reconsider. She dubbed it bad luck for a single woman to buy a house. To her, it was too permanent of a decision to make and intimidating to men. What she failed to clarify was it was intimidating to little dicks because the men who had them were the ones who had a problem with single women owning homes. Besides, I've dreamt of owning a townhouse in the city since the day I walked into one to train a client.

I pulled out my phone from my clutch purse I still held and tapped into my music app, cuing up a playlist to listen to.

My client's townhouse was immaculate. Views of the city from her living room window. A water view from her backyard that faced the East River. Her home was stunning and set the bar for what I should strive for when I saw it at 25-years-old. I worked hard, made real-life sacrifices so I could get here.

And at 34, I was damn happy to have arrived.

I strolled over to my chest drawer, placing my phone on the dresser's surface along the way. After opening the drawer by its crystal pull, I snatched up a pair of pink biker shorts and an orange sports bra without even considering if they matched. I wasn't posing for any ads tonight. Recording any workout videos to post online. This was only for me.

Exercising was my self-care.

My love of it started out of frustration. I never imagined I'd make a living off it beyond going to the gym. I got paid for being fit. Modeling workout outfits, promoting sports foods and nutrition. But my genuine love, my career which was also my passion, was personal training.

My phone on my dresser vibrated with a call. I stole a glance at my wall clock, then closed the distance between me and the device. One quick look at the incoming call flashing on my screen made me close my eyes and tilt my head back.

I already knew why she was calling.

"Stas, what are you still doing up? It's late."

My sister, Anastasia, kissed her teeth. "Apryl, it's 10pm not 2am."

"Hmph." I slid into my biker shorts, adjusting the waist band once it was on. "I thought new mommies were supposed to sleep when the baby sleeps."

"Who's the new mommy?" She questioned. "Because I already did this six years ago, and the evidence is asleep in her room."

"I'm referring to the adorable two-month-old I can't get enough of."

"Oh that one?" She sucked her teeth. "He never sleeps."

I snickered.

"Besides, I couldn't sleep until I got all the details on how your date went."

"Horribly," I confirmed. "The date was the caricature of all dates."

"No," she whined. "What happened?"

"What didn't?" I shook my head as if she could see me. "The manipulative twit swindled the idea of a woman's independence to the tune of leaving his wallet at home, so he didn't have to pay for his *fucking* meal."

"Shut the fuck up."

I removed my clip-ins and gathered my hair up into a high ponytail, twirling my relaxed strands around each other until they formed a bun. "He aspired to be a stay-at-home *dad*, Stas."

"Really?!" Her voice climbed an octave. "That's surprising. He sounded like the perfect find."

"Maybe for someone else." I rolled my eyes, making my way to the stairs. "Hopefully they were there to help him pay for his meal because I had the server split the bill behind his back, then I bounced."

"Well, look, don't let that discourage you," she started. "This is your first date after being out of the game for eleven years and getting over the breakup of it. Give yourself grace."

Just the mention of that relationship again rubbed me wrong. The greatest heartbreak I'd ever experienced still sent a pang to my gut.

I hated that for myself.

My ex probably didn't think of me anymore, especially after what he did. Meanwhile, I'm still triggered by only the mention of what we had.

I hated that for myself, too.

I heard my nephew, Raphael, stirring and fussing on the other end of my phone as I jogged down my stairs headed to the basement. "Raphael doesn't like his mama up so late, interrupting his sleep."

"Didn't I tell you this child doesn't sleep?"

I laughed.

"And Raphael could get the best sleep in the expensive crib his father built instead of being all up under my arm in *our* bed."

I arrived in front of the door to my basement and pulled it opened. "You know your arms are the best, Stas. Your baby sister knew that first."

"*Mm-hmm.*"

I could smell my equipment before seeing them as I made my way down. A strange thing to say, but I could. Its scent was one of those things I loved so much, but I couldn't explain why. It was just my thing; I guess.

"I'll talk to you later." I turned on the light in the basement.

The illumination from the overhead ceiling lights fell on my treadmill, stationary bike, weight stand, and stair master. My eyes homed in on the treadmill.

"I'm about to work out," I told her, eyes unwavering.

"At 10 at night?" she challenged. "I would think you'd be getting ready for sleep."

"I'm holding tension in my back. I need to work out."

"You're the only person I know who considers exhausting themselves by exercising to be a way to relax."

"Love you and goodnight Stas," I said. "I'll call you in the morning."

I placed my phone on *Do Not Disturb* and left the device on the couch I kept down there.

Lifted my legs one at a time and held my heels against my glutes to stretch my hamstrings. Did the same with my arms, pulling my arms over each shoulder.

I had no interest in stretching for too long tonight. I needed to jump right in.

And I did.

I walked up the band of my treadmill, gliding my hands along the railing before powering it on. I warmed up with a short power walk before increasing the speed and selecting an incline. The belt rolled as the treadmill's running deck elevated, causing me to work harder. I felt the burn in my calves first and blushed at my body's way of challenging me.

My heart rate increased, and sweat gathered at my temples. I consciously took control of my breathing, inhaling, and exhaling with the beat of my feet slamming against the treadmill's belt as I ran. Music played around me with high-powered motivating lyrics to keep me going.

I was in my happy place - in control of everything. I decided if I kept going or if I wanted to stop. If I wanted to go harder or take it slow. I was in control. That was my security. I couldn't imagine at this stage in my life a man providing anything close to this.

And regardless of all I had and everything I still planned to get, the thought of never being able to duplicate this satisfaction in human masculine form after having my heart ripped to pieces scared me.

Four

"How many?"

I turned my ear in the hostess's direction. "What?"

"How many are in your party?"

Her Chinese accent made it hard to make out her words not only because it was heavy but also because the restaurant we were in was so damn loud and busy.

An all-you-can-eat buffet.

I hadn't been to one in years, in over a decade, actually. But something about King Star Buffet was calling my name. And my appetite.

I'd only stepped out my condo to get some fresh air... and because my fridge was empty.

The call from Brielle's father, Mr. Chadwick, didn't help with keeping me comfortable indoors either.

"Everett," he said when I answered.

"Mr. Chadwick?"

"How are you?"

Terrible, thanks for asking.

"As good as I will be, I guess," I said instead.

"Good to hear."

I shook my head.

"Look, I spoke with the board of investors and we've agreed to offer you $500,000 an episode instead of the $200,000 we discussed for you to host Neutral Corner. How does that sound?"

It sounded great. Which I told him. I also told him I would continue to think about his offer.

"Take your time," he insisted. "Kyle's contract ends by the end of this summer, so I would like for you to step right in at the start of September. It'll also be a great time to announce that engagement between you and that daughter of mine."

No pressure, right?

The deal would be lucrative and I'd make an excellent transition from boxer to host post-retirement. It was perfect. What sucked was what I'd have to do to get that kind of opportunity.

Marry his cheating ass daughter.

So, at seven in the evening on a Friday night, I was hungry, stressed, and overwhelmed in my condo, so I went for a walk to find something to do.

It was too early to hit up a bar, so I settled for my latest pastime: eating.

I lowered the rim of my L.A. Dodgers baseball cap over my eyes.

"It's only me," I mumbled to the Asian hostess.

"Huh? I can't hear you—"

"Only. Me!" I shouted. "I'm here alone."

Having to acknowledge that made me cringe.

That was really my reason for needing to leave my condo. It was quiet and empty. Though I subscribed to a minimalist home setup, that's not what made it feel empty.

I couldn't remember the last time I spent a Friday night alone at home. Brielle and I often had something planned or my sister Eryn called wanting to hangout. If they didn't occupy my time, training for a fight, traveling to promote it, or going away on vacation to relax, occupied the rest.

Never did I ever have nothing to do on a Friday night.

I had all this time and nothing to do with it, so the easy way I could think to pass the time was to eat.

"$20."

"Huh?"

"$20 to eat," she explained. "Includes unlimited drink and the tax."

"Oh." I pushed my hand into my black joggers' pocket in search of my wallet. I singled out a $100 bill from the cash compartment and handed it to her.

The hostess handed me back my change. Her straight black strands feathered the air as she twisted her head from left to right, searching the room. "Not too many seats, yeah? Very busy. You pick a seat. Sit anywhere."

I scanned the room, my eyes falling on tables filled to the brim with families and couples, all socializing and eating. The place was your usual buffet setting. Basic wooden tables and chairs, plain walls with Chinese decorations and a sign stating a two-hour table limit for all customers.

I lowered the rim of my cap. The last thing I needed was to be recognized by anyone here, even if that wasn't an actual concern. It would just be difficult to explain me being there to the people who knew me.

The space smelled of fried rice, soy sauce, fried poultry and seafood, amongst other things. Sugaring the air were Chinese donuts, a rainbow medley of jello, and random fresh fruits. And somehow, all those scents could co-exist in the air and not make me sick to my stomach.

In fact, I was hungrier, smelling everything.

I didn't waste any time going to secure a table. Instead, I grabbed a warm plate and began piling things on.

I hadn't been to the gym since that Monday when I kicked myself out the building. Besides the fact I was feeling a way about that, I hadn't returned because I simply didn't have the desire to work out.

My desire to eat was greater.

What was I exercising for, anyway? I was officially retired and had nothing to train for. My time was mine again, and I had nothing to do with it. It was time for me to relax.

Wasn't that what retirement was all about, anyway?

My plate was full of food. Fried rice, fried whiting, crab legs, and baked clams, broccoli in garlic sauce left room for nothing else to fit. But when I spotted the last fried chicken wing in the silver chafing dish, I had to have it too. I'd lifted the fried wing piece and placed it on my plate when a small child sighed loudly while looking at the empty pan.

"Mom," he whined, "that man took the last one."

"I'm sure they'll bring out more," she promised

"But I don't want to wait! I want that one," he retorted, pointing at my plate.

And the old me probably would've let the kid have it, but this me wanted to sit and eat my food in peace.

So I did, albeit walking away from a tantrum.

One plate of food became two and two became three. It was two hours later, and I was on my fourth full plate of food. I could've stopped, but I figured, what was the harm in getting more?

But when I stood from my seat to head back to the serving stations, my abdomen tensed, then cramped before a wave of nausea swept me from the depths of my belly to the base of my throat, hitting me like a storm. I heaved twice before clamming my hand over my mouth while rushing away from my table.

Thankfully, the restroom sign was prominent on one of those walls, guiding me to the men's bathroom. But seeing that was half the battle, because I couldn't get there fast enough. I heaved again on my way there, but instead of it being just a sign to get to the bathroom, the food I ate covered in bile pushed up my throat and out my mouth, my hand failing to catch it all.

"Oh my God, *ew*!" I heard behind me as I pushed through the bathroom door. "Was he throwing up?!"

My hand dripped with hot vomit as I bursted through the stall door, missing my clothes, but not the floor around the toilet. I hurled the rest of what I'd eaten into the ceramic bowl, including what I had that morning. Mounds of undigested food fell into toilet water in chunks. I hunched my 6'3 frame over the public toilet, releasing the contents of my stomach. When there was nothing left to regurgitate, my body didn't get the message. I dry heaved so much, I had to drop into a squat and eventually into a seat on the floor, dropping my head further into the toilet.

Yes, it was disgusting.

The situation was grave.

I've overeaten before. I'd done it several times. On cheat days before working out, it wasn't uncommon for me to binge before hitting the gym.

But I hadn't been working out.

I'd been consuming at a rate that wasn't my norm.

And the sad part was I didn't care.

I pushed up off the floor by placing a hand on the stall's toilet seat. I peeked down as I lifted myself up, cringing immediately. Below my Nikes were splatters of vomit that didn't make it into the toilet, there on the stall floor.

"God," I exclaimed, running the back of my hand against my mouth. I flushed the toilet and headed out to the sink.

I stared ahead of me. My reflection in the mirror over the sink made me divert my eyes. The bags beneath them, the fullness in my face. I looked horrible.

I'd only started eating without burning calories four days ago and already I was noticing a difference.

But again, I didn't care, and I wouldn't allow myself to understand why.

What I allowed myself to do was finish up in the bathroom, turn my cap forward, and to return to the buffet, with a fresh new warm ceramic plate to fill.

My belly was empty again, and to be honest, I wasn't hungry. But I moved around the serving stations, using tongs at every chafing dish to plate another round of food. My fifth plate, but I guess because I vomited the four from earlier, it shouldn't count.

I returned to my table, prepared to dive in, when the hostess from earlier approached.

"Two-hour limit." She pointed at a sign near the front where I had entered.

I glanced in that direction.

When I arrived, I remembered seeing the sign, but didn't think twice of it.

"I'm almost done—"

"Two-hour limit," she repeated. "We have customers waiting." She gestured at the chairs near the front of the restaurant where people sat waiting for tables to empty. "You eat four plates of food already." She leaned in closer and whispered, "You throw up on the floor outside the bathroom. I saw you."

"You were watching?"

She pointed at me. "Two-hour limit—"

"Aight, aight. Fine." I jumped to my feet and dropped my fork. "Took my $20, but want to tell me how long I can eat."

"Very busy today. Plus, you eat too much. Made yourself sick."

"Whatever," I mumbled, making my way away from the table.

Getting kicked out of the all-you-can-eat buffet should've been another sign that something wasn't right, especially after throwing up in the bathroom and still going back to eat again.

But it wasn't.

It was just the incentive I needed to hit up a bar.

———

My ringing home phone forced me awake. I turned over to my back in bed and extended my arm for the cordless phone, lifting it off its dock.

"Yeah," I rasped.

"Mr. Peters," Jacob, my condo building's doorman, said on the other end of my phone. "Sir, your sister has arrived."

"No." I groaned. "Tell her right now isn't a good time."

It wasn't at all. Eating like shit, then staying way too long at the bar last night was taking a toll on me the next day.

"You've had enough champ," the balding bartender insisted when I gestured for him to fill my glass with a fourth round of bourbon straight.

For a Friday night, my local bar around the corner from my condo was fairly empty. On a busy day, it saw little traffic, but tonight, it was slow, I'm sure of any bar. I wasn't fussing. Its lack of patrons made it the perfect spot for me to grab a drink or three.

Now four.

Not my usual number.

"My father is in Arizona this week on business. So, I know where he's

at," I told him. "I don't need you to be my dad. I need you to bar tend. Just fill this glass for me, old man."

"You usually only have one."

"And you rarely say over two words to me when I come here."

He placed both hands on the bar's surface. "Because you're not a regular and you don't tip well."

"Man, look—"

"Whatever it is you think this next glass will offer, I promise you're mistaken."

I kissed my teeth and looked away.

"Your last fight with Kevin Claymore was legendary," he stated, still not lifting the bottle to pour. "What an excellent way to go into retirement. On top. Bravo."

I grunted.

"I saw the special on that sports network before the match. About what you had to do to get ready for the fight." He whistled, I guess impressed. "Lean meats, no carbs, vegetables with every meal, not a spot of sugar." He counted on his fingers. "You wouldn't even take a sip of wine and when you come here, which is rarely, you have one drink, that's it, and you barely finish that."

I leaned back in my seat.

"I said all that to say go home, champ," he insisted. "Please."

I listened. And thankfully, I left the bar to go home, because after eating at the all-you-can-eat buffet and having only three drinks, I felt like shit on shit. Everything in me, with a joint, ached. I'd been doing too much and could only come to that conclusion after the fact.

"Sir—"

"Jacob, tell my sister to come back later—"

"She's already headed up, Mr. Peters."

I sighed heavily, draping an arm over my eyes. "Jacob."

"Sir, she signed in and told me not to bother calling you to let you know she was here. I tried to stop her, but—"

"You'd have better luck trying to stop a runaway freight train. But thanks for trying."

The ding of my private elevator made me growl again.

"She's here now, Jacob. Thanks for warning me."

"My apologies, sir."

"None needed."

"Everett!" I heard shouted from my living room. "Where are you?"

I shut my eyes tight. "Enjoy the rest of your day, Jacob."

The click and clack of my sister's high-heels grew louder the closer she got to my room. I ended the call and dropped the phone on the side table, then grabbed my down comforter and threw it over my head.

I couldn't deal with her right now.

Eryn, my sister, was a hurricane in human form. Big personality with no filter. And she was younger than me by four years, but you would never know it.

"Nigga!" she hollered, her voice bouncing off my bedroom walls and echoing around me. "I know your ass is not hiding from me."

And loud. Did I mention she was loud?

I felt the covers being pulled off my head before locking eyes with her.

Big brown ones with long natural lashes stared back at me. She wore a form-fitting Barbie pink party dress with a neckline that was too low and a hem that was way too high. "Where the hell have you been, Ev?"

My sister and I had been in L.A. for six years and she still had the strongest Brooklyn accent you'd ever hear on a black woman.

"It's too early for the volume you're coming at me with," I accused, pulling at the covers.

She caught the bedding midair. "It's 3pm. Early where, Everett? Not here."

Eryn left my side and walked to my floor-to-ceiling windows, pressing the button to retract my blackout curtains. The fabric pleated, then invited in the California sun to light up the dark space.

I squinted at the light before pinching the space between my eyes when that same light became too harsh to bear first thing after waking.

"I haven't heard from you in days." She crossed her arms at the window. "I've been calling, and you haven't answered once. I only showed up here because this guy I hung out with last night lives and works at the precinct in this area."

"A cop?"

"I love my men in uniform."

"Please don't."

She giggled.

"Last night?" I examined her getup again. I scanned her from her long straight hair, pulled back into a braided ponytail, past her outfit that gave off the impression she'd just left the club and not someone's apartment. My eyes settled on the straps of her high-heeled sandals.

"Why are you still wearing that outfit if you two hung out last nig...?" I stopped myself when the answer became clear without her needing to confirm. "You know what, never mind."

My sister was far from the shy type, so I was sure she would've told me. She spent the night at the gentleman's home. That's why she was wearing the same clothes, I could conclude without confirmation. Because this was the first time I'd ever heard her mention dating anyone and the fact she didn't mention a name and only where he worked, she probably didn't know this guy well enough to have spent the night. But I'm sure she slept there, because Eryn believed in one-night-stands more than she did committed relationships.

At least now she did.

"I didn't make it home last night." She shrugged. "So, we—"

"Save it." I sat up in bed. "We agreed after I moved out of our condo after that year of living together that you would never tell me about what you do in your private life."

We'd moved to Cali six years ago after Eryn decided she was tired of living in New York. She'd broken up with her ex after graduating from college six years prior and hadn't gotten over the breakup. Eryn figured a change in scenery would help and immediately wanted out of the East Coast. I was in search of a new boxing coach, so I agreed to move with her to Los Angeles. We shared the condo she now lives in until I couldn't take the random men she kept bringing around, then crying over and that I grew tired of having to talk myself out of kicking their asses. It became toxic. So, for the sake of our relationship, I moved out, giving her space to be herself while not creating scenarios to ruin my career or land me in jail.

She peeked down below my neck and focused on my abdomen. I was shirtless in bed with only my boxers on as clothing. Though the covers still concealed my underwear, my upper torso was on full display.

Her brows squished together, forming lines between her eyes.

I peeked down to see what had her attention. Someone else would've ignored the slight fold in my stomach. But Eryn wasn't someone else.

In the short time between Valentine's Day and now, I'd put on a little weight.

More weight than I thought I could put on in six days.

The kind of weight to create the tiniest fold, but Eryn knew me well enough to not let it slide.

"Wait." She squinted. "Is that the start of a *gut* I see forming?"

"Eryn—"

"Everett, what's going on?" she interjected. "Your eyes are bloodshot red, your skin is flushed and you look like shit."

"Thank you."

"I'm serious. I haven't seen you with any kind of fold in your stomach since..." she contemplated. "Since *never*, actually."

"I'm in retirement," I offered. "I can afford to let myself go a little."

"Bullshit," she spat. "You're one of those my body's a temple types." She squinted more. "How'd the engagement dinner go?"

I closed my eyes and leaned my head against the headboard. "Not well."

She walked over and took a seat at the foot of my bed. "Not well, how? What happened? Did she say no? I know she didn't say no—"

"I didn't get the chance to ask."

Eryn gestured with flailing hands for me to continue.

"When I went to hide the ring for her to find, I found a box of sex tapes in her closet."

Her brows wrinkled more. "Sex tapes?"

"Brielle has been cheating since 2017."

Her eyes went wide. "So, practically your entire relationship?"

"Yup." I leaned my head back against the headboard. "The sex tapes were of her with other men. At least I think the other sex tapes were of her with other men. I didn't view them all. Only the one I singled out, which was of her having a threesome with two men."

"Stop!" She jumped to her feet. "Stop playing with me! You mean to tell me this *fool* was dumb enough to tape herself cheating?"

"She admitted it was a kink, then claimed she did it for me."

"Oh, did she climax with them for you, too? Did you feel it? Was it good?"

I tried to exhale the tension her comment caused in me.

Eryn rolled her eyes. "How kind and brave of her to take dick from other men because she loved you. *My* God."

I cringed. "Don't be so damn brash."

"Brash?!" she scoffed. "*She's* the brash one."

I looked away.

"Nah, actually? She's fucked up. What she did to you was *so* fucked up."

Silence fell between us. For years I've come to the defense of Brielle whenever my sister spoke ill of her, so this was new. Hearing Eryn talk down on Brielle and Eryn having reason to do so was new.

"I never liked that bitch, I swear." Eryn gritted her teeth. "I fucking hate her. You should've listened to me about her."

"Don't do that right now," I said low. "Before this, Brielle did nothing for you not to like her—"

"Yet," Eryn cut in. "She had done nothing for me not to like her *yet*. I told you there was something about her I didn't like. But your fetish for turning out good girls wouldn't let you see past her fake pick me ass. She wasn't a good girl, Everett."

"Fetish?" I questioned.

"Yes, *fetish*, and don't act like you don't know what I mean."

"Whatever."

"Brielle looked like a good girl, but she was always so fake and disingenuous to me. Very *'whatever you like'*, then hop on one foot and bark like a dog at your request. She made me sick."

"God," I groaned.

"Always smiling sweetly all the time, but that Kodak grin never reaching her eyes. Just fake as fuck, so of course she'd do some foul ass shit like this behind your back and say she did it for you, *ugh*!" She punched her hand. "That little manipulative trick ass *bitch*."

I shook my head, rolling my eyes up to look at the ceiling. I really didn't want to get into this. Not first thing after getting up.

"Look at you." She sucked her teeth. "She did you so dirty and a part of you still wants to defend her."

I focused on my sister again.

"Oh. My. God." Her jaw dropped.

"Here we go with the dramatics."

"You still love her," Eryn accused. I say accused, because her voice dropped with disdain. "You still freaking love her!"

"You don't have a relationship with someone for five years and stop loving them overnight, Eryn. Of all people, you should know that."

She rolled her eyes at me. "Don't give me that shit. And we're not talking about me." Eryn walked over to me, pointing a finger in my direction. "You still love her even after what she did. You probably would take her back if she begged the right way. Wouldn't you?"

I swallowed hard, wanting to deny the claim but deep down not knowing if Eryn was wrong, either.

Because I did still love Brielle. Our relationship, as far as I thought, was great. She was a good girl. And she did everything to my liking and at my request and, yeah, I loved that about her too. Brielle held me down even when I was away from home for weeks at training camp. Traveled to matches with me. Supported me and cheered me on in everything. I knew I would marry her after our first date. She was the one for me. And although I wouldn't admit it, not even to myself, her actions crushed me. Completely blindsided me. So much so, I didn't know what to do or how to process everything. And I didn't know if I would refuse taking her back, either.

"Just tragic." Eryn grunted. "So, the engagement doesn't go well and you two break up and you don't think to tell your sister?"

"I'm still processing."

"How are you feeling, though? You haven't said how or what you're feeling."

Disappointed.

Crushed.

Hurt.

Lost.

"I'm cool," I chose instead. "What I look like being hung up over the shit Brielle did?"

Eryn blinked in response.

"There are more women in this city, in this world, than there are men. I'm not trippin' off this."

"But you loved her, still do from what I can see. And she cheated in a major way. I mean, I hate her, but I should call her for advice. She had what I would call a great ass night. Two men? Yes, please, sign me the fuck up."

I gritted my back teeth.

"But she was *yours* and she cheated on you, Everett." She looked me in my eyes and added, "You have to be feeling something. You can't be Dr. Liz Peters's firstborn and not be able to say how you're feeling."

She was right.

I knew exactly how I was feeling, but admitting it made me feel weak. Saying I've felt an emptiness since everything went down the night, I should've popped the most important question in my life doesn't make me feel like a man. Acknowledging I unknowingly shared a woman - I was more than ready to make my wife - with men she's labeled strangers doesn't make me feel like *the* man, either.

I'm EP. *The* EP.

A world heavyweight boxing champion. A guy who had women swinging from his arm from the time he was a junior boxer. For years, too many women have thrown themselves at me. So much, I found it difficult to be disciplined and faithful in past relationships. I always felt I was an extraordinary man, and because of this, I didn't feel like I should live the ordinary life of being a one-woman man. But then I realized that one noble woman is worth more than however other many swinging from my arm. It was when I met Brielle at a private club where I hosted an event and she didn't look like or act like the other women. She didn't look like she belonged at a club. She didn't even know who I was. Sweet faced and innocent, but with heat in her eyes, the kind that hinted she knew how to turn the bad on when needed. I wanted to covet her and bring that heat out, but only for me. Not for her to go sharing that with other random men because she had a kink or a worry that she wouldn't be able to keep me happy. So yeah, my heart hurt. And she still had a piece. But I would never admit that.

"I'm cool," I repeated with a stone face. "I feel nothing."

FIVE

APRYL

"And you?" The server asked. "What can I get for you tonight?"

I smiled up at her. "I'll have—"

"She'll have the roasted chicken breast with vegetable pilaf," Reid, my date, interjected. He looked at me and added, "You'll love it. This restaurant is nationwide famous for their roasted chicken."

We sat across from each other in a crowded restaurant and lounge in midtown, Manhattan.

We'd met on HeartMates and set up a date after two conversations. He seemed intelligent and assertive. A young black investor on Wall Street with an excellent vocabulary and a beautiful award-winning smile. After my first date a week ago, I consciously filtered out the men, being sure to only entertain the career men from now on. They didn't have to make what I made, but they needed to make something, and I felt I found that in Reid. He was perfect and checked off all the "don'ts" on my list.

The problem? He was a complete and utter controlling narcissist.

Something I only found out a few minutes ago.

"I'm the man who likes to order for his woman."

I arched my brows. "*His* woman. Am *I* your woman already?"

He found that amusing. "Well, of course not, but I'd like to think we're working our way to there. Why else would we be out on a date?"

"Uh-huh." I palmed my wine glass filled with water.

"You must try the Chardonnay when you're done with your water."

"I don't drink."

"We'll have to change that, won't we?"

"Excuse me?"

His impish smile taunted me behind the rim of his wineglass. "I'm realizing now you're an alpha woman."

"A what?"

"Alpha," he repeated. "Headstrong, confident, a leader."

A pageant-like smile pulled at my lips.

"I don't like that."

I released my smile immediately.

"I usually steer clear of women like you and can often identify your type in photos alone. Your sweet face threw me off."

I folded a few strands of hair behind my ear. "Should I apologize for my face deceiving you?"

"I mean, if you wanted to apologize, I would accept."

"I'm sure."

"Don't get me wrong. I can see how I can use your kind of leadership energy," he added. "To run a household."

I jerked my head back.

"But there would need to be an understanding that I'm the man of the house. Therefore, my word holds more weight."

"Here is your artichoke and spinach dip," the server announced as she placed a bowl of bread and a dip on the table. "I'll be back with the rest of your order in a few minutes."

I hate artichokes.

And I should've admitted that, but I didn't want to ruin the date... although I'm pretty sure at this point Reid was doing a great job ruining it all on his own.

For a restaurant and lounge, the space was busy. Cooks yelling orders so loud patrons could hear it while eating. The wait staff needing to squeeze behind and between chairs just to make their way around the room. The place was popular, but I would've loved something more intimate.

That's what I get for allowing Reid to choose. Not that I had a choice. He told me where we would get dinner. Never asked. And I thought that was better than the date with Darryl, being that I had to plan everything.

"A celebrity personal trainer," Reid stated, drawing me back into the conversation. "I looked you up. You're a big deal."

"Yup." I nodded. "I worked very hard to be a big deal."

He shook his head. "There's that alpha again."

That did it.

"I haven't known you long enough to be sure of this, but based on what you're telling me, alpha women aren't what you take issue with."

He flashed that beautiful smile that now seemed menacing.

"I think it's actually confidence that intimidates you."

"Hmm..."

"Do you have a problem with confident women, Reid?"

"I have a problem with alpha women who mask their forceful personalities with being confident, yes." He nodded. "But I like you. And you don't look like an alpha. You just have the qualities of one, so I'm willing to work with you. I'm sure you can turn them off."

"Why would I want to?"

"You didn't even know what it was before I mentioned it."

"I knew what an alpha woman was before you mentioned it, Reid. You confused me by bringing it up. And even if I didn't know what it was, it doesn't matter." I sat up in my seat. "If an alpha is what you've identified my personality to be, then you've seen me for me and if you're asking me to change that, I'm already not okay with it, regardless of whatever label you give it."

He scoffed. "No man would ever go for that."

I rolled my eyes.

"A man wants a woman who listens and knows when to take a step back behind him."

"Wow."

"You're a leader, that's cool, but if you were to make it to a second date with me, it would be with a focus on marriage and children, which you don't seem like you're ready for."

Maybe I should get drunk.

"Make it to a second date?" I leaned back in my seat and folded my arms. "Are you supposed to be a prize?"

"I am." He shrugged. "I look great on and off paper."

"Same."

"Yeah, but you're a woman." He gestured at me. "You don't get better with age, you get worse."

"The fuck?"

"You exercise for a living."

"Asshole," I retorted. "Exercise for a living is a lazy thing to say."

He snorted. "I mean, I can see you do well for yourself, but marriage with me would have you prioritizing our relationship and our children over your career."

"Even if I had my career first?"

"Careers are not living things, Apryl." He sat back in his seat again. "People are. Relationships are. And a marriage and the nuclear family define a woman."

"Define?"

I should've deleted the app.

"Yes. So a woman's overall focus should be on making her marriage last."

I nearly lost it. "Well, that counts me out because I don't think this date will last long enough for us to have dinner together, much less make it to marriage. Nor do I want it to."

"Your loss," he chastised. "What are you, 31?"

"34," I gritted.

He cringed. "Time is not on your side. You don't really have the option to spend your time however you like, including waiting for your version of Mr. Right."

I pushed my chair back and stood to my feet. "Well, then I better get going, huh? I shouldn't spend another minute of my precious time on trash ass men like you then. Because you clearly are *not* Mr. Right."

I singled out a $100 bill and placed it on the table, and walked away.

Reid said a few more words, but I tuned him out. My mind was already sorting and deciding which exercise equipment I'd spend the night working up a sweat on.

———

"I almost caught a case last night."

My sister, Anastasia, or Stas, as I called her, turned to peek at me over her shoulder.

"That guy I told you I was going on a date with. Reid, the investment guy?"

"Right," she replied, turning completely to face me. "He's the one with the fantastic profile photo. He was—"

"A complete narcissistic asshole."

On a chilly late Sunday afternoon, I sat parked on my sister's kitchen stool in her kitchen watching her prepare dinner for her family.

Stas has always been about this life. I'd remember her taking good care of her Cabbage Patch Dolls and playing pretend with her Easy-Bake Oven. She was always the wife and the mother and I the pretend child.

Stas was all of five years older than me, but she was like my second mother, except I could be super honest with her.

"What happened?"

"I don't want to get into it." I dropped my head into my hands. "This is exactly why I didn't want to date again. Exactly why I kept to myself for the last two years because, my God."

She sighed.

"Can I get a healthy medium? Or am I stuck with two extremes? The gold digger 2.0, or a controlling narcissist who may be a budding abuser."

"I'm sure this is just two one offs," she rationalized. "The most important thing is you're ready. Putting that energy out there will attract what you're looking for. It's that list of yours that's the problem."

I lifted my head out of my hands. "My list? What's wrong with my list?"

She placed the knife on the cutting board and walked to the island where I sat. "It's unrealistic Apryl, I've told you that."

I pursed my lips.

"Your list is restrictive. Does not work a 9-5 job with no plans to move up in the company. His body fat is not higher than eighteen percent. Does not rent an apartment. Is not in a relationship. Does not have a woman who *thinks* she's in a relationship with him—"

"Everything on my list sounds realistic to me."

"Auntie, Auntie," my niece, Luna, ran into the kitchen to me. "Look! My Barbie has on workout clothes like you."

"Oh, LuLu, she is fly!" I winked. "And I love her fit."

"Her name is Apryl, like you too."

I smiled even bigger. "How lucky am I to share a name with a doll, so fly?"

Luna was one of my favorite people in the world. At only six, she was my sunlight in a world so dark. I adored her.

"LuLu, go back to your room to keep playing," Stas instructed. "Auntie and I are talking about something important."

I pursed my lips at Stas.

"It *is* important," Stas insisted the moment Luna was out of earshot. "You're probably having these bad dates because of that townhouse I told you to hold off on buying."

I sucked my teeth. "Don't give me that."

"You have the house, the car, the career, the lifestyle. You have everything, Apryl." She took a seat on a stool opposite me. "What will a man feel he can contribute to?"

I cringed.

"Men like to feel wanted. Needed. With all you have, what can a man complete?"

"Nothing." I stated sternly. "I don't want or need a man to complete me. I want him to enhance me more than I've enhanced myself."

She sat quietly.

"Make me better than I already am. Set the bar higher than I have for myself. I have a townhouse. Why can't my man have two? I have a successful career. He's more than welcome to have one as well. I will not wait to be married with children to start my efforts to go for mine and what I want out of life. No. I won't do that."

"You are so headstrong."

"And you're a *pick me* and you don't need to be."

She scoffed.

"Kwamé doesn't ask for you to do any of the things you do, but you do it anyway. He hires personal chefs, house cleaners, and nannies and you've turned them all down because the image of a woman being a mother and not having to wear herself thin is an image you identify as cheating in the game of life."

Stas rolled her eyes.

Because she knew I was right. I loved my sister more than anything, but she and I have always butted heads on her thinking. She often called me a feminist, but I've never identified as one. I was a woman who didn't want to give up on myself or accept less because I was a woman. I believed I deserved the world not *because of* anything, only because I said so. Period.

"Careful Apryl," Stas warned, standing on her feet. "You're sounding like mom, and you see how things are working out with her."

I twisted my lips to one side.

"She's uncompromising too. And *very* alone."

I swallowed hard.

Our mother is who I believed I got my thinking from. She's been single since Anastasia was ten and I five. She's dated, but we've never met the men. My mother has been single my entire life, and I didn't want to be like her, even though she was the vision of perfection.

"Like mom," I started, "I'm comfortable being alone. Unlike her, I don't *want* to be."

"Then get rid of the list," she pleaded. "Get yourself a man, stop dating, and finally settle down."

"All I heard you say was *settle* and I won't."

"I said *settle down*."

"Yes, *settle*." I moved closer to the island's natural stone counter. "If you always tell me I create the situations I find myself in whenever I hit a roadblock, why can't I use that same energy to create the romantic life I want?"

"Okay," she conceded. "Good point."

"I want what I want, and I'll get it. I just know I will."

Stas's cheeks dimpled as she smiled.

"My man is out there somewhere. Fake laughing with his girlfriend he knows doesn't appreciate him, but he won't leave her ass because he knows the dating scene is trash and he wants no parts of it."

She giggled.

"But he's out there. I just need his ass to stop sleeping on what love really is." I sighed. "He needs to wake the hell up, stop wasting both of our times, and come get me!"

Six

"EP, wake your ass up!"

I groaned at my agent, Daquan's voice booming through my phone. He interrupted my sleep with his call. Had my phone ringing back-to-back before I could peel my heavy eyes opened to find my device to answer.

"How are you sleeping at 5pm, bro?"

"I had a long night," I rasped.

"Doing what?!"

Eating, drinking, dealing with thoughts that caused me to do too much of the aforementioned from midnight until ten in the morning. You know, my new normal.

I didn't want to deal with people the night before, so before midnight, I took a trip to the liquor store to pick up a bottle of dark rum and vodka, grabbed a couple of burgers, fries, and other fried stuff, brought it all home and had a time last night.

I finished the food and emptied the bottle of vodka, too, and finally passed out from it all at 10am the next morning. It was depressing, and I felt every bit of horrible hours later.

"I was chillin' last night, man. I'm retired, ain't I?" I replied, irritated. "What's up? What you want?"

He sighed.

"Calling me with this bullshit."

"Eryn told me what happened with Brielle, man. Damn. I'm..." His voice trailed off in an exhale.

I shut my lids tight and squeezed them together.

Brielle had been around long enough for our names to be synonymous with each other in our circle. Jay Z and Beyonce, Tamia and Grant Hill. Everett and Brielle. We were a pair.

"I'm sorry, Ev."

"That damn Eryn." I kissed my teeth. "What was she doing calling you with that, anyway?"

"You know, Eryn has always kept me in the loop of anything that could affect your game or could bring you down."

And they've fucked.

"We're partners on your team, Ev."

'Cause they've fucked.

The first time I found out it was by accident. He'd called me one morning from his apartment and I heard her voice in the background. I couldn't be too sure. But I confirmed everything when I caught them secretly making out outside of my dressing room after one of my biggest fights in my career in New York. I never made it known that I knew, nor did I break Daquan's jaw for messing with my sister, since he should've already known she was off limits. We'd known each other from our hometowns in Brooklyn, New York. He agreed to move out to Cali. No questions when I told him I wanted to move. Plus, his consistency with always keeping me booked and paid kept him on my good side, but I didn't like that my sister was calling his ass with my personal business.

"Whatever," I replied. "I'm good. It happened. What's up? You got something for me other than your sympathy that I can't do shit with?"

"All business, huh?"

"It is when you calling me, waking me up out of sleep." I balanced myself on my hand to pull myself up to press my back against my headboard. "I know I don't have any fights lined up."

"I got something better," he promised. "I was taking mental notes during our meeting last month."

"Okay...?"

"I have an opportunity that will have you giving back while doing what you love too."

"You gonna cut to the good part, Day?"

He chuckled. "There's a community center opening in Brooklyn in July. In Bed-Stuy. They're opening a pool there and could use a celebrity face to draw in the news outlets to publicize the opening and attract future donors. I know the director of the facility and called him and he was more than happy to hear from me. He's agreed to have you there for the opening to teach swimming lessons to the young black boys and girls in the neighborhood."

I sat up immediately. "Oh, word?"

"Word." He chuckled again. "Everyone knows your love of swimming and your advocacy for young black children learning how to swim, so although it's not boxing, it aligns with your brand and interests. It's a good look and a great way for people to see you beyond boxing, especially in retirement. It could open the doors to other opportunities, lucrative ones. Now, the community center gig ain't paying much—"

"It doesn't have to," I interjected. "It don't even matter 'cause I'd do it for free." I nodded, an appreciative smile pulling at my lips. "Matter of fact, let them know compensation isn't necessary. I'm there. And it's in our part of Brooklyn, too? Yeah, we can guarantee I'll be there."

"Aight!" Daquan shouted, enthusiastically. "That's what's up. All right so I'll reach out to them and let them know your appearance is a go."

"Yeah, do that. And Day?"

"What's up?"

"Thanks man," I told him. "I can always count on you to look out for me. To keep my purpose always in mind, especially when I'm not there to remind you."

"Always," he said back. "We'll talk."

I ended the call, threw my phone down on the bed, and leaned my head back against my headboard.

See, that was why I kept Daquan around. Though he overstepped boundaries sleeping with my sister, he's always came through and presented me with options I didn't know were possible.

I've advocated for the teaching of swimming for young black children in the inner cities since the start of my career. Most swimming lessons cost money that many parents living check to check, and even on government help, couldn't afford. Tact on the stigma that most black people don't know how to swim, this can be a recipe for stagnation. Losing my friend Chase at a young age and my mother signing me up for swimming lessons after made me understand the value of learning an essential skill. Learning how to swim not only helped with my coordination as a boxer, it opened the doors for new experiences. It made life a little more limitless for me. I've wanted children who looked like me to experience the same freedom. And now a lot of them will.

"Yes." I smiled.

The opportunity to teach swimming even for only a day, to use my image to draw in the right crowd, made me feel valuable.

I lowered my view to my abdomen. As my sister had pointed out, a gut was forming. It wasn't too noticeable to outsiders, I'm sure, because of all the muscle I've built over the years, but it was there.

I moved my eyes to my phone and lifted it off the mattress with plans to dial up Eryn, but noticed the notification from Brielle's social page informing me she'd posted a photo.

Why was I getting notifications about her social activity?

Because besides consuming more than I should have, I'd become a glutton for punishment.

I'd tired of constantly checking Brielle's social feed every day and seeing no updates. Seeing what she was up to, keeping up with what she was doing, gave me insight into how sorry she really was about what happened. I was waiting for the remorseful post, either subliminal or direct. The post that showed her heart hurt as much as mine or possibly worse because what we had was real. It was beautiful, and it was ours, and she fucked it all up. I hoped that the post was coming. But I pulled up a photo of her back to the camera, but her hand in a man's hand as she guided him toward Caribbean blue waters and white sand.

The caption: *New stunning beginnings to match a stunning sunrise.*

I knew it was a man's hand instantly. The broad hairy forearms made that very clear.

The longer I stared at the photo, the harder it hit me.

She really doesn't give a fuck.

She is not sorry at all.

And that remorseful post I've been waiting for isn't coming.

That fact had me balling my hand into a fist and punching the mattress a few times.

I threw the covers off me, jumping out of bed with a heaving chest. My veins pulsed in my neck as I felt my pressure climbing. The room seemed to spin a little because I was so angry. I had the urge to punch something, break everything, to give this rage a home to let live, but I barely kept things around to break with my minimalist setup.

I still had that half-empty bottle of dark rum in the kitchen from last night, though.

Drinking after a night of binge eating and drinking, and it not being a wise idea, crossed my mind, but needing to numb the feeling of rage and pain took priority. So I stomped my way to my kitchen, snatched the bottle off my counter, and took the bottle to the head, deciding a visit to the bar would have to come next.

———

"Drink, drink, drink, drink..."

Their voices were so high pitched and slightly irritating, but I couldn't complain since they were in the right setting for their vibe.

I refused to return to the bar that was just around the corner from my condo, so I hailed a cab and took it less than a mile to a more popular bar in Los Angeles.

The Purple Cat was one of those franchise-like bars with locations in L.A., New York, and Miami. I came here because I knew I'd blend in because of the crowd.

Being noticed wasn't a concern for me. I didn't care to be bothered, though. Plus, I found I was more recognizable in my boxing trunks and with gloves on my hands than with a backward Los Angeles Dodgers cap, white tee, and black joggers.

"Whew!" The table of women hollered at the top of their lungs, drawing my attention to their section for the fourth time since I entered the bar.

There were eight of them in total. One lady wore a tiny white veil in her hair and the matching sash that read Bride-to-Be. They were loud, too loud for this small hole-in-the-wall joint.

Everything in the Purple Cat was black and purple. Though there were lights all around the room, the owner kept them dimmed low enough to still make out faces, but not bright enough to remember them. Every time I'd glance in the bride-to-be's direction, I found her looking back. At first, I thought it was all in my head, but I confirmed all of that when she built up the nerve to approach me at the bar.

I'd chosen this seat at the far end near the restrooms for a reason. I wanted to go unseen and to be left alone.

So much for that.

"Do I know you from somewhere?" were her first words to me. "I feel like I know you from somewhere."

She approached at the right time... or should I say, the wrong time. I'd swallowed at least three Glencairn glasses of bourbon and had gestured to the bartender for a refill, which he obliged. Unlike my local bar, the bartender didn't recognize me, nor did he try to talk me out of ordering another round. All he cared about was me covering my tab, which I'd already given him my card to do. He was happy, and I was drunk. It was shaping out to be a good night.

"That's the line?" I asked her without looking. I sipped my drink, feeling as it left fiery trails as I swallowed the slightly sweet, rich spirit.

"What do you mean?"

My head was light, and the room appeared unreal. Even she seemed unreal standing beside me. She wore a skintight white mini dress that left nothing to be desired. Her breasts hung out as if they were both fighting to be free of the Jersey fabric's hold. Her eyes were glossier than her lips but, even inebriated, I could see the sex in her eyes.

I was pretty sure the liquor helped me identify the sex in them faster than usual.

"Your pickup line." I took another sip of my drink. "Was that the line?"

She giggled, then smiled big.

On the surface, she wasn't my type. She gave off 90s, raunchy rapper Foxy Brown vibes - sexy, boujee with absolutely beautiful brown skin and eyes that slanted up toward her temple on each side. She was attractive, and that was probably why I couldn't keep my eyes off her since arriving at the bar, but one thing that was a turnoff was that I could tell this would be easy, so I wouldn't learn anything about her. The other obvious thing was she was disloyal.

Her energy was more than an innocent flirtatious I'm-out-with-the-girls-just-having-fun vibe, and given how raw I still was after Brielle, I didn't like her being so open to me when she clearly had more permanent plans in the works.

But she was sexy, and I was drunk, so...

"Yeah." She bit her bottom lip. "That *was* the line. Did it work?"

"Depends." I licked my lips. "Was that how you landed the groom-to-be?"

Her lips quirked up, and she looked away, embarrassed maybe.

Excited to do something she might regret, perhaps.

I was curious.

Was this how Brielle did it? Was this how she picked up those men, knowing she had me at home?

"Zara!"

I turned to the voice to see a tall, slim woman with high cheekbones and the gait of a model headed our way.

The woman who sat beside me, whose name I now knew to be Zara, clenched her jaw.

"Zara, what are you doing?"

"Minding my business, Gia." Zara replied. "Something I encourage you to do."

Gia glanced over at me and did a quick scan of me. She glanced at Zara, then focused on me again and announced, "She's getting married on Sunday."

"Gia!"

"Zara, you are," Gia chided, folding her arms. "And the way you're leaning in and flirting, someone would think you weren't engaged."

I nodded and returned to sipping my drink. Gia was a good friend. I wondered if Brielle's girls tried talking her out of talking to the men she eventually slept with.

"Didn't I tell you to mind your fucking business?" Zara stepped off her stool and got in Gia's face. "Don't think I don't know."

"Don't know what?"

I moved my eyes between them.

"I know what you did with Jamal."

Gia scoffed. "I don't know what you're talking about."

"You two slept together," Zara revealed through her teeth. "Don't even try playing in my face about it, either."

Gia released a curt laugh this time. "What are you talking about?"

"I saw your text to him when I went through his phone last week, Gia. The text of you begging him to end the engagement and choose you because you two were always supposed to be together from the start."

Gia's eyes went big for only a moment before she regained composure and blinked them free.

The table of women was as loud as they were when I first arrived, not at all realizing the tense situation happening at the bar's counter.

"You shouldn't have gone through your fiancé's phone, Zara," Gia stated.

I inhaled a deep breath and looked away.

Were there any loyal, honorable women left in this city?

"Bitch," Zara spat. "The only reason I haven't kicked your ass yet and why you're still a bridesmaid is because I see Jamal doesn't give a shit about you, and whatever night you two shared meant nothing." Zara got closer to Gia's face and added, "You've known Jamal all your life and had to beg the man and he still didn't choose you. How sad."

"You know what's really sad?" Gia retorted through her teeth, "It's that Jamal asked a *hoe* to marry him after knowing her for only a year and he hasn't realized yet she's a *hoe*."

I'd turned away from them, but I could feel the anger emanating from them behind me.

"Hey," I heard whispered in my ear. "I'll show you exactly how I landed the groom-to-be, if you're interested."

I should've offered a resounding no. Stayed in my seat, drank the rest of my drink, and returned to my condo to pass out and wake up at an incredibly unacceptable hour the next day.

But I was interested. Not in how she got her man, but in how a woman willingly ruins a relationship.

"Zara!" Gia called as Zara and I walked away. "Zara!"

"Fuck off, Gia," Zara shouted as we neared the restroom's door and stepped in.

This was so dumb. In my inebriated state, I knew this was unwise. The hurt in Zara was obvious, and I was dealing with hurt feelings, too. And it crossed my mind that I was about to do the same thing those guys did with Brielle, but I needed to know. For my sanity, I had to know.

She flicked the switch, and the bathroom illuminated with light. Up close and with more light, I could see Zara, although beautiful, stood before me as drunk beyond belief like me. Her eye makeup was a little smeared, her lipstick a bit faded. She moved closer and I could see she was a little dead in the eyes. Her eyes didn't sparkle with excitement or mystery; they were just there, completely unreadable.

She placed her hand on my shoulder and ran her palm down my arm, her eyes moving about my form. "You have the most amazing arms."

I said nothing, just kept trying to read her.

"What did you say your name was?" she asked, licking her lips. "I feel I should at least know that."

"You can call me E."

"E," she repeated, tossing her head back in a drunken laugh, losing her balance a little. I had to catch her to keep her on her feet.

This was so wrong. How could she not see it was wrong?

"I don't have any condoms," I informed.

"No worries." She balanced herself on the arches of her heels to kiss my neck. Against my skin she confirmed, "I have plenty."

Her white veil tickled the side of my jaw with her so close. She smelled of alcohol and floral perfume. Brielle was more of a sweet fragrance woman, always had been.

I asked Zara, "Did you plan to sleep with someone tonight?"

Zara stepped back to look up at me. "Why do you ask?"

"You have condoms on the weekend of your wedding."

She sucked her teeth. "Are you letting that bitch out there get in your head?"

I stepped back to keep my balance. I'd been drinking for a few days, but the liquor here seemed stronger because I'd never gotten this drunk at a bar.

"Don't allow her to trick you out of your position," she slurred, struggling to stay on her feet as she swayed from side to side. "She fucked her best friend, *my* fiancé. The two of them have finally done what they wanted to do all these years, and it was not what my fiancé was expecting, which is why there's even a wedding still happening on Sunday." She lifted her wrist to glance at her wristwatch. "Well, tomorrow now, since it's officially midnight."

"So, are you trying to get him back? Am I the accomplice in a payback?"

"I'm *trying* to *fuck* you," she explained. "I am literally giving you full access to my pussy, and you have questions?"

Plenty of them.

I wanted to know what was going through her mind. How she thought she'd feel afterwards. I actually wanted to have sex with this woman to see if she'd enjoy it, knowing she was getting married the next day. I figured if I understood her, I'd understand Brielle, and maybe understanding Brielle would help me get over this fucked up feeling I couldn't shake.

But... I couldn't go through with it.

"Are we going to fuck or what, E?"

I backed away from her while shaking my head. "Nah."

"Oh my God, seriously?!"

I turned the knob on the bathroom door, prepared to step out when I saw a man who matched my height but was slightly slimmer, standing on the other side, blocking my exit.

He looked at me, then glanced past me and into the bathroom at Zara.

"Jamal?" Zara questioned behind me.

There's a rule in boxing that every coach teaches their student before they let them into a ring. It's a rule my coach often repeated to me whenever I'd break it.

Never take your eyes off your opponent.

It's a rule that is so deeply imbedded in me that under no circumstance do I do it. It is why I remained undefeated throughout my entire career and why poor health didn't force me into retirement. I hung up my gloves willingly and was in excellent health.

The urge was there.

The urge to glance back at Zara to confirm what I knew deep down in me to be true. That Jamal was her fiancé, and he was standing only inches away from me. The years of boxing training and that one rule to *never take my eyes off my opponent* trumped that urge.

It's the only reason I saw the punch coming before he even lifted his arm at his side.

I leaned to the left and immediately put my hands up. I pivoted out of the bathroom's doorway and maneuvered around him.

"You thought you would get away with fucking my fiancée?" He swung again, and I ducked out of the way.

"You two stop before I call the cops!" I heard shouted behind the bartender's counter.

"You just gon' ignore that Bride-to-Be sash around her, huh?" He swung again, and I moved out of the way once more. "You probably would've gotten away with it too with your punk ass if my best friend ain't call to tell me what was up."

"You bitch!" Zara shouted. "You called him?

"I sure did," Gia sneered back.

I heard Zara running past before she declared, "I'm gonna beat your ass."

She sped past and I probably would've followed her with my eyes if Jamal hadn't stepped forward again to throw another ill executed hook.

I moved slower than usual. The liquor had me seeing things as if I were viewing them through a prism.

"Jamal, Zara, stop!" A woman yelled somewhere behind us. "You two are getting married tomorrow."

I was drunk, but I knew better than to counter any of his punches. He threw punches like an amateur. There was no doubt he'd been in a street fight or two, but he didn't fight in a way to protect himself. Only to cause damage, hoping the person he squared up with didn't know what they were doing.

But I did, which was why I wouldn't throw a punch back. Because if I did, it wouldn't be to throw another one. It would be to end this.

So I kept him in sight and kept leaning out of his punches. Kept reading his expression and predicting what he'd do next.

My balance was terrible. The room was spinning. But I felt when I was bear hugged from the back and pushed off my feet, landing cheek first against one of those wooden tables in the bar.

The rotating lights flashed through the bar's windows, tinting everyone in blue and red.

"You are under arrest," I heard announced behind me, as what I now could confirm was one of Los Angeles's finest. He pulled my arms one at a time behind me, handcuffing my wrists together, and all I could do was close my eyes and grit my teeth at the metal cutting into my skin.

"I didn't even get to fuck," I mumbled to myself as the officer yanked me to my feet and escorted me out of the bar.

———

If there is one thing that sticks in my memory, it's the smell of things. Whether they are sweet or foul, scents have a way of sticking with me for a lifetime, and the holding cell at a precinct in downtown L.A. was no exception.

It smelled of rusted metal, dried shit, cheap cigarettes, and stale coffee. Not one scent was independent of the other. It was a unified smell of funk that did well with sobering me the hell up. The precinct's holding cell was all I needed to confirm jail and prison wouldn't be a place I'd like to go. Not that I thought anyone really wanted to go to any of those places, but if the holding cell was this bad, I didn't want to know what the inside of a commissary smelled like.

To the left and right of me were rows of occupied cells. The cell to my right had a gentleman asleep and snoring on the bench and in the cell to my left was Jamal, who hadn't stopped staring at me since he quit pacing moments ago.

"You're EP," he finally said, approaching the bars of his cell.

They lined the cells side by side with a guard at the far-right end near the exit door.

I glanced at Jamal, then looked forward. I was no longer drunk. In fact, I went through phases of sobering up. That's what happens when you have nothing else to focus on... realize when the liquor wears out, making everything heavy, including your thoughts.

"I thought you looked familiar when you opened the bathroom door at the bar," he continued, "but I wasn't sure, since, you know..." He diverted his eyes around his cell. "I was angry and wrapped up in the moment."

I shook my head and ran my hand down my mouth.

"You could've knocked me out, caused some actual damage."

"*Hmph*," I huffed.

"Why you didn't throw a single punch?"

"Because I could've knocked your ass out and caused some actual damage." I glared his way. "Just like you said."

He swallowed hard and stepped back.

"And I didn't want to do that, not the weekend of your wedding," I added. "Not that it matters anymore, since we're not getting out of here until Monday."

"Wh-what?"

"It's officially the weekend, so courts are closed," I reminded, dropping my head into my hands. "We won't get in front of a judge to post bond until Monday."

"Oh my God."

"And by the way," I added, "We didn't do shit in that bathroom. You pissed your girl off fucking your best friend, though."

His brows wrinkled. "What?"

I said nothing in response, only stared back at him.

"Fuck," he whispered and lifted his fist to his mouth. "She knows?!"

"Oh yeah." I nodded. "Read some text on your phone and your best friend confirmed everything when your girl confronted her about it."

"No! Shit," he hissed, turning away to pace again.

"Why would you fuck your best friend, who is in your soon-to-be wife's bridal party, anyway?" I looked his way again. "Did you *not* want to get married?"

"I—" He dropped his head into his hand. "Shit!"

He ran his hand down his face and moved back and forth inside his cell, mumbling things to himself that I didn't care to make out.

I exhaled and grunted. "It's gonna be a long ass weekend."

The taps of leather hard bottom soles echoed around the space as a tall black gentleman with a button-down shirt tucked in his slacks made his way down the lot of cells.

He stopped in front of mine and smiled a brilliant white smile that made him look a lot like basketball player Derrick Rose.

He chucked his chin. "Hey champ."

Up close, I noticed the ring of keys dangling from his hand. He singled out a key, placed it in the cell's keyhole, unlocking the cell with one turn. The meeting of metals echoed next before he slid my cell door open.

He gestured with his head. "Step out."

I stared at him for a moment.

"You're going home."

"What?" Jamal exclaimed in his cell beside me. "I... I thought we were here through the weekend."

I tilted my head to one side and didn't move.

The gentleman with the badge clipped to his front waist and the gun in his holster smiled again at me. And it was genuine. Referred to me as champ, which meant he knew who I was.

Still, I was hesitant.

"I thought the courts were closed and I have to see a judge."

"Don't worry about it." He gestured with his hand this time. "Come with me and I'll explain everything."

"I know better than to trust L.A.P.D."

He smiled and pointed behind him with his thumb. "Your sister's here. Eryn?"

My brows and all the tension in my face relaxed.

"Look." He walked closer to the cell to speak lower. "I can't get into any of that here. Just come with me and we'll sort everything out."

With that I stood from my seat on the steel bench, paid another glance Jamal's way, then stepped out the cell as instructed, following the guy out of the funk.

A short walk later, and finally out of the room of cells, the guy with the badge turned to me to say, "I'm Coleman, but you can call me Cole. I'm a huge fan."

"Thanks."

"That last fight with Kevin Claymore was insane." His eyes lit up. "The way you countered with that jab, cross, then hook." He acted out the move, punching the air. "Legendary."

"I appreciate it."

"The officers logged nothing," he informed next, continuing to walk up ahead again. "They didn't book you two when you came in. Only planned to have y'all sober up in the cells back there. If they knew who you were, they wouldn't have even cuffed you. I heard you didn't swing on dude, much less hit him. That's honorable because..." He whistled. "Ain't no way he would've left that bar with an intact jaw if you did."

We'd finally entered the precinct. Given the hour, the precinct was empty, but the phones still rang, and voices scattered in the small space.

I saw Eryn seated at one desk inside the precinct.

"Like I said," Cole addressed my sister as we walked closer. "The officers didn't book him or the guy we brought him in with, so he's all good."

Eryn stood to her feet, adjusting her off the shoulder crop top over her leggings. "Perfect, thank you, Cole." She looked my way next. "I will take it from here."

"And will you call me too?"

She smirked while looking away, and I felt like throwing up.

"And I don't mean dodging my phone calls and only calling me to see if we arrested your brother, which you never told me was EP."

"He *hates* when I tell people he's my brother."

"To get free shit," I added. "Yes."

Cole chuckled.

"Hey," I said to him. "What's gonna happen to the other guy? He's getting married tomorrow and technically we didn't fight—"

"We'll release him in the next hour." Cole fanned the air. "The officers just wanted to get you guys out of the bar before you damaged property. The owner of the Purple Cat is good friends with the commissioner. Officers arrested you two to protect the property more than anything else. Getting arrested will leave the other guy a little shaken up for the aisle, but he should be good."

If he made it there after all his drama.

I didn't care to think anymore about it, so I told Cole, "Cool," and left with my sister after she bid Cole farewell with a hug.

"How'd you even know I was here?" I asked the moment we were close to the precinct exit.

"Tracked your phone here." As we stepped outside, she pushed her hand into her designer crossbody, pulling out my phone. "I got it from the officers who arrested your dumb ass."

Eryn rolled her eyes when I took the device out of her hand as we made our way up the city block.

The precinct was within walking distance of my condo, so I knew I could get there on foot. We walked in that direction.

"I called you three times before heading to sleep and you didn't answer, so I got worried considering your latest shift in behavior, which, by the way, what the fuck?"

"I went out for a drink."

"And a fist fight over a girl?"

"Her fiancé found us in the bathroom."

Her brows piqued. "Excuse me?"

I folded my arms over my chest.

"What the hell were you planning to do in the bathroom with her, Everett?"

"What you think?"

She grunted. "Everett, seriously?"

"I was drunk." We stopped at the crosswalk. "I wanted to see how far she would take things since she was planning to get married the next day. Made sense to do it but again I was drunk." I shrugged. "I wanted to know if she had someone at home, how far was she willing to go to jeopardize what she had."

She shook her head. "I swear. Ever since this shit with Brielle, you've been spiraling hard. I don't know what the hell you need to do to get a grip, but you need to do it like yesterday."

I blinked in response.

"No one should ever get you like this." Eryn looked me up and down. "You're gaining weight at a speed I've never seen you do before, like ever. Which I don't mind. You know I've always carried a little extra myself. Your gain is barely noticeable to others, I'm sure, but if you continue like this, beyond vanity, your health will fail, especially with you getting drunk like every night. And now you're getting locked up over bride-to-be pussy? At almost 39? It's a miracle they didn't book your ass. Can you imagine the field day the press would have with that shit?!"

We stood at the crosswalk even though it was our light to cross.

"You went your entire career, staying out of trouble, avoiding gossip, and having nothing to mess with your money. Getting arrested, booked, and a mugshot would've been a grim look, Ev. Post-retirement too? You've been concerned about how you'd make money after boxing? When the phones stop ringing with offers, you'd have reason to worry. They hate jailbirds a lot."

"Eryn—"

"Do something, Everett, please. Because bro, I am worried." Eryn looked up at me with tears in her eyes. "I don't know what that something is, but do something. You are not in the right city to be losing your shit like this."

I inhaled a deep breath and dropped my head forward.

She was right. I was trippin'. For the past month, I had been trippin' and to no one's detriment but my own.

So I nodded, pulling her into a tight hug, hearing as she sniffed her tears back.

"Aight," I said to her. "I hear you. I'm on it."

Seven

"Not to be repetitive, but I can't get over how stunning you are in person."

I blushed.

"Your profile picture and your photos online don't do you justice."

My cheeks officially ached from smiling for so long.

On a Saturday evening, just before 9pm, I sat in GrayArea feeling pleased with myself for not keeping my word on deleting HeartMates, because it had finally come through.

"This soufflé you suggested is delectable," he complimented next. "Beautiful and with great taste. Am I lucky or am I lucky?"

I giggled, lifting my hand to cover my mouth so I wouldn't embarrass myself by accidentally spitting out my dessert.

His name was Ivan Brown. It happily surprised me to see we were both a match when I received the alert that Ivan hearted my profile picture. He was a serial entrepreneur from Texas, so he had a southern twang in his deep voice. Waited outside the restaurant to greet me when

I arrived. Held the door and pulled out my seat. A gentleman, for sure. He looked good and smelled better. Even as I sat across from him, I somehow got whiffs of his expensive cologne whenever a pocket of air passed between us.

The man was fine. Both fine in features and as a normal date.

Thank you, God.

"You know we have to do a second date, right?"

I grinned so hard.

And he said all the right things. Ivan checked off all the boxes on my list.

I'd finally found the perfect one.

And right on time, because I was growing warts on my lips from kissing so many frogs.

Not really, but Ivan kept hope alive for sure.

"Definitely a second date," I agreed, lifting my glass to take a sip of water, smiling behind my rim.

He grinned back, and my heart melted. The date was winding down and had gone so well. I sat across from him, mentally pairing my first name with his last.

I inhaled a steady breath to calm my heart from wanting to fly out of my chest, since it felt like it had grown wings the second we exchanged our first words that night.

The man was perfect and so was the night.

Apryl Wilde was finally getting what she deserved as a willing participant in the dating world.

The server approached our table with the checkbook and placed it between us. I had lifted my hand off my lap, prepared to lean forward and pick it up when he already had his card in his hand.

"I got it," is all he said without paying a second glance.

Ivan slid his card into the book's jacket and gestured for the server to come and get the book.

"I had such an amazing time," I told him.

"I did as well." He winked. "You are a delight."

I blushed. "You cannot imagine the experience I've had since re-entering the dating world."

"Oh, I can imagine." He snickered. "It's slim pickings out here."

I pointed at him. "An understatement."

"When you've found the perfect find," Ivan added. "It's like you've got to hang onto them for dear life." He belly laughed, and I did too.

"It's a jungle out here for sure," I concurred.

Relief.

This man didn't have a single flaw, and the date was as flawless.

Wait until I tell Stas how much of a success this was!

After the server returned the booklet and Ivan retrieved his card, I gathered my things, prepared to leave, and float all the way home.

I'd lowered my eyes into my bag for only a moment to pick through my things for my rouge lipstick, to dab a bit more color on my lips before stepping out, but I caught when Ivan gestured to someone behind me.

Thinking it was the server and giving it no other thought, I asked, "So, about that second date—"

"Ivan?" the feminine voice questioned behind me.

I tossed a glance over my shoulder and did a double take. The woman stood over my shoulder dressed in a crop sweater, high-waist jeans and leather boots. She was shapely and had a lot of curves, slightly more than me. What was clearer was the confused look she wore on her beautiful, heart-shaped face. My eyes moved between Ivan and the woman for a short while before Ivan smiled and intoned, "Paige, good! You're on time."

Perplexed would be for the lack of a better word to describe the moment.

The mystery of this woman grew more when Ivan introduced us.

"Paige, this is Apryl. Apryl, this is Paige."

We exchanged smiles, both of our brows showing signs of confusion.

"Paige, this is my first date with Apryl, and it went really well." Ivan looked at me and flashed his teeth my way. "Apryl, this is going to be my second date with Paige since our first date last week went really well as well."

I had to take a deep breath to ground myself at that moment, since it felt like I had stepped into a warped universe.

Paige folded a few locks of her curly hair behind the bend of her ear.

"I'm sorry," she started. "But Ivan, did you... double book or... something?"

"That was what I was about to ask." I couldn't mask the quavering in my voice. My heart was racing, making me breathe harder than normal. "Because I'm a little confused."

And I was, but even confused, couldn't explain exactly what I was.

"Oh, there's nothing to be confused about," he stated, pressing his back to his chair. "Paige is the mother of an adorable little boy who turned seven last month and Apryl is a very successful businesswoman with a bank account I wouldn't dare compete with. You two have something the other doesn't and I refuse to choose between you."

The wrinkles in my brows deepened.

"So I figured, if things went well, you two should meet because I plan to date both of you."

I was so stunned I couldn't give a reaction. So Paige did it for us both.

"The fuck?!" she exclaimed, a touch too high. "Ivan, are you serious right now?"

"Very," he doubled down.

"Okay, so." She folded her arms. "Dating two women is fine, although I don't agree with it, but what happens when you form a connection with Apryl and I?"

"We'll all start our relationship," he answered matter-of-factly.

My jaw dropped even further at the audacity.

"Wow." Paige expressed with humor. "If you believed in polygamy, you should've led with that because I would've told you I didn't, and I would've sent you on your way."

"Same," I finally chimed in. "Because I'm all about monogamy."

"Monogamy is so dated." He fanned the air.

"Well." I leaned forward in my seat. "If you feel so strongly about that, why don't you go search for women who are compatible with your thinking and leave those of us who don't believe it's dated alone? Like you found us." I shook my head. "This is so lazy of you."

"The way I see it is," Ivan said, leaning in too, but he folded his hands on the table and took the posture of someone trying to negotiate a deal. He repulsed me. "I am a great guy."

I rolled my eyes away. Paige made her annoyance more audible.

"I'm good looking, make good money and own my home. I'm an excellent conversationalist. I know exactly what women want - love and money - and if you two give it time, I can show you how incredible I am in bed, too."

Yup. I'm deleting the app.

"Aside from all that, you two really have no other choice, do you?" He pointed at Paige. "You're a single mother with a *job* and not a *career*. You have no goals and you're looking for marriage. There's barely any man who'll want you."

Paige's eyes went wide.

"And you." Ivan pointed at me. "You make too much money and you're too settled into your lifestyle for a man to feel like a man in your presence, which men hate. You're also well into your 30s with no kids and no plans to have any. What will I do with you? Enjoy only you for the rest of my life? Please don't lie to yourself. The clock is ticking and I'm sure you can hear it."

"*Motherfucker,*" I whispered.

"I am a catch. I am *the* catch, and you two would do well by getting in line with what I'm offering."

Great, so he's a sociopath.

I abruptly pushed my seat back to stand up. The legs of the chair made a harsh screeching sound against the floor beneath them. I was done with him.

"Girl," I said to Paige when I was on my feet. "You want this seat?"

"To hit him with?" She quizzed. "Sure. To sit? Hell no."

"Cool. Ivan?" I turned to glare down at him. "Thank you for dinner and fuck you for wasting my time."

———

"Paige? The girl who he planned to join our date told me Ivan was her thirteenth date since joining the app. Thirteenth!"

I sat on my sister's kitchen stool the next day, a Sunday, like I've always done, retelling my dating disaster from the night before.

The rain outside pelted her kitchen window, the clouds above tinting the room with a slight gray hue.

The day matched my mood. I was down badly and over it. I felt completely defeated.

My head was in my hand when I grunted. "This was only my third date and I've decided I can't do this anymore."

"Stop using the app, but don't quit dating," Stas suggested while seasoning chicken breasts in a metal bowl. "You're just getting out there after Troy."

I rolled my tongue in my mouth in response to her saying his name.

It had been two years since my and Troy's breakup and still the mention of his name caused a sharp pain to shoot through my chest near my heart. He'd literally broke my heart, ruined eleven years of what we built. And unfortunately, while I was over dating, I was still not over him.

"You haven't dated in over a decade."

"Because the dating scene is trash." I scooted to the edge of my seat. "See, you don't understand how bad it is, Stas. You married your college sweetheart and didn't have to encounter the filth that is out there who are being labeled as candidates. It's bad, sis."

"Give it time."

"Stas, I am done." I shook my head. "Last night sealed the deal for me."

"Apryl."

"I have no clue what factory is producing these men, but these assholes are defective as hell. Malfunctioning in public. Saying some real off the wall and adjacent Handmaid's Tale bullshit. The state of the dating scene is at a level orange. It's a dating recession in this bitch. A whole ass mess and I cannot. I will not."

"So that's it?" She stopped moving around her kitchen to gather seasonings to give me her full attention. "You're just going to quit like that?"

"Yes." I nodded. "Just like that."

She shook her head.

"I'll be fine. The only thing I'm going to have a hard time with is not having sex."

She pursed her lips.

"I've been celibate and not by choice. Managing that hasn't been hard, but I can no longer lie to myself about being able to live without sex. I want sex. I *love* sex and I miss it dearly, but I'm not willing to deal with the losers attached to the dick. They're maddening."

"You value intimacy," she acknowledged. "Always have."

"I do, very much, but it's like I said; I'm comfortable being alone. I just would love not to be. But if being alone is what I must be to avoid gold diggers 2.0, narcissistic control freaks, and sociopaths, then so be it. I value peace more than sex, more than anything, and peace is not out there with these men. I'm not willing to sacrifice that in exchange for intimacy."

She nodded. "*That* I get."

We were quiet for a moment, her returning to preparing dinner and me returning to my thoughts.

If I had it my way, I wouldn't know a thing about what the dating scene was all about. I loved being in a relationship. I thought Troy would be my last. The disappointment still eats at me.

"What if," Stas offered, breaking the silence, "what if you got rid of the list, went after exactly what you wanted, and anything or anyone who isn't in alignment with what you want, you don't even try to see how you can be flexible. Instead, don't even give them a second of your time. Stay firm in your vision for what you want from a man. No exceptions. Similar to what you're doing now, but not focusing primarily on their potential flaws."

I looked over at her. "What?"

"I've never liked your list and the fact that you follow it so religiously. The other day I realized why. It's negative and restrictive."

I blinked in response.

"Each line begins with *does not* and it's negative, which opens the door for you to attract negativity."

"Okay, Ghandi."

"No." She giggled. "Hear me out. The law of attraction is working either way. You saying *doesn't,* but listing the attributes after *doesn't,* is you using the law of attraction to get what you *don't* want. Now, if you know what you want, minus the list, and if you encounter a person who meets none of the things you want, you'll just know not to bother." She shrugged. "What are the odds that all of your dates have gone to shit after you created that list when you started dating again?"

"Look." I threw my hands up. "The only reason I made that list was to have a starting point since I haven't dated in years. I'm not at all married to that list. I'm willing to try what you're suggesting. But I don't think it'll make that much of a difference, if a difference, at all."

"I'll take that. And I'm positive the tide will change."

"All right, salt of the earth."

She stared at me, confused.

"Ghandi, tide, salt... get it?" I quizzed. "The Salt March where Ghandi and his supporters walked 240 miles to defy British policy by making salt from sea water to protest the British tax on salt in India back in the day?"

"Witty... random and very corny," she teased. "You were always the pretty history geek."

"Oh, whatever."

She snorted.

"Apryl, any man would be lucky to have you."

My smile melted into a frown, and I swooped my hand across the back of my neck. "I don't want any man. I want *the* man meant to enhance me and make me better than I already am."

"So, go *only* for that, no list necessary." She grinned.

EIGHT

"Everett, my love," my mother answered on the other end of my phone. "It's been too long since I've heard your voice. How are you?"

I laid in bed on a Sunday afternoon with a headache that wouldn't go away. Though what happened at the bar occurred two days ago, I was still feeling the aftereffects of that endless night.

A pounding headache to match an upset stomach was making my day drag. My choices left me nauseated all-day.

This was getting old.

Eating all the wrong things in excess, drinking way too frequently, then waking the next morning to my energy levels being in the trash and not understanding how to get them back up. It was getting old and so was I. All I wanted to do was lay in bed, and for someone who worked out six days out of the week for at least three hours at a time, this was a major downgrade and wasn't a routine I could stick with. Something had to change.

Eryn's voice played in my head on repeat after I returned home during the early morning hours on Saturday. She was right. I needed to get a grip.

So, I called the one person who I knew could help me do it.

"I know, ma, I'm sorry for not calling."

"You don't have to apologize." She snickered. "More important things are keeping you too inundated to call your mother, right?"

I chuckled. "Ma."

She always had a way of having Eryn and I analyze ourselves and our choices with her leading questions. And she always had plenty of them.

My mother, Dr. Liz Peters, a licensed psychotherapist, offered therapy in her basement office in the brownstone I grew up in, in Brooklyn, New York. Being the child of a woman who studied how people thought, behaved, and felt for a living made for an emotionally advanced childhood.

Every decision she made and action she took was part of her being a loving mother and the other part, a distinct scientific approach. Her focus was always on helping us face our emotions head on and to understand and manage our behaviors. The result? We'd either not do shit to get in trouble or get in trouble and do our best to hide it, wishing she'd beat our ass if she found out, which she never did. Because talking it out, trying to pinpoint the motivation behind our actions and having to tell her word for word in therapy sessions that would last the entire day, was way more torture than any ass whopping would've provided.

At least that's what we thought.

My mother never just said what she thought of my sister and my choices. She'd only ask leading questions all posed so Eryn and I would come to the conclusions ourselves.

Eryn always found it frustrating to talk to our mother. My sister would much rather be a closed story and keep everything to herself. This only made our mother more intrigued and determined to crack my sister's book open.

"I'm fine," I answered.

"Let me ask you again, because your voice doesn't match your answer. And maybe next time, you can pretend harder. How are you, Everett?"

I snorted, then sighed.

"Not well, ma," I admitted. "It's been a difficult few weeks, if I'm being honest."

"You're being honest now," she said. "Is what you're going through something you can't change?"

"I could change it."

"Then that's good news."

I sighed into the phone again.

"New York's no California in the winter, I'll admit," she explained. "We had a snowstorm the other day in Brooklyn, but the snow has been clearing up since the sun is out a lot now."

I draped my forearm over my eyes.

"You should fly out," she offered. "Your room is still waiting on you to occupy it and yes, it's cold, but that's what makes hot chocolate in Bryant Park possible."

I licked my lips at the thought of getting hot white chocolate from the boutique chocolatier right across from the park in Manhattan.

I needed to get out of L.A. for a little, even for just a week. Trying to cope with the Brielle situation had nearly got me locked up for real.

I needed distance between myself and the scene of Brielle's crime, California.

"Aight, ma, you had me at hot chocolate." I smirked. "I'll be back home this week."

———

"I'm flying out to Brooklyn tomorrow evening."

Later that day, Eryn showed up at my condo with dinner. Grilled salmon, wild rice, and grilled Brussels sprouts she picked up at the local clean eating restaurant. It was two minutes from my condo's lobby. I knew this because I passed it on my way to other things.

I almost forgot how good something could taste without being breaded or deep fried, dripping with oil.

After my announcement, I noticed Eryn stopped chewing for only a moment before continuing to eat.

All she replied with was, "Oh?"

"Yeah." I nodded, forking another piece of salmon into my mouth. "I called mom earlier and you know how she does. Won't just come on out and ask me to come home and visit?"

Eryn kept her eyes down on her recycled container filled with food.

"Daquan called me two days ago about an appearance he hooked up for me in Brooklyn."

"*Hmph*," she huffed.

"I'm taking part in a community center opening this summer. Gonna teach the kids how to swim."

"That's... great."

"It's a one-day gig," I added. "I'm thinking I might stay out there until the summer, though, just before the community center opens. Sublet the condo here." I shrugged. "I found some people to rent it out to for three months, so I'll be back in July, then will fly back to New York for the community center opening later that month. I got movers coming here in two hours to move some of my stuff out of here and put it in the storage unit I rented until the end of June. I figured I can get my head together out east, fly back with a rational mind before returning to NYC again to meet my obligations for the gig. When all is done, I will return to Cali."

"I see," she said next.

Eryn was always so weird about New York since leaving. She hadn't been back, not once in the six years we've been living out here in California. It was home for us, but she'd developed an aversion to going back to our home state.

My attention returned to inside my container when she suggested, "I think it'll be good for you to head back to New York for a bit."

I peeked up at her.

"Daquan ran the idea he had by me before calling you with it. I told him he was right on time, considering what happened to you and Brielle." She unscrewed the cap off her water bottle. "I personally would find it to be torture to return to New York, but I think the time away from Cali will help you get your mind right again."

I studied her for longer, watching as she returned to pushing around her food.

"Baby sis."

She peeked up at me.

"You finally ready to tell me why you hate New York so much and why things get weird between us whenever I bring up New York?"

She shrugged, stabbing her plastic fork into her food. "There's just too many memories of heartbreak there, that's all."

She always gave the same answer, but would never elaborate. My sister was a closed book. If she shared anything with someone, they would have to consider themselves lucky because she didn't let anyone into the inner workings of her mind, not me and not even our mother.

"What happened between you and Simeon? You're always so cryptic when sharing what went wrong with y'all."

She placed her fork into her container and sat back in her seat.

"Did he cheat on you?"

"Of course not."

"Hurt you physically?"

I balled a fist to brace myself for her response because if it was anything but a no, I would have no choice but to track him down and crack his skull open with my bare hands.

"He would never," she confirmed.

I placed my plastic fork in my container. "Then what happened?"

"I don't really want to get into it. Simeon didn't cheat on me. He didn't beat my ass. He just wasn't ready to give me what he didn't have, and I was. That's it."

"That tells me nothing."

"Can we change the subject, please?"

I exhaled.

"Let's think more about you and going back home, and this dope opportunity," she insisted. "I'm sure you already know mom will have a therapy-inspired outing planned for you."

I tightened my lips to hold back my laugh. "She already has one planned and used it to get me to agree to come home."

Eryn wagged her finger. "She's a tricky one, that one."

I snickered. "You should come too."

She bit at her bottom lip nervously.

"Take a brief break from the corporate office and the grueling task of extinguishing celebrity gossip fires."

"Nah." She shook her head, her long hair falling in her face. "I'm trying to get promoted at the firm, so there are no off days for me, which you know I would love. What I wouldn't do for a day in bed, sleeping all day."

Eryn was a PR Marketing executive at Opal Sands Marketing Agency- one of the elite marketing agencies on the West Coast. They were the reason she wanted to move to Los Angeles. She loved her career with every breath in her body. Which was kind of scary for me.

Eryn lived, ate, and dreamt of marketing. When she wasn't working, she was thinking of working. Barely enjoying the fruits of her labor. She found momentary releases through one-night-stands and excessive shopping sprees. And if she wasn't doing that, she was sleeping. The woman loved to sleep.

"Bring me back a cheesecake."

I looked her way again.

"When you come back, bring me back a cheesecake."

"You know I'm not planning to come back until late June, right?"

"That's cool." She forced a grinned. "I just need some way to ensure you come back to L.A."

"Eryn."

"Cali could never compete with your love of New York, of Brooklyn. Love it so much you tattooed Bed-Stuy at the side of your forearm. The most love you gave Cali was wearing your blue Dodgers cap occasionally."

I folded my lips in my mouth and bit them closed because she was right. New York was home and the only reason I moved to California was because Eryn wanted to flee the East Coast for reasons she probably will never discuss. And then I got to Los Angeles, and a year later met a girl, Brielle, and fell in love, and decided this was my new home.

But with the prospect of returning to Brooklyn to stay until the summer, I could already feel my spirits lifting.

NINE

I could see the snow caps in a bird's-eye view from my rounded-corner window. Clumps of white on everything and sugared on bare tree branches.

The captain tilted the private plane to the left, offering a view into the distance. Pillars of skyscrapers appearing behind light fog that could've been frosted air. I shivered at the prospect of what I was seeing being true. It would be cold outside when we landed, and I sincerely wasn't ready.

The last time I came to visit was during the summer on business about a year ago for a fight at The Garden. Although I had time to catch up with my mother and my father, along with close friends, my visit was brief. Too short.

The flight attendant visited my club seat to collect the remaining food items and an empty champagne glass, reminding me to, "Please stay seated, Mr. Peters, until we have landed."

There was a shift immediately. I didn't sense the same weight on my shoulders or the toxic thoughts stalking my mind. I was there, in the present, and back in New York City.

The landing was a breeze and so was the jog down the jet's stairs into a waiting black car where the chauffeur placed my bag in the trunk for my convenience.

I traveled lightly for a three-month stay. I figured anything I needed and didn't bring, I could buy. My stay would be temporary anyway, so there was no desire to over-pack.

As soon as my driver joined in the traffic, a chorus of honks and revving engines was there to greet us. Rows of black and yellow cars, box trucks, and rental bikes zipped up and down the blacktop roads and white-lined bike lanes. The buildings, as always, were all so tall, they seemed to kiss the sky. People impatiently jaywalked or waited at cross-walks, all distracted with scrolling on their phones. Their exhales were all visible as white transparent smoke. March in New York was chilly and unforgiving.

"Hopefully that groundhog didn't see his damn shadow," I mumbled to myself about the groundhog tradition while pressing my back to my seat.

There was an event in Pennsylvania on Groundhog's Day where everyone depended on a groundhog not seeing his shadow in February of every year, so spring could arrive sooner than later in the east.

The expressway took us from Queens to Brooklyn. Queens was a short distance from Brooklyn, so soon after my landing I'd arrived in Bed-Stuy.

We drove down Fulton Street, the heart of Bed-Stuy, and I barely recognized the area. Well-structured buildings, coffee shops, bakeries, a bookstore that appeared busy. But the most obvious were the equal sightings of black, brown and white people along the shopping strip when once it was mainly black people who breathed life into these Brooklyn blocks. It was like running into the 20-year-old who, when you last saw them, was in diapers. My city had continued to grow without me and the feeling was bittersweet.

The driver turned onto the block where the brownstone I grew up was. The houses were the same, but the vibe was different. More quiet, more mature. Where there was once just a sidewalk, now had trees with green slow-release watering bags around the foot of them. The neighbors now had small planters on their steps, like my mother's.

She always kept plants on her stoop. Said it attracted life.

The driver pulled the car over and hopped out of the vehicle. I got out slowly, taking in the new environment of my old neighborhood. Traces of what I remembered were everywhere beneath all that Bed-Stuy had become. I'd have to get used to it.

I climbed the stairs with the bag the driver retrieved and handed to me, and headed up to the big red door with the acorn reef.

As I reached the top of the stairs, my mother opened it.

Big salt and pepper curls are where my eyes went to first before settling on the eyes that smiled without the help of her lips.

Elizabeth Lorraine Peters. Veteran psychologist to everyone, especially in this hood. But to me, the woman who gave me life.

I was nineteen months old when my mother earned her master's in psychology. She took me up on stage with her and my father captured her on camera in her cap and gown and with me in her arms. She and my pops could have left Bed-Stuy after she earned her master's. But she refused. She wanted Eryn and me to experience the culture, even though everyone who didn't live here couldn't understand her loyalty to the hood. Her loyalty to remaining here had roots in her providing therapy to the people, unknowingly.

Her approach to the sciences was one that was gentle but direct. She wasn't anything like what most would perceive a psychologist to be. So much so, I didn't know I was being counseled. No one knew when they spoke with her. Not until we were so deep into what appeared to be a light discussion. But by the time we realized what she was doing, my mother would've helped us uncover something about ourselves that we then became curious to learn more about.

But she was my mother first, and the hug she gave me when I walked into her open arms was proof of this.

"Everett," she said in my ear as she hugged me tightly.

I had to bend my legs a little at the knees to meet her 5'4 height.

My mother took me by the hand to guide me over the threshold. "Come in, son."

Evergreen and patchouli scented the air, always have.

She kept a bowl of dried flowers and leaves near the entrance, so from the entryway to our living room smelled like a florist's shop.

Everything looked different. The runner that extended from the entryway, down the hall where the living room was on the other side of the wall.

Inside, the living room always reminded me of the brownstone living room in Spike Lee's *Mo Betta Blues*. A large, beautiful bay window facing the street, an antique upholstered sofa, and the matching loveseat and armchair positioned opposite an intricately designed coffee table carved out of wood imported from Africa.

The drapes were still heavy. Photos of my mother, Eryn, and I still crowded the mantel. In one of those pictures was my father, a constant reminder that we were once a family who lived under the same roof.

My parents separated and then divorced when I was a kid. The divorce was the calmest I'd ever seen and nothing like the horror shows we see on TV. Our parents were never the affectionate types in front of us, though I remember hearing them get intimate at night a few times. The only thing the divorce changed was my father's address. He was still around though, had keys to the brownstone - probably still does. My father was at every birthday and graduation.

He always traveled the world as a money broker, an entrepreneur. Never the type to be still, he and my mother could not have been more opposite than they already were. But they shared a love for Eryn and I.

"You look good."

I turned to my mother to see the smile on her face wrinkling the corners of her eyes.

"You look like you've been bulking up for something." She took a seat and patted the cushion beside her. "Got anything in your plans?"

I obliged, taking a seat while shaking my head. "I put on a little weight post retirement, is all."

My mother stared at me for what felt like minutes, but really it was seconds. And all she said was, "Okay," when she spoke again.

"Do you want to run your bag upstairs before we head out?" she asked next.

"Definitely," I answered.

"I'll call a cab in the meantime."

The stairs still squeaked whenever I walked on them and I could still see inside my room through the gap beneath the door as I climbed the last few steps.

Inside, my room still smelled like cedar wood thanks to my bedroom's cedar chest. While the house downstairs had changed, everything in my room remained the same. A full-size bed, a study desk, a dresser with a mirror and posters of Muhammad Ali and Mike Tyson on my wall.

I'd moved out of the brownstone when I was eighteen, but my mother made sure the house cleaners didn't neglect the room whenever they cleaned the rest of the house.

There was something about returning home. Everything felt more like home this time and not like I was visiting with plans to go back.

My mother and I sat inside the chocolatier's boutique. The decadent multi-layered scent of every kind of chocolate sugared the air. Sweet as vanilla to spicy, like chili peppers. The chocolatier mixed chocolate with unfamiliar and familiar flavors, which created a unified aroma I could only describe with a moan. Exactly how I always remembered it from the day I first visited at 10-years-old. The space was small and thankfully, there weren't too many patrons in the shop, making it the perfect spot for my mother and me to sit and chat.

She blew into her mug of dark hot chocolate before taking another sip. My cup of hot white chocolate sat on the coffee table in front of us. I focused on the wavy white lines swirling out of my ceramic mug.

"How's California?" She asked.

During our ride to the city, she did most of the talking, updating me on the things about her practice. She planned to travel to Hawaii again in autumn, where she will provide therapy for a mental health retreat. After attending for the first time the year prior, she loved it so much she had to return to provide her services.

"Cali is Cali." I shrugged, leaning forward to pick up my cup. "I definitely needed to take a break from it."

"Take a break from what?" My mother probed, voice as gentle as can be, questioning directly, like always. "It's just a state. A non-living thing. What could it have possibly done to you to make you need a break from it?"

"Something happened, ma."

She nodded, then returned to blowing in her mug of hot chocolate.

I dropped my attention to the mug in my hand. "I've been eating and drinking a lot. More like excessively."

"Oh?"

"Yeah." I took a sip of my drink. "I got arrested last week."

I peeked over at her, prepared to see the disappointment, but my mother wore an even disposition, like I knew she would.

"What happened?"

"I was out at a bar and this bride-to-be—"

"No," she interjected, placing a hand on my knee. "Not what happened at *the bar?* What caused the excessive eating and drinking?"

I ran my hand down my face slow. "Always straight to the root, huh, young lady?"

She smiled, and dimples appeared around her mouth. "It's always a great place to start."

I inhaled a deep breath and asked, "Do you remember Princess Latimore?"

"I do." She nodded. "The first girlfriend you ever brought home. The only girl you've ever brought home before Brielle, actually."

I nodded too. "I think you also remember Princess because you really liked her."

"Good observation." My mother giggled. "Princess was your perfect pair, and I liked that every time you spoke to her or *about* her, you smiled from your heart and with your eyes."

I bit at my bottom lip. "She was a good girl."

I looked out into the boutique briefly, reminiscing about my first love at 19-years-old.

"I'll never forget your face when I told you I messed things up with Princess." I cracked up. "You were livid with me."

"I wasn't livid," she clarified. "Just *very* disappointed."

"I know," I acknowledged, "and because of that, I told myself I wouldn't introduce you to any more of my girlfriends, just in case you end up liking them and I mess things up again."

I sipped my white hot chocolate, closing my eyes at the buttery sweet taste of velvety cream coating my tongue.

"I had several relationships after Princess. Six, to be exact, and I messed them all up. Lying, cheating. Lying about cheating." I wagged my finger. "But that seventh one? My relationship with Brielle? I said I'd change for her. Messing things up wouldn't happen."

"How'd that pan out?"

"Well," I snorted. "I brought her home. You loved her just as much as you loved Princess and I made sure I was the best boyfriend a boyfriend could ever be... and then she rewarded me by messing things up. And in a major way, I can't get over."

I ran my hand down my low-trimmed beard.

"And I can't say shi—" I cleared my throat. "And I can't say anything about it because that's my karma."

"Your karma," she repeated. "*Hmph.*"

"What?" I grinned at her. "Too spiritual for the scientist?"

She laughed out loud before looking around herself and giggling. "Maybe a little. But what I want to know is, if you're not able to feel through what happened, how are you coping?"

"Coping?"

"*Mm-hmm.*" She placed her mug on the coffee table in front of us. "When you feel what you feel anytime you think about what Brielle did, how do you ride that wave of grief? How are you grieving what you two had if you don't allow yourself to acknowledge the pain you feel from the death of it?"

I gave it some thought, finding myself coming up with nothing.

"I remember after your friend Chase's funeral; you were so closed off. I tried like hell to get you to talk to me about what you were feeling, and you'd always tell me you were fine. I, of course, couldn't think for you, but I suspected you felt guilt for not being able to help him the day he drowned in that park."

I nodded slowly.

"You started eating sandwich cookies. Sandwich cookies in the morning, afternoon, and night. And it got to where you were going through a three-row pack a day. And I didn't want to tell you anything about it because I knew you wouldn't admit to it. So I fed two birds with one seed. I signed you up for swimming so you'd learn how to swim and not develop a phobia around water, and I signed you up so you could stay active. The less time you had to eat, the less time you would spend doing it was my logic."

"I remember that."

"But then your grief materialized in needing to hit things and then you started fighting in school. Your father behind my back signed you up for boxing, which he knew I didn't agree with. It took many years and a few therapy sessions with my therapist to see his motivation and mine were the same. We just picked different focuses, is all." She placed a hand on my knee and squeezed it. "You've always turned to eating your feelings when all else failed. It was unhealthy then, and it's more unhealthy now. And if you're doing unhealthy things, I can't imagine you have time to do the healthy ones."

I lowered my view to my fingers.

"When was the last time you went for a swim?"

"It's been a while."

"Worked out?"

I shook my head.

We were silent for a moment, allowing the sounds in the chocolatier boutique to fill our listening space.

"How do you feel about what Brielle did to you?"

I inhaled a deep breath and admitted in an exhale, "She broke my heart. It shattered completely to irreparable proportions. She was my plan. She was *the* plan, and she ruined it. But I'm disappointed more than anything. Disappointed that I even feel this way after what I did to my relationships in the past. I shouldn't have a place to say anything about what she did. I should feel guilt more than feeling betrayed."

"You may acknowledge the hurt Brielle caused you, Everett. Yes, you hurt others the same, but that's not a reason to not acknowledge she hurt you and that it disappointed you that what you envisioned for you and Brielle didn't come to fruition. Trying to numb that realization by attempting to eat and drink your feelings is not a remedy. Choosing to consume to distract yourself from what you must feel to move on is a punishment that has no purpose. Stop making it an option. It solves nothing. Instead, it becomes a solid foundation on which to build an additional problem."

I leaned back in my seat.

"It happened. Everything has happened. What will you do now to move forward that doesn't entail punishing yourself for things you no longer do?"

I shrugged.

She turned my head to look her way. "Acknowledge and accept you're in the aftermath of a storm, then rebuild and grow in the wake of that storm, that's what. You know what you must do, Everett. Do it and quit feeling sorry for yourself. Life must go on, my love."

———

"Meki," I said into the phone. "What's good, man?"

"E *motherfuckin'* P," he said back.

I let a smile wrinkle the sides of my mouth.

"What's going on?"

"Man." I leaned my back against the hotel's leather headboard.

My mother insisted I stay in my room in the brownstone, but I needed space. Being home always recharged me. Remembering where I came from was food for the soul I didn't know I needed. But staying there didn't make me feel like I'd get anything done. Plus, I was still recovering from the conversation my mother and I had and I knew if I was under the same roof as her, she'd dive more into the situation. I just could not talk more about Brielle and the aftermath of our breakup. So I booked a suite at The Braxton Hotel, reasoning I'd stay there for a week tops. That would be enough time to find a place of my own.

"I'm in New York," I informed him.

"Oh, word?"

"Yeah, until the middle of June, at least."

"Dope," he replied. "We gotta link up."

I blew air through my lips. "That's why I'm calling."

"What's up? Talk to me."

"I... uh." I chewed gently on my bottom lip. "I have a small appearance coming up in Bed-Stuy. A community center is opening in late July near my old neighborhood and they want me to teach the children how to swim on opening day. You know, for the optics."

"That's what's up, Ev," he complimented.

"Thanks. You think you got availability in your calendar to train me?"

Meki earned his living as a personal trainer. Got his start working at a celebrity trainer's gym before he branched out and opened his own gym in New York three-years-ago. Meki always had the vision and the cash to do it as a descendant of 20th century black elites who were entrepreneurs and engineers, but he didn't have the experience. So he worked under the tutelage of celebrity trainer Robert Kurt, gained experience, and opened his own gym with his own roster of top tier trainers in the Upper West Side of Manhattan.

"Definitely," he answered. "I gotta remind you, though, that Cadence is in her last month of pregnancy, so that might affect things a little, but I can definitely get you to the gym, and we can do something. What are we working on?"

"I gained a little, so I need to burn the fat off and tone up, nothing too much. You know I'm not too into tone up exercises or whatever."

"Retirement treating you well, huh?"

Though Meki and I were pretty cool, letting him in on the shit that had me eating my feelings just didn't seem appealing to me.

"Stop by the gym on Wednesday," he instructed. "We won't have a session, but we'll prep. We'll check your BMI, give you a fitness assessment, so we'll know exactly what to focus on once the fun begins. Sounds good?"

"Sounds great, Meki." I nodded slowly. "I appreciate you."

TEN

The hard-pumping music greeted me the moment I pulled opened the gym's glass door. The squeak of sneakers entered my sound space next. I inhaled the scent of fresh linen, rubber, and traces of sweat. I'd just entered my second home.

"Hey Apryl," Michelle, the front desk receptionist, greeted with a wave. "Your 9am is already here. She told me to tell you she's on the treadmill."

"Thanks girl."

I power-walked toward my private room at MK's Sports Lounge and Gym. When trainer Meki Knight approached me two years back to come train at his gym, I was against the idea.

I'd built a career of my own, privately training clients, mainly celebrities, and wanted nothing close to a job. He promised it would never be that. Also, he promised I could use the space to train my clients, and he'd work around my schedule so he could slide in his own high-paying clientele and split the earnings from their sessions 50/50. I couldn't say no after that.

Plus, I was still raw from my breakup with my fiancé and losing who I thought was a good friend. I needed a distraction. So, I told Meki sure, and I made the sports lounge and gym my second home.

There was no place like MK's Sports Lounge and Gym. The location, disguised as a tiny setup from the door, was actually revolutionary. It was the largest sports lounge and gym in the city and it was black owned.

Two stories of gym space made up the fitness center, with an upstairs lounge overlooking the entire fitness space. Anyone who wasn't a member envied the wellness experience. That's because Meki didn't open the gym to the public. It was exclusive entry only, and you had to be invited to apply for membership.

I breezed past the open-plan area that served as a space for HIIT and boot camp classes, then peeked up at the mounted screens televising what the cameras captured in the equipment room. I glimpsed my client running on the treadmill as I continued toward my dressing quarters.

I wrapped around the corner and spotted Meki standing by one of the floor-to-ceiling windows that offered a view of the Manhattan skyline. Beside him was a tall, brown-skinned man with the broadest shoulders and the hilliest arms. He had a natural V-shape to him, but not exaggerated. At his size and width, I assumed he was a bodybuilder or someone in a similar career. The guy wore a maroon sweatshirt and the matching joggers, and stood next to Meki, engaged in their conversation. Every time he spoke, he did it with his hands, too. They were large, veiny, and had tattoos on the back of both palms.

I continued to my dressing room, throwing glances over my shoulder, trying to make out his face. It wasn't all that visible, since the rim of his cap slightly shadowed everything north of his lips.

Something about him, though, was distracting me. I couldn't get a good look at his face, but the energy he gestured with and his overall presence made me curious who he was.

I put my things away, checked myself in my full-length mirror, then made my way to my client. Couldn't help but to look Meki's way to steal a look at the gentleman he spoke with again. Meki spotted me and waved. The guy looked my way and this time I got a better look at him.

Penetrating ebony eyes, full bow-like lips. Strong jawline highlighted in a perfectly low-trimmed beard and a thick neck like a football player. He looked like a Kehinde Wiley portrait come to life of a powerful, virile warrior dressed in Jordans and a Yankee's fitted, if there were ever a portrait like that.

He was black art.

And he intrigued me.

I waved back and probably would've walked over had my client been just a little late. Instead, I approached the receptionist's front desk to get a quick look at my calendar, but really, to be nosy.

"Hey girl," I said to Michelle. "How you doin'?"

"Surviving and maintaining," she answered, handing me a bottle of water, which I usually asked for when I arrived at the gym. "You only have two in-studios today. Your first one's on the treadmill in the back and your next is at one this afternoon."

"Thanks," I told her while unscrewing the cap off my water bottle, and stealing another glance Meki's way. "So... who's the guy talking with Meki over there?"

Michelle smirked. "He's *so* fine, right? I didn't recognize him at first without all the boxing gear, but when Meki introduced us, it clicked."

"He's a boxer?"

"*Mm-hmm.*" She nodded. "Retired though, but undefeated. That's Everett Peters."

I furrowed my brows.

"You probably know him better as EP."

"Oh, okay, yeah." I nodded this time. "I've heard of him."

Vaguely. People in high places have mentioned him. I also heard Meki name drop him a few times in passing. Boxing wasn't a sport I followed, so I've never sat and watched many fights. Probably would have more if I knew about this guy. I turned to look Everett's way again. His build made sense now.

"He's a pretty big deal," Michelle added.

I shrugged, turning to face her again. "I don't follow boxing."

"Girl, neither do I." She giggled. "I just like watching men move aggressively in nothing but shorts."

I snickered. "Is Meki training him or something?"

"I don't know yet," she answered. "They arrived together, and Meki took him in the back, where we usually do fitness assessments before training begins, so... maybe?"

"*Hmph.*" I lifted my watch in view to check the time. "Let me start my session. I'll see you in a little."

"Have a good one."

During my walk over to my client, I checked over my shoulder once again to get another look at Meki's friend.

Everett Peters.

I couldn't keep my eyes off him.

He was a presence I couldn't ignore, but I had no desire to investigate any further. I was quite content with the little information I had on him.

So, I thought.

ELEVEN

I glanced in the direction I last saw her, watching as she exited toward the back.

"She looks familiar," I said to Meki while pointing her way.

"That's Apryl Wilde," he informed.

"*That's* Apryl Wilde?" I raised my hand to my low-trimmed beard to stroke. "She looks *different* in pictures."

"You mean she looks *finer* in person?"

I looked over at Meki to see him smirking at me.

I told him, "You need to get that look off your face."

He bent over laughing, and I scoffed.

Not only did she not photograph well, photos failed to capture how much of a masterpiece her body really was. Contoured waist that seemed cinched by a corset under her skin, well-rounded bubble butt that looked to be all muscle. All that with the face of an angel and eyes as brilliant as the diamond studs in her ears. She walked around the gym without the slightest clue about how magnetic her presence was. *Fine* was an understatement.

"Took a lot of convincing to get her to agree to work out of here." He shook his head, pulling out his phone. "Had to sign her as an independent contractor and add a clause in her contract that states she can train her own clients here. But she's worth it. Apryl's excellent for business."

From what I knew, Apryl had built a mini-fitness empire mainly online and from her living room. Community fitness videos, downloadable exercise guides, workout supplements, the works. Got a few endorsements that had her face in ads. A beautiful face in person but one that did not photograph well on billboards because, damn, she was breathtaking.

"Cadence is on her way up," Meki announced, breaking my focus. "I just got her text."

"Cadence?" I questioned. "Isn't she, like, ready to pop any day now?"

"Not any day soon enough." He shook his head. "Seven days overdue. She's tired of being pregnant. Cae did everything the midwife told her to do. Drank the tea and all that, and wifey is still pregnant seven days past the due date and hating it. So she's stopping by to spar for a bit. She thinks that'll do it."

"Who's she sparing with?"

"Me," he answered matter-of-factly.

I chuckled. "So you're about to box your wife, man?"

"Let her get in a few hits so she can get out her frustrations with me for doing this to her, as she says? Yes." He nodded. "Absolutely."

I laughed some more.

He gestured with his chin. "She just walked in."

All I saw was her belly as Cadence waddled her way over to us, dressed in a sports bra and maternity fitness leggings with the waistband over her baby bump.

"Oh, snap!" She hollered. "Is that *the* EP?"

"You know better than to call me that." I extended my arms for her to walk between. "Look at you all big—"

"All what?!"

I glanced at Meki and he shook his head.

"All *big* ready to spar, duh," I said instead, pulling her into a gentle hug.

"*Uh-huh.*" She giggled while wrapping her arms as far around me as they could go. "Are you here to give me some pointers?"

"EP doesn't need to give you pointers," Meki insisted. "You've been throwing right hooks at me since the day we met. You're good."

She jabbed him in the arm.

I met Cadence about a month after she and Meki got engaged. He'd told me about her in passing when they started dating, for lack of a better word, but after he moved to California, he introduced us. They'd moved back to New York for Meki to open his own gym. They also planned to start a family and wanted their children born on the East Coast since they both were born on the East Coast too.

"Anyway." Meki held his fist out for a pound. "We'll be in the back. Take a walk around, get acquainted with the place. I'll be back up front so we can discuss your assessment."

"Sounds good." I pointed at Cadence. "Aye, take it easy on him, aight?"

"I'll try." She joked, taking Meki's hand, and they walked to the back of the gym.

I turned to the floor-to-ceiling window. I pushed my hands into my pockets and gazed out at the skyline. There was something so captivating about this city. Even in near zero-degree weather, from the comfort of a warm gym, the skyline looked picturesque with dots of capped snow here and there atop skyscrapers. The city wasn't all hype. It was iconic just for existing.

"Everett." A deep voice called behind me. I turned to find another familiar face.

I smiled. "Simeon?"

He chucked his chin, closing the space between us. When he was close, he held out his hand for a handshake and I obliged, pulling him in for a brief hug too.

Simeon and my sister together were like living black Barbie and Ken dolls. An exquisite couple. Matching dark skin tones, perfect height ratio. They were a handsome couple until they weren't.

"What's going on, man?" I asked when I stepped out of our hug.

"Ah, everything's going well, thank God," he answered, displaying his always perfect rows of pearly whites. "Yourself?"

"All right," I shrugged. "Getting used to retirement life."

"I heard," he said back. "Read last month how you gave the gloves a rest. Is there a chance you'll grace a ring with your presence again?"

"Nah." I shook my head. "I still have got my mental faculties, and my health is great. I know when to bow out gracefully."

He nodded.

"So, uh." Simeon scratched the back of his neck. "How's Eryn?"

I smiled, happy to see he wanted to know.

"Eryn is Eryn." I shrugged. "Big marketing exec out in Los Angeles. Still vibrant. Still social. And still very single."

He chuckled. "I moved to California three years ago. Moved my agency over there after my client, Dallas Roque, signed with the Oakland Flames."

"Oh, shit." I lifted my fist to my mouth to hide my excitement. "*You're* Roque's agent? That's what's up. Congrats."

"Thanks, brother."

"*The* Simeon King," I recited proudly. "Glad to see you doing what you've always wanted to do, man."

"I appreciate that, thank you," he said back.

"You should reach out to Eryn," I suggested. "Since you're out in Cali now and all."

Simeon glanced down at his running sneakers before looking out the floor-to-ceiling window. "I doubt she'd want to hear from me, Ev."

Simeon and my sister were college sweethearts until they ended things shortly before their graduation. And it's a mystery what the catalyst was that ended their relationship. She wouldn't tell me and, based on Simeon's response, I doubted he'd be the one to tell me either.

"You got your phone on you?"

His eyes shifted to mine. "Yeah," he answered, patting his gray joggers' pocket. "I got it."

"Here." I held out my hand. "Let me give you her number."

"Everett—"

"Just a call, Simeon," I insisted. "At the mention of your name, she reacts similar to the way you just did when I mentioned you calling her. You two should talk."

He inhaled a deep breath. "I mean... I'll take her number, but—"

"That's all I'm asking you to do," I told him.

Simeon placed his device in my hand, and as I keyed my sister's number into his phone, I asked, "If you're in Oakland now, what are you doing back here in New York?"

"I'm here for *her*," he answered, accepting his phone back and pointing across the room.

I followed his gesture with my eyes to the woman Meki identified as Apryl Wilde earlier.

"Dallas has got this sports nutrition brand he's working to grow — Pure Roque. And I want to pitch to Apryl to endorse."

As he spoke, I watched her walk with a woman to one mat, sharing words with the woman before the woman got in position to perform an exercise flat on her back. Apryl stood over her, scanning the room, only stopping when her eyes landed on me. She did a double take when she noticed me staring back, and then she refocused her attention on her client.

She reminded me of Tatyana Ali. Long straight black hair, soft dainty facial features, and eyes that lit up like a fairytale princess. Apryl had a sweet face like an angel but a body of a seductress.

"So beautiful, right?" Simeon voiced beside me, pulling me out of my daze.

I blinked myself back into the moment.

"That's exactly why I want her on his brand," Simeon explained. "I figured I'd accept Meki's invite to join, purchase a membership here, stop by a few times before going in with my pitch."

"Smart." I nodded, moving my eyes back her way.

Apryl dropped into a squat to correct the woman's form. I tilted my head for a better view of her ass, getting lost in the natural curves of her body.

"Try not to drool though, damn," Simeon teased.

I shoved him and he broke up laughing.

"I'm in New York for another four days," he told me. "Let's meet up for lunch."

"For sure," I said. "Let me get your number and we can set up a time to do that."

Shortly after, Simeon was off to work out, and I remained in the same spot, sneaking glances at Apryl.

Looking at her, one wouldn't know she was worth millions. A modest celebrity in her own right, she trained some of the best, making a career out of sculpting the bodies of some of Hollywood's elite, notably actress Chloe Rae. I know this because Apryl's name got around. I didn't know her personally, but she endorsed a few of the sports brands that sponsored me when I fought. Though I'm sure she was a smart woman, her body was her money maker. She was a hustler. I could respect that.

I tracked her all over the area I stood and where she worked with, who, I would now assume, was her client. In the time she spent in the same space as me, our eyes met several times, each time both of us diverting our eyes away but somehow attracting each other's attention again.

She was fine. This was true. But admiring her from afar was all I wanted to do.

TWELVE

APRYL

I waved at a neighbor as I climbed the cement steps to my mother's front door. The flurries from our last winter storm had melted, leaving puddles where there were piles of snow. I sensed traces of warmth in the air, although it was subtle. Early March in Brooklyn never hinted spring was near, only that winter would stick with us for a while longer.

I approached my mother's front door and singled out the key to her house. The house was once mine and my sister's as children too, but since we've left, my mother has renovated it so much, you can't tell children once lived there.

The moment I stepped inside, I smelled something simmering in sauce cooking on the fire. I assumed it was something quick my mother put together because she wasn't the slave over the stove kind of person. It was only her, and she was a simple woman. In that regard, we were the same.

I heard her sucking her teeth behind me before I saw her.

"Apryl." She shook her head. "What did I tell you about letting yourself into my house like this, girl?"

In her hands were a bunch of flowers she probably bought from the local florist. She liked to buy herself roses... and candy and take herself out.

My mother, Camille Frasier, was the treat yourself type. She and my father split when I was only five, and she's never been in a relationship serious enough for me to see it.

"Mama, you know I have the key."

"Of which I didn't give you."

I had it made without her permission and for good reason. One of my greatest fears was coming to visit, knocking on her front door, and she not answering. Then I'd have to call the police to break in her door, only to find her dead with her eyes eaten out by one of her ugly ass cats.

One of those ugly cats moseyed up next to me and ran the side of her furry body against my leg, making me jump back.

I hated those damn things.

I used my shin to move the yellow-brown feline away, and it hissed at me.

"You better not kick my cat," she said calmly over the island in her kitchen.

"They shouldn't have walked up to me."

She sucked her teeth again. "I don't know what you don't like about them. You got so much in common with cats."

I rolled my eyes as I entered her kitchen to join her.

My mother wore her long, thick, dark auburn hair pulled back in a low bun. Around her hairline were prominent strands of gray. Except for that, you couldn't tell my mother was in her early 60s.

"Hard to please, fierce tempered, affectionate once you get to know them, and quite loyal." She focused her attention on the flowers she arranged in a glass vase. "Just like you."

"They're gross."

She shook her head.

The kitchen was the largest part of the house. With one large window with a view of the backyard, a big high island that reminded me a lot of my sister's kitchen island. Stas had the island in her home remade to look like this one to remind her of the home she grew up in. Pots and pans hung off a steel beam below the low ceiling. Everything was the same as always, except for the kitchen table.

That day, unlike any other day, there was a setup for two. She positioned two plates and a set of utensils laid opposite another set of utensils and plates.

And two wine glasses.

"Are you..." I glanced her way and back at the table. "Are you expecting someone?"

"I am," she answered curtly.

My mother had been single from the time I was a child. I never recall meeting her dates, or her bringing any men around. It was her and her friends or her by herself.

The opposite of my father.

My dad had not been single all my life.

He was married.

Three times.

And all of them have ended in divorce.

I never understood that. How my mother would know my father had moved on three times and for her to not marry once.

She's never exchanged vows. Hadn't had a boyfriend, at least to my knowledge, in decades. She's dated, I know of that. I would recall her saying she had a date on some weekends, but I've never met those men.

"Is Ms. Rema or Ms. Tonya stopping by?" I queried. Those two were my mother's best friends. She'd known them from childhood.

"No."

Short ass answers, ugh!

"Mama, why are you being so short with me?"

"Why are you all up in my business?"

I jerked my head back. "Well, excuse the heck out of me."

"You're excused." She giggled. "Apryl, you don't need to know everything happening in my life, beloved." My mother made her way over to the pot of food I smelled simmering when I walked through the door. "I'm having company over. That's enough for you to know."

"Do they have a name?"

"They do."

I narrowed my eyes. "Will you tell me?"

She stood over her stove, stirring the pot. "I won't."

I fought back my smile.

She doesn't have to tell me it isn't a date anyway, because the chances of it being one at my mother's age are slim to none.

Over the years, she has settled into the idea of living alone. She takes herself out, buys herself flowers like the new bouquet she recently added to her vase in the water. She even went to the movies alone.

The idea of it all made me cringe.

"I want to check out this movie tomorrow, but Stas is too busy to go with me," I complained to my mother one weekend last year over coffee in her kitchen. "And I can't get one of my girls to go with me because of their schedule."

She shrugged. "Then go by yourself."

I hiked my top lip up in disgust. "To the movies?!"

"Yes, to the movies." She took a sip of her latte. "It's not like you can talk at the movies, anyway. It's the perfect place to go alone. I do it all the time. I always enjoy myself."

"Uh-uh." I shook my head. "That's like going out to eat alone."

"Which I do too," she admitted causally.

I shook my head as I lifted my cup to blow into.

"Learn to love your own company and have fun alone. You shouldn't depend on others to have a good time and enjoy life. Time is of the essence. You shouldn't wait for people to help you live yours."

The premise was one I could respect, but I couldn't do it. Couldn't do it then and definitely couldn't do it now.

My eyes landed on the bowl of caramels sitting at the center of the island. I licked my lips at the sight of the wrapped candy in the crystal bowl, momentarily reminiscing on its taste. As a teenager, I gained most of my weight by eating too many of those things. I could afford to have at least one caramel these days, but I resisted and snatched my attention away, refusing to unwrap one and toss it in my mouth.

"How have your dates been?" She asked, unknowingly helping me to quit gawking at the bowl. "The ones you set up on that awful app I'm still waiting for you to get rid of."

"Horrible," I answered. "One train wreck after the other. I think I'm not cut out for this."

"You are." She stood opposite me on the side of the island. "Just stop looking."

"If I stop looking, how will I find anyone, mama?"

"Only God knows that, Apryl."

I wanted to roll my eyes, but I knew better. Instead, I listened.

"The good thing is you're putting yourself back out there after Troy."

This time, I rolled my eyes.

"When you are ready and open to something, life moves in alignment with what you want."

"Sounding a lot like Stas."

"Well, she is my child."

I glanced at the kitchen table again, at the plates and wine glasses. "Is that what you did? Be open and ready for something? Is that what's got you having dinner for two tonight?"

She blushed.

I arched my brows at that.

"Wait, I was only joking," I said. "But judging by your reaction—"

"It's time for you to go, beloved." She announced. "I love you, but I have to get ready."

"And open, huh?"

"Aht!" She threw her kitchen towel at me, and I ducked out of the way. "Goodbye."

"Oh, it's like that!" I stood up from my seat. "Okay."

She laughed. "I'll call you later this week and *please*, stop using your key to this house, girl. Thank you."

Thirteen

I combed through the clothing I packed in my designer keepall in search of a tee to throw on. It was mid-day, a few minutes after 2pm, and I was getting ready to head out for my first training session at MK's Sports Lounge and Gym.

It had been almost a month since I'd worked out. I hadn't done so much as a sit-up or a leg lift. I knew Meki was going to put me through it. Before moving out to Los Angeles six years ago, Meki used to train me privately in my home between fights. And after I moved out to California, I'd book time with him. He was brutal and very skilled in the art of fitness. I knew I'd have to put in the work that would make me sweat out all the shit I'd been eating and drinking for the past month. And I was more than ready to do it.

I'd just poked my head through the neck of my shirt when my smartphone rang with a call.

"What's up, man?" I said into the phone when I noticed Meki's name flash on the screen. "I'm getting dressed right now to head out—"

"Cadence went into labor this morning," Meki interjected. His voice was slightly shaky. "We're in the hospital now."

"Oh, shit." I paused, walking. "So, the boxing exercises worked?"

"A little too well." He exhaled a stuttered breath. "She's good, contractions rolling through at a reasonable pace and she's handling them amazingly, like a G, but listen, I can't make it to the training session today."

"I mean, obviously," I told him. "You got something far more important going on right now."

"It's surreal, if I'm being honest." He exhaled into the phone again. "I'm about to be someone's dad, EP." Meki sighed deeply. "Wild shit, right?"

"Indeed." I smiled, genuinely happy for my friend.

"I'm not gonna leave you hanging, though," Meki continued. "I reached out to Apryl and asked if she could train you and she agreed."

My smile dropped. "Apryl?"

"Yeah, Apryl Wilde," he answered. "Remember her? The one we were discussing at the gym?"

How could I forget her? The area of the gym where I waited for Meki to return offered a photogenic view of the world famous New York City skyline, but Apryl was my preferred view during my visit to his gym. She pranced around like a peacock, completely unaware of how magnetic she was to those watching, myself included. She had the sweetest face and demeanor and the sexiest physique. Her ass poked out and curved at the perfect angle, like a perfectly drawn painting. But while I enjoyed her in her element, training with her was not as attractive.

"I remember Apryl," I told him. "But I don't know about her training me."

"Why not?"

"For one, what I need? The intensity we usually work with? I don't think she can give me that. I haven't worked out in almost a month. Believe it or not, I'm out of shape. I was out of breath climbing those stairs at your gym the other day."

"I noticed," he chimed in.

"Okay, so I obviously need something heavy, something rough. I need my body sore after the workout to jumpstart everything."

"And she's the one to do it. Trust me, bro," Meki countered. "Whenever I'm looking for a workout that will knock me on my ass, I schedule a session with Apryl. All the trainers at the gym do. Don't let her face and her endorsements fool you. Apryl's not about the red carpets and flashing lights. She's more than the hype. She's a major beast! And she's an expert on weight loss and toning. Cadence already booked her sessions with her for after the doctor clears her to work out. Apryl is no joke, I promise you."

It wasn't only that, though. She was a distraction. Just the thought of her was making my heart race before I'd executed a single exercise. She's too fine and I'm still too raw from my breakup.

"Give me someone else, Meki."

"There isn't anyone else, EP," he explained. "That's what I'm trying to tell you. To get you in the type of shape we discussed in time for the community center opening in Brooklyn? All the other trainers have booked calendars and won't be able to train you consistently. I'm taking a few weeks off starting today to be home with Cadence and the baby. The other trainers will be available on some days and not on others. Apryl's calendar had no room in it either, but she agreed to squeeze you in on a time slot when I told her why you were there - to train for the community center opening."

"Aight, look." I ran my hand down my mouth. "The truth is, I find her to be a distraction."

"A distraction?"

"Yeah, you know," I said next. "She's too attractive. She's beautiful or whatever."

He was quiet for a moment before busting into a hearty belly aching laugh on the line.

"What the fuck is so funny?"

"Yo! Are you crushing on Apryl Wilde or something?!"

I sucked my back teeth.

"You are, huh?" He chuckled some more and I couldn't say anything against it.

Because maybe I was?

My reputation proceeded me. The animal that everyone knew as EP in boxing gloves was down badly. I knew it would show during my workout. I likely wouldn't be able to keep up. With Meki, that would be fine. He'd probably talk shit and hurl insults to get me back in the right state of mind. But with Apryl, I couldn't let her see me like that. I didn't want to embarrass myself.

And I shouldn't have cared.

But I did.

"Use her as inspiration," Meki suggested. "Make her your muse or whatever. When you're thinking about quitting in the middle of a rep or you feel too tired to execute the next set, glance her way and use her as motivation to keep going. That's one of the many things women are good for. They make us want to go the distance to impress them. The male ego relies on a woman's applause. We thrive off that shit."

I rolled my shoulders back. "Meki, I hear you, bruh, but—"

"Get off the *fucking* phone, Meki!" Cadence screamed in the background. "Are you kidding me? I'm in labor and you're on the phone, kee-keeing in my gahdamn ear? Get over here, please. I'm practically getting ripped open from the inside!"

"Aight baby, I'm coming. Give me just one more min—"

"Now!" she roared. "Oh God, I'm having another contraction, *ugh*!"

"I gotta go, Ev," he said into the phone. "3pm and be on time for your session with her. Do *not* be late. *Please* don't be late."

Before I could utter anything else, Meki abruptly ended the call.

"Fuck," I whispered to myself.

Fourteen

APRYL

He's late.

I stood at the front desk, every so often checking the time on my phone or the wall clock behind our receptionist, Michelle. I'd rolled my eyes so many times, they were getting irritated.

When Meki called me, letting me know his wife, Cadence, had gone into labor and he needed for me to fill in for him at his friend, Everett's, session, I said no.

Between running my online fitness business, renegotiating contracts with the companies I endorsed, and trying my best to balance my social life and my career, I didn't have the time. But then Meki shared with me Everett's reason for being in New York - to attend a community center opening where he'd be teaching young black children how to swim in the inner city. I thought his decision to be the face of that was honorable. It was a cause I could get behind.

But his being late? I couldn't get behind that at all.

I flared my nostrils and folded my arms, growing more pissed by the minute.

One thing I hated more than anything was having my time wasted. I usually wrapped up my stay at the gym by 2pm to head back home to start my next leg of work. *My* work. But here I was, 3:16pm, waiting for this man to show up for a session that was to benefit him...

... and me, if I'm being honest.

Yes, I agreed to assist Everett in getting in shape for his appearance at the community center. According to Meki, Everett had put on a little weight shortly after retirement and required a little tune up. The way I saw it was, if we got him in tiptop shape for his appearance, better than he planned, he could name drop me as his trainer, the person responsible for helping him get ready for the community center opening, and I could finally have another well-known celebrity attached to my name and not Chloe Rae's. That woman had become the bane of my professional existence, and I needed her name finally removed from all my accomplishments so I could really be free of my past.

"Where the hell is this guy?!"

I noticed the top of his baseball cap and then the tops of his shoulders as he walked up the stairs. I straightened my back and peered his way. Everett took his time climbing the last few steps. He walked into the gym as if they printed his name on the street sign outside. Over his ears were headphones, and he wore a black sweatshirt and matching joggers. A designer gym bag swung from his shoulder and the handle, from a jug of water, hung from his fingertips.

I'd only seen him twice, but it was enough to notice that Everett had this bop in his walk that was so Brooklyn.

The light bounce on his feet was signature. Every step he took was so subtle and accentuated by the soft sway in his shoulders that was almost rhythmic. He took up space when he walked and it was as if the air parted when he made his way around a room.

Some of the gym members working out paid him a glance as he passed before they returned to focus on what they were doing.

His eyes found mine, and he kept them on me, chucking his chin my way and turning to head toward the private trainer dressing rooms.

"Where is he going?"

"Oh!" Michelle started over my shoulder at her seat behind me at the front desk. "Meki told me to tell you that Everett will use Meki's private dressing room instead of the locker room before and after his sessions to provide more privacy for Everett."

I rolled my eyes again and paired it with pinched lips. "Meki can tell Everett where to go to change, but can't tell him to be on time? Meki knows how much I *hate* when people are late."

Besides him arriving sixteen minutes past the hour of his scheduled session, Everett made me wait another ten minutes before he finally emerged from the back.

By that time, anger coursed through my veins.

And I rehearsed in my head the verbal lashing I'd deal him the moment he stood opposite me, but when he turned the corner from the secluded area of the dressing rooms, I nearly swallowed my tongue.

Gone was the sweatsuit. He changed into a pair of shorts that showed off his columnar legs. Covering his torso was a faded muscle tank with more faded words printed on the front and the back.

His eyes locked on mine the moment we were in each other's sights. Also gone was his cap, allowing me full access to a view of his beautiful face.

Honestly, all professional fighters looked the same to me. I always associated them with having pronounced brow bones and squared jaws. Exaggerated muscular torsos, broad shoulders, all poured into boxing trunks and gloves. With them fully clothed, I couldn't tell who was who. They could stand next to a gym rat and I wouldn't be able to tell the difference.

There was no mistaking what Everett did. He wouldn't be able to work a regular job if he couldn't fight in a ring.

His arms were enormous, his hands proportionate to his size and big too. He had tattoos, several of them, but they were all inked artfully on his golden-brown skin, causing no clutter to the eyes admiring him. The tattoos were mostly words and names, like Bed-Stuy tatted in block letters down the side of his forearm. The other ink on his body was tribal graphics, extending from his shoulder blades to the thinned skin on his wrists.

Everett kept his eyes locked on me until he was standing inches in front of me.

I could feel my pulse in my neck and the hairs standing up on my arms. He made me nervous. His presence was intimidating. I was 5'6, not too much shorter than him, but the man had a way of towering over people in demeanor. Directly in front of me, I couldn't maintain the tough veneer, but I sure as hell wouldn't show it.

"Follow me," I ordered, moving around him, grabbing the clipboard I placed on the front desk and taking steps toward our open-plan area for HIIT exercises. Everett's sessions would be private, according to Meki. That meant the area where he'd work out would be closed to the other members in the gym. This part of the gym was for training private clients, often celebrities, to offer the assurance of privacy.

Everett followed as ordered, taking steps a few feet behind me, quietly.

We arrived in the back and I tossed the clipboard onto the seat of the bench press machine, then turned to face him.

"You're late," I started. "I don't like that."

His brow arched, and he twisted more to face me.

"When someone gives you a preferred arrival time, you shouldn't walk in at that scheduled time. You should arrive five minutes earlier. I'm surprised you don't know that."

"Meki's wife went into labor and he told me at the last minute," he explained.

Everett's voice was like pure honey. Nice and easy, and like a soft touch to my ears. His expression was even and endearing as he explained. The man's eye contact never wavered, looking me fixed in my eyes. His stare was intense, making my heart feel like it was beating in my ears with his words.

"I'm aware," I confirmed. "That doesn't negate you being on time. He gave you a reasonable heads up at a time that still would have had you here on time."

"I wasn't sure I was going to show up."

It was my turn to arch my brow. I raised both, in fact.

"I'm not all that confident you can train me in a way I need to be trained."

My hands were on either side of my waist when I asked, "And why's that?"

For the first time, his eyes lowered from mine to look me up, then down. "I'm not looking to have a body like Chloe Rae. She was your client, right? You're credited often, everywhere, on and offline, for her famous ass she loves to show off."

I took a breath at the mention of her name.

"Female trainers focus too much on core workouts and spend way too much time on toning. I hate toning." He shook his head. "I'm not trying to be in here doing squats and lunges up and down that hall back there half the time. I'm not looking to gain a fat ass."

"First." I closed the space between us. "*That's* very sexist."

"It is," he admitted, with no qualms about it.

I bit down on my back teeth. "Second, that's presumptuous of you to think that's my fitness plan for you."

He blinked in response.

"And last, squats work not only at the core. It's a full-body workout. It gets all the muscles activated all at once, but you would know that if you weren't trying to do my job and not yours."

"What's my job?" He challenged.

"To be on time," I snapped back. "And don't give me this nonsense of it being a last-minute schedule change. You had plenty of time to adjust."

He squared his eyes in a way others would cower at the sight, but I wanted to choke him.

"See, right now," he went on, "you're pissed. I acknowledge that you're pissed, but I think it's cute at best... comical at worst."

My head jerked back.

"I see Ashley Banks from The Fresh Prince of Bel Air when I look at you. You two are like twins. Same sweet, innocent face. Not intimidating at all. If she got mad on the show, it was adorable, sometimes laughable."

I scoffed this time.

"Like a charming teacup Yorkie, circling around barking at people's ankles. I hear it, but it has no effect on me."

My eyes ballooned. "Did you just compare me to a dog?"

He shook his head. "Nah. This ain't gon' work. I'm out." Everett turned away from me and started toward the direction we had entered.

I inhaled a deep breath and decided on my exhale that this was war.

"Get your disrespectful ass back in here and on this fucking mat."

He paused in step for a beat, taking his sweet time to turn and look my way.

"I was going to go easy on you," I told him. "Because Meki explained you're a little out of shape."

I couldn't see it.

God built this man like a statue.

"But now, I have to make you pay for not only wasting my time, which is money, but for also fucking with me."

He snorted.

"Fifty push-ups," I ordered. "And I don't care how many sets you have to do them in. Just get them done."

He remained on his feet and didn't move a muscle.

"Sixty," I told him next. "The longer you make me wait for them, the more I'll pile on. And Everett?"

He stared at me, no answer.

I closed the space between us and told him, "You will not leave this gym today until you give me every one of what I told you to give me."

He stared right into my eyes as if he were trying to look through me and didn't blink. I was so close to him, I noticed everything about his facial features that would go unnoticed by someone not in his personal space. Like the tiny scar on the bow of his top lip and how feathery his long lashes were.

But I refused to give into intimidation.

After a second more of this, he asked, "Do you know who the fuck I am?"

His voice vibrated in my chest. He wasn't loud or anything. Everett spoke from a place of authority, though. Like a man used to giving orders more than taking them.

"Talking to me all reckless and shit." He stepped more into my space and, for a moment, I wanted to shrink from his boldness. "Do you have any idea who you're mouthing off to right now?"

His dark eyes peered into me. And instead of cowering, they emboldened me.

"Yeah." I took a step forward and positioned myself right under him. I could smell traces of the soap he must've showered with warming on his skin. "I do.

His Adam's apple bounced with a swallow.

"I'm talking to the man who's about to give me the sixty push-ups I asked for, plus the ten extra I just piled on because he keeps trying me. I don't like that shit at all, and I want to show him how much I really don't like him fucking with me."

He groaned low. I wouldn't have heard it had I not been so close, but I did. And the throaty moan made my nipples hard.

I stepped back and dared him not to follow my orders with a daring stare of my own.

I parted my lips to raise the number to eighty when I noticed he still didn't move, but I stopped as he lowered himself down to his knees in front of me, still watching me, and balanced his upper body on a plank on his hands, executing his first series of push-ups.

His biceps flexed under the weight of him.

My heart was hammering now, and I tried but failed to get hold of my breath.

Everett grunted with each rep. I counted nineteen before he lowered himself to the floor and turned over on his back.

"No resting."

"Fuck that," he shouted back, out of breath.

I bit at my bottom lip, knowing I had a decision to make. I couldn't let him slide. He challenged me and now I had to apply pressure and exert my dominance over a man who was extremely dominant himself.

I squatted beside him. "Get up."

He opened his eyes and glared up at me.

Everett looked so damn good in that position, on his back beneath me. The only thing missing to make the sight more perfect was if I straddled him.

"Get up," I repeated. "You've had enough time to catch your breath. I counted nineteen reps. We'll call that a set. You owe me at least two more sets."

He grunted and exhaled, returning to his hands to plank.

The sounds he made sparked arousal in me. Sex was always on my mind, but I practiced self-control. I'd be lying if I said it had not been even more heavy on the brain, and his grunting helped nothing. I wanted to cross my legs to calm the throbbing happening between them, but there really was no use.

He collapsed again, punching the mat beneath him out of frustration, I suppose.

"What's taking you so long to give me these push-ups, Everett?"

"You're not taking it easy on me," he huffed, pushing himself up to sit. "Seventy push-ups out the gate? No warming up beforehand, nothing?"

"Warming up is what you do when you get here on time. And the push-ups were twenty before you opened your big ass mouth, remember?"

"Yo, fuck—"

I tilted my head to the right and asked softly, "*Fuck*, what?"

His chest rose and fell. He broke eye contact with me and returned to his position on his plank to resume his push-ups.

He grunted at each one and collapsed shortly after.

"Let's go!" I shouted, clapping each word hollered. "And that'll teach your ass not to play in my face ever again."

———

"Honestly, I think we're going to continue to clash." I spooled pasta around the prongs of my fork. "Because he is absolutely a pain in the ass. *My ass,* to be exact."

The buzz of chatter swarmed around us like bees as I sat amongst my sister, her husband, her two children, and she and my dad, Martin Wilde.

We were all out to dinner at an American-style diner. It was kind of a thing for us. Pick a day out of the month to meet up with our dad to hang out at a not-so-fancy place. It became a thing after my sister Stas had her daughter Luna, and he complained about us being too busy for him. How I got lumped in on the *us* and *busy* claim still perplexes me.

"He's egotistical, a brute, and abnormally stubborn, amongst other things." I chewed my food hard. "I might have to throw him back to Meki and let Meki know I have to pass."

Everett's behavior at his session earlier still had me very pissed. Although it ended hours prior, he'd upset me to no end and challenged my patience in ways a client had never done.

"And this is a new client?" My sister inquired. She held her son, Raphael, cradled in her arms as she fed him from his bottle. Luna sat on the other side of Stas between my sister and her husband, Kwamé, nibbling on a chicken nugget.

"A brand spanking new client," I answered. "This was his first session. He insulted me during his *first* session."

"He's a celebrity too?" My brother-in-law, Kwamé, asked next.

"An athlete, yes." I forked more pasta into my mouth. "I guess you could call him a celebrity, too."

"Well," my father chimed in, dusting the yellow lint off his black shirt. There were several lines of it throughout the fabric of his shirt, but not enough to be visible. I wouldn't have seen it had I not been sitting so close. "You gonna tell us his name, or are we playing charades for dinner?"

I cracked a smile. "Everett Peters or EP, as Meki calls him."

My father's face contorted. "EP? *The boxer*, EP."

I placed my fork on the rim of my plate. "Yeah, he fights."

"Yeah, he fights?" My dad bust up laughing, lifting his napkin to wipe his mouth. "That man does not only *fight*, Apryl."

I blinked in response. "He also doesn't *follow* orders well, so…"

"EP is a living legend, Babygirl." My father sat up in his seat like an eager child and not like a man in his early 60s. His eyes must've caught another collection of lint on his sleeve because he dusted his shirt once more. "The man has thirty-six wins and not a single loss, has been fighting professionally since he was fifteen years old, really since he was eleven, but that's a whole 'nother amazing story in his boxing journey. EP has made his way through the circuit and dominated each phase of his career. I'm talking KOs as a junior boxer *and* a youth boxer, fighting against other kids his age, of course. By the time he reached an open age at eighteen, his KOs graduated to TKOs and it was *over* for these other guys, and they knew it. 'Cause his fists were weapons, baby. *Whew*, some of them refused to get in a ring with EP because of those hands and how fast they moved!" He laughed. "I'm pretty sure they popped a few bottles of champagne to celebrate after he announced his retirement two months ago, because he had them eating mats in the ring and petrified for years."

I blinked my eyes repeatedly, completely confused. Listening to my father rattle off Everett's stats like some kind of groupie was off-putting. Everett's whole "do you know who the fuck I am" spiel makes sense now according to what my father shared, but Everett's stamina during his workout was not adding up.

"The man you just told me about cannot be the same one I trained, or *tried* to train today," I explained. "Because the man I worked with this afternoon could barely give me twenty push-ups without needing to stop to catch his breath."

"Well, then shit, that ain't EP." My father chuckled, dusting off lint from his shirt again.

I squinted at him.

"Because Everett Peters's training is rigorous," he continued. "And I've seen your workouts, Babygirl. Your exercises are nowhere close to what EP's gotta do before a fight. Not by a mile."

"I resent that." I folded my arms. "My workouts are high-intensity exercises. High octane. They are quite intense."

He shook his head and focused on his food.

"And *EP* could barely keep up."

"Have you looked him up?" Kwamé quizzed. "Like, Googled him?"

"Nope." I lowered my eyes on my pasta. "And I won't."

"And why not?" Stas asked next.

"After the whole Chloe Rae situation, I avoid Googling my clients. The public figures, at least." I shrugged. "I learn too much when I do. Get too invested in their personal lives. Then I can't maintain professionalism with them."

"Apryl, please," my father insisted. "That was a one-off with that Hollywood demon."

I loved my dad for that. Chloe became *that Hollywood demon* when he found out about her betrayal, and she has been *that Holly-wood demon* ever since.

She didn't start that way. Chloe started as my client four years ago. Then she became my friend. Her infectious bubbly personality drew me in and her stunning beauty. Chloe was ultra-feminine, and I liked that, because I was too, so I felt comfortable in her presence. She had just signed on to do a huge blockbuster movie when she reached out to me to train her. You know the brand of blockbuster film. The one that has all the explosions, quick-paced movie scores, the big buff guy jumping out of insane moving things and the buxom beauty who lusted after him. Chloe became that buxom beauty when she landed the leading role as the movie's siren, and my fiancé, Troy, was the big buff guy jumping out of insane moving things and getting the girl in the end.

Took his role a little too seriously... a role I went to bat for him to get, no less.

"Well," I half shrugged this time. "Keeping true to that rule has kept me focused and unattached to my clients and my work, allowing me to do my job without getting my feelings involved."

"Look him up," my dad insisted. He pinched yet another piece of lint off his shirt. "He may not have too much online material, since he's not as popular as a Mayweather or Wilder. EP keeps to himself and doesn't go to the popular places to be seen, nor does he do a lot of interviews, but I'm sure you'll find something on him."

I squinted at the collar of his shirt, then leaned toward him, pinching a piece of the lint off his shirt this time. When I brought it closer in view to examine, I noticed it wasn't lint at all. It was short hair, like from an animal.

"Is this cat hair?" I asked, looking his way.

"Uh, no, I don't think so." He cleared his throat before returning to eat.

"*Hmph*," I huffed, dusting the hair on the restaurant floor. "Looks like cat hair to me."

FIFTEEN

EVERETT

"Ahh!" I grunted, falling to my chest. "Shit."

I could feel the disappointment emanating from her before looking up to find her glaring down.

"I need a full thirty seconds of that plank, Everett," Apryl reminded me. Her hands gripped her tiny waist, brows so wrinkled I feared they'd stay that way and she'd blame me for it, then make me pay with more exercise. "That was only seventeen seconds. You've got to push through the pain. Come on!"

We were in MK's Sports Lounge and Gym on a freezing Wednesday afternoon, butting heads again.

I should've kept my mouth shut the first day. She clearly had a vendetta now and had been trying to prove her point ever since.

I pushed myself up again, balanced my weight on my arms and legs on a plank and tried like hell to exhale the tension through my teeth as I maintained my position.

Meki was right, Apryl's a beast. She's a beauty too, but more so a beast.

I'll admit - the sweet face had me fooled, making it clearer that I had Apryl fucked up. And she'd been making me pay for that since the session started. This was our second time training, and I'd been around her long enough to determine there wasn't anything sweet about her.

"Very good," she told me once I completed my planks. "That only took 100 years. Let's get into lunges, your favorite."

I hated lunges. She knew that.

Apryl put me to work the moment she saw me step up the gym's stairs for our appointment when I arrived. Like a lioness in the wild waiting for the gazelle to sink her teeth into its neck, she was waiting for me at the front desk with the receptionist, like she did for our first session.

That first session was a lot, but gave me insight into a woman I really thought I had figured out but I knew nothing about. Because the way she got in my face and refused to back down was... extremely sexy.

I couldn't deny. Apryl was my kind of fine, but she was very unapproachable. She wasn't easy to talk to. And we've had little opportunity to talk to each other since my first session. I'd been trying to find an in with her, but my attempt at making small talk earlier did not help.

"You don't photograph well," I pointed out to her while warming up with a walk on the treadmill.

Random as all heck but, whatever. I didn't want to be my direct self, since the situation called for a suaver approach. Plus, it had been a minute since I had to strike up a conversation with a woman I found attractive, and charming has never been my forte.

Apryl stood to the right of me, attention down on her phone until I opened my mouth.

She knitted her brows above her beautiful brown eyes when she focused on me. "Excuse me?"

"The ads you're photographed in. You don't photograph well in them."

The pinched expression on her face deepened. "Are you trying to offend me?"

"No, I'm just..."

She stepped forward and pressed a button on the treadmill, causing the belt to move quicker.

"For that, you can give me two miles."

Ruthless and with no patience. Some might call her a bitch. She intrigued me.

"Thirty seconds of lunges," Apryl instructed, pointing ahead of us using her chin. "To the equipment and back again." She peeked down at her watch. "And start."

Meki was officially on paternity leave and wouldn't return until the end of the month. He and Cadence welcomed a beautiful baby boy, Mekal Meki Knight, who looked equal parts of Meki and Cadence. My friend is a father now. I hoped to one day join the club.

"Where's your head right now, Everett?" Apryl shouted down the hall. "I need those lunges deeper. Bend those damn knees." She turned to the side to show. "Like this. Bend them. Get lower."

I underestimated her, just like I underestimated the significance of the weight I put on. Although it wasn't visible, the twenty-three pounds I gained in the short time made it harder to execute her exercises. I should eat these, allowing them to roll off me like water. I would normally knock these out in seconds, but my joints ached. Holding up my body weight seemed like an impossible feat, and I couldn't maintain breath control to save my life. This was so embarrassing.

I completed the last set of lunges and walked the rest of the way back to her. My body was hinting at needing a break. Which I knew she wouldn't give me.

"You're not focused," she told me.

"I'm doing what you asked me to do, though, right?"

"No, not right. And that's the thing. You aren't doing them right." She ran her hand across the back of her neck, dropped her hands at her sides, and sighed. "I'm trying to understand how an athlete of your caliber, according to Meki, at least, is struggling—"

"Aye!" I interrupted. "I ain't struggling with shit."

That was bullshit.

I was barely hanging on, but I'd be damned if I admitted that to her.

She shook her head. "Your form is horrible, stamina the worse.

You're giving me forty-five percent of the effort I am used to getting from my clients—"

"Then go train their ass," I told her. "The fuck I care about what the hell they do during *my* damn session?"

Her hands were at her waist again. "Don't get mad at me. Be mad at yourself..." She poked me in the chest for emphasis. "... for giving me a piss poor performance. Subpar all the way around."

I flared my nostrils.

She was brutal. And as she ripped into me with her words, her expression was even, her face still pleasant.

I bet she has the most beautiful sex face.

"See, not focused."

I grunted, placing my hands on top of my head to make catching my breath easier. "What time is it?"

"Got somewhere else to be?"

"Yeah." I nodded. "Everywhere else but here."

"Okay." She peeked down at her watch. "It's get-your-ass-on-the-leg-press o'clock."

I inhaled a valiant breath and shook my head. "I can't do anything more today."

I wanted to tell her more, explain to her that although the weight I'm working to shred, isn't much, I can feel the exercises in my bones and my bones are feeling every bit of the thirty-eight years I've used them. But I didn't have the guts to explain myself.

She folded her arms. "*You're* telling *me* you're done for the day?"

"Yes, the one doing the exercises and getting in shape said they're done for the day." I lifted the bottom of my shirt to clean the sweat off my face. "You've been working with me since the time I arrived."

"Your session is for an hour, Everett," she reminded, ripping her eyes off my stomach to meet my eyes again. "You've only worked out for forty-seven minutes. And you're not done until I say you are."

"Quality over quantity, Ashley Banks," I told her, turning to leave. "And I'm done when I say I'm done, and I'm done."

———

"I can't believe you did that, Everett," my sister, Eryn, chastised in my ear. "Such an ass sometimes."

I shoveled a handful of barbecue chips out of the bag and dropped them into my mouth. I'd just gone through one family-sized bag and had opened a new one to empty it the same.

Later that night, after my session with Apryl, I sat on the couch in my suite, undoing all the work I did at the gym. I chewed on the chips; each time remembering how I felt being scolded by Apryl. She wasn't wrong, and she wasn't the harshest trainer I've ever had. But her words held a little more gravity than any of the other trainers I've worked with, for reasons I wasn't ready to admit.

"I'm not an ass. She is." I licked chip dust clean off my lips. "Walking around there, talking her shit, screaming out orders like she's about that life."

"She's a trainer," Eryn reminded me. "She's there to train you and you're not making it easy."

"*She's* still in her feelings because of our first session. Apryl needs to learn to let shit go and not make things personal."

"Or," Eryn cut in again. "She sees she has to be hard on you because look what you're doing now."

I stopped chewing.

"Crunching in my ear for the last hour on something I know isn't healthy."

"Yeah, aight..."

"Making her job difficult, because I'm pretty sure you shouldn't be eating whatever you're eating."

"She stressed me the fuck out," I defended. "I needed a pick-me-up."

"You *need* to find your discipline."

"I've eaten like this all the time," I insisted, taking another handful of chips. "I'd eat my junk to my heart's content, then go to the gym to work it all out."

"Which I always found to be unhealthy," she countered. "And you've been getting into the gym and being lazy."

"It's harder now, Eryn." I admitted between using my tongue to clean my gums. "Maintaining what I already worked years to build was simpler than having to lose what I've gained. This weight, my age..."

"Excuses are monuments of nothingness—"

"Whose side are you on, baby sis?"

"The side that's right," she answered. "The side that will get my brother back in the state of mind of a man who thinks with his head and not with his emotions. That's the side I'm on."

I sighed again, folding down the top of the bag and moving it out of sight.

We were both silent on the line when Eryn asked, "How does she look?

I grimaced. "What?"

"Apryl. How does Apryl look in person?"

I cleaned the corners of my mouth with the tip of my tongue. "Better than she looks in pictures."

Way better.

She was an endless beauty. The longer someone stared at her, the more things they would find about her physically to admire. Her face was pleasant, her eyes an erotic story. Her skin was so smooth like sun kissed manuka honey, and she had toned curves like the winding roads I used to love getting lost on in California because of the views. Apryl was a masterpiece from head to toe. A showstopper. And I was a fan.

"That tells me a lot." Eryn giggled. "You must like her to respond so short."

"I wasn't short."

"That's probably why you keep giving her a hard time. You don't know how to flirt and choose big jerk every time."

I furrowed my brows. "What the hell are you talking about?"

She laughed this time.

I kissed my teeth. "I may not be a Prince Charming kind of dude, but I know what I'm doing. I know the art of the approach."

"You do, and your angle is jerk, nigga," she defended. "Every time you like a woman, you offend her. You think you're complimenting, but it always gives big jerk energy. It always gives tease the girl in the playground when you like her, but more mature."

I immediately thought about the brief conversation Apryl and I had earlier when I was on the treadmill after telling her she didn't photograph well.

I was being honest, but I guess Eryn had a point.

"So, are you going to quit?"

I snorted. "I don't know how to spell the word 'quit', kid."

"Good," Eryn replied. "Great. Because you need this, Everett. And as hard or difficult as Apryl may be, she's staying on you, which is a good thing. It lets me know she takes her job seriously, and she's invested in helping you achieve your goals."

"You got all that from me telling you she kicked my ass at the gym?"

"Yup, and the fact she hasn't cussed your ass out for being a stubborn brute yet proves you're not the only one who has a little crush."

"I don't have a crush."

"Yes, you do. You both do."

I arched a brow, considering her words before deciding, "Nah, I don't think she does."

"Oh, no?"

"*Uh-uh.*" I shook my head, sitting up in my seat. "I'm going to believe she can't stand my ass, much less have any kind of crush on me."

"Everett, I know women," she insisted. "We do not give our patience to everyone. Only a selected few. And we reserve that privilege for the people we either love or like a lot."

I scanned the floor, considering my sister's words. Not that Apryl having a crush mattered much. I wasn't interested in giving any woman any of my attention this soon after my breakup.

"And I would never steer you wrong," she promised in a sing-song tone. "Remember that."

Sixteen

Every light in my townhouse was off except in my bedroom. I sat in the middle of my king-sized mattress with my laptop open in front of me. It was almost midnight, and I'd spent the last five hours trying to talk myself out of web surfing for information on Everett.

The conversation with my father during our family outing two days ago played on my mind on repeat.

"He's a beast."

"He's incredible."

"The guy you're talking about can't be EP."

Training today was another tough session. Everett was hard-headed, stubborn, and a pain in the ass. He was immovable, and it frustrated me because he really made it difficult for me to do my damn job.

"Ugh," I groaned, reminded at that moment of how frustrating Everett was.

I inhaled a breath next and pulled my laptop to me, waking it up with a tap on the mouse pad.

Some would say my refusal to Google clients was ridiculous. And it was, to an extent. Simply viewing it as only Googling would give that impression, but it's more so my history of getting too close to my clients after learning more about them than my heart could handle.

My ex-fiancé, Troy Vanderbilt, was a former child actor. He guest starred in a handful of popular sitcoms in the 80s and 90s and had been acting since he was in diapers. More recognizable by face than by name, we met during a time of self-reconstructing in both of our lives. He wanted to transform his image from childhood actor to Hollywood heartthrob. I wanted to prove to my parents that dropping out of college my sophomore year - and forfeiting a full-ride scholarship - wasn't the worst decision of my life by beefing up my resume and gaining credibility as a celebrity personal trainer. A relationship was never something I planned, especially not with Troy. But I looked him up when he found my listing on Craigslist and he reached out, and I formed a connection with the man before his very first session, mainly because of what I learned about him from my online search.

Troy came from a family that relied on him to be the breadwinner at an age he couldn't talk to protest their decision. He earned a great living as a child actor but had to file for bankruptcy by the age of twenty because his parents had spent all the money he'd accumulated down to the last dollar. I was determined to get him back on top after learning that.

I navigated to my internet explorer and began typing in Everett's full name in the browser window.

Actress Chloe Rae was another mistake. I'd heard of her but knew nothing about her past, her career as a former model turned actress. Mutual friends told her my area of expertise in helping women maintain curves while getting fit and she was on my phone booking her first session. Like with Troy, I Googled Chloe, formed an attachment after learning she'd lost both parents as a teenager in a freak car accident. She'd do interviews, complain about being typecast and put in a box as a black Hollywood actress. Her struggle to break the mold resonated with me. So, I made a promise to myself I would help make her bigger and better than all of her Hollywood peers, shattering whatever glass ceiling the old white Hollywood bigwigs tried to keep her under.

I had no plans for Chloe to go from client to close friend. I guess that happens when you bond with people and take your work to heart. But it was that same heart that blindsided me to both Chloe and Troy's betrayals.

Since then, I've refrained from learning anything more from my clients besides what they shared with me. Their personal lives outside of their revelations were none of my business. I wasn't interested in getting to know them past what they told me they wanted from their fitness goals.

But Everett had me going against my word.

I had to see what my father was talking about, because the man who I've been training is far from any beast I've ever encountered at MK's Sports Lounge and Gym and I was one session away from accepting defeat and giving the bare minimum until Everett's session days were up.

The first thing to populate on my screen were photos. Everett stood in one of them, dressed in boxing gear, with his gloved hands up at his face, only revealing his eyes. Those enormous arms of his were like rolling steep hills covered in ink. Veins highlighted his strength up and down his biceps and forearms. Abs lined up like large cubes of ice. He was far more muscular than he was now.

That intrigued me.

Other photos of Everett included him standing face to face with opponents, towering over them. The look on his face was intimidating, damn near petrifying. He stared at me through the screen and I got goosebumps. Flared nostrils beneath dark piercing eyes, jaw so tight I could see its muscles through my laptop's screen. I clicked over to the video tab of my search and selected the very first still at the top of the list.

It was a documentary, following Everett weeks prior to his last fight before retirement. The doc captured him rising as night still cast darkness over the day. Shadow boxing as the sun rose behind him. Three hours of strength conditioning that included him having to outrun a car and push a tractor wheel up a hill.

My nipples hardened at the sight of him being so active. So strong. Resilient. Grunting and pushing. Roaring through the pain, but still going. At no point did he give up. Regardless of how rigorous the exercise was, Everett kept at it, completing each instruction his trainer hollered when I, myself, may have had to say enough.

His tenacity blew me away.

When the short half an hour doc was done, I sat there for a moment, stunned, eyes scanning my walls in disbelief.

"What the hell happened to him in such a short time?"

I refused to accept this was the twenty-three pounds Meki claimed Everett needed to shed, holding Everett back. Though that amount of weight was significant, it shouldn't have been this debilitating, making a prized athlete find it difficult to complete elementary workouts.

I ran my fingers through my hair, then pulled on the strands near the end.

"I don't understand."

While others would brush off thoughts like this, I viewed them as problems that needed solving.

A serial problem solver, as my sister Stas called me.

I sat for a moment longer, only stopping my racing thoughts when the metaphorical lightbulb went off in my head.

I shook my head when the idea crossed my mind again after I tried to dismiss it.

But what if what I have planned is the only thing that'll work?

I knew it wouldn't be right to suggest it. Many times in the past, getting too close and going beyond what I was required has backfired.

But I needed Everett more than he needed me. I couldn't go another year having my name tied to both Troy and Chloe. And as long as I remained in control of everything with Everett, I would be fine.

"Just don't get too close," I told myself.

I couldn't get close. Because what I was about to offer to do was absolutely insane.

———

I didn't wait for him by the front desk like usual. To be honest, me waiting for him there before his session was an intimidation tactic, making my face the first face he saw on arrival. Truth was, Everett intimidated me. He made me have to work overtime not to shrink myself in his presence and surely that was at no fault of his.

The gym was quiet that day. It was a cold and rainy Friday. The beginning of spring was the next day, so the weather was giving the season a head start.

On rainy days, the weather challenged the most committed, and many didn't show up to workout.

Everett did.

That was a good sign.

He swaggered into the open-planned area where we held our boot camp and HIIT trainings. This was where we stretched and warmed up. Everett looked ready today, which I needed to see to get inspired to go along with my plan.

Donned in a pair of black performance shorts and the matching drop arm tank top, Everett arrived dressed the part, but his demeanor suggested he'd much rather be somewhere else.

"I'm surprised you showed up," I teased when he was close.

He brushed his hand down his face and stopped in front of me. "Definitely considered not showing up." He glanced around himself. "Would've made sense since it looks like a ghost town here this afternoon."

I smirked. "But EP always works while everyone else plays, right?"

His brows knitted.

"You recited that in the documentary you filmed prior to your last fight with Kevin Claymore. You recited it several times, actually. *Work while everyone plays.* Said it while you ran miles. While you shadow boxed before dawn. Got it tatted on the back of your calf."

His top lip quirked up in a smile. "You watched the doc?"

"I looked you up." I nodded, crossing my arms over my chest. "I rarely Google my celebrity clients for personal reasons, but I had to see what everyone else sees."

"What do you mean?"

"People pair your name with beast way too many times for me to believe it, but it contrasts heavily with what I see you do here at the gym."

"We're starting early, huh?" He asked. "Can I get on the mat first? I haven't warmed up yet and you already gettin' at me?"

I giggled. "I'm saying your reputation proceeds you."

"*Mm-hmm.*" He pinched the underside of his beard. "You have a funny way of expressing that."

"Everett." I shook my head. "I watched you run beside a car for miles on end. You pushed truck tires up incredibly steep hills. Shadow boxed for hours. I watched you bench press over two hundred pounds and witnessed with my two eyes your stamina being through the roof. All in this doc you filmed only a few months ago. What the hell happened between now and then?"

He sucked his teeth.

"And don't take it the wrong way," I explained. "I need to know what *happened*. Because the man I've been training and the man I watched in the documentary are clearly the same, but then they are not."

"I underestimated what an extra twenty-three pounds of fat would feel like for me when working out. Then there's my age, and my lack of motivation, and you get *this*."

"You push through it. It's only twenty-three pounds and you are able-bodied." I wrinkled my brows. "Haven't you ever had to pack on pounds before a fight?"

"See, you don't understand. Look at you." He gestured at me. "You don't even look like you have fat anywhere besides in your ass."

I arched my brows, knowing it wasn't always that way.

"Muscle and fat feel different, at least to me they do. This isn't twenty-three pounds of muscle. I got fat here, Apryl. It's pure fat." He patted his soft abs. "And even though it's not hella noticeable, it's there. It feels different to me. It's weighing my ass down, woman."

I twisted my lips to one side and lowered my chin to my chest.

I'd decided what I'd do from last night and, as an idea, it seemed crazy. Actually, going through with it was going to be insane.

"I want to propose something to you, but I need something from you in exchange. A guarantee."

"A guarantee?"

"Yes." I nodded. "A promise to give me everything for what I'm proposing."

He lifted and dropped his shoulder, then gestured at me again. "What are you proposing?"

"That I gain twenty-three pounds and we lose weight together, as a team."

He stared at me for a moment without blinking. After so long of a silence, he asked me, "Apryl, why the hell would you do such a crazy ass thing?"

I inhaled a deep breath. "Because you're right, I don't understand. I may have fat nowhere besides my ass, as you say, but it wasn't always like that. I was overweight my entire childhood and teenage years. Nothing worked. My parents tried everything to help when I was a child and I took on the effort as a teenager, trying every fad diet until my freshman year in college, when I decided enough was enough. I developed and patented a fitness plan that worked like magic and I sold that plan for millions to millions of other people, just like me, struggling to get in shape. But although I remember what it was like getting in shape, I remember it differently. I don't remember what part of my mind I needed to hack to stay committed to my commitment to losing weight. So... I want to reconnect with it to help you." I ran my fingers through my hair. "I've tried everything with you, to get you to give your all, and I see you have, but honestly, it hasn't been enough."

"So you're going to put your body through stress, throwing off your biorhythm by suddenly gaining weight... for me? Because I haven't been performing in the gym?" He laughed. "Why the fuck would you do that?"

"Because I need you as much as you need me."

The furrows in his brows deepened.

"The media have tied my career to a woman who has become the bane of my existence, and I can't go another day being linked to her." I shook my head. "Not a career I worked hard as hell to build from the ground up when the people closest to me thought it would be the biggest mistake in my life to do it." I angled my chin up. "Chloe Rae does not deserve credit for that shit. Getting you in shape in time for your appearance will give me something fresh and new to be linked to. I'm using you and I'd like to do it respectfully. Twenty-three pounds is just weight for me, anyway." I ran my hand down my neck. "At least I *hope* it'll just be weight for me."

His eyes softened. "What did Chloe do to you?"

"I don't want to get into that right now," I insisted, refusing to go back to a dark place. "Let's make a deal."

He stared at me.

"I need to understand what you feel, and you seem to be motivated by others. I'm the same." I admitted. "I'll gain twenty-three pounds, give or take, and we'll lose it together. As a team."

He expelled a cynical laugh. "You're crazy."

"A little." I tightened my lips to contain my humor. "I go to lengths most trainers wouldn't dare think about for their clients. But a lot of trainers are never in the same position as their clients, so I never compare myself or do what other trainers do."

"That's an understatement." He shook his head.

"Your community center appearance is important to you, so it's important to me."

He nodded slowly. "I appreciate it."

"Show me your appreciation by holding up your end of the bargain." I glanced around us at the mats and weights. "We won't work out today or for the next month or two."

"Oh, word?"

I pointed at him. "But I want you to stay active in some way. You can choose what that some way is."

"I can swim." He lifted, then dropped his shoulders. "I love to swim."

"Okay. Swimming will work." I smiled. "I'll also arrange an eating plan for you with a list of approved foods you can have. You need to abide by my plan like it's your Bible." I held up a finger. "The only time you can eat like shit will be with me when you take me to the places you like to consume your crap."

He belly laughed, then bit his bottom lip, maintaining a smile. "Oh, are we going on... like... dates?"

I ran my fingers through my hair again to stop myself from blushing. "Let's call them assignments."

His smile grew wider.

Everett was more handsome with the corners of his lips wrinkled in a grin. I had to take a breath to continue speaking.

"Because I have to gain in a short timeframe, I'll give myself two months to put on the weight."

"I can't believe you're serious right now."

"I need you to," I replied, staring him in the eyes. "Because this *is* fucking crazy, okay? What I'm proposing is insane, but I'm confident I know what I'm doing."

"Shit, I hope so." He looked away. "That's a lot of pressure to put on me to perform now, you making such a commitment. I won't be able to give any excuses if you're trying to lose weight, too."

I winked. "That's the plan."

He flashed his teeth.

"So." I walked closer, holding out my hand. "We got a deal?"

Everett accepted my hand and looked me right in my eyes. "Deal."

A chill ran down my spine when our hands touched. So prominent, so effective, I couldn't brush it off as being nothing even if I tried.

I slid my hand free and cleared my throat in my attempt to regain composure. "Great."

"So, now what?"

"You take me to your favorite spot." I smirked. "Because I'm hungry."

SEVENTEEN

I sank to the bottom of the pool, only stopping my descent into the water when my feet touched the pool's floor. The building that housed my new condo had an indoor Olympic-sized pool. I'd been using one of the building's amenities daily since moving in the month prior.

Everything was silent and still underneath the water. The only sound noticeable was the rhythm of my heart beating in my chest.

Living in New York again has been the relief I didn't know I wanted. And Apryl had become a friend I didn't know I needed.

Our relationship did a 180-degree shift after that day at MK's Sports Lounge and Gym. Although I never really hated the woman, I wasn't quite a fan of her bossy ass either. I liked she wasn't a pushover, and I underestimated how good of a trainer she was, I'll admit, but I didn't think things would work out in our professional relationship and I was very wrong.

As promised, we hadn't worked out in two months. During that time, she kept me on a strict low carb, high fruit and vegetable diet. I could only deviate from her plan whenever we went out to eat at my favorite spots. I wasn't sure how that plan would work, having to spend time with her outside of the gym, but our first meet up had to be the best time I've ever had.

"Oh my God," she moaned, closing her eyes. "This is unreal."

At her request, we were at one of my favorite spots whenever I was in New York.

Four Amigos.

It was a small Mexican restaurant in Boro Park, Brooklyn. The strip of block where the restaurant sat was like little Mexico. Several other establishments were other restaurants, Mexican markets, or barbershops and hair salons.

Night had fallen in Brooklyn, so the neighborhood was lit by string lights and paper lanterns blowing in the icy wind of the night.

Apryl and I sat across from each other in the cramped restaurant. On arrival, I could tell she was uncomfortable with the crowd. She stroked her arm repeatedly with her hands and hadn't uncrossed her arms since walking in.

But after the hostess walked us to our table, and we ordered our food, and the server brought it out to us, she'd loosened up after her first bite.

She looked beautiful tonight. Her long waist-length hair pulled to the top of her head and wrapped in a bun. I'd only seen her in gym clothes, so it was a delight to see her in a sweater dress, long black boots, and a short puffer coat to keep her warm.

She was on her third taco when she'd finally come up for air.

"Good?" I asked before biting into mine.

She chewed and nodded her head, unable to speak. Her eyes briefly rolling to the back of her head was enough proof the meal was hitting the spot.

"This white sauce." She pointed at her taco. "It's amazing. I think I'm in love! What is it?"

I smirked. "Sour cream?"

Her giddy smile morphed into pursed lips. "Oh, shut up."

I threw my hands up. "What did I do? You asked."

Her mouth bulged with food. "You didn't have to say it like that."

"How'd I say it?"

"Like I was making a big fuss over something as simple as sour cream."

"Is there something wrong with being in love with basic things, like sour cream?"

She shook her head and laughed at herself.

I shared in her amusement, reaching for a napkin to clean my mouth. "Don't get out much, huh?"

She reached for her folded napkin to clean her mouth as well. "I haven't eaten like this in... over a decade."

I wrinkled my brows. "You haven't had tacos in a decade?"

She shook her head. "My strict diet never allowed for it."

I stared at her, waiting, hoping she'd continue.

Just like Apryl, I'd done my research on her online as well. The only difference is, there was little information that gave me insight into who Apryl was. How she started in her career, the millions of lives she's changed with her workout program, even her friendship with Chloe Rae. All of that was available by a boatload. But anything in-depth about the woman who sat across from me? Nonexistent.

"I used to be overweight for most of my childhood and teenage years."

I recalled her mentioning that during our last session.

"Teenaged me, used to eat any and everything. When stressed, I ate. Happy, I ate. I celebrated and grieved with food." She took a sip of water. "So, when I decided I wanted to take my weight-loss journey seriously and not make it another unfulfilled new year's resolution, I cut out everything. I submerged myself in all things health and wellness, reading everything I could get my eyes on during my first year in college. Spent more time reading books on fitness than on my studies and it showed." She burbled. "I studied for so long, I determined on my own it wasn't what I was eating, it was the amount of what I ate causing the problem. So I ran with that. I cut out more things and put myself on a restricted diet. Brown rice, vegetables, lightly seasoned lean proteins, and shakes. I figured, if it doesn't matter what I eat but it's the amount of what I eat that matters, what would happen if I stayed away from the bad stuff all together?" She shrugged. "So that's what I did. For over ten years, I stopped eating things like this." She pointed at her near empty plate.

"God." I licked food particles off my lips. "You're so intense with every-thing for no goddamn reason."

She stared at me for a long while, then burst into uncontrollable laughter. I couldn't help but to join in.

That night was the best date that ever was. It became the start of a friendship I never knew was possible between Apryl and I.

Every Saturday since, like clockwork, we'd meet up, and I'd take her to a place I liked to eat. Mexican, Thai, soul food kitchens, you name it. We waited three hours once for a table to open at a popular Korean restaurant to eat world famous Korean barbecue in Jamaica, Queens.

The gap between waiting for our table and actually being seated became the perfect opportunity to get to know each other better, more intimately.

"Let's play a game," she proposed outside of the restaurant as we waited.

"All right," I agreed. "I like games."

"Cool." She grinned. "It's called twenty-one questions. We ask each other any and everything and we must be honest, regardless of how we think we'll judge each other's answers."

I twisted my lips to one side. "Should I be nervous about this?"

Apryl giggled. "We'll stop at the twenty-first question. Ladies first." *She winked. "If you weren't a boxer, what would you be?"*

I stared up at the night sky, thinking. The moon was out, bright and silver, casting a subtle glow over the city.

"A race car driver."

Her mouth fell open. "Really?"

I nodded. "For sure."

"You drive well?"

"Amazingly."

"Hmph.".

"What about you?"

"Probably a nutritionist," she revealed. "Or what I was in school studying to be before I dropped out."

"Which was?"

"A teacher."

I pushed myself off the brick wall we leaned against. "Nice."

She smiled the most beautiful smile I'd ever seen before. She looked away shyly.

"You'd be more famous than you are now," she added. "If you went the race car driver's route."

I held up a finger. "Which is why I stuck with boxing instead of changing careers."

She nodded, still smiling. "I'm actually surprised you're not more famous."

"Don't be."

"You're undefeated, a lot more skilled than the boxers known by face than by name."

"That's something done on purpose." I stared out ahead of us at the blacktop road and the cars driving over it. "You can't maintain privacy when everyone knows you. Go everywhere without bodyguards. I'm known more by name than face. And people who know me by face can hardly see it because I'm always rocking a hat." I tapped the rim of the Yankee fitted I wore tonight.

My ex, Brielle, hated that about me, my desire to stay low-key. She loved name dropping me at restaurants and in front of club doors and I made it difficult for her to make a name for herself as an athlete's girl-friend by me being turned off by fame.

"I feel you though." Apryl nodded. "For me, that's why I accept I don't photograph well, like someone so kindly pointed out."

I chuckled.

"Makes it harder to be recognized in public," she added. "Which I love."

"You know." I turned to face her. "When I said you didn't photograph well, I wasn't trying to offend you."

She turned to face me, too.

"I only meant you were sexier in person."

We locked eyes, and she smirked.

"Oh," she said. "I thought you were just being an asshole."

I shook my head. "I just don't know how to flirt. I'm way too direct."

"Oh," she responded again, folding a lock of hair behind the bend of her ear. "You were trying to flirt that day."

"Operative word: trying."

She giggled.

"Looking back at it, I should've just told you how beautiful you are."

"Were," she corrected, peeking down at herself. "Not with this extra weight I'm packing on for you." She poked me in the chest.

I licked my lips, my eyes fixed on her hips. "I think you look sexier with it."

Her jaw dropped slightly before a smile appeared on her lips again. Apryl parted them to say something when a voice interrupted us.

"You wait for the table to open?" The Korean hostess said at the door.

Apryl and I perked up immediately.

"It's ready!"

That outing fortified our bond. And each outing after helped us grow closer. Conversations flowed better, comfort levels elevated. We went from sitting opposite one another in restaurants to standing beside each other as we scarfed down hot dogs after waiting in a crowded line at Nathan's on Coney Island in Brooklyn. Our engagement became innocently physical to intentionally erotic.

"This is disgusting, Everett," she exclaimed as we stood over a stand-up table at a Greek restaurant in Brooklyn Heights. We'd caught a movie an hour ago, something new for us. For the past few weekends, it has only been us going out to eat, but I insisted we switch it up when it was getting monotonous. So, we watched a film at a theater on Court Street, walked a few blocks to a Greek spot I'd never been to, and we were about to bite into a gyro. After only a few weeks, I noticed a change in Apryl's body. Her hips were wider, around her midsection thicker. As if it were possible, she got finer with each pound she packed on. Her ass had become a point of focus for me as it spread to my content. It was becoming harder and harder not to touch it, or to maintain a platonic relationship with Apryl.

When we ordered the gyros, I insisted we try the stuffed grape leaves, which were made of rice, meat, and vegetables. At first glance, she was sure she'd hate it, and after biting into her first one, she was certain she didn't like them.

"You're not eating them in a way to enjoy them," I insisted.

She chewed what she bit off and gagged a little after swallowing what remained.

The pinched expression on her face was so damn adorable. The fullness of her face had softened her features, made her look more feminine than she already looked.

"And how am I supposed to eat these things without wanting to throw up?" She glanced at the other stuffed grape leaves on the plate and stuck her tongue out in disgust.

I picked up one of the stuffed grape leaves and used my free hand to take her by the chin.

"Here," I told her, holding the grape leaf to her lips. "Open."

She stared at me for a beat before she slacked her jaw and opened her mouth.

I placed the grape leaf at her mouth's opening and instructed, "Don't bite it, suck on it."

She arched a brow at that.

"Go on," I encouraged in response.

Our eyes remained on each other as she wrapped her lips around the outer edges of the briny outer layer and began sucking out the rice, ground beef, onions, tomatoes, and seasoning. I watched her chest rise and fall in her cotton pullover. My dick stiffened in my joggers. If we weren't in a room full of patrons, that probably would have been the night I jumped her bones in public.

When the grape leaves were almost empty, I told her, "Now open up," and I slid in what remained of the wrap.

We maintained eye contact as she chewed bits of the grape leaves, and she swallowed, not gagging this time.

It went without saying things changed between us. But I was in no position to acknowledge the obvious after promising myself I wouldn't start another relationship of any kind with any woman so soon after my breakup with my ex, Brielle.

"So," she started, "that was extremely sexy, I'll admit."

I smirked. "Agreed."

"But these are still very disgusting, Everett."

"Well, sucking the filling out isn't how you eat them, anyway, so..."

She gasped.

I popped one in my mouth and added, "I just wanted to see you suck on something."

Apryl punched me on the arm and I cracked up. She did too and before long, our laugh transitioned into a bellyful chuckle between us.

That was two weeks ago.

I closed my eyes and sunk deeper into the still hollowed pool, squaring my shoulders and squatting under water to feel the pressure against my shoulders to weigh me down. When I couldn't hold my breath any longer, I frog jumped once until my face penetrated the surface and I inhaled lungs full of air. Leaning back, I floated atop the water, staring up at the pool room's ceiling.

I looked forward to Apryl and my outings. She'd finally gained the twenty-three pounds which she informed me of at the start of the week. Apryl also mentioned our outing, scheduled for later in the week, a Saturday night, would be the final one.

Tonight was Saturday night.

I was unsure how I felt about our date night routine ending, but I wouldn't make that known. I enjoyed our time together and would make tonight's final one equally exciting.

Our last outing would be bittersweet because, although I knew we'd strengthened our bond in our client-trainer friendship, I wanted more, but I wasn't ready for what would happen after I got what I wanted.

I put all those conflicting feelings out of my mind though, to turn over onto my stomach, begin kicking my legs and paddling my arms to move about the pool, with plans to complete one of many laps around the cool water.

Cool, calm, and supportive, I realized at that moment that Apryl and water were a lot alike, and likely why I was falling for her when I shouldn't have been.

Eighteen

APRYL

I couldn't lie to myself, even if I tried. Though my reflection in my mirror didn't bring me down the way I thought it would at the start of this journey, my energy was terrible. My vitality was in the dumps. I could barely get out of bed these days to carry out my daily routines, and that was something I never thought I'd ever have to experience again.

Tilting my head from left to right, I stared at my midsection and smiled. Even with a little extra weight on my stomach, my body looked... good.

Soft, rounder than usual. But good... even though I felt like absolute shit on the inside.

I blinked at the fold of my stomach, slightly hanging over the waistband of my panties. Guided my eyes down to the cellulite, denting my thighs.

I'd always had stretch marks and cellulite from my overweight days, but to see them so prominent now after only two months of overeating with the goal of gaining twenty-three pounds to lose at the gym? It was shocking but relieving. I wasn't obsessing over it being there. Seeing it took the pressure off, desiring perfection all the time. Even if I was two pounds over.

Is this what Everett felt? Or did the extra weight bring him down emotionally?

Through my lens, men weren't as hard on themselves as women were with their bodies. Muscle gain was all men cared about and Everett never seemed hung up over the weight he gained. He just knew he needed to get the extra pounds off him for the optics during the opening of the community center appearance he had in two months.

I poked at my stomach, watching the flesh jiggle a little. My abs were there. Not as defined, but I'd worked so hard and so long to get them; there were indentations in places my abs used to be toned.

Although I wasn't a fan of excessive eating, I was kind of loving how my body showed every ounce of the twenty-five pounds I'd gained. It made me feel really feminine. Like one of those Baroque paintings in Ruben, but sexier and in ebony.

I snickered at the thought.

The evolution of Everett and my friendship was another thing I didn't expect to like.

I mean, can I really call it a friendship? Am I supposed to feel like fucking my friend?

I don't know if it was the foods I was eating or the fact I'd successfully penetrated the armor of a man I found to be illusive and difficult only to find how amazing of an individual he was, but my attraction to Everett had grown immensely.

Saturdays couldn't come fast enough each week. I had to force my phone out of my hand to keep from texting him most weeknights to see what he was up to.

He was a great date. A way better date than I'd been on with the help of the HeartMates app. If you could call it help. And Everett and I weren't dating.

Tonight will be the last night of our eating out. He'd booked a table for us at a spot that hosted mukbang seafood boils. He offered for us to check it out a couple of weeks prior, but I couldn't stomach another all-you-can-eat type setting after our visit to a Brazilian restaurant. The amount of meat we ingested would likely remain in our system for months undigested.

The Brazilian restaurant was the first time we got the closest... physically.

"I hate it already," I groaned. "I hate crowds."

Wall-to-wall people crowded Taste Rio at eight in the evening on a warmer than usual Saturday in April. Everett had run out of favorite places on our quest for me to pack on the pounds, so this spot between Fifth and Sixth Avenue in Manhattan was new to both of us.

"Don't be grouchy right now," he insisted. "Just chill. Take in the atmosphere."

I rolled my eyes to myself.

"I think it's kind of dope in here," he said next. "Crowd and all."

I'd gone from wearing jeans for our meetups to sweatsuits for the comfort after eating. Everett had always been the joggers type and wore a pair of gray ones for the night, along with the matching pullover.

As soon as we arrived, we crammed ourselves into the closest line inside the restaurant. We had to give a name to the hostess so she could seat us. Throngs of patrons packed the restaurant, crowding the lines just to give her our names. There were three long lines, full of people pushed up against each other like a pack of sardines. Everett stood behind me in line. A few times, he'd accidentally bump into me from behind, and my ass would brush against his crotch. Happened so many times, I expected it. Maybe I looked forward to the accidental bump.

I guess the friction occurred so much that when we bumped into one another once again, I noticed some stiffness there that wasn't there before.

I didn't want to assume, so I glanced over my shoulder, lowering my eyes to his crotch, to, sure enough, see Everett was wearing a hard-on. The outline of his dick didn't show he was fully erect, but there was definitely some blood flow happening down there, and his gray joggers failed to hide that fact.

I rolled my eyes up at him in time to see him repress his laugh and look away, licking his lips to hide the smirk pulling at the corners of his mouth.

"You all right back there," I joshed.

His smirk became a full blown beautiful beam of light. "Couldn't be better."

That night, I returned home with a belly so full of meat and pastels, it had become upset. I was also full of salacious thoughts and fantasies of Everett sliding that hard-on into every orifice I had that he could fit his girth into. The thoughts became so consuming I had to relieve myself with my silicone rabbit. But that still wasn't enough.

I needed sex as much as I needed to exercise, maybe the former more.

Exercising had always been my substitute for sex, and without them both, I was losing my mind.

"Thank God tonight will be the last night of this shit."

Because although I enjoyed my time with Everett on these mini-food excursions, I was over food.

I grabbed a pair of leggings and pulled them up to my waist, one foot at a time, before throwing on my designer hooded sweatshirt. Then I turned to exit my room so I could grab my coat near the front door, leave my house, and not be late.

———

The spot was loud and disorderly.

Event organizers hosted Mukbang Boil under a tent in Bryant Park in Manhattan a few blocks from Times Square. The tent was huge, but the space was minimal. People were tapping my chair with their metal chairs every time they pushed it back to make more space or to get up and leave.

I'd bitten into my buttered corn and propped the side of my head up with a fist. The meal was so underwhelming. I was over it.

Everett sat across from me wearing clear gloves. In one hand was a crab leg and the other a stainless-steel crab cracker.

"I am so *tired* of eating." I tossed the rest of my corn into the plastic bag with the rest of my food.

Scatters of shrimp tails and crab leg shells laid all over our table like the scene of a seafood murder. My mouth was on fire because of the extra lemon pepper sauce I requested. I literally could eat no more.

Everett licked the side of his mouth with his tongue.

I want to fuck him so badly.

I dropped my forehead against the table and grunted.

He cracked up laughing across from me.

"I'm happy my shitty mood is humorous to you."

"Aww," he teased. "Is Apryl having one of those grumpy nights again?"

I sucked my teeth, and that just added to his entertainment.

Mukbang Boil was a pop-up restaurant that changed its location every week. We had to make a reservation days in advance so that they prepared our meal and reserved our table in time for our arrival.

"Do you ever feel like shit during the week, Everett?"

He took off the clear gloves and leaned back in his seat.

"Like, I've been feeling *really* shitty since I've been eating like this." I pushed the bag away from me. "I'm tired all the time, angry—"

"Lethargic, low energy," he added.

I peeked up. "Yes! You feel that too?"

"All the time," he stared past me. "It kind of comes with the territory of eating like crap."

"*Ugh*," I exclaimed. "This can't be life."

He shrugged. "To me, it's better than feeling the other stuff."

I tilted my head to the right in response. "What other stuff?"

The sound of chatter buzzed around us in our silence.

Everett ran his hand down his face, pointed at me, and said, "The only reason I'm going to share this with you is because you've become somewhat of a homie these last eight weeks."

I nodded and waited for him to continue.

He leaned forward in his seat and sighed. "The community center opening wasn't my primary motivation for leaving Cali for New York."

"Okay..."

"I had a nasty breakup that sent me to a place mentally that was destructive."

I blew air out of my mouth. "I know *all* about nasty breakups."

His lips curled up as he laughed. "I doubt your nasty breakup could touch the heels of mine."

I offered a sardonic laugh of my own. "I'm positive mine trumps yours."

He tapped the table with his index pointer finger. "I found out my girlfriend was cheating on me with multiple men via sex tapes. I found the recorded DVDs on Valentine's Day, which was also our fifth-year anniversary, while trying to hide her engagement ring so she could find it when I proposed to her that same night."

I arched both brows.

"But the best part about it was she tried to convince me that her cheating was to benefit me."

"Damn," I exhaled. "Well, I acknowledge your cheating ex, her sex tapes, a fucked-up Valentine's Day, and her delusion, and I challenge you with my fiancé, who insisted we keep our relationship and then our engagement a secret for both of our careers, cheated on me with my new best friend while filming a movie. Oh, a movie I busted *my ass* to get him hired so he could star in it with her."

He cringed. "Oh, shit!"

"*Uh-huh*, but that's not the hardest part." I inhaled a valiant breath. "Because she and I were best friends, her name became attached to my brand. So every success I experience, every dollar I earn, she's mentioned and credited for building everything, not excluding the laborious work that pre-dated her. So instead of being known for my accomplishments, everybody credits her for building my career. To this day, including *you*, Mr. Peters. So it's damn near impossible to get past her and my fiancé's betrayal. Because I'm reminded of it *every* fucking day."

"Fuck," he whispered, and cringed again. "I mentioned her when talking about your training, huh?"

"Yeah, you sure did."

"Okay." He threw his hands up in surrender. "I'm sorry. You win."

"*Mm-hmm*." I nodded. "And lose."

"Shit." Everett leaned in closer. "Chloe fucked your fiancé?"

"Several times behind my back and he ended up leaving me for her, even after I begged him not to."

"Man."

"I *begged* him not to leave me after *he* cheated, Everett. Can you believe that? Do you have any idea how low that shit feels? How low that is? To beg a cheater not to leave you?"

He kissed his teeth. "Damn."

"Their relationship didn't last long enough for them to be photographed on the red carpet together at the movie premiere of their movie."

My heart ached as I recalled.

"I went to bat for him to be in that film and I thought it would be so perfect to have him and my new good friend, Ms. Chloe Rae, act together. I wouldn't be weird about the kissing or intimate scenes because I trusted them both." I squeezed my eyes closed. "Just dumb."

"You're not dumb." He shook his head. "You weren't wrong for trusting."

"Tuh!" I rolled my eyes up to keep the tears from falling. "He did an interview recently. For a major publication. He's got this movie he's starring in. It's not as big as the one with Chloe, but it's big enough to keep the buzz going."

Everett remained focused.

"The interviewer asked him what his biggest upset in life was and guess what he said?"

"What?"

"He said with his entire chest, his greatest upset was his breakup with Chloe. Not going bankrupt at twenty after his parents squandered all of his child-acting money, not prematurely claiming Chloe as his girlfriend publicly but insisting he and I keep our relationship private so he could give off the impression of being single to maintain his female fan base. Of course, not breaking my heart after I worked tirelessly to help him get back on top of acting or lying to me when I always told him the truth. Oh, no. His biggest upset was his two-minute-long relationship with a woman who refuses to confirm she was ever with him." I shook my head. "Meanwhile, I'm going on tragic first dates that get worse after each one before it. The best date I've been on has been with you, and it wasn't a date."

He chuckled.

"And now I'm sluggish, horny, and sad as fuck." I could feel the tension building in my neck and shoulders. "How do you deal with this feeling every day?"

"I jerk off every night, so that handles the horniness."

I pointed at him. "Why does it not surprise me you addressed that issue first?"

He cracked a smile. "And," he continued, "there's lots of alcohol and bars in California and New York to drown the rest."

"Welp." I closed my eyes. "I don't drink—"

"You do tonight," he interjected.

I opened my eyes to the smirk he wore.

"No." I shook my head. "I haven't had a drink in over a decade."

"And you didn't have sour cream for that long either, but you had some with me."

"Sour cream, alcohol, hmm..." I held my hands up, mimicking a scale. "Not the same thing."

"Well, I drink and you're doing everything I do until Monday, right?"

"Everett..."

"So we're getting drunk tonight, Ms. Wilde. Come on."

Before I could protest anymore, he grabbed me by the hand and pulled me out of my seat and toward the tent's exit.

————

"I tell you I have drunk no kind of alcohol in over ten years and you buy a tray full of shots? Are you kidding me?" I asked over the music. "We couldn't have started with a beer or something? I'm drunk after the first shot, Everett!"

The bass line in the hip-hop song playing reverberated around us, blasting from speakers all around Club Déjà Vu. It was Everett's idea for us to stop there for *one* drink. Not a tray full of shots.

Women dressed in nearly nothing, danced in cages, or swung on suspended swings wearing nipple pasties shaped like pools of whip cream with cherries on top.

The bouncer let us in without a question after recognizing Everett. Before we could make it past the corridor leading to the club's bar, the owner offered VIP if Everett simply spoke into a mic and waved at the club goers. Everett negotiated the skybox and a private server instead for more privacy, and here we sat alone with a few bottles of expensive champagne, a tray of tequila shots and sliced lime all on the house.

"You're not drunk." He tossed back another shot. "Tipsy, maybe. Here." He handed me another.

I accepted the shot glass against my better judgement and tossed the contents back, mentally mapping the alcohol's descent down my throat, leaving fiery trails in its wake. I quickly reached for a slice of lime to sink my teeth into the wedge.

"You know," he said with a laugh. "You don't have to eat the lime after *every* shot."

"Oh, I'm sorry." I pressed my hand to my chest. "You must think I have an aluminum pipe for a trachea like you."

He hollered a laugh.

"I need a little help to swallow hard liquor."

"Apryl, please. Tequila barely classifies as hard liquor."

The aftertaste from my previous shot still singed my throat, making me cringe when I swallowed. I reached forward for another lime, the last one, to chase the taste.

"Now we're out of limes." He used his chin to gesture at our private server, pointing at the empty tray of limes. "Should I have her bring more salt as well?"

"Shut up," I mumbled over the lime wedge. "I'm drunk."

"You're not drunk."

Despite his reasoning, I knew I was drunk. And with the new shot coursing through my system, if I wasn't drunk before it, I sure was now.

We were so underdressed for the club. Women walked around the club floor beneath us with their asses and breasts hanging out. Guys wore expensive printed tops unbuttoned way below the neckline and paired their outfits with designer slacks. They all finished their looks with a piece of gaudy ass jewelry, unapologetically wearing their incomes.

Over a short time, my two shots became four, and that four doubled to eight. And when Everett handed me the ninth, I could barely accept the shot glass without spilling some of the tequila.

I was definitely drunk... now.

My head was wavy and my body light. Thoughts circled my mind in a fog and it felt good not having to think for a little and to be in the moment.

A nice, relaxed feeling settled over me, allowing me to lean back in my seat and to close my eyes, basking in the feeling of nothingness. What I was consuming was so toxic and I was sure I'd pay for my choices in the morning when I had my head in my toilet, but in that instance, I felt great.

"Twenty-one questions," I slurred, starting our little game.

"Shoot."

"What is something no one knows about Everett Peters?"

He chuckled lazily beside me. I could tell without looking at him that the liquor had him inebriated beyond belief.

This was such a bad idea.

I opened my eyes to confirm my assumption, and I found Everett with his head slung over the neck of the couch, super relaxed.

His thick neck and protruding Adam's apple. His laid-back posture and relaxed demeanor. It all looked so inviting.

I knew I had to be drunk when the sudden feeling of leaving my seat to straddle him came over me. We were alone. For the hour we'd already spent in the skybox at the club, our private server had only returned once to bring more limes before Everett sent her on her way. A lot could happen in this space between Everett and I... all by ourselves.

But that would be foolish.

Our job together wasn't complete and doing that, everything that happened after the straddle, would not differ from how close I got to my ex Troy and former friend Chloe. I could not keep my promise to myself about not making the same mistake twice.

So, I opted to shake that thought free of my mind to calm the desire. I closed my eyes again and leaned my head over the neck of the couch.

"Something people don't know about me. *Hmmm.*" He hummed. "I'd say..." He paused for another beat. "That I like to eat pussy."

My eyes shot open, and I lifted my head off the couch's neck to turn my head to face him.

"Excu... What?!"

He opened his eyes a second later and turned his head to face me.

"That is *not* what I meant when I said tell me something no one knows about you."

He snickered low, too weak to bust out laughing, which I was sure he wanted to do.

I pressed my fingertips to my lids. "My God."

"Hey, you asked," he defended. "And it is something no one knows. I genuinely love to do it."

"Oh-kay," I continued, barely able to keep my eyes opened. "I'm drunk enough to explore that revelation."

"And I'm wasted enough to divulge," he added low.

I forced myself to sit up on the large plush couch to face him. "So... do you go around putting your mouth on random women's pussies to satisfy your love of eating them?"

"Of course not," he answered, head turned my way. "That would be nasty and compulsive, which I am."

I laughed.

"But not nasty and compulsive to the point of doing some stupid shit, like putting my mouth on random women's pussies, as *you* put it."

"Okay, so..." I shrugged. "Set up the scene for me. What does that look like?"

He sat up and faced me, licking his lips slowly. "I'm a fan of the taste of pussy. The unique essence of a woman. I love it. Crave it in most cases. And no, I don't go around eating every woman's pussy I date. That would be *very* unsanitary."

I quirked a brow.

"I'm nasty, but I'm not *that* nasty. The standards I have are there."

"Oh, of course." I nodded, balling my lips to keep from laughing. "I'm sure they'd have to pass a written exam or a pussy assessment to qualify too, huh?"

"See you're playing." He smirked. "But I'm serious." Everett licked his lips again, then leaned in close to tell me, "I'd eat your pussy if you let me."

We were mere inches away from each other when I skipped a breath.

I swallowed hard. "You'd do that?"

"With pleasure," he whispered back, the scent of tequila sweet on his breath. He bit his bottom lip and lowered his sight to my lap. "You look like you taste good. I'm willing to bet every dollar I got you taste *real* good. You might be the best meal I've ever had."

"Straight, no chaser, huh?"

"Remember," he reminded, "I'm not good at flirting. I'm better at being direct."

I couldn't control the rise and fall of my chest if I tried.

"Well..." I looked him in the eyes. "I squirt when I come."

Everett responded by closing his eyes briefly, exhaling a low groan to himself. I had to press my thighs together to calm down.

"Would wetting the sheets be a problem for you?"

"*Ab-so-lute-ly* not." A lusty smile slowly formed on his lips. "I find shit like that to be a joyful surprise. Like opening a bag of food and finding out they put more than I was expecting. You're that extra scoop of fries."

I snickered. "You and food." I held a finger up. "And squirting sounds good in theory until when it's actually happening."

He rubbed his chin. "What do you mean?"

"Quickies, as a squirter, is out of the question, especially when your partner sees it as a hindrance. Gotta put a towel down always. Can't have random sex in public. Worried clothes would get wet."

"Your ex felt that way?"

"Did he feel that way?" I scoffed. "He hated it." I dropped my sight on my left ring finger in thought, remembering having to disconnect mentally while having sex so I could orgasm in peace and not get hung up over him being disgusted when I came because I always squirted when I climaxed. Without fail. I was so dumb back then tolerating that. "He considered squirting to be pee."

The furrows in Everett's brows deepened even more. "Excuse me?"

"He called it *diluted pee*." I cackled. When he first said it, it wasn't funny. "I remember using this as a coping mechanism and justification for him cheating on me. That he was finally relieved to be with someone normal again. Someone who didn't have such an uncontrollable bodily response to enjoying sex."

"He's a fucking loser," he declared, shaking his head. "He should not have made you feel that way."

"Yeah, well." I looked away.

"I mean…" Everett ran his hand down his beard. "Calling it *pee* takes the sexiness right out of it."

"Oh, completely," I seconded. "There was also nothing sexy about him practically running to the bathroom to get me off him after we were done. Or when he'd change the sheets, the moment he got out of the shower."

"No, he didn't."

"He did," I answered. "He wasn't a fan of wet spots."

"Listen to me." He pointed at himself. "I *love* the wet spots. And squirting?" He shrugged. "If it's pee, then it's pee."

I laughed.

"For me, it does something for me, seeing the social proof I did a body good."

My heart was racing. Between my thighs, hot enough to keep a drink warm.

"Everett, this conversation is inappropriate. We shouldn't be having a conversation like this."

"It's already being had and I'm not trying to stop it. Do you want to stop?"

The music elevated a notch in the skybox as the club's DJ transitioned his set from one genre to the next.

I shook my head slowly, giving my answer.

"I had a squirter once," he continued, leaning forward to pick up another shot of tequila, tossing it back when in hand. "Only once. She wasn't my girlfriend, although I had one at home."

"What?"

"Yeah." He nodded. "I was a fuckup. A liar and a cheater. Very disloyal, which is why I don't really have a foot to stand on to hold resentment against my ex for what she did. I'd imagine it was karma arriving on time for me."

I stared at him, conflicted with how to feel about that. I assumed that was how priests felt listening to confessionals.

He was honest, though. I respected that.

"The woman, the squirter, was just some lady I met at a private party and fucked in a coat check." He stroked his beard's stubble. "She couldn't control her release or the evidence of it, and I loved it. It was sexy as hell. I had parts of her all over my dick that night, the condom at least. Unfortunately, I'll never get to see her again, but I think of her often."

"Because she squirted?" I asked.

He nodded. "I'd never been with a woman who squirted when she came. I had plenty of women who creamed, which I love as well."

"Oh my God." I giggled at his nonchalance, discussing something so private.

"Didn't take me long to realize squirters were my new fave. Feeling that warmth sprayed all over my dick." He bit his bottom lip and moaned.

I dropped my jaw.

He *is* nasty.

"Oh, please don't act shy now."

"I'm... not." I tried to hide myself, blushing. "I'm also not too hot at the fact you're a cheater."

"*Was*," he insisted. "I was young back then, too. Just coming into money, only exercising discipline as it pertained to maintaining my belt. There were a lot of women around me. I didn't know how to say no to them, nor did I think I needed to."

"*Hmph.*"

"I'm not like that now." He stared forward. "Probably wouldn't have been so bothered by my ex cheating if I was still the same way. It probably would've been best that I stayed that way, actually."

Everett leaned forward again to grab another drink, and I reached over to stop him. I noticed a pattern.

Overeating and over-drinking when discussing uncomfortable things.

"Everett, you can feel what you feel. Your feelings are valid despite your past, okay?" I assured him. "You cheated on women and that was wrong, but you stopped. You fell in love, and you expected your ex to be loyal like you were being to her and she wasn't."

He clenched his jaw.

"You're allowed to feel hurt by that. Your past doesn't negate the pain. It doesn't dictate otherwise. You feel what you feel and your feelings are valid."

"Ha!" He glanced at me. "You sound like my mother."

I smiled. "Wise woman."

"And a psychotherapist."

"Really?!" I perked up in my seat. "That's so cool."

"Just like squirting for you sounds good, in theory. Having a psychotherapist as a parent sounds great in theory as well."

I held back a giggle.

"And your squirting is not a reason for your ex to have cheated on you," he added. "Even if it's allegedly diluted pee."

This time, I gave into that giggle.

———

Everett and I spent another hour at the club before deciding to leave. Club Déjà Vu was closer to my townhouse, so I walked home instead of hailing a yellow cab.

"I can't let you walk home alone. I'll walk you," Everett said, following behind me before I could tell him otherwise.

It was after 1am, and even given the hour, the streets were still bustling with energy. As we were leaving the club, people were just arriving. They didn't call New York the city that never sleeps for nothing.

We arrived at the bottom of my townhouse's steps when I announced, "This is me."

Everett angled his head to look up at the door, then the windows, his eyes visually climbing the polished stone to the roof of my townhouse's structure.

"Wow," he exhaled. "This is all you?"

"Yup." I angled my chin up and relaxed my shoulders. I'd gotten so much slack over the years on my decision to buy a townhouse alone.

"This is incredible." He gazed at me, impressed. "Big boss shit. I like it. I like it a lot."

My head jerked back. "You... like that?"

"For sure." He nodded slowly, smiling while still examining the outer structure of my townhouse. "It's all yours. Something you own.

An investment. Owning property in New York City is a smart move and solid long-term thinking. Very dope. How many bedrooms?"

I was so flustered by how much he was pouring into me, I couldn't remember the amount of rooms myself. "Umm, four. No, five."

He bobbed his head, impressed. "Five is very good."

Yup, I'm going to fuck him.

Everett pointed over his shoulder. "I'm gonna go catch a cab now that I see you're at your enormous door." He joked. "Monday, right—"

"Do you want to come in?"

Yes, I said that doing anything remotely physical with Everett would be bad for business and kind of like me going down the same path of getting too close to my clients, which, yes; I said I wouldn't do. But I really wanted him in my bed that night.

He lifted his baseball cap to scratch the top of his head. "Ummm..."

"You can sleep on the couch in my living room," I reasoned. I didn't want to be so forward to let him know he wouldn't know what the couch felt like beneath him because he'd be sleeping with me in my bed. Maybe. Because *if* we slept at all, sleeping would be the last thing we did.

Literally.

"It's late," I added. "And we're drunk."

"The walk here helped me sober up a little."

"Just come in," I pushed, turning to climb my steps. I'd reached the middle of my cement staircase when I turned to see him still standing at the foot, so I gestured with my head at my front door while continuing up the stairs.

I didn't turn back again until after I placed my key into the door's keyhole and opened it, then walked through the arched entrance, kicking off my sneakers. The only time I turned to look behind me was after Everett closed the front door.

I pulled my hair out of the bun I twisted it into, feeling the strands cascading down my shoulders. "Can I get you some water?"

"Yeah, thanks." Everett ran his hand up one column's groove. His eyes measured the height of the arch over my entryway. "19th century built?"

"Yeah." I padded to the kitchen and stopped in front of the fridge. "You know architecture?"

"I know New York City real estate. I've been studying it for a year, looking for another viable stream of income that's recession proof to keep my money flowing and growing while retired. Until I find something more lucrative, that is." He toed off his sneakers and swaggered into the living room, eyes still scanning.

I handed him the water when I entered the living room, watching as he unscrewed the water bottle cap.

We stared at each other as he chugged the bottled water near empty.

Anticipation stuttered by breathing and made my pulse race. My patience was dwindling. I wasn't sure how much more small talk I could entertain.

He swallowed what remained in the bottle and chuckled to himself over the spout. Twisted on the bottle's cap, and placed it on my coffee table before he confirmed, "I'm not sleeping on this couch tonight, am I?"

"Nope." I shook my head slowly. "You're probably not going to sleep at all tonight, actually."

Everett made a shrugging expression with the corners of his lips.

"Cool, then..." He pointed over my shoulder at the kitchen. "I'm gonna need another bottle of water. For sure."

I got the water, but instead of walking it back to him, I walked it to the stairs that led up to my bedroom.

"You can drink this one upstairs."

He smirked and took steps to approach.

I led the way, refusing to look back until we were in my room. When we arrived, I allowed him to walk in so I could close the door behind him.

Just like downstairs, he looked around, scanning my room from wall to wall. "I like your style a lot."

I gave the room a once over. "I can't take all the credit. My interior decorator did all the work."

"I'm not talking about your house." He turned to face me. "I'm referring to the way you move. How you go for yours. You're a little aggressive. I like that."

He closed the space between us, taking slow steps toward me.

"You don't make things a mystery." He tilted my head back, so I'd look up at him when he was close. "Real grown with it and I like grown."

My eyes danced along his face, visually devouring his stunning African features. Full nose and lips. Dark eyes so rich they only reflected as brown beneath my lights. His mannerisms were simple yet sexy. He exuded confidence, clearly comfortable in his masculinity. The man was gorgeous inside and out, despite his flaws. Definitely worth crossing the line for.

Everett took the water bottle out of my hand and glanced away to sit the bottle on the surface of my dresser, an arm's reach away. "I'll drink that after we're done."

He refocused on me, pressing his hands on either side of my head on the wall behind me.

"Can I be honest with you?" he asked, lowering his eyes below my neck.

"You should always be honest with me," I answered low.

"I've wanted you from the moment we locked eyes at the gym."

I balanced myself on the arch of my feet, angling my mouth with his. When I was mere inches away from his lips, I whispered, "Same," before crashing my mouth into his.

He received my kiss fearlessly, grabbing me by the back of my head and darting his tongue into my mouth, wasting no time.

Our tongues twisted and twirled around one another, our eager exhales caused the heat in our breaths to caress our faces. Everett leaned me back against the wall and kissed his lips off mine to guide his mouth down the sensitive skin on my neck.

I thought my eyes would cross from the sensation of having his mouth on me. Refused to stop the moans from humming from my lips when he drew the skin into his mouth and sucked ever so gently.

I caressed the back of his head as he continued trailing his tongue down my neck, kissing my breasts through my clothes, continuing his journey down my form. Everett snaked his hand up my sweatshirt, pulling me from the moment instantly. Not because what he was doing didn't feel good. It felt great. I just remembered how meaty my midsection had become to me.

I had the finest man in my townhouse, and all I could think about was him seeing my fupa.

"Wait." I grabbed him at the biceps. His arms were so hard, the muscles clearly there. Where exactly was this extra twenty-three pounds? Because I swear I felt I was the only one who had gained weight.

"What's the matter?" he whispered. Everett continued to massage my ass through my joggers while squatting down in front of me.

"Umm." I swallowed hard and looked away, briefly, embarrassed. "I'm not..."

He blinked in response, standing slowly at his feet.

I bit at my bottom lip nervously, then sighed.

"Look, the weight I gained went straight to my stomach and ass." I ran my hand through my hair. "I'm not as toned as I was the first time you locked eyes with me at the gym."

He smirked, then chuckled.

I rolled my eyes. "Why are you laughing at me?"

He held the smile on his lips. "I'm not laughing *at* you. I'm laughing at your concern."

I pushed my tongue into my cheek.

"Let me let you in on a little secret." He moved in closer. "I couldn't care less about shit like that. Are we clear?"

Everett leaned back to read my expression.

"No man," he continued, "not a real one, at least, is going to stop sex or worse, step away before getting any from a woman he's attracted to because she's got some extra weight in her stomach or her ass. Not this fucking man, that's for sure."

I couldn't stop the smile from pulling at my lips.

Okay. Good answer.

"So do me a favor." He ran a finger down the side of my face and moved a few strands of my hair over my shoulder. "Think no more about what you think I want to see and concern yourself with what you want me to do, although I promise I need no guidance."

"Oh?" I inhaled a deep breath, lifting my arms to run my hands down his chest. "So you're saying you got this? No direction necessary?"

"None," he confirmed with a nod.

They always promised high.

That thought made me roll my eyes away, and I was turning my head when he caught me by the chin to keep my face in line with his.

Everett ran the pad of his thumb from the top of my lip to the fullest part of my bottom. He looked me right in my eyes and didn't blink when he told me, "I'm going to fuck you *so* good tonight."

And it wasn't what he said, but how he said it that let me know it wasn't him who wouldn't be able to keep up with the pace.

It was me.

I was in his arms with my legs wrapped around his waist before I could think of a witty comeback and on my bed, before I could tell him I didn't have any condoms.

His lips were on mine again, hands everywhere but at his sides. We moved like we'd rehearsed this very thing several times in our heads. I know I did a few times after a couple of our recent meetups.

We pulled and tugged on our clothing until there was nothing left but skin on us.

He scanned me from the top of my head to my feet and leaned in close, caging me between his hulking arms to whisper, "Beautiful," into my ear. Everett kissed me from my ear to my neck, my neck to my breasts. He left a hand on my right one and traded his lips for his tongue as he continued down to my thighs. He pushed my legs back with one hand, exposing my waxed pussy, and wasted no time putting his mouth to work between my lower lips.

I thought I'd break my back by how high it arched once his tongue licked the tip of my clit. He polished my pink pearl ever so lightly with the tip of his tongue, delivering feathered strokes against the sensitive surface. I jerked each time he flicked up, then down. Lowered my view to him when he took the ball between the soft pillows of his lips. He picked a rhythm and a direction for his tongue and committed fully to it. Never missing a beat, never going off course, flittering with continued purpose.

He moaned so much between my legs, elevating the warming feeling running through me. Sounded like he was feasting on his favorite meal, the way he vocalized his satisfaction with pleasing me.

He teased my perineum with his fingertips, brushed those same fingers near my opening. Lifted his gaze to mine as he lapped at my clit knowingly. Everett wanted me to see his tongue twist and turn on me. His low-lidded stare turned me on and tuned me into the gradual transition from unbearable sensitivity to coming. I used my feet to lift my hips up, then down, dragging my pussy against his flicking tongue, feeling possessed by his tongue's routine.

I wanted to tell him I was there, and that I was about to burst, but he rendered me silent when he applied pressure with that same tongue and drew tight circles around the circumference of my clit at a speed I didn't think was humanly possible. I swallowed my words, inhaled a breath I doubted I'd exhale, and I imploded, releasing a silent cry that lifted me from my recline on my bed. He held me down with his grip on my breasts, thumbing my hard nipple as he continued licking and moaning in sync with me. He moaned like he experienced my orgasm, too, and it was a turn-on I never knew existed. I was nearing the end of my ride when he released the pressure of his tongue. His licks got softer, feather-like again, with breaks of kisses to my pussy lips.

He raised his head, and it was high enough for me to see the results of his actions running down the facial hair around his mouth. Everett slowly licked my wet release clean off his lips, and used his hand to swipe down his beard, then grabbed my legs by the calves to push back to my ears so he could get to work again.

Everett wasn't lying. He absolutely loved eating pussy. The proof was in how eager he was to return to his place between my thighs.

He duplicated the same amount of focus and delivery. I laid my hand on his head as he reburied his face between my thighs. He kept his eyes on me the whole time, sucking and licking my clit and my folds.

Sensitivity from coming seconds earlier morphed into a hunger to come again. I circled my waist in time with his twirling tongue. Between his moans, the sight of his head bobbing and circling between my thighs. Punctuate all the aforementioned with the actual feeling of my imminent orgasm, seesawing me between sanity and mania. I was losing my *fucking* mind on my bed.

"Everett!" I fisted the sheets and braced for another orgasm. "Please."

He firmed his tongue and circled my clit more deliberately, slowing and loosening his grip on me only when my body stopped trembling.

I was boneless after that. Completely depleted, but aware when he took a break from whipping his tongue across my clit to reach for his joggers.

I heard the crinkle of the condom wrapper, then lazily watched him smooth the latex down his very erect dick. His erection poked forward like a compass, as if it were guiding him back to me.

Everett returned in front of me and instead of dropping to his knees again, he used the crease in my hips to slide me to the edge of the bed to get closest to him. I spread my legs and placed a hand against his soft abs. He pulled me closer to him, sliding into me the rest of the way. Everett kept his low-lidded gaze on me as he sunk deep, then deeper.

His strokes were slow at first, delivered with the controlled thrust of his pelvis. His hands were everywhere again, skating his fingers against my nipples.

I hummed my moans, tried my hardest to bite back my cries of ardor, but it was useless. Everett felt too good for me to hold back.

"*Yeahhh*," he growled low, surrendering to a deep moan. "I can tell we're gonna have *a lot* of fun tonight."

A pulsing rush stronger than the one he created with his tongue ripped through me, causing my walls to flutter, my back to arch once more, and a warm sensation to gush out of me. It spilled between us, creating moisture and slick sounds where we connected.

I squirted each time he pulled back from pushing forward.

"Damn, Apryl. *Damn*," he groaned, sweeping four fingers back and forth against my clit as he continued thrusting in and out, using the proof of my release as lubrication. "You're a fucking goddess, baby. *Gahdamn*."

That wavelike feeling returned stronger than before because of his constant stimulation. I contracted and released repeatedly, squirting uncontrollably at his command. We made such a mess.

His work on my clit and his thrusting sounded like he was playing in the water. And the sound alone was about to make me come again.

"Wait, wait." I closed my eyes, feeling consumed by the feeling. "You got me coming *too* fast, too soon."

He licked his lips slowly, lifting my legs to push my knees back by my ears, maintaining his pace.

"Nah, you're good." He slapped my ass, then caressed that same spot to soothe it. "You're *great*. Absolutely perfect for this kind of action. Just like I *knew* you would be."

I fisted my sheets, arched my back, and gave in to his deep thrusts with a moan.

"You *loved* yelling orders at me at the gym." He smirked, then slowed his pace a little. "Ain't that right, baby?"

I locked eyes with him, exhaling in defeat.

"With your bossy ass. I ain't forget." He bit his bottom lip. "And I'm not trippin' off that no more, so no worries. But tonight you're gonna take some orders from me, aight?" Everett ran his tongue down two of his fingers, returning them to my clit to stroke. "The only difference is, I'm gonna whisper mine and you're gonna *love* them. You're gonna love them a lot. Come here." He flipped me over and slid in from behind in a collapsed position. Everett placed his forearms on either side of me, caging me in, and thrusted faster this time... and harder. "I ain't even close to done with you yet." His lips were at my ears when he added, "And there aren't enough wet spots. So, be good..." He flicked my earlobe with his tongue and told me, "... and come some more for me."

We definitely aren't sleeping tonight.

NINETEEN

EVERETT

"So," my sister started. "What did you do last night?"

I moved around my condo, picking up this and that, straightening up my space on a cool and sunny late Sunday afternoon. I'd gotten up from a deep sleep earlier that afternoon, much later than usual since returning to New York. I returned home early in the morning and had to catch up on the hours I missed by sleeping in. My circadian rhythm had improved since starting the food plan Apryl assigned to me a couple of months back. Despite the weekend binge eating we'd been doing to help her pack on the pounds, I was getting my energy back.

It was because of her I returned home after five in the morning from her place. The woman had a sexual appetite as big as mine, so we went at it off and on for hours.

Just the thought of our time together sent blood rushing to my dick.

"Chilled," I answered my sister. "I *chilled* last night."

I buried my fingers in Apryl's hair as she lifted and dropped her ass with an unmatched hunger on top of me. Her bed made no sound. The headboard didn't bang against the wall. But the sheets were loud as hell and slick from all the wet releases I fucked out of her.

I gritted my teeth, doing my best to control my nut, but she was making it so damn hard to put her pleasure first.

She was a goddess like this, in this state. Fully in the moment and committed to performing. It was like she never got tired. Instead, she got energized by the orgasm she experienced before the new one she was trying to chase after now. Apryl was an athlete. She complained about not having energy because of what she'd been eating and not exercising, but her stamina tonight had reached gold medalist status.

She locked eyes with me and I almost lost it. Licked her lips really slowly and let her jaw slack after. Our bodies made slick sounds between us as she rode me like a seasoned jockey.

I loved to watch my dick disappear inside of her and reappear, only to do the same thing again. We'd tried every position, but I was sure my favorites were missionary - where I could witness her reactions - and this one with her on top for the same reason, but seeing her also in control.

Her pussy glistened at this angle. The sight of her was so enticing I craved another taste. Promised myself I'd help myself to one when it was my turn to lead again.

"You're so close," I told her.

We'd only been intimate for a short time, but it was long enough for me to learn her body's signals. I could feel her imminent orgasm in the contraction of her walls and the slight trembling she did each time my dick brushed against her spot hidden within her.

I tightened my grip on her hair and grabbed her jaw with my other hand. Ran the pad of my thumb down the fullest part of her top lip, and slid my finger into her mouth, stopping at the joint. She bit down gently on my finger, rolling her hips faster and moaning louder. And when I matched her speed with upstrokes of my own, she came undone, coming for me.

"Suck it, Apryl," I whispered. "Give me a show."

And she did, sucking on my thumb, moans muffled now, eyes rolling with no control, while wetting me and the sheets some more beneath us.

It was a damn good night.

"*Chilled* how?" Eryn probed.

I kissed my teeth. "Why are you so nosey?"

"I'm bored, Everett, clearly," she whined. "Cali isn't the same with you gone."

I poked out my lip, pouting, sincerely empathizing with her. "I miss you too, Eryn."

My sister wasn't the sentimental type, so whenever she allowed herself to be, I always met her halfway.

"I hung out with Apryl last night." I took a break from cleaning up and sat on my couch. "We hooked up at her place."

Eryn gasped.

I closed my eyes and shook my head in response. "Don't start with that."

"How could you say that so casually, like hooking up with your trainer, is nothing?"

I shrugged. "I mean... it was definitely more than nothing. It was *everything* but... I sure as hell am not about to divulge that shit to my sister."

"But I bet if I was Meki or someone else with a dick, you would."

I wouldn't. If it had been any other woman I'd been with, maybe. But what happened between Apryl and I felt damn good, beyond the physical, and I wanted to keep the details down to the small ones, from our time together all to myself.

"Apryl and I... we had fun. I'm feeling her." I suppressed an excited smile. "Our time was nice."

"Our time was nice," Eryn mocked in a faux deep voice. "Such a fucking gentleman."

I chuckled.

"Well, look, you could've felt something for packing peanuts, and that would make me happy. So long as you're not feeling anything for that bitch, Brielle, I'll celebrate."

"Calm down, Eryn."

"What I'm saying is I'm happy for you."

It's amazing. Even after all Brielle did, I couldn't help but to still hate how Eryn spoke of her. I had to stop that.

"About exes, though," Eryn digressed. "Guess who materialized out of a distant memory into the form of a phone call to yours truly?"

"Who?"

"Simeon fucking King."

I sat up from my recline. "Okay, good, so he called you."

"Everett, why did you give that man my number?"

"I ran into him two months ago and he asked about you, so I gave him your phone number and told him to reach out and find out how you were doing."

"*Ugh!*" she groaned.

"How did you know I gave him your number, anyway?"

"Because he said so."

"What did you two talk about?"

"Nothing, because I didn't answer."

"What?! Eryn."

"Sent that sucka straight to voicemail and logged his number under the name 'The Past' which is where his ass belongs, because I'm not taking any of his phone calls today, tomorrow, or anytime in the future. Never."

I crossed my arms. "Man, will you *please* tell me what happened between you two?"

She said nothing.

"He won't say shit, you won't say shit, but look at how you react to only the mention or discussion of his name.

"Everett, please."

"Simeon was your college sweetheart. You two were in love until you weren't. He got up and left New York, and you became depressed for six years after. Literally, the only thing that snapped you out of feeling down all the time was when you decided you wanted out of New York. And you've been treating the state like a stain you want off you ever since. Eryn, tell me what happened."

She released a trembling exhale.

"Did he hurt you?"

"No, not physically. He..." Her voice trailed off before she took a deep breath. "He wasn't ready to give me what I gave him."

"What the fuck does that mean, Eryn?" I clenched my jaw. "You tell me the same cryptic thing every time and I don't know what it means. And I don't know if I have to hop on a plane to Oakland to manhandle this man and have him answer for whatever shit he did to you."

"Oakland?" She asked. "He's in *California*?"

"Yup." I nodded. "Moved out there three years ago. He's Dallas Roque's agent. You would've gathered all that info if you answered your damn phone."

"Oh, my God! Three-years?!" she whispered. "He's close. Not close, close. But, close."

We were silent on the line. I didn't want to say anything, and I was still waiting for my sister to tell me what happened between her and her ex.

"I have to go," she announced.

"You're about to call him?"

"Hell no," she maintained. "But I need to, *umm*... I have to go. I'll... I'll call you next weekend."

Before I could say anything further, she ended the call.

Twenty

I waved at a neighbor people-watching from their porch as I climbed the stairs outside my mother's house. From the time I'd opened my eyes, all I'd thought about was last night.

I stood on my mother's porch, singling out her key from my key ring of others, trying my hardest to get my mind straight. There were moments on my Sunday afternoon when I could get a break from my thoughts, but mostly, I was continuously being drawn to last night with Everett.

That man could barely give me a solid few minutes of planking, a solid few minutes of anything, but had the stamina of a wild horse.

Any man who could keep up with me in bed was a champion. My appetite was insatiable, a complaint my ex often had. But Everett matched my energy until the end. Matched it so well, he intimidated me with his skills.

Was he as satisfied as I was?

Because every move I made, every trick I performed, it was as if he'd seen it all before, and that left me feeling... unsure.

I inserted the key into the keyhole and opened my mother's door. The house was quiet, the lights off. My mother was a retired EMS dispatcher who now volunteered her time at soup kitchens or voters' voting booths. But there were no elections this week and her days at the soup kitchen were Wednesdays and Fridays.

I'd only taken a few steps past the front door when her cats moseyed themselves up to me to brush their bodies against my leg. It took everything in me not to kick them away.

Instantly, I was concerned. My mother always kept her cats in her room to keep them from getting into her stuff while she was away. And she'd have to be away if the lights were off.

"Ooh!" I heard faintly from the back of the house.

My heart dropped. I hightailed in that direction immediately, wanting to shout that I was there to help, but couldn't get the words to materialize. This was my nightmare in waking life.

My mother was in distress and alone.

"Oh!" she cried again, and I panicked. "Goodness, lawd, have mercy!"

I followed her voice to her room and pushed open the door that was ajar.

Expecting to see my mother on the ground helpless and in pain, I walked in to see this woman on her back with her legs in the air, naked, having sex.

I slapped my hand to my mouth. "Oh my God!"

What's more shocking was that between her legs was my naked father.

I slapped my hands to my eyes next.

"Apryl!" she yelled.

"Mama, what the hell?!" I wanted to cry so badly, hoping if I cried enough, I'd cry my eyes out of their sockets.

"Apryl," my father tried next, "Babygirl, take your hands off your eyes. We're decent now."

"No, thanks." I shook my head, hands still in place. "I hope to never ever be able to see you again."

"I done told you to stop walking in my house like that." My mother sucked her teeth. "Girl don't listen."

I dropped my hands from my eyes to look their way. "What were you two doing? What are you doing here, dad?"

As if I needed an explanation when I was doing the same thing only hours ago and the whole reason I was on this earth was because they did what they were doing now.

But these were my parents, who separated when I was five. My father had married three times and divorced as many wives, none of those marriages ever being with my mother.

What the hell was happening here?

I felt like my brain was short circuiting trying to make sense of what I was seeing - my mother and father... together?

How?

Why?

Huh?

This must be a warped universe.

I wanted out of it immediately.

Drop me the fuck off at the next planet. Please!

"I have to go," I announced, turning and walking face-first into the wall beside the door. "Shit!"

"Apryl!" they shouted at the same time.

"I'm fine," I confirmed, while running full speed toward the front door.

What a way to ruin a Sunday.

The next morning, a Monday, I waited for Everett on the large floor mat in the open area where we hosted HIIT trainings and boot camp sessions.

For two months, I've fantasized about returning to the gym. That's how much I couldn't wait to get back into exercising. I got a little sleep the night before because of my excitement at restarting my routine.

And because I was thinking of my mother and father...

And Everett...

I had a lot on my mind, but I was beyond grateful to be back in the gym to work out.

These past few months, I've continued to train clients at MK's Sports Lounge and Gym, strictly giving instructions and no demonstrations to keep my metabolism at bay to pack on the pounds.

It's been torture.

The eating, the not working out, the drinking.

All too much.

Today, though, that will change, and I was looking forward to working up a sweat.

Although Everett has helped me do that already.

Between the moments of trying to sort out, and forget, what I caught my parents doing the day prior, I replayed in my mind the moments I shared with Everett, on repeat. We'd only had that one night, but I... missed him?

Or something.

I don't know.

What I know is, when I caught sight of him as he swaggered around the corner to enter the open workout area, I skipped a breath.

Or two.

No, three.

His eyes found mine the second he entered the area, and he didn't break eye contact once.

I cleared my throat, running my fingers through my hair, mentally kicking myself for not properly preparing for our interaction with each other after our hookup.

We hadn't spoken to one another since our night together. Not through text either. So it was like the morning after. The sequel.

"I'm going to head out," he announced low, stepping off my bed completely naked in search of his clothes. They laid like confetti sprinkled here and there around my room. I watched as his ripe ass rose and fell with his stride, shoulders so squared it was like the air parted for him to walk.

The sky outside was still dark, but there were slight breaks in the sky trying to let the new day in.

I peeked at the time on my alarm clock and read 5:04am in red.

"Get home safe," I said, honestly unsure of what to say. This man had me coming and squirting like an overnight downpour and the best I could tell him was to get home safely.

He found it funny, chuckling at my failed attempt at not making things awkward. "Later, Apryl."

"Good morning," he greeted me when he was close. He wore compression tights beneath jogging shorts and a loose-fitting white shirt over it all. Everett also wore a heavy-lidded stare, stripping me to my core. It was like I stood before him naked again. That's what I felt as he looked at me.

"Hey, hi, go-good morning." I closed my eyes and folded my lips into my mouth to stop my rambling.

He ran his hand down his low-trimmed beard and chuckled, revealing his always hidden but dangerously beautiful smile.

I sighed with exaggeration. "Can you stop?"

He tilted his head to the right. "Stop, what?"

"This." I gestured at him. "That *'it's all good. I do this all the time'.* The thing you're doing. It's giving this-ol'-thang energy."

"Well." He smirked, then shrugged.

I slacked my jaw.

"Nah." He broke up laughing. "I'm messing with you Apryl." Everett checked over his shoulder and I did too. When it was clear we were alone, he approached, only stopping when he was mere inches in front of me. I leaned my head back to look up at him.

He said, "But it *is* all good and although I *did* this all the time, I get why you might be in your head right now."

He used his pointer finger to move a few stands off my shoulder blade, redirecting my hair down my back.

I shivered from the chill he caused to run down my spine.

"So sensitive." A sexy grin spread across his lips. "You do not know how much I love that."

"You were fantastic the other night," I admitted, pressing a hand to his chest. "Very high stamina."

"Why, thank you. Did you leave your review of me on Yelp? Every star rating counts."

I punched him in the chest. "Shut up."

He laughed again.

This side of Everett was nice, comforting.

He and I were speaking for the first time since the other night and it should have been awkward and it wasn't, and that was throwing me off.

"You were good too," he complimented.

"Was I?" I squinted at him. "You seemed really tough to read."

He furrowed his brows.

I ran my hand through my hair again. "You gave off the impression that everything I did that night... you'd seen it all before. It was hard to figure out what you liked."

"It shouldn't have been hard to figure out," he disclosed. "What I liked was pleasing you. I loved it, actually."

I said nothing.

"You turned me on by just being turned on, and every time I watched and felt you come, it satisfied me all the same."

"Sounds selfless."

"Sounds that way, but to be honest, it's actually selfish," he countered. "Not to sound like *that* guy, but I've had a lot of sex with a lot of different women, Apryl. I went through the stage of having sex just to say I did it, to focusing on my nut and my nut alone. Doing it so much that way got boring. I eventually found what really excited me about sex and when I did, I understood sex and my role in it. And that's when the fun began."

"Oh?"

"I turn 39 on the 21st. Things change the older you get, especially as a man. You're 34, based on your website's bio. Which means you're in your sexual prime." He tilted my head back. "I can tell you've been selfless for too long. Start being selfish too, at least with a man like me, if the opportunity ever presented itself again."

The idea of experiencing the night we shared again caused me to pull on my walls. What I wouldn't do to have him between them again, but realistically, it would never happen.

"I doubt it'll happen again," I said with my mouth, but deep inside me, I prayed I was wrong.

"Yeah." He bit his bottom lip and nodded slowly. "It's probably for the best we didn't do that again anyway, 'cause I'd get addicted to you."

I balled my lips to keep from smiling.

"'Cause you? You're dangerous." He wagged his finger at me, backing away. "Sexual napalm."

I gasped exaggeratively while pointing at myself. "Who, me?"

He nodded. "Hell yeah, you. And I don't need that after my ex... even though I would like to have it. 'Cause you might make me a fiend, fuckin' around with you and that juicy fruit between them thighs."

"Juicy fruit?"

He winked. "I said what I said."

I rolled my eyes and laughed to myself.

"Well, I need no more of what you were slinging after my ex, either." I licked my lips, knowing I was lying through my teeth. "Besides, I gotta kick your ass for the next few weeks in here and I can't have anything jeopardizing our deal."

He pointed. "Exactly."

I gestured at the mat. "Shall we get started?"

He nodded. "On your go."

"Cool." I got down on the mat. "Let's warm up."

About fifteen minutes into our workout, I realized my excitement was no match for reality. And by half an hour, I came to terms that I'd underestimated how much twenty-five pounds could slow me down.

Fatigue left me tired and nauseous. I'd taken off two months and gained a little, at least what seemed like a little to me, but it was weighing me down. Now granted, it was our first day back, but I was feeling the burn of having to exert myself more than usual. It was frustrating.

"Oh my God." I grabbed a towel to clean my face. "I can usually go a full minute performing bilateral waves with these battle ropes."

I'd only lasted ten seconds.

"I told you," he commented through his heavy breathing. "The extra pounds slow you down. Don't matter how much you did before it. With it on you, it's like starting from scratch."

It hadn't been an hour. This was only the first session back, but I finally saw it - things from Everett's perspective, and this was only the first workout.

My chest rose and fell as I scanned around me at the kettle bell, battle rope, and the rest of the equipment I'd set aside for our workout.

I immediately realized I'd have to rethink our entire routine. The reintroduction of the go hard or go home thinking would need to take a backseat or we'd get nowhere and not in shape.

"We can't work out like this," I determined, more so to myself. "We have to build up to this."

"That's what I was trying to explain to you, but you were so hardheaded."

I pushed my tongue against the inside of my cheek.

"Push through it, Everett," he mocked in a high-pitched tone. "It's only twenty-three pounds, Everett."

"Be quiet."

He snorted.

"I said all of that because you're an athlete. I'm a personal trainer. I believed it didn't matter how long it's been since a workout because the process should be like learning how to ride a bike, only needing to learn things once. If you were a vigorous gym rat before gaining weight, and I worked out twice a day, getting back in shape shouldn't be this hard. But I was wrong." I ran my fingers through my hair. "Very, *very* wrong." My mouth fell open with that realization. "We're going to have to start from scratch, Everett."

"Yes." He nodded. "And it's all good." He clapped his hands once next. "'Cause we just have to reverse course and make it right. We can do it."

"We can." I nodded, my mind recalibrating the plan. "Okay. All right... *ummm*... we'll focus more on calisthenics. Let's power walk a mile on the treadmill, then jog an additional mile, then return to the mat. We won't use equipment for our first few days back. From there, we can reassess after I evaluate our progress."

"Aight, boss lady." He smiled.

I refused to hold back my smile.

Everett gestured at the treadmills down the hall. "Let's get it."

Twenty-One

I squinted and leaned over my steering wheel to peer through the windshield. It was my attempt to steal a glance at the road up ahead. Trees with leaves that looked like they hadn't shed the season before, framed the way to a location Apryl told me to meet her.

She called me bright and early that day. Surprised me when I answered and she wished me a, "Happy Birthday, old man."

It made me smile, both hearing from her and realizing she remembered my birthday.

"And who told you today was my birthday?"

"You did. Mentioned it a week ago when we returned to MK for our first session back. You said you were turning 39 on the 21st. It's the 21st! So, happy birthday, old man."

My smile remained.

"Got anything planned?"

I shook my head and said, "Meeting up for our session later."

"Cool, because I canceled our session today. It's a holiday. EP day."

I chuckled. "But what if I was looking forward to the session?"

Not to work out, but to see her. As hard as I fought it, the more I was around her, the more I enjoyed being in her company. Her personality was infectious, and she was a cool person once she let her guard down. The sex we had two weeks ago helped as well.

"I have something better planned."

"Oh?"

"Mm-hmm," she answered. "I'm going to text you an address and the time to be there. Wear something comfortable."

I arched my brows. "Are you going to tell me what this place is?"

"Of course not."

I smiled in response.

"It's a surprise."

The GPS told me to make the next right and then another left and gradually the scenery changed in front of me.

In the far distance, I noticed pizza-shaped checkered flags flapping in the wind and a road much different from the one I drove on.

A patch of grass formed an oval lawn in the middle of my path. Gates framed by small walls were the next thing to catch my eyes. By the time I caught sight of the luxury vehicles parked in a domino line beside the racetrack, I knew where I was.

My face lit up.

Speedway Racetrack, sprawled in big black bold letters, decorated the sidewalls. I pulled up to the security booth and gave the guard my name at his request. He pointed to the parking area for me to park my car. The moment I powered off the engine, I heard a rapping on my window.

An excited smile tugged at my lips when I got her into my view.

With the weather warming up and some pounds slowly getting burned off in the gym, Apryl had been wearing outfits that stressed and showed off her curvy fit physique. Although she was still curvy, she was slowly getting her fit shape back. She was soft, and I loved it.

"The birthday boy is here," she said as I stepped out of the car.

I pushed my hands into my joggers' pockets. "And where is *here*?"

"As if it weren't clear, silly." Apryl turned to gesture around herself. "It's a racetrack!"

"I see that." I looked around too. "What are *we* here for? I thought we had a very strict, Monday through Friday gym routine."

She giggled. "Is EP becoming a gym rat again?"

I fanned her comment off with my hand.

"Well, you could consider today to be a cheat day. Your new cheat day."

I wrinkled my brows.

"Instead of going to stuff your face with food that's no good to you physically or mentally, you're going to live out one of your passions until you've tackled them all. And what better time to start than on the day of your birth? New beginnings."

I glanced around me again to take in more of the surrounding scene.

Foreign luxury cars sat parked a few feet away from us. The racetrack was empty. No people, no other vehicles as far as the eyes could see. It looked like it was just us.

"I remember you telling me that if you weren't a career fighter, you would've gone into racing cars professionally."

I tilted my head to one side.

"Although I can't do anything about the lost time, I figured I could rent out the racetrack for a few hours so you could race those cars over there to your heart's content."

"You were listening to me when I said that?"

She blushed, then looked away shyly. "It would've been hard for me to forget, since your reply was definitely original and unexpected."

I took a breath to calm the beating of my heart. She tried to minimize something that was so damn impressive.

She was paying attention when I spoke to her.

"Anyway." She jabbed at my arm and I found her terrible boxing stance humorous. "Shall you get started?"

The next hour entailed me sitting behind the wheels of Lamborghinis, Ferraris, and my favorites, Porsches.

The Porsche glided against the racetrack like its tires were sharp knives and the track was like butter.

Apryl sat beside me in every car, hollering and cracking up with me as I adjusted the clutch, pressed my foot down on the gas, gripped the steering wheel in every vehicle and whipped around the track like a seasoned racer. Not once did she get scared or uneasy. And we were going down that track at top speed. An adrenaline junkie, like myself. We were getting high off the now.

Apryl rented the track for two hours, and for those two hours I tested out all the exotic cars they had on the lot.

By the time we were done, my heart was racing, my head pounded from all the excitement, and my face hurt from smiling so hard.

"That was." I shook my head and exhaled. "Wow."

She laughed, sliding the band around her bun out of her hair, to wrap it around her strands again. "So you had fun?"

"Fun?" I asked, turning to glance at the track again. "I haven't felt this alive in... months."

She blushed. "That's excellent."

I wanted to grab her by her t-shirt and pull her close to me. Wrap my arms around her and tilt her head back to plant a kiss on her lips, hoping our kiss transitioned into something else.

But I nodded instead. "It is."

I wondered if she knew the restraint I was practicing, keeping my distance from her at that moment. I could see the flicker in her eyes as she moved hers to my lips, then back up to my eyes to regain eye contact.

I exhaled through my mouth and tried my best to hold it together.

God, please don't do this. Don't make me fall for this woman right now.

"This was one of the best, if not *the* best, gifts I've ever gotten," I told her. "Very thoughtful. Thank you."

"You're welcome." She pointed ahead of us. "I had them set up lunch for us in their dine-in hall."

"You had everything planned, huh?"

She winked. "I sure did." Apryl reached for my hand next, and there was a spark of static between us that forced her to jump back.

She gasped in response, and I laughed, taking her hand again, threading my fingers with hers.

"Come on," I told her.

I realized the spark meant something, but I didn't want to show that. The look in her eyes when I peered over at her after taking her hand again let me know she knew it meant something, too. It also let me know I wasn't the only one practicing restraint between us... which was a significant discovery that changed everything for me.

Twenty-Two

I climbed the last step to my mother's front door and pushed my hand into my crossbody bag, blindly searching for my key ring. I'd done the routine so often, I only stopped myself when I singled out and angled the key in front of the lock. My presence at the doormat reminded me of what happened the last time I opened my mother's house door with the key I had a locksmith make without her permission.

I swallowed back the feeling of wanting to throw up my breakfast on her front porch and quickly returned my keys to my bag, opting to lean to my right to ring the doorbell instead.

She was at the threshold, opening the door less than a minute later, giggling when she recognized me standing feet away from the screen door.

"Oh goodness," she chastised on the other side of the mesh before opening it. "You are so damn dramatic."

Her finding humor in my disgust did nothing to ease my stomach turning. I had to damn near wrestle with the flashbacks of her and my father having sex the day I walked in on them two. I've wrestled them so fiercely in the short time I've been there, I'm already exhausted before taking a seat on the kitchen island's stool.

Since I caught them in the act, I haven't been to the house. I spoke to my mother on the phone once after, just to check in on her. But I did well not to ask her about what I walked in on and she didn't bring it up either on our call, thankfully.

I'd seen my father shortly after at dinner with my sister and her family and could barely meet his eyes.

"Apryl, can you please stop this?" he begged. *"You're making this awkward."*

I wasn't sure how I did that. Fine, I sat next to my sister instead of by my father at the diner we usually frequented, leaving him alone at the opposite end of the table, which I never do. We always sat beside each other, but I couldn't pretend I wasn't uncomfortable in his presence.

"I'm sorry I'm making it awkward, dad, but it's too soon after..." I gestured with my hands. "You know."

Stas's husband, Kwamé, snorted and my sister slapped him on the arm.

"Oh, come on." Kwamé laughed. "It's funny, babe." He focused on me when he insisted, "Apryl, quit making things uncomfortable for pops here. It was something that happened once."

"The once she walked in on," my father mumbled under his breath. "Her mother and I have been seeing each other and doing all of that for some time now."

I gagged, then gagged again.

"Ew, what?" Stas said, which I could only show.

"Okay, let's just shift our discussion," Kwamé recommended, before clearing his throat. "Who wants to try the baked apple pie?"

We tabled the conversation of what occurred the day I caught my mother and father having sex, and it would remain tabled indefinitely if it were up to me.

Once I was inside my mother's house, my eyes were scanning from the front of the entryway, all around the living room, and zeroing in on the kitchen ahead of us.

I turned to her, refusing to take another step into the house until I knew it was safe to. "Are you... alone?"

She laughed this time, and I rolled my eyes to myself.

"Apryl, please stop it and come on," she said, walking past me, headed to the kitchen.

I was on guard as I followed her. I hadn't seen my father since our dinner and I didn't want to. It was hard enough seeing my mom.

"Want some coffee?" She asked casually.

"No," I answered curtly, still scanning.

"Your father isn't here." She confirmed, her back facing me as she poured herself a mug of caffeine. "So you can take a breath."

And I did, loudly, to her amusement, before I plopped down onto a seat on the stool.

"Mama, I *really* don't find any of this funny."

She turned to face me.

"Like..." I ran my fingers through my hair. "What on earth were you two doing that day?"

She parted her lips to speak, and I held up a hand to stop her.

"Please don't tell me *what* you were doing. I *know* what you were doing."

"Oh, okay." She smirked.

"I just mean, why on earth were you two doing *that* with each other?"

She chuckled. "It was us doing *that*, our business, that allowed *you* and your sister to be here."

"Well, I wasn't there for it and I wish I hadn't been here for what I saw you two doing the other day."

We were silent for a moment, allowing my mother to take a few sips and to enjoy her coffee.

I wanted to know everything, but then I wanted to know nothing at all. It was jarring, being aware of my parents' situationship.

Do they have a situationship? Should I ask?

Because that's what Stas called it when I told her about what I caught them doing that day over the phone.

"No way," she whispered.

"Way," I confirmed. "I saw it. Like, I literally saw them both in action and I want to unsee it so badly."

She cackled. "What does this mean? Is this like a relationship, a booty call? Oh my God, is it a situationship?"

"A situation, what?" I shook my head. "No, I don't want to imagine our parents being in a situationship. I don't want to imagine them being in any of those things you mentioned."

"This is so weird," Stas said with more breath than tone. "Isn't that weird?"

"Very." I whispered back. "We didn't raise them to be like this. I don't know what's gotten into them."

Stas burst into a fit of giggles.

But I'd wished for this every Christmas from when I was five and until I was twelve. And when it didn't happen, I came to terms *they* would never ever happen. My father married three times, never asking her once to be his wife.

And she always made it seem like it didn't faze her. Never to search for a husband or a boyfriend of her own. My mother chose herself and settled into a single life without a care for much else.

So why was she entertaining my father *now*?

"Why are you going backwards?" I asked. "And why now?"

She peeked up from her mug and focused on me.

"Dad has moved on three times over," I reminded her, as if she wasn't already aware. "Started *several* new lives with other women and you haven't had so much as a boyfriend."

She nodded.

"How did this begin again between you two?"

My mother smiled, walking the mug to the island and setting it down.

"About three months ago, we ran into each other at the market." She smiled while taking a seat opposite me on a stool. "I was ready to checkout and was heading down the aisle leading to the register. I saw your father in the aisle trying to decide what brand of pasta to pick up. Naturally, I considered turning down another aisle just to avoid him, but he glanced up at that very moment and did a double take at me." She giggled this time, her expression making her look twenty years younger. "He called me over, asked me which pasta he should choose for his pasta sauce. I gave him the suggestion and continued on my way."

Her golden-brown complexion took on a rosy hue around her cheeks. This woman was blushing.

"I'd just checked out and was making my way back to my car when your father chased me down in the parking lot and invited himself over to my house to fix him dinner. He dubbed me the best cook ever, and he also admitted to never knowing what to do on a stove. He said he was coming over for dinner. It was audacious, but your father has always been the audacious and charming type and I've always fallen for it. Plus, we have never had the relationship where he and I couldn't sit for dinner. So we did, and it was the best date I'd ever been on, Apryl." She pressed her hand to her chest. "He kissed me that night after we'd cleaned up and I slapped him clear across his face because excuse me, no. He did not ask, and I'm a lady." I laughed and my mother did, too. "But that night became the start of a new routine for us that blossomed into something beyond my wildest of imaginations and instead of impeding it, I went with it, like I did everything else in my life, and it's been the best decision for me."

"So, like," I started. "Are you two... together?"

"We are."

I cringed, but said nothing in response. I was processing, mentally computing this new reality I'd given up on decades ago.

"And why now?" my mother asked next. "Because I like this version of your father. This version of him gets it and agrees with this version of me."

I wrinkled my brows.

"We all go through changes at different stages in this life, metamorphoses, that continue to shape us into the people we will be. When your father and I met and had your sister, then you, we were young and still growing and we weren't patient enough with each other to grow together. There's only so much you're going to know at twenty-four, and we knew little. But I knew what I wanted, and that wasn't your father. He knew what he wanted, and that wasn't me. And I accepted that because I accepted who I was. I knew what I wanted and what I would compromise to have it, and despite creating two lives with him, your father had yet to show he was worth me compromising for a life I knew I wouldn't be happy living. So, I created the life I wanted and learned to be comfortable alone and with myself.

"And your father learned how to be a husband after having no real representations of one in his life before his three marriages. He did not know how to be a suitable partner, but he learned with women who wanted to teach him how to be. How to love beyond limitations. And that's beautiful. I'm happy for them because it couldn't have been me."

I snorted.

"And that's not to throw shade, as y'all say." She joshed. "Everyone knows what they rightfully deserve. I felt I deserved more than he was giving, and I was right. Because the man I have been spending time with as of late is not the same man I refused to spend a lifetime with decades ago. He's returned to me differently, *wonderfully* transformed. People change when they want to change, and that's what your father did. He communicates better, expresses his feelings more fluidly, and I noticed that during our time together. His growth attracted me and eventually my admiration grew into a physical desire—"

"Got it," I cut in, not wanting her to proceed past that. "I got it. Please don't continue."

She chortled.

"Wow." I shook my head. "Well, this explains the cat hair he had on him a few months ago when we went out to dinner with Stas and Kwamé. I can't believe I didn't put two and two together. I'm usually good at that."

I stared past her and out of the window.

"My parents are in a relationship with each other." I pressed my hand to my cheek. "This is the twilight zone."

"Always so dramatic," she accused, before sipping her coffee again.

And maybe I was.

I was also curious.

If my mother could find romantic love after being without it for so long, surely, I could too.

My mother turned to the stove to start dinner, and I pulled out my phone. I tapped into HeartMates, feeling inspired to restart my dating search and, with new vitality, to make the app work for me.

TWENTY-THREE

T*he trees are so green and plentiful out here.*

That was the thought running through my mind as I sat in the spacious boot space of my Range Rover, staring out ahead of me.

Apryl gently nudged me with her elbow to get my attention to hand me a bottle of water and the turkey sandwich she made and brought from home.

When she called to invite me to hike in Watkins Glen State Park in Upstate New York, I couldn't say no. I knew her reasoning for inviting me had more to do with the hike supplementing our workout and less about us hanging out, but even if I didn't want to work out, being in her presence was motive enough to tag along.

Apryl offered the option of a hike at the right time. That morning I'd received a call from Mr. Chadwick, Brielle's father, the man trying his best to get me to marry his disloyal ass daughter. I hadn't heard from him since arriving in New York, and I was more than thrilled about not hearing his voice during my stay in the city. His phone call was an unpleasant surprise.

"Everett, son, do you hear what I'm hearing from New York?"

"Hear what, sir?"

"The days falling off the calendar."

"Mr. Chadwick—"

"Kyle's contract is up in three months. The offer for his position and your drawn-up contract is still sitting and waiting at my office table for you to sign."

"Mr. Chadwick, I appreciate the offer but—"

"I've increased the dollar amount to $700,000 per episode, and I'm still offering you the opportunity to renegotiate your salary after your first year on air."

I sat up straight in my seat immediately.

"I'd advise you to renegotiate for one million an episode, son."

My brows piqued, like they had a life of their own.

"You'll earn one million per episode by next year, which I'd be more than happy to approve for my son-in-law, huh?" he tried.

I gritted my teeth in reaction.

"The best offer any host in history has ever received in their first year hosting any show on The Sports Report Network," he stated. "Ask anyone, they'll tell you. But don't utter a word to them, because they'll hate you for nepotism."

My heart raced.

"Come on, Everett." He complained. "What more do you want? I'm offering everything but the goddamn kitchen sink here. What do you say?"

I told him I would consider the offer.

The possibility of earning one million an episode in one year deserved at least some consideration... right?

But now, his offer was up against some stiff competition.

Apryl.

She put a spell on me when she gifted me with that day at the racetrack. That's how it felt, at least. Because I couldn't stop thinking about how thoughtful the gesture was. I tried like hell to keep our sessions strictly professional the week after, but the more I saw her the more I craved being around her. And the more I craved being around her, the more I craved being *inside* her.

She pointed out ahead of us at the bird flying.

"A Lark Sparrow," she remarked, referring to the bird. "I usually see her babies in Central Park. This one is an adult."

I glanced over at her and took a bite out of my sandwich. "How do you know it's an adult?"

"The face pattern," she answered. "The black, white, and reddish-brown pattern is usually brighter on adults and duller on immatures."

I chewed, still looking at her. "Just full of all kinds of random facts, huh?"

She looked at me and giggled, shaking her head. "Sorry. I'm a bit of a geek."

"No apology necessary." I smiled back. "I like your brand of geek."

We stared at each other for a beat before she looked away, refocusing on her sandwich.

After returning from the hike minutes ago, we spent the rest of the time eating out of the Range Rover's boot space. This part of the SUV was like the truck's loading dock. I'd had the Range custom made to my specifications, which included lining the entire boot space with soft floor mats. This made this part of my truck the perfect chill spot for Apryl and myself. I flipped down two rows of seats, which made the back of the Rover resemble a van, and created a space large enough to accommodate my stature and hers. We initially were going to take Apryl's four-door, but it was a little too cramped for me, given my height. It's a good thing we made that change, because now we could sit comfortably after a long hike and enjoy lunch in front of the beautiful scenery.

I scanned around us in the surrounding area. There were a few other vehicles, about three, parked at the lookout, but they were all spaced out by several feet and nowhere within close distance to us. Apryl and I were practically alone out there.

For the next hour, we watched the sun prepare to set in front of us as we finished our sandwiches. The sunset, her presence, the renewed energy I was feeling pumping through my veins from the physical work we were doing on ourselves. It felt like a moment. For the first time in a long time, I felt fantastic.

Not fantastic because of anything.

Just fantastic, period.

I looked over at Apryl, who stared forward, clearly in thought. Her side profile was like a painting's, one an artist would create using curves and shadows to recreate the beauty they've seen at most once. Apryl's full lips and her cute button nose looked picturesque at this angle. Her long lashes slightly feathered the air each time she blinked. In her element, just sitting there, she was a sight to behold. A stunning woman with a heart so pure it accentuated how attractive she was to me.

Shit...

I'm falling... hard.

I guess I was a little too wrapped up in watching her because she turned her head briefly to glance my way and caught me staring in wonderment.

She rolled her eyes and smiled, returning her attention back to the view. "You're staring."

"I am."

"Stop doing that."

"And *why* would I do such a crazy thing?" I scooted closer to her and noticed the moment she took a deep breath and closed her eyes. "You're the best sight out here."

"I bet that's the line that gets you all the girls." She peered my way. "Huh, EP?"

I shook my head slowly. "All the girls don't take me hiking and make me lunch."

She kissed her teeth. "I made a sandwich."

"What do they say? The way to a man's heart, blah, blah, blah."

She snorted a laugh and dropped her head forward.

I lifted it again, using my finger against the slope of her chin, and she locked eyes with me once our eyes aligned.

I wanted her.

I've wanted her.

That one night we shared, although what we did lasted for hours, was too brief for me. I said I couldn't fall for another woman, but my head and my heart are rarely on the same page.

And call me crazy, but I felt Apryl might know this feeling.

She took another one of those deep breaths and pressed a hand to my chest. "We've been good."

I nodded.

"Not discussing what happened after the mukbang and the club, not making things awkward after."

"That's true."

"And that allowed us to stay focused." She dropped her hand and looked me in the eye, adding, "We should stay focused."

"Okay," I nodded my understanding. "So what do you suggest I do to calm this craving I have for you? Because..." I ran my hand down my low-trimmed beard. "I want to taste you right now."

She arched both brows and tilted her head to one side, smirking. "You want to do *what*?"

I licked my lips and chuckled.

Apryl shut her eyes and bit her bottom lip, then smiled. "Everett."

"Apryl."

"I have a habit of getting too close to my clients and..." She ran her hand through her long hair. "I kind of want to break out of that habit, you know?"

That was responsible and something I should've respected. But the attraction I had to this woman made me feel impulsive. The good impulsive. The change your life for the better impulsivity. She wasn't with anyone, neither was I. The only thing that would keep us apart was our client-trainer relationship, but there were no obvious rules against us being more besides what would be the right thing to do, which was to keep things professional.

I combed my trimmed beard with my fingers, shifting my attention in front of me, then back to her.

"Well, shit. Do you mind breaking out of that habit after me, though?"

She laughed. "What?"

"Pick somebody else for that and do the right thing with them." I pressed my hand to my chest. "Because me? I don't want the honor of you being good and behaving with. I don't want to be the first in that."

"Oh, I bet." She flashed a girlish grin, looking away again.

"Because what I want right now?" I scooted even closer with her attention off me and leaned in close to her neck, pressing my lips to that spot. "Is to lick your cum off my lips."

A soft moan hummed from her mouth and her breathing quickened.

"I want to make your body vibrate beneath me, in this truck, by this view."

Her eyes searched mine for something before she briefly closed them and took another breath.

"I'd mess up the lining back here," she tried this time. "Get it wet and everything."

I wrapped my hand around the strands of her hair and tugged on them, hard enough to lean her head back.

"Was that supposed to change my mind, Apryl?" I kissed my way from her neck to her ear. "Because that just made me want to do what I want with you even more."

"*Mmm.*"

"'Cause if that's your argument," I told her, "I vote we fuck this lining up and everything else back here. Give me a reason to detail this entire SUV."

She turned to look at me with a slack jaw, and I crashed my lips into hers. I leaned my weight against her, encouraging her to lie back.

"What I tell you about that, anyway?" I trailed my tongue from her lips to her neck. "Haven't I told you I don't mind your body's response to me making it feel good? No man in their right mind would."

She moaned, placing a hand against the back of my head.

"So please know it doesn't bother me at all." I drew in the thin skin and sucked. "I love that about you. You know that."

With my mouth busy against her neck, I grabbed either side of her leggings' waistband and slid them over her hips.

"I've been sweating all day," she said, this time not realizing she was selling me instead of convincing me to stop. "And there are people all around us."

Her panties and leggings were both off by the time I told her, "The other hikers parked their cars at least a mile apart. They won't see us and even if they did, I really don't care."

I pushed her legs back and got into position, diving face first between her thighs.

When I told Apryl I loved her taste, I wasn't lying or exaggerating. She had an essence to her. Most would say I was lying if I told them it was sweet and satisfying. But it was to me. She squeezed her thighs against my ears, canceling out any sound around me. All I could hear was the slip and slide of my tongue against her tiny pink ball and her doing her best to muffle her moans with tight lips. She placed a hand against my head and arched her back, peeked down at me every so often before rolling her head to the crown in ecstasy.

I held onto her by the crease in her hips. She rolled her body from those hips, running her pussy up and down my lips. I moaned at her moaning, sincerely feeling pleasure from her pleasure. I loved the act of pleasing her, making her body do all the things that would make her feel like she was not in this world.

She dug her fingertips into the back of my head and laid still. I lapped my tongue from left to right and noticed that her folds contracted and released against my lips. Warmth hit me next, and I quickened my tongue's twirl until her body jerked in my grip. Then I slowed it up as she caught her breath, feeling my beard drip with her release. I was so hard at that moment I could feel my dick throbbing to the rhythm of my heart.

I didn't expect Apryl and I would hook up after hiking, but that didn't stop me from being prepared if we did. So, as she laid there still, trying to catch her breath, I removed my joggers and boxers and was about to cover my erection with the condom I slid out my wallet, when she wrapped her slim hands around the length of me, tipped her head to her right, and sucked my dick into her mouth.

The move took me by surprise, forcing me to stumble back. And she didn't lose her grip or position, tightening her jaw around girth and bobbing her head up and down on me.

I dropped my head, trying my best to regain control. Because at that view, looking down to see Apryl's mouth on me, her ass slightly in the air, and her sucking my dick like someone who knew what the fuck they were doing, I was about to bust in any minute.

How embarrassing that would be!

I gathered her hair and held it at the crown of her head and did my best to control her pace by directing her on and off me, which she allowed me to do for a few beats. But then she started twirling her tongue around the head while bobbing up and down, and I had to clench my teeth to keep from losing my fucking mind.

I gently pulled her off using her hair and returned her to her back, quickly sliding the condom down my erection along the way.

A practiced skill.

I took her by her jaw and whispered, "That mouth is a problem," as I tunneled into her. "And so is this pussy, damn."

She moaned, placing her hands on my backside to guide my movements. Apryl and I performed in all the positions the boot space would allow. We laughed when some positions were too awkward for the space and orgasmed hard in the positions that worked like a charm.

I wasn't sure what this was, this thing between Apryl and me. But I knew I liked this space between who we were and whatever it was we were becoming. I liked it a lot. Maybe too much.

Twenty-Four

Blender blades whirring and crushing tiny rocks of ice greeted Everett and me as we stepped through the glass door. At my insistence, we were visiting Just Juice Bar - a local spot only blocks away from MK's Sports Lounge and Gym.

The tiny space was full of life and inviting, with its bright ceiling lighting, friendly staff, and endearing scent of fresh pressed juice in the air.

"Nice spot," Everett commented over the whirring and hip-hop music blasting.

"One of my clients owns it." I nodded my head in time with the song playing. "Eva Gordon. Her husband is Jaleel Gordon."

"Jaleel Gordon," he repeated. "The Bronx Baller. Dope." Everett gave the place a once over. "Very dope."

I nodded again.

The juice bar was my favorite place to visit after an intense workout.

It was always like my motivation and my treat to myself after a busy exercise day.

Just Juice had a few tables in the establishment, but that didn't stop people from hanging out, sitting up against either the window wall or the grass wall to suck down their juice through paper, drinking straws.

There was a table empty near Everett and me, one I knew wouldn't stay empty for long.

"You can grab a seat and I can get the juice," I told him.

His face scrunched up before he shook his head. "Or, you can go sit your pretty ass at one of those empty tables and *I* can get the juice."

I fanned his comment away. "It's cool. I can—"

"What juice do you want?" He interjected, challenging me to continue with his arched brows.

I exhaled in defeat. "Citrus passion."

He winked. "I got you. Now go grab us that table."

I smiled and turned away to make my way to one.

It was a unique feeling having someone take care of something for me, again. I'd gotten so used to handling everything on my own these past two years, it's become second nature to know I can do it myself. It was always like that.

My relationship with my ex, Troy, spoiled me a little. He used to take care of a lot of the things I considered mundane. After we broke up, it was a shell shock having to do all the things he once took care of, like taking out the trash, fixing things around the apartment we shared. I think that was one reason I was hell bent on buying a house as a single woman. I never wanted to rely on a man to do anything ever again, and buying my townhouse was the biggest way I knew to do that. Despite that, I thought it was cute and kind of chivalrous of Everett to insist he wait in line to get our drinks. It was something small, but it felt nice having someone do something as *small* as that for me again.

He was good at not making things weird between us, too. Earlier at the gym, our first time seeing each other after our second unplanned hookup, you wouldn't have even known anything happened over the weekend. It was business between us, but far from stiff. Everett was more focused and eager to carry out my orders and, most of all, respectful, with the occasional tongue-in-cheek remarks. He joked a little and would always make sure he touched me somehow, but he played things cool and made things seem like everything was strictly business with us at the gym. He valued privacy. I loved that. And I found his maturity with balancing sex and work to be very sexy.

I sat at the table as instructed and pulled out my phone to browse through my emails as I waited for him. A notification popped up as I was scrolling through my inbox, informing me of date options within my area. I downloaded the HeartMates app again after my talk with my mother. I figured the best way to keep hope alive in a bleak dating scene would entail me putting myself out there and weeding through the bad seeds to secure the perfect find. If anything, they would serve as good practice.

"Here you go," Everett said over my shoulder.

I closed the app immediately, placed my phone on the table, and I twisted my waist to accept my drink.

"Thank you," I said to him, wrapping my lips around the straw. I closed my eyes and sucked down a good portion of the drink before coming up for air. "*Mmm*," I moaned when the nicely chilled fresh juice did the job of quenching my thirst.

He chuckled softly and sipped his drink through his straw. "*Mmm*," he moaned this time, nodding his head, then going in for more.

"Right?!"

He swallowed the juice in his mouth. "Yeah, this is legit."

"I'm obsessed!" I giggled, picking up my phone to snap a picture of my drink. "What did you get?"

"Mango Madness."

"*Mmm*, yes." I dropped my head back between my shoulders before making eye contact again. "That's my other favorite."

He winked. "Noted."

I blushed, looking down at my phone to upload the photo to my social stories, being sure to tag Eva.

"Photo sharing?" He queried.

"Yeah." I shrugged, placing the phone down. "My followers love knowing every low-calorie thing I like to put in my mouth."

"Hmph." He smirked. "Then you should let them know what you put in your mouth this weekend." He winked. "It was definitely zero calories, and filling."

I gasped, and he found my reaction funny.

Even though Everett did a fantastic job of not making things awkward between us after our hookup, he never skipped a chance at saying something suggestively adorable and nasty in the same conversation. Earlier during our session, it was him saying he couldn't wait to work out with me today... so we could sweat together again. In this moment, it's his memorizing my favorite drinks... then slyly mentioning what we did last weekend.

It was kind of cute. He was sweet in his own way.

My phone chimed with another notification from HeartMates. The device was in the middle of the table, where I'd placed it and left it, with the screen's face up. The notification wasn't a basic tiny banner, it was larger than usual and included a picture of a guy with locs and text saying he'd liked my photo and the system acknowledging we were compatible. My eyes immediately bounced up to see Everett's attention down on the screen.

I wanted to disappear.

He tilted his head to his right as he lifted his gaze to mine and asked, "What's HeartMates?"

I bit inside my cheek. "It's nothing. Just an app."

"What kind of app?" he questioned next, taking another sip of his drink, waiting for my reply.

My cheeks grew warm, and I shifted in my seat uncomfortably. Although I had decided I would put myself out there dating wise, discussing it with anyone besides myself and my sister made me uncomfortable.

"It's a dating app," I confirmed.

The wrinkles in his brows deepened. "Why do you need one of those?"

"I don't need it," I replied, defensively. Again, although I was okay with my decision to list myself as an available candidate on the app, I hadn't gotten comfortable sharing that fact publicly. "I use it to assist with my search. Like a job recruiter, but instead, the app is helping me find suitable candidates... if that makes sense."

He took his straw to his mouth again to take another swig of his drink. "How's that been going for you? Using the app?"

I cringed, then shook my head, grabbing my drink to continue drinking too. "It's been a little of a disaster. I actually deleted it after a few terrible dates. I only reinstalled it a few days ago."

"And why'd you do that?"

I pursed my lips. "Are we playing a game of twenty-one questions here?"

"Nah." He shook his head, placing his drink down on the table beneath him. "I feel you are way too fine and too much of a catch to be on an app like that. It almost seems wrong for someone else to strike gold on something I like myself. I'm trying to see how I can get ahead of the competition."

He was so direct, one of my favorite things about him. He also had my full attention.

A smirk pulled at one corner of my mouth. "Come again?"

"That's exactly what I'd like to do." He pointed. "Make you come again, and again, *and again*, and again—"

"Oh, my goodness." I laughed, and he did, too. "I was just telling myself how well you've been good at not bringing any of that up."

"Well, I am bringing it up," he insisted. "And for good reason. What's your actual goal with this app, anyway?"

I blinked in response.

"Like..." He scooted to the edge of his chair. "What's the primary motivation behind posting yourself on this app as a candidate?"

I shrugged, twirling my straw in my drink. "To just date, I guess. Companionship, maybe. I just wanna go out on dates, enjoy the company of someone other than myself, and have fun."

"You trying to marry any of these guys?"

"Whoa!" I held a hand up. "No... I mean, maybe?" I lifted my shoulders and dropped them. "I'm not opposed to the idea of marriage. I don't know if I want it right now, but I would like the option to be there, you know? But no, I'm not *outwardly* looking for that from the guys on HeartMates. I can barely find a guy there I can enjoy a few hours with, much less someone to spend a lifetime with."

He twisted his lips to one side and nodded. "Well, shit, stop wasting your time, then. I can do that for you."

I lowered my chin, keeping my eyes locked on his.

"You want to go on dates, hang out, and have a good time? I can do that. We've already done that a few times, already unintentionally. So." He shrugged a shoulder. "Let's do it on purpose."

I couldn't stop the eager smile pulling at my lips, even if I wanted to. "I didn't know you were interested."

"Oh." He fell back against the back of his seat. "She didn't know I was *interested*."

I bit back my smile.

"I've had my face between her thighs twice..."

"Everett," I whispered, looking around. "*Shh.*"

"... I've damn near splashed around and swam in her wet ass pussy, happily I must add..."

"Oh my God." I glanced around us while scooting to the edge of my seat, seconds away from slapping my hand to his mouth. "Would you *shhh?*"

"... but she gonna look me right in my eyes and tell me with a straight face something crazy, like she didn't know I was interested," he finished, smirking. "Since you need me to say it with my mouth, yes, Apryl Wilde, I'm interested. I'm very interested in going on dates with you."

Direct, and in plain English.

See? *So* sexy.

I licked my lips and shyly looked away briefly. If wasting my time with all those other losers was what I had to do to get here, I would gladly have done it all again.

"I figured," I started. "Since you just got out of a relationship—"

"Don't worry about any of that," he interjected. "I know I'm not. I don't think about that whenever I'm hanging out with you. It's the furthest thing from my mind. You wanna go on dates, I wanna take you on dates. Let's start there."

My heart might as well have grown wings. My whole body honestly because I could float and hit my head on the ceiling. Beyond his words, the sincere look in his eyes, the passion and the urgency in his voice, did it for me. Everett was being real, vulnerable. He wasn't acting interested; he *was* interested, and the shit was so damn sexy to me.

"So." I ran my fingers through my hair and batted my lashes at him. "What are you saying?"

He lifted my device off the table and held it out for me to take. "Delete the app and let's discuss where we're going out on our date on Friday."

I bit my bottom lip as I accepted my phone from him, prepared to do exactly that. "Okay."

"Okay," he echoed, and winked.

———

"After you," Everett said with one hand on the door and the other gesturing for me to walk through it.

I giggled as I stepped along, turning to glance at him over my shoulder. "You know we've been out together before, right? And you've already gotten lucky. Twice. No need to be extra."

"Oh, no, no, no." He wagged his finger at me. Our entrance prompted the hostess to ask for our names to confirm our reservation. "Those other times don't count. We're on an official date tonight, Ms. Wilde. I'm gonna be all the extra I can be."

I suppressed a giddy smile.

"Peters," he replied to the hostess. "Party of two."

Our pick for the night was an Indian restaurant, Ashoka Grill, in Park Slope, Brooklyn. We ran through viable ideas of going somewhere upscale, but didn't want to be seen. I thought about something cute, like a picnic in the park, but we didn't want to deal with the bugs.

"Let's find somewhere low-key and off this concrete island," he suggested earlier in the week.

Ethnic food in Brooklyn seemed to fit the criteria.

Every New York City foodie with an internet connection raved about Ashoka Grill. They all gushed over the traditional and modernized menu online and how delicious every single dish was, down to the rice pudding.

They decorated everything in red. Red lighting, red walls, red table-cloths. The only thing that wasn't red was the wall window offering a street view of the neighborhood on the other side.

It was nice and quaint, perfect for our little date.

We approached our table and Everett grabbed the back of the chair I planned to sit on, pulling the chair out and waiting for me to take my seat.

He did not know what these thoughtful gentlemen's acts of kindness were doing to me. That, and what he wore tonight.

Everett was always the joggers and t-shirt kind of guy. I'd only known him for a short while, but it was long enough to conclude all of his outfits had some kind of jersey cotton fabric to them. Very sporty, all the time, and that was fine. I lived in leggings and sports bras, so I wouldn't say a thing about it.

But tonight, he switched it up. Tailored dress shirt with the sleeves rolled up to the space below his elbows. He left two buttons undone, showing off his pronounced collarbones - collarbones that had become more visible because of the weight he'd shed. His jeans were simple dark blue denim, but the cut made his legs appear columnar, strong. The designer white canvas sneakers he donned to complete his look added to this laid-back sexy swag. I couldn't help but to fawn over him silently.

"You look exquisite tonight," he told me when he took his seat. "Very Dorothy Dandridge in Carmen."

I pointed. "That was the exact look I was going for. Thank you." I smoothed my hand down one of the milkmaid braids I plaited and pinned around my head. I'd literally chosen the off-the-shoulder green satin dress I picked up from a vintage boutique last summer because it reminded me of that era.

"You look good yourself."

"I know, right?" He winked.

I rolled my eyes, prompting him to laugh.

The server brought menus for us, and we selected what we wanted from them. For drinks, we ordered mango lassi and, for appetizers, samosas. The chicken and salmon masalas were the most raved about option on the menu, so we went with both as well.

The restaurant was quiet. Only two other patrons were present, engaged in their own conversation. Indian music was playing from an unseen sound system, setting the mood.

Everett looked at me through heavy lids. We were totally delaying the inevitable. I didn't know what was on his mind, but if it was anything close to what I was thinking, neither one of us was going home alone tonight.

"Twenty-one questions?" I proposed, taking a sip of my drink.

"I love this game, so sure." A smirk pulled at his lips. "Permission granted to ask anything you want."

It was a silly game; I know that, but playing it with Everett allowed me to learn so much about him. Things that wouldn't normally come up in conversation. He was so fascinating, and his responses to a lot of the questions since we started this little game, back in the spring, always made things interesting.

I pointed my eyes up at the ceiling, rummaging mentally through questions to ask.

"Taking too long, Ms. Wilde," he teased. "Now it's my turn."

"No, no." I shooed his attempt to rush me away by waving my hand in the air. "I got it. I'm just trying to find the best way to word it."

"Just spit it out," he instructed. "Overthinking will only take the fun out of the game and games are supposed to be fun, not analyzed."

He was right.

"Okay," I conceded. "What's your newest favorite thing to do since returning to New York?"

"Hmph." Everett placed an elbow on the table and took his fingers to his low-trimmed beard. "Apryl."

"Yes?" I answered.

"No." He licked his lips. "I'm answering your question."

I narrowed my eyes, confused.

"My new favorite thing to do in New York…" He smirked. "… is Apryl."

I scoffed a laugh. "Everett."

He shrugged and took a sip of his mango lassi. "It's been quite the pleasure... and the exercise. You're a great person, exceptionally beautiful and intelligent. A go-getter with a heart unmatched. But on some physical shit? I *love* sex with you. It's my new favorite pastime. I'm trying to make it my *every time,* to be honest."

I arched a brow and did a horrible job of puckering my lips to hide my smile.

"Sex is pretty cool with me," I boasted. "I'm surprised you enjoyed it so much with me when, the whole time, I had to get over the fact you intimidated me a little."

He showed his palms and shrugged. "How'd I do that?"

"You're great." I crossed my legs underneath our table to calm the excitement happening there at the thought of Everett and my past hookups. "Like really, fantastic at it. Most guys aren't. They like sex a lot, but do not know what they're doing. Not you. That was surprising our first time. Having to come to terms with not being able to out-fuck a man was a process."

"Well, I'm happy you came to terms with that because I'll always make sure you come first and I'm not interested in having a competitor. I enjoy being in control."

"But don't you ever lose yourself in the act?" I asked. "Relinquish control or maybe get caught slipping?"

He licked his lips.

"You like to watch, but have you ever let someone watch you?"

"That's a very rare sighting."

"I think I have found my new goal," I teased.

He laughed. "See? That's one reason I love sex with you."

"Oh?"

"You don't know how to relax, so I enjoy giving you no choice but to."

I took a long breath in and let it out through my mouth.

"It's like I told you. I get pleasure from pleasing you. My pleasure comes from watching and feeling you enjoy yourself with me. I'm not concerned about whatever tricks you can do, how long you can last on your knees, how much of me you can take in your mouth... although all that shit sounds good to me, too."

I laughed lowly.

"What's paramount to me? What will always be a point of interest with you - if not my main point of interest - is if I feel good to you. Good enough to make your body prove it. I measure that success when you can confirm your satisfaction without words. That's a conversation I reserve with your body."

I ran a hand over a braid. "That's a lot of pressure to put on yourself, no?"

"I love sex. So, it isn't pressure when I'm doing what I love."

I pursed my lips. "Yeah, but everyone loves sex."

"Everyone *claims* to *love* sex, but all they *like* doing is coming."

I tilted my head to one side.

"And by coming, I mean making themselves orgasm using other people's bodies. Most who say they love sex love it selfishly, which isn't fun at all. My focus is on making you come first. I wanna see and feel it happening. That's my high, that's my pleasure." He nodded slowly. "I love the act of fucking *and* being intimate in other ways. I love it more than actually coming."

I arched a brow. "Now that's interesting. Why is that?"

"I enjoy controlling the range when having sex." He smirked.

"The range?"

"Sex with me happens in phases, sections, like a four course meal, and I enjoy it most when I intentionally suppress my nut."

The conversation had me forgetting to breathe. So in-depth, slightly erotic, definitely tantric, but still very clean. Everett intrigued me. "Sections?"

"Yeah, like music." He bit his bottom lip. "Good sex is like an excellent song with sections. It can start fast and end slow or start slow and end fast. There's an intro and rhythm. A cadence and a buildup to a crescendo before I mellow everything out. I compose scores when I fuck."

A smile pulled at both corners of my mouth. "Do you now?"

"*Mm-hmm.*" He nodded. "I like to start my songs slow, then go real fast."

I inhaled a shaky breath, reminded in that instance of his technique.

"High intense, chorus of moaning, making percussion instruments with our bodies, hair pulling, a little choking - not too much - lip biting, work you up to the state where you do not know where to put yourself or how to brace for the orgasm that takes you by surprise."

I shifted in my seat, feeling warmth grow between my thighs.

"That's my jam," he stated, taking a sip of his drink. "Then I like to smooth all that out after, you know? With some soft and sensual strokes." He smirked. "Move lazily, but not too lazily, just slow enough to ground you back here with me so you and I can catch our breaths."

"Oh, when did I get pulled into this?"

"You've been in it." He licked his lips and grinned boyishly. "I just revealed our plans for later tonight."

"*Our* plans?"

"Yup, *ours*," he echoed.

"Are you trying to monopolize my time, Everett?"

"Nope. I'm looking to make the most of it."

We held our stares for a few seconds.

Our server arrived at our table with our meals, setting our plates down in front of us.

I glanced down at my plate, ribbons of steam wafting from my meal. It looked delicious, but I didn't want that at all right then. I wanted what Everett planned to serve.

I wouldn't admit that, though.

"So..." Everett finished his glass of mango lassi. "Should we tell our server we're getting these to go?"

I shifted in my seat, my body responding to what he was suggesting.

"Everett?"

"*Mm-hmm?*"

"I'm not sleeping with you tonight."

"Perfect." He smiled widely. "'Cause I don't plan to sleep tonight either."

We entered through his high-rise condo's door locked at the lips. Everett and I could keep ourselves composed and patient during our black car ride from Brooklyn back to Manhattan. Longing stares, suggestive glances, so much lip licking to chap them. By the time we entered his elevator, I couldn't take the wait anymore. So, I jumped him.

Playing it cool had never been my thing, anyway. And Everett had me in the danger zone since our talk in the restaurant.

Everett didn't bother with the lights inside the condo once we were on the other side of his door. Not that there was a need for any. His condo had floor-to-ceiling windows with the curtains drawn back. Manhattan, from my view, resembled a field of confetti. The lights from skyscrapers, and the gleaming litter of headlights and taillights from a distance all lent light to his condo, making the space glow in the dark.

Everett pushed me up against a nearby wall and turned me so my back faced him. I pressed my hand to the wall's cool surface, dropping my head back between my shoulders, leaning my head against his chest.

The food we brought back from the Indian restaurant was in the white "Thank You" plastic bag he dropped by his front door.

We didn't eat any of it at the restaurant and likely wouldn't eat it at all tonight.

He gathered my satin dress at my hips, rolling the fabric up with his grip, while drawing the thin skin on my neck into his mouth. He sucked gently and strummed his finger along the seams of my panties in the space where my pussy was.

"Turn around," he directed in my ear. And I did, watching as he lowered down in front of me, bringing my lace underwear down to my ankles. He lifted one of my legs, placed it on his shoulder, and dove right in.

God, this man loved to eat, and I loved to be his meal of choice.

Everett was an expert. The way he licked and lapped at my clit, his tongue never moving haphazardly, or without a plan, was all the proof he understood the assignment. I tried to hold back the intense orgasm creeping up shortly after we started. I didn't want it to end so soon, but my body had made up its own mind, surrendering to a release that had me squirting all over that man's face and screaming in his home, prayerfully not waking the neighbors.

The only reason we made it to his bedroom was because that's where the condoms were... and the stunning view.

I didn't think it could get better than the living room, but the head of his California king bed pushed up against one floor-to-ceiling window, allowing that wall window to serve as a headboard, was an aphrodisiac I didn't even know I needed.

We made quick work of our clothing, flinging our things about the room. Everett lived a minimalist lifestyle. There was barely any furniture in his room, in the condo, from what I could see, but the quality of where he laid his head reflected his wealth.

It took a little convincing to get him to lie up under me. My hands pressed the window behind his bed, using the glass as my leverage. I let out a huge breath when I sat down slowly on his dick, moaning as the head and the thick shaft tunneled deep into me, inch by inch. My lips parted like silk rose petals around his girth. He groaned under me and held onto my waist, running his hands up to my breasts every so often to pinch and roll my nipples between his fingertips.

The stimulation and warmth made me tremble. My view was getting blurry by the minute as my eyes rolled because of the friction. My back arched out of my control to help brace myself for what was coming.

"There it is," he whispered, sitting up from his recline to suck my nipple into his mouth. He wrapped an arm around my waist and held me in place and took the lead. Pumped his pelvis upward, delivering well-timed deep upstrokes, escalating his pace until he was slamming into me with controlled vigor, fucking me while I was on my knees over him. And there was nothing I could do about it, nothing I wanted to do about it except to come all over him.

So, I did. Hollering, moaning, and whining through a pulsing orgasm that made me tingle all over. Slick sounds created from him thrusting in and out of my wet pussy, colored the moment erotically, making him groan and grunt. By the time I reached my end, he was starting his ascent. His jaw was tense, attention misplaced, his guard down. He became rock hard inside of me. Aware of this, I planted my hands against the glass behind him again, then lifted and slammed my ass up and down against him, hard and fast, repeatedly. My walls were still fluttering from my release, my body still trembling, but I wanted the reward of having a front-row seat, the perfect view of watching him climax.

And he didn't disappoint.

Everett's eyes locked on mine knowingly. I recognized the defeat in them and the need to regain control.

Out of breath, I pleaded, "Don't hold back on me." I lifted, then dropped in rhythm. "I wanna see you. Please let me."

And he did.

Instead of fighting or hiding it, he allowed his lids to grow heavy, shading his eyes. He grunted in time with me lifting, then dropping myself up, then down on his hard-on. Bared his teeth and breathed through them before dropping his jaw and then leaning his head back against the glass window. Everett arched his neck and his Adam's apple protruded while he released the deepest, longest guttural moan I ever heard him make. Deeper than any man I'd ever been with. It ignited something in me. Made me keep going, even though I had little left to give. But I didn't stop until he stopped shuddering and finally released the tension in his shoulders on the window glass. Everett uttered soft curses, slowly gaining control again.

He didn't want a competitor, but I found a new desire that night – bringing him to the point of no return... and watching as he unraveled. A big brawny man, egoless and completely fine with submitting to pleasure for an audience of one. It was endearing, vulnerable, and very sexy. He wasn't the only person who liked to watch. I loved watching him come because he didn't hold back. Allowed me to capture every angle of his sex face, shamelessly. No ego, no hiding. Just feeling.

It was *such* a turn on.

I took his face in my hands and kissed him long and hard, and he reciprocated the energy. He grew erect between my walls, dismounting me, discarding the condom, retrieving another, then pulling me to him again by my ankles.

"Thank you for that rare sighting," I rasped. "It was everything I imagined and more."

One corner of his mouth lifted in a shy grin. "You liked that, huh?"

I nodded as he raised my legs, held one back using his forearm, and guided himself into me with no hands.

"I *loved* it," I confirmed, dropping my head to one side, overwhelmed by the feeling of him filling me to the hilt so soon again.

He said he didn't plan to sleep tonight, and I was more than happy not to, either.

For the rest of the night, Everett and I made more music with our bodies and choreographed our own routine that gave me several more views of him enjoying me and I him.

I wasn't sure what this thing between us was becoming, but I understood the gravity of the night.

We did more than go on a date and fuck after.

We were starting something new... a new thing neither one of us had the heart to manage.

Twenty-Five

"Therapy?" Meki questioned on the other end of my phone.

I sat beneath a giant blue umbrella outside of a Kips Bay diner that offered outdoor seating. It was an hour before noon, so the sun wasn't too harsh for time out under it. My father and I made plans to meet up since he was in town for a few hours and I was available after my early morning session with Apryl.

It was actually at our session Apryl posed the idea of us going to therapy together.

"Nothing serious or anything," she explained after suggesting therapy. "I read online once attending therapy with the person you're dating is a good idea. Sets expectations. You can decline though, but..." She shrugged. "I think it would be good for us."

Were we dating?

I sure as hell wasn't about to ask her about it.

When I proposed we *date*, I meant for us to go *on* dates. The thought of some other man spending time with her made me uneasy.

Like leaving a flawless diamond in the middle of Herald Square, knowing it's a diamond, and literally waiting for someone to find it lying there. The idea of some other man finding this amazing woman on an app was torturous when I found out she was on one. I couldn't bear the thought, so if dating was what she wanted, I could do that.

Meaning go *on* dates.

Not start a relationship, per se.

I wasn't ready for all that.

I also wasn't ready for the pussy that woman put on me only a few nights ago.

She had me showing up to our session an hour early just so I could spend more time with her.

Sprung off that ass, I know.

"Yo, is that normal?" Meki asked next, I guess filling the silence from his previously unanswered question. "I know it's been a minute for me, but is this what people are doing now? Going to therapy before getting into relationships?"

I wanted to get ahead of something that wasn't anything yet by telling him Apryl and I were seeing each other outside of the gym. Our last scheduled session was for next week, so I figured the timing was perfect. Meki was spending less time at MK 's Sports Lounge and Gym after the birth of his son, so I barely had time to see him when I was there to get trained by Apryl. He'd transferred all of his clients, including me, to the other trainers at his gym and was handling only administrative work from his new loft in Brooklyn. He'd purchased the loft in cash after returning to New York from California.

So I called him while I sat waiting for my father to join me and revealed Apryl and I were involved. Not on anything official, but after the night we shared, something had popped off between us. Then I mentioned the therapy idea she had dropped on me earlier that day.

"I really don't know if it's normal," I answered, scanning the surrounding area for a familiar face. "But honestly, at this point? After what she put on me the other night? Apryl could ask me to take a long walk off a short ass bridge and my only question would be if she wanted me to do it now or later."

He bellowed a laugh.

The cooing of his son on the other end of his phone, followed by Meki's shushing, made me smile.

"She got you whipped as fuck, huh?" He asked low.

"Man, like butter." I shook my head, raising my hand to the bridge of my nose to pinch.

Meki chuckled low this time. I guess because the little man was near.

"How's the daddy life?"

"You curious just because or for self?"

I kissed my teeth. "I told you one thing about me seeing Apryl, and here you go with the leading questions."

He laughed low again.

"I'm curious for both reasons, I guess," I replied.

"The daddy life is the best thing to happen to me," he answered in a serious tone. "This guy who ain't let me sleep since his ass arrived has made me love his mother ten times more than I did before him, which I never knew was possible, and I loved Cadence a lot pre-Mekal. He's made me feel like the richest man alive since he's got here."

I nodded. "That's real."

"I'm tired as all hell. Little man won't sleep unless he's lying on someone's chest, mine specifically. But I feel blessed beyond my wildest dreams, man."

I smiled widely, genuinely happy for my friend. "Good shit."

"Great shit," he added. "And Apryl's an exceptional woman. A self-starter, very determined. She's a big boss, and fine, of course. You two match."

"Yeah." I nodded, stroking the short hair on my beard. "The therapy thing is unique, but it'll probably be cool. I don't think there's anything the doctor could ask me that my mother hasn't already peppered me with questions about. Plus, maybe this therapy session could be good, considering Apryl and my relationship history, you know?"

"You gotta tell me what happens," Meki insisted. "'Cause I ain't never heard of going to therapy while dating."

Are we dating, though?

I wouldn't ask Meki that or field his opinion on the matter. Not that I could, anyway, with my father making his way up the block.

"I got you," I promised. "Aye, yo, I see my pops with his old B-Boy bop in his walk, making his way up the block. I'll hit you up later."

"No doubt." He chuckled. "Give him my best."

"Will do."

I ended the call as my father was approaching and I stood to greet him.

My dad, Craig Peters, has always been the bachelor type and always dressed like one. Designer sunglasses. As usual in a dress shirt - forever unbuttoned at the top and never with a tie. Consistently paired the relaxed business casual look with tailored slacks and expensive leather shoes, regardless of the season. A single man since I was ten-years-old, on his own, without a serious relationship to show for his adult years on this planet. It was almost like his marriage with my mother was a dream, like it never existed. That's how long he's been single. I'd probably believe Eryn, and I materialized out of thin air if it wasn't for how identical we were to our dad.

"Champ," he stated when he was close enough, splaying his arms to receive me.

"Pops." I embraced him, smiling when he hugged me with all his might and patted my back twice, only to hug me tight again.

My dad wasn't around a lot growing up. He was an entrepreneur, still is. A loan broker for big corporate business owners, often with clients overseas. So he traveled often, practically lived in airports, planes, and hotels. I always believed it was his choice to put me in boxing training without discussing it with my mother first, caused their marriage's demise. But it was when I got older, I could identify the real culprit - his absence at home.

"I ordered nothing," I told him as we took our seats across from one another. "I wanted to wait for you to get here."

"A gentleman." He removed his sunglasses, setting the frames on the table in front of him. "I think I'm going to start with a coffee. Get some of this tired out of my eyes."

"When did you get into town?"

"Six this morning." He pinched the space between his eyes. "I have a meeting in Dumbo later this afternoon and another in Queens tomorrow morning, then I'm flying out tomorrow night to broker a deal in Shanghai. I plan to stay out there for at least two weeks to see what I can cook out there. That's a business city. Shanghai."

I shook my head, smiling. "Always jet setting."

"Always making money," he corrected.

I nodded in acknowledgment.

It was always clear to me what I didn't want to be, whatever my father was. As a child, I never knew what he did for a living. I just knew he made money because that was how he presented it to me. I also knew he was never home, and I understood whatever I became when I grew up; it couldn't be whatever my pops was.

"How's your mother?" He asked, leaning back in his seat. "I haven't had time to hear her beautiful voice since coming back."

"She's good," I answered. "Her practice is doing well, as always. And she looks fantastic—"

"As always," he interjected.

I smiled. "You know it."

He chuckled, shaking his head. "Don't I know it? *Hmph.*"

Their relationship was always fascinating to me. Even as a child, I knew it was different. I never knew how different.

My father spoke of my mother so fondly, like she was a good friend and not his ex-wife. And she always did the same. Growing up, I thought everyone's divorced parents were like that. So, imagine my shock when I learned my parents should've hated each other's guts, but never did. I wasn't sure if that resulted from my mother being a head doctor or my father being so cool and laid-back, but whatever the reason, their relationship was great and it was quite clear Eryn and I lucked out with growing up with divorced parents.

"And how about you?" He questioned.

Our server briefly stopped at our table to take our orders and stepped away to give our orders to the restaurant's cooks.

"I'm... better." I ran my fingertips down the sides of my beard. "New York has done good things for me since I've been back."

"Translation..." He smirked. "I've met *someone* out here who has done good things *to* me."

I hollered a laugh, and he did, too.

"Your sister told me you've been... *busy*."

I sucked my teeth. "Eryn stay sharing my business like Tic Tacs."

He laughed.

"That's all right," he commented next when he got the strength to. "There's nothing wrong with some company, especially after what you've been through."

"Word."

"Is it serious?"

"I'm not sure." I thought about sharing Apryl's therapy plan with him in that instance, but decided against it, knowing he'd have more questions I wasn't ready to answer. "But I know I like her... a lot."

"Then get serious," he offered, sitting up in his seat and leaning forward in it to balance himself on the table on his elbows. "She a young girl?"

"She's 34."

"*Hmph*." He stared off into the distance. "Yeah, she's at the age where seriousness might be the only thing she's looking for."

I ran a finger over my lips, considering that.

"Is she a good woman?" He posed next.

"A great one," I answered without hesitation.

"Then don't waste her time." He kissed his teeth. "'Cause there ain't nothing right about wasting a woman's time. What Bob Marley say?" He continued. "The biggest coward is a man who awakens a woman's love with no intention of loving her."

I jerked my head back, taken aback. "Damn."

"*Mm-hmm*."

"Deep."

"Very."

I pointed. "He also had fiftyleven kids."

"His personal life doesn't negate the facts." He explained. "And all those kids, including the offspring of those kids, have not embarrassed or tarnished his legacy. The man knew something. You can't create all that without the love not being a major component."

I made a quick shrugging motion with the corners of my lips. "True."

"What are your intentions with this woman?"

My dad was asking heavy questions, questions I did not know I'd have to answer when I moved back to New York temporarily.

"Uh…" I scratched the back of my head.

He found my reaction funny.

"To be honest." I smiled up at the server, who briefly returned to our table to drop off our food and drinks. "I didn't expect it to get to a point where I would have any intentions."

He arched a brow.

"She's my trainer."

"*Hmph*," he huffed once more. "Eating where you shit again, huh, son?"

"Nah." I laughed. "Not really. See, we started hanging out as a part of this program she put together to help get me back in shape. And that hanging out turned into… uh… into—"

"Fucking," my father finished.

I shut my eyes for a moment and laughed. It really did sound worse than it actually was.

"Fucking," I echoed. "Yes. But now that is turning into something else that has me agreeing to go to therapy with her later this week."

"Problems already?"

"There's actually no problem at all."

His brows gathered over his eyes, understandably. I didn't understand her reasoning myself, so I had no clue how to explain it to him.

"It's important to her, and now it's important to me."

He smiled knowingly.

"I don't know why she wants to go, but I'm willing to go because she asked me."

"So your intentions are good."

"For sure," I confirmed. "But I plan to leave for Cali right after the community center opens."

"Plans can change."

"Yeah, but I didn't prepare for that change." I shook my head. "I'm on a short lease. My condo barely has furniture. My bed has no headboard. I pushed the mattress up against one of the floor-to-ceiling windows in the bedroom. And although the shit looks dope, it's a clear sign I'm not here to stay."

"Plans can change," he repeated before taking a sip of his coffee. "The question you have to ask yourself is if you're willing to get out of the way of that change to let the magic happen or stick with plans that may have not been God's plan all along."

I blinked several times in response.

"I had a good woman once." He sat his mug down, moving on to unwrapping his utensils to eat. "But I also had plans. And when those plans were changing, I didn't want them to. I wanted to be a millionaire before forty, by any means necessary. That *by any means* cost me time with a wife who grew tired of coming second to my work. So I achieved my plans, becoming a millionaire before forty. A *wife* wasn't a part of that plan, so I wasn't a *married* millionaire before forty. I was a divorced one. A decision I regret more and more every day as I level up in age."

He had my attention.

"Love isn't something you only do. It's also something you're in. No one wants to be in love alone." He sipped his coffee. "Plans change, son. They're supposed to change. And if this woman you've been entertaining is worth a change in plans, pursue that."

"So soon after Brielle, though?"

"That's not a question for me." He forked a piece of his omelette into his mouth. "You tell me."

I sighed. "Tell me you were married to a psychotherapist without telling me you were married to a psychotherapist."

He raised his fist to his mouth to cover it while he laughed with his mouth full.

I shook my head.

"All I'm saying is get serious. This is your final year in your 30s. You're getting older. Women don't get dumber the older they get. They get wiser, they know what they want and often it's not a man who's willing to waste their time. Figure out what you want to do and do it. But do it fast because time has no patience."

My pops.

Rarely around but when he came around, he came bearing gems.

———

"Therapy?" Stas questioned with deep wrinkles in her brows. "For what?!"

We sat in her kitchen on the island's high stool, an island that resembled the one in the house we grew up in. She and I were waiting for dinner to finish so I could eat and escape her judgement.

I crossed my legs in my seat. "Yes, therapy. And please save your opinion. I'm not interested in one."

"Why on earth would you ask that man to go to therapy?"

"Because he's fine as hell, with eyes that make me melt, a bright white smile that finishes the job his eyes started, and he has the charm and charisma that was never written in fairytales, but should've been, duh! Not to mention..." I held up a finger. "His dick had to have been hand sculpted by God because he sure fucks like one."

"Uh..." We heard near the kitchen's entrance.

When I turned to face that way, I noticed my sister's husband, Kwamé, standing at the threshold, eyes bouncing between my sister and I.

"Hey, Kwamé." I waved nervously, turning in my seat to face my sister again, tucking my lips into my mouth and squeezing my eyes shut. "Didn't know you were back home."

"I can tell." He joked. "Stas, is dinner ready yet? Or should I go stab my eardrums out in the office with my fountain pen after walking in on this very private conversation?"

She rolled her eyes. "You're so mellow-dramatic."

"And completely traumatized after overhearing my sister-in-law, who I've known since she was practically a baby talking about an act that makes babies," he added.

"You've known her since she was thirteen. She's a grown woman now, and has found a man who fucks like a God, as you heard."

I snorted.

"Christ," he exclaimed.

"Dinner will be ready in fifteen minutes, babe."

"Sorry Kwamé," I told him, turning to face him briefly. "Love you."

"Love you back," he replied, his voice trailing off. "Please be mindful of your nosey niece, who likes to eavesdrop on conversations in this house."

"Noted," I mumbled.

"She's busy watching cartoons," Stas assured. "She's not moving from her spot in front of the TV unless we drag her from it."

I inhaled a deep breath.

"Therapy when you two aren't in a relationship yet?" She asked, setting the conversation back on course. "Apryl, this might be too much too soon. What did he say when you suggested it?"

I shrugged a shoulder. "He agreed. We go on Friday."

She shook her head. "And what do you plan to gain from this therapy session?"

"I don't know yet." I folded my hands on the table. "But I read in this article that going to therapy before you start a relationship irons out any kinks and snags that may pop up unexpectedly when a relationship starts."

"Oh, my goodness."

"Listen." I sat up. "I know you remember the shit I went through after Troy and Chloe. There were red flags all over that play before they got involved behind my back. Red flags on both their ends and separately, that I ignored. I like Everett. I need to make sure liking him is healthy beyond the physical. We need a good start... if we plan to have one. Therapy is going to help with that."

"Just nuts."

"Hey!" I jabbed the island's counter beneath me. "You haven't dated in decades, so you don't know what single women are facing in these treacherous ass dating streets. Therapy is the least a man can do when dating."

"*Are* you two dating?"

I blinked a few times, perplexed by the question.

"Like I know, you two have been hanging out, but that was still just work for you. And I know you two started hooking up because of that. But *are* you two actually *dating* now?"

"I mean..." I shifted my eyes out her kitchen window to stare at the sunrays shining through the glass. "I don't know exactly, but I guess we are... kinda... a little... I think. We did not sign a contract or an agreement. So, I don't really know."

"That sounded like a long-ass winded no. You should've just said no."

"Look here." I pointed at her. "You will not talk me out of this."

She held her hands up in defense.

"Therapy will be good for us," I asserted. "It'll be great. We are insanely compatible, we've got the physical attraction down to a science. We simply need to exercise communication skills and transparency and we'll be golden. If we decide a relationship is what we want, we'll be so ready for one."

"Are you ready for a relationship, though? Like, do you want one of those things?"

"Will you stop doing that, *ugh*!"

"What?" she asked with a smirk. "Make sense? Question your choice of doing something with an end goal you aren't sure you want? Which part?"

"I like him, okay?" The conversation and the doubtful thoughts it was evoking made me so nervous. My hands were perspiring. To dry my sweaty palms, I ran my hands down my thighs. "I like him a lot and I think I could love him. But before I do that, I need to know if he's worth loving."

Stas's eyes softened.

"I need to know this time..." I stared down at my hands. "Because another heartbreak will kill me."

"Apryl." She leaned across the counter to take my hands. "It will not kill you."

"It will," I insisted. "To my core. And I can't experience that again. I don't want to feel that kind of disappointment ever again. So, we're doing therapy because I'm insecure about the new feelings I'm having for Everett. I'm falling too hard and too fast. He was only supposed to be a client and now he's feeling like a dream come true. I need to pierce through the fog to see what's real and what's just got my head in the clouds because he makes me come really fucking hard."

She snickered.

"So ask him, Apryl," she reasoned. "Ask him all the questions you want him to answer so you'll feel secure."

"I don't know what to ask. Plus, the article said a therapist will be more objective-based and will know how to navigate through our thoughts to help us delve deeper into the root of our responses. They'll help us sort through our thinking and make sense of our answers and our concerns... well, *my* concerns. I want a third party on this."

"You can't hack *being* in a relationship. It's not something you can decode. A relationship is an experience." She folded a lock of hair behind her ear. "The trust and strength in a relationship develops from going through the *healthy* highs and lows. Relationship highs do not test your bounce back muscles. The bad times play as big of a role in a successful relationship as the happy times. You're trying to skip the bad parts and its lessons in a relationship you're not sure you want to begin with, but you won't just say that."

"I don't know if I want a relationship." I threw my arms up in defeat. "I don't. You're right. But I want the option to have a good one. And if the option exists with Everett, it will be clear in therapy."

"So damn headstrong." She stood from her seat to approach her stove. "When you decide to do things, you do them even when people try to talk you off the ledge."

I stuck my tongue out behind her back.

"Saw that," she confirmed, while plating the lamb chops and red wine stew over brown rice near the stove.

"I'll take a little extra today," I told her, referring to the food. "Three spoons of rice instead of two and a lamb chop should be enough."

"A *whole* lamb chop?" She turned to look at me. "Not a tiny crumb of meat and a sprinkle of rice, like always?"

"Oh, shut up." I laughed, then shrugged. "After my brief experiment I did with Everett to assist with him getting in shape, I've eased back a lot on maintaining a super strict diet."

Her brows arched.

"I wanna keep a little of this soft on me. I'm in love with the toned soft look these days." I looked away shyly. "And coincidentally, Everett is too."

Stas did a terrible job, fighting back her huge smile as she turned to face her stove again. "I hope this whole therapy thing works out for you."

"I know it will," I replied confidently. "Not too much sauce though, please."

Twenty-Six

"That was... interesting," I expressed the moment we stepped through the heavy glass door.

At mid-day on a Friday, the streets bustled with traffic on the blacktop road and the city concrete. New information cluttered my mind. Everett and I had just stalked out of the high rise after our visit with the therapist, who has an office in the building. And thankfully we'd stepped out at the right time because I needed the air, pronto.

I glanced at Everett, and he seemed so very unfazed. He was also forthcoming and transparent during our session. More transparent than I was expecting.

I wasn't ready...

I wasn't ready at all, actually.

"So," Dr. Reyes began. "Based on the intake form filled out by Apryl, I'm aware this is a brand-new relationship."

"We're not in a relationship," Everett politely corrected.

"Yet." I glanced at him, then focused on her again. "We're dating right now."

He took my hand and gave me a closed-mouth smile. "We're going on dates. Not dating in the traditional sense."

Dr. Reyes's thick brows arched slightly.

Her office was cozy, cozier than I was expecting. I'd never been to the office. Simply booked the appointment online and filled out the intake form. She was the relationship therapist interviewed in the article suggesting dating couples seek therapy before becoming serious. So, I figured no vetting was necessary.

Her desk sat in front of an expansive wall window that stretched from one end of her office to the next. The office was enormous, and she accounted for every square space in the most beautiful of ways. It gave comfort and chic. And yet, I was uncomfortable.

"I want to be honest," Everett started. "My mother's a psychotherapist and she's always encouraging transparency, so I want to keep it real."

Dr. Reyes smiled. "Very much appreciated."

His transparency, though, yes, I appreciated, was annoying me and the session only started minutes ago.

"Apryl, you look uncomfortable."

Spot on.

"'Cause I am." I folded my arms. "I'm trying to understand why Everett felt inclined to point out we aren't in a relationship."

"Because we aren't," he clarified in the gentlest voice. So gentle I couldn't with sense get mad. "I know this is important to you, and I know how important it is to be honest in these things."

"In what things, Everett?" Dr. Reyes quizzed.

"Therapy," he answered.

"And how do you feel about Apryl's idea of you two attending therapy this soon in your relationship?"

"We aren't in a relationship."

"She knows!" I shouted, then cleared my throat when I realized I was a little too loud with that one. "You don't have to keep reminding her."

He bowed his head in acknowledgment, then admitted, "I think it's foolish for us to be here. This therapy session is way too premature of a move for us."

My jaw dropped.

"I get Apryl's reasoning, but I don't agree with it. I like her though, a lot, and want to support her."

I glared his way and mumbled, "Are you kidding me right now?"

And that man really looked over at me with the most genuine disposition, asking me, "What did I do wrong?"

Nothing. He did nothing wrong. The therapy session was just not what I was expecting.

In the hour we spent sitting across from Dr. Reyes in the plush loveseat for two, we went to places in conversation concerning Everett and my relationship - or whatever it was we had - that I wasn't at all prepared for. We picked at the scabs of our recent past heartbreaks only to discover we hadn't quite healed from what seemed to be old wounds. Everett admitted to still having love for his ex despite her betrayal, and I admitted I would consider talking to my ex if he called. Well, I did not exactly admit it. It took a lot of tooth pulling to get that fact out of me.

"Would you answer?" The doctor asked.

"I... I would let it go to voicemail."

"Would you return the call?"

"I mean." I shrugged. "Maybe. Yeah, but only so I wouldn't seem rude."

"He broke your heart," Everett chimed in. "I think the least you can do is to be rude."

"You said you still loved your ex."

"That's different."

"Apples to oranges," I sniped back. "But still fruit."

"Let's stay focused," Dr. Reyes insisted with a warm smile.

But what took the cake was when Dr. Reyes asked the last question of the session. The question that left my mind cluttered with thoughts even after we left the therapist's office, and as Everett and I stood on the pavement feet away from the glass lobby door.

"This question is for both of you and is an opportunity to ask anything you want of each other fearlessly."

I swallowed hard, already nervous.

"The question is - what is one thing you would ask each other that

you've been keeping to yourself out of fear of getting an answer you wouldn't like?"

I gave it some thought and came up blank. I figured we didn't have this issue of being afraid to ask things. Our silly game of twenty-one questions allowed us to ask whatever we wanted. And we've asked the most daring ones already.

I could confidently know we were good here, for the first time in our session. Finally.

"I would ask Apryl if she'd agree to moving in together."

That relief didn't last long.

My eyes nearly popped out of my head. Like literally ballooned in their sockets to the point of causing dull pain. The revelation completely took me off guard.

I whipped my head in his direction so fast and in obvious shock.

Everett causally met my gaze.

He lifted and dropped a shoulder. "I just thought of this question last night. Figured I'd just go for it just now."

That was fair, but still very absurd.

Despite that, "Excuse me?" was the only thing I could think to ask, because what I really wanted to ask was, "what the entire fuck?"

"Apryl," Dr. Reyes started. "Keep in mind this is a safe space free of judgement. I asked with a focus on doing so without the fear of being judged or the thought of being rejected for asking it."

I wished she would just shut the fuck up.

"Why on earth would you want to ask that?" *I asked Everett, ignoring the doctor. "I own a townhouse."*

"I know you own a townhouse, but that's not a problem," he replied. "We could still own something together. Your house could still be your house. And if you wanted, you could list your house as an Airbnb."

"An Air what?!"

"Apryl," Dr. Reyes chimed in again.

And I ignored her again as well.

"Why would I have random strangers stay in my house?"

"It was only an idea."

"A bad one," I mumbled.

Dr. Reyes drew in a breath and released it just as quickly. "Apryl—"

"We are so done here," I interjected, standing to my feet. *"Thank you, Dr. Reyes. You've done enough."*

I couldn't get out of there fast enough.

"You seemed so comfortable up there," I told him.

He slipped his hands into his cargo shorts' pockets. "I'm a therapist's kid. Feels like I've been in therapy my whole life. So, our session upstairs was light work."

"That was not what I was expecting."

Therapy seemed so easy as a thought. My expectations didn't mesh well with reality. I wanted her to mediate, to help me find questions, to ask to field Everett's replies, to clue me in on if he'd be a suitable candidate for me to do whatever I had planned.

Selfish, but whatever. That was my idea!

Dr. Reyes psychoanalyzed me. She did her damn job. Oddly, that... annoyed me.

"Well." He tipped his head to one side. "What were you expecting?"

I turned to face him. "Definitely not you asking to move in."

He gestured with his hands nonchalantly, as if all of this wasn't a big deal to him. "It was a new question I've been mulling over for the past few days after the other night we spent together. I'm also on a short lease, so—"

"We've only been seeing each other seriously for a few weeks now. Why would we move into a place together? Why is that even a thought already?"

"Why would therapy be for you?" He asked back.

Shit. Touché.

"I own a house."

"Which you've reminded me of several times this afternoon."

"I bought a house so I wouldn't feel I'd need a man to make such a big life decision."

"And I admire you for that."

"So much so, you suggested I put my house on the market to be shared by strangers."

"Apryl, *please* gorgeous." He dropped his head back between his shoulders before meeting his eyes with mine again. "I don't want to go back and forth with you." Everett approached and pulled me close to him by my lower back. I exhaled against his chest. "It's a beautiful day. You look stunning, as always. And I'm hungry, and I know you are too, which might be the reason you have an attitude with me right now."

My stomach growled on cue, causing me to roll my eyes.

A smile appeared on his lips. "Let's get something to eat. Go back to my place." He licked his lips. "So we can make sweet love and not war. How does that sound to you?"

Like my favorite song.

I tried to fight my smile, but had no choice but to let it shine through.

He bent his legs at the knees to get eye to eye with me. "What do you say about that?"

I nodded my answer, and he smiled back.

"I guess we can do that."

While sharing time and space with him excited me, I couldn't ignore the fact that I might have made a mistake. Because therapy may have done more harm than good.

At least for me.

———

She tried to slip from my arms without me knowing.

"And where do you think you're going?" I asked, tightening my arm around her waist and pulling her back into the spot on my bed she'd fallen asleep in.

The hour had to be after midnight. After returning from the therapy session hours ago, we ate the halal food we ordered for pickup and did what we did best, enjoy amazing sex, before falling asleep in my bed afterwards.

"I have to go," Apryl said lowly, trying her best to uncoil my arm from around her.

I closed my eyes and nuzzled my nose into her hair from behind. "Just spend the night."

Instead of trying, this time she removed my arm from around her waist with better force.

With so much force, I opened my eyes to get a good look at her because the energy had definitely shifted.

She'd been in some kind of mood ever since we left the session. Quieter than usual while we ate and a little more submissive in bed when we had sex. She was holding back, and I'd let her hoping she'd get past it, but it looked like I was wrong.

"I'm not spending the night," she mumbled, moving around the room, picking up her clothes. Apryl stepped into her panties when she found them, then snapped on her bra when she found that. Not once looking my way.

"Why not?" I pulled myself up by my arms, leaning my back against the cool wall window behind my mattress. "It's late and no big deal. You've done it before."

"I have a house," she spat, poking her head through the neck of her top and then her arms through the sleeves.

I attempted to exhale my annoyance. "Apryl, what does that have to do with you spending the night?"

"I have my place," she tried. "I don't need to spend the night."

"Of course you don't *need* to. I'd *like* you to."

She turned to face me after dressing herself in her final article of clothing. "I didn't buy my townhouse, so I could spend the night out of it."

"You bought it because you had it like that and I love that shit for you, for real. If I've made you think I had a problem with it, Apryl, please know I don't. And please don't think owning expensive ass property bothers me in the least 'cause it doesn't. At all. I'm proud of you for that."

She ran her fingers through her hair.

"Why do you keep making it a point to let me know about this house today?"

"Because you keep making it a point to make me forget I have one."

My posture collapsed in response. "What's going on with you?" I gestured with my hand for her to walk closer to me. "Come here, let's talk."

"I think we need to take a break."

"A break from *what*?" I shot back.

"This thing, whatever it is, we're doing."

I blinked a few times in response, growing more annoyed with her the longer we spoke like that.

"The therapy session made a lot of things abundantly clear about us, one of which being neither one of us has given ourselves enough time to heal from our relationships with our exes."

"We knew that," I reasoned. "We knew we'd been dealing with the baggage from our last relationships. But we've been enjoying each other's company and accepting it for whatever it is right now. That's the real reason neither one of us wants a relationship, right?"

She looked away.

"Right?" I repeated.

"You still love her."

I sighed heavily, running my hand down my mouth. I inhaled her scent on my hand unintentionally. Breathing in her essence on my fingers was the only thing keeping me from losing my patience with her. "Apryl, come here."

"No." She shook her head, a slight smirk appearing on her lips. "Because if I come over there, I already know what to expect based on how you just said my name."

I licked my lips slowly, knowing she was absolutely right.

"We will not keep talking," she added.

"'Cause talking is overrated."

"Everett."

I closed my eyes again and leaned the back of my head against the glass behind me.

"Next Monday is your last session with me."

I leveled my head to look her way again.

"You're back in excellent shape, more than ready for your community center appearance in Brooklyn next month." She shook her head slowly. "You don't need me anymore."

"I never needed you." I clarified. "I wanted you. I still want you. And I'm a man who sees what he wants and makes it what he has."

"You want me as what?"

I inhaled a deep breath, not all that sure myself.

"Everett, I want a relationship. I just don't want one right now. But I would still like the option of having one, you know?"

I nodded. "I know."

"And the way things have been moving with us makes me want one, but only to keep having you around and that isn't—"

"Healthy," I finished.

"It's not. Especially not after what I've been through." She threw her arms up in the air, then let them fall at her sides. "I bought a house."

I scoffed a laugh.

"I bought a house to prove to myself I could do it without tying my plans with a man, because if I'm with a man, I want to be with him because I want to be with him. Not in fear of losing him or him choosing someone else over me. Or worse, feeling if he leaves, I'll lose a part of myself." She shook her head. "No. I don't want him to complete me. I want him to enhance me. And I don't want to go back on what I want for myself. Moving in may not do that, but right now, from my purview, it will. And it could very well be the baggage blocking my current view of what you are propositioning. That's why we need a break."

New York will never be my permanent residence again. I was here because I needed to get out of L.A. for a little after that shit with Brielle and the negative effects of it all. Despite that, I always planned to return to California because I'd built a home there, a life. My sister was still there and the reason I moved out west to begin with... but I would have made the change for Apryl. Because whatever this was we were doing, what it was becoming? Felt good, natural, and made me want to do it forever, but officially and with titles.

I wouldn't say any of that scary shit to her, though. Look at her reaction to the idea of spending the night.

But she was right. We weren't ready for all that other stuff yet and it made little sense to ignore that fact.

So, I pulled the covers off me to get off my bed and get dressed.

"What are you doing?"

"Taking you home... to the house you bought." I smirked.

"You don't have to do that, Everett." She pointed over her shoulder at the wall window behind her with her thumb. "I can catch a cab."

"I'm taking you home," I told her while poking my head through my tee. "And if you don't like it, you can fuss about it on the way there. Let's go."

TWENTY-SEVEN

I bobbed my head to the bass line from the song, blasting through my headphones as I made my way down an aisle at my local organic gourmet market. On a Sunday, it wasn't as busy as usual. It may be because I was shopping mostly from the produce section.

I filled my cart halfway with green bags of produce and clear bags of protein. Lettuce, kale, salmon, chicken breasts, you name it. If it was leafy, a lean protein, a vegetable or a fruit, it was in my cart.

I committed myself to the food plan Apryl gave me. Making sure not to deviate, not even for a greasy snack, although I'd gotten the urge to do it every day since I started following her plan. The same way, I've had to fight the urge to call her after that early Saturday morning.

"Here we are," I announced, pulling the car over to the curb in front of her townhouse.

The neighborhood was quiet, although there was one jogger out for a midnight run, a man walking his dog along the opposite sidewalk, and a food delivery guy riding his moped up the block.

"Thank you." She unhooked her seatbelt and reached for her doorknob.

I immediately clicked the automatic lock button to lock all the car doors.

She laughed.

"I know you don't think you're getting out of this car before giving me a proper goodbye."

"Everett—"

"You said we needed a break," I reminded her. "Does that mean you can't kiss me goodbye?"

"I'm going to see you on Monday, in two days."

"I want a kiss there, too."

She looked at me. "Everett."

I unhooked my seatbelt and leaned over the center console in her direction, sliding my fingers into her hair when I was close and using my grip behind her head to pull her to me. She moaned when our lips collided and I parted her lips with mine to slide my tongue into her mouth to take our kiss deeper. I kissed her like I wouldn't see her for one hundred days instead of two, and I still wasn't happy about it. I let her know without words, I'd miss her. Her soft moans she let escape made me stiffen in my joggers. I wanted to come in her house so damn badly, so I could come in her too.

She broke the kiss, pressing her forehead against mine, trying her best to catch her breath. Apryl leaned her lips against mine again, to steal another kiss.

"Quit trying to make me change my mind," she said against them.

"I'm trying to make you change your clothes from off you to on your bedroom floor."

She giggled and pecked me once on the lips. Apryl unlocked the door and pulled at the handle again, to open it and step out.

I respected her wishes. Didn't follow her up her stairs to her front door or call her after that early Saturday morning, even though I'd come close to calling.

She wanted space. I'd give it, respectfully.

I wheeled my cart to the register for checkout. I had the grains at home and only went to the market to buy produce and protein.

With my bags in hand, I made my way out, walking my way back to my condo's building. I had plans to cook something then head out to Brooklyn to spend time with my mother, who didn't have any clients today.

My energy was high. I crushed my fitness goals beyond expectations. The old me and the new me made a whole new me I really liked. It was a good place to be.

The closer I got to my condo's building lobby door, the more in view a woman standing at the entrance became. Instinctively, I furrowed my brows and squinted my eyes when I thought I recognized her from the back.

I pulled my headphones down from my ears, then jerked my head back when I was sure it was her.

"Brielle?"

She turned. Her black curls whipped in the air and bounced on her bare shoulder blades as her eyes lit up at the sight of me.

I stopped walking, my shoulders sagging without my control.

"Everett!" she shouted, power walking so quickly toward me in sky-high stiletto heels. I had no time to process what to do when she got in front of me.

She knew what to do, though.

Wrapping her arms tight around me like she had no plans to let me go. The grocery bags occupied my hands, but I don't think I would've hugged her back if my hands were free, anyway.

"Oh my *God*." She ran her palms up and down my arms. "You're so solid. More solid than I remember."

"What are you doing here?" was the only thing I could get out.

"I'm meeting with a buyer in two hours." She grinned proudly. "I've breathed life into my stylist business since you've been gone. I reconnected with a few people to get some of my clients exclusive pieces. A local designer invited me out to their showroom here in New York, so here I am."

"What are you doing *here*?" The paper bags' handles were cutting into my skin. "How do you know where I live?"

"Jacob, your doorman at your condo in L.A. clued me in on where you were getting your mail forwarded." She shrugged. "I figured I'd try the address. When I arrived, your doorman here said you'd run out but should be back soon, and he was absolutely right."

Brielle had a certain charm that men couldn't resist. She didn't have to work hard to get information from the opposite sex. Her inviting smile, bright eyes, and bubbly personality made it seem like she was doing them a favor, accepting the information that she requested from them.

It was a head trip I've fallen for more times than I'd like to admit.

"Well?" She anchored her head back to measure the height of the building with her eyes. "What floor are you on? Are you going to invite me in?"

"Are you fucking with me?"

She adjusted the gold chain on her Chanel purse over her shoulder and fluffed her glossy curls with her manicured nails. "Everett, let's not do this out here."

"Let's not do this at all."

I took a step to walk past her and she stepped in my path.

"Brielle, move."

"Everett," she whispered. "Please."

I inhaled a deep breath and released it shakily.

"Invite me up so we can talk."

Passersby paid us no mind as they went about their weekend day, minding their business, like New Yorkers knew how to do.

The fucking nerve of this woman to pop up here unannounced after all the shit she did, expecting me to let her in my place.

The reason I was in New York was to escape her bullshit, and here she was, again, with more.

"Nah." I shook my head and moved around her. "I'm not dealing with this."

She started sobbing loudly behind me as I took two steps towards the building's lobby glass door.

I squeezed my lids closed, willing myself to keep walking and ignore her, but her cries only got louder.

Now, New Yorkers may mind their business and the rest of the world might find them to be jaded, but a beautiful woman crying in the middle of Manhattan would garner the look of a person or ten. I didn't need that kind of attention.

I hated it when she did this. Brielle's tears were her weapon and hard to ignore. She knew that. I often believed she used those tears as a weapon on me, able to make her eyes water on cue to get everything she wanted.

So fucking manipulative.

I couldn't walk past the doorman and he notice her crying outside over my shoulder. Not when she was just in there asking for me. He'd immediately link her upset to me and would definitely tell a friend, and then the media. I'd been in this condo for a short while, keeping my head low and minding my business. My short lease was almost up and I'd practically gone about my business here unnoticed.

I didn't need this shit Brielle was bringing.

"Come on," I said through my teeth, refusing to look her way. "Let's go up."

The hurried clicks of her heels against the concrete over my shoulder and the eventual grip of her arms around my waist from behind was proof enough that she heard me. I wanted to recoil from her touch, but gritted my teeth and beared instead.

I walked out of her embrace and grabbed the handle of the lobby's door to hold it open for her to walk through ahead of me.

It was like she wasn't crying outside by the time the elevator doors closed with us behind them.

Typical.

Brielle rambled about her flight to New York and how much the city changed on the way up to my condo.

She stepped inside my place before me after I unlocked the door, her eyes scanning the place like some kind of drone, recording everything to memory.

"You barely have any furniture in here."

I ignored her, placing my bags on the marble counter in my kitchen.

"You didn't plan to stay long. Good."

I stood facing her now, folding my arms over my chest.

"I knew as much." She smiled sweetly. "Jacob in L.A. told me you arranged for your Range, that you shipped from Cali to New York, to be returned and delivered to your L.A. condo's garage for your return in July."

"My doorman sure was loose about my business with you." I poked my tongue into my cheek. "Is he on one of those DVDs you kept in that box?"

She gasped. "What?"

So damn dramatic.

"Of course he isn't. I didn't sleep with him." She drew her mouth into a straight line.

'Cause he wasn't a model, is what I'm sure she would've said if she knew it was safe to.

"He just sees how much I miss you. How much I love you. He understood me wanting to know your whereabouts, is all."

She would've fucked him, though.

I shook my head at the thought. "Brielle, what are you doing here, woman?"

Brielle walked closer, placing her purse on the island in front of me. "I've missed you so much. I respected your wishes regarding calling you, but when I found out you'd move to New York for the summer, that crushed me. Then when I got the call to fly out here, I knew I had to see you while here."

I looked away when she made her way closer.

"I considered calling you, but I knew you wouldn't have answered, so." She shrugged. "I decided to just... pop up."

Brielle ran her fingers through her curls. "We never had time to talk about what happened."

"Nothing to talk about."

"You never gave me an opportunity to explain myself."

"I didn't need you to explain shit, Brielle. You fucking cheated on me and recorded every single time you did it."

She cringed, then exhaled loudly. "Okay, I deserved that. What I did was stupid—"

"I agree."

"And I wish I hadn't done it."

"I bet you do."

"And I know it's asking for too much..."

"Then don't ask for it."

Her bottom lip trembled. "I want you back, Everett. I really do. It was foolish of me to do what I did and I should've thought more of it, but I figured if there was anyone who would understand my mistake, it would be you."

I lifted both brows. "Oh? Are we supposed to bond over breaking people's hearts right now? Is that what this is?"

"You once told me you would want the opportunity to show your exes you had changed."

I blinked rapidly.

"It was during one of our drunken nights where you admitted if you could speak with your exes, you'd show them how much you've changed with me. How you can commit to one person the way you committed to me?"

"And look what that got me."

"All I'm asking is for an opportunity to show how sorry I am. To show you how much I've learned from my error and how much I want to fix things."

Slowly, I shook my head.

"I'm not asking you to take me back, although I'd be more than happy to be your woman again. I'm asking for an opportunity to show you I've changed. To show you, I'm still worthy of being your wife. I made one misstep."

"You made a box of missteps."

"Everett, *please.*"

I wanted so badly to scoff at her shit. To kick her out next and to ask her to not think about me in the future because I was done with her, done with her shit. But as audacious as she was being... she was right. I said those things about wanting an opportunity, and I meant that. Realistically, I never expected to be taken back by any of my exes, but I wanted to show them I'd sincerely changed, like I promised I would after breaking their hearts. I didn't feel obligated to give that opportunity to Brielle, but then I kind of felt I needed to practice what I preached. Plus, I wanted not a single doubt about what could have been if I didn't give her a chance to prove she was better. I wanted no blocks to exist because I didn't follow my gut on this.

I had nothing else happening to me, anyway. My sessions with Apryl were ending. She'd made it clear a relationship wasn't what she wanted right now. I was moving back to Los Angeles, and I already knew I could never view Brielle as my wife ever again after what I saw on that DVD. I really had nothing to lose and much to gain. I was sure Brielle would show me in more ways than one that I made the right decision to break up with her. Now, it was time I made her see that for herself.

See, she was definitely trying to play a head game with me, like always. Which was the first clue she hadn't changed since I ended things between us. But I'd play along.

"All right," I agreed. "Fine, let's do it."

Her eyes lit up.

"Let's see where this goes."

Twenty-Eight

APRYL

I spent the entire session smiling with pride as I watched Everett at work.

He gave me the push-ups I asked for, plus twenty extras. Ran the four miles on the treadmill like it was nothing but a mile. Completed drills like he inhaled air and out worked me in more ways than I was expecting during our workout routine on the mats. Compared to his very first day with me at MK's Sports Lounge and Gym, his last day was a cakewalk. His stamina had increased, body fat was now nonexistent, and his muscle mass had improved exponentially, both in numbers and visually. Sweat rolled down the peaks of his arms. The man was back in fighting shape, more than ready to stand opposite an opponent in the ring if he wanted to.

I was back in shape but with softer curves and at the weight I started with before offering the idea of gaining weight to lose it with him. I'd altered my diet, so it wasn't as strict as before, and I've been really loving a more flexible eating plan.

We were a success story, but Everett was the fairytale.

"Excellent work today," I told him, as we cooled down with stretches on the mat after our last workout. "You completed everything like a beast in here today."

He nodded. "I appreciate it. Appreciate you."

I tilted my head to one side in my attempt to read him.

His energy was different. I noticed it from the moment he walked in.

Big contrast to the way we left things that early Saturday morning in his car when he dropped me home.

"Are we good?" I asked him low, scanning the area in front of us before lowering my focus to him, searching for his eyes. "I feel like things are a little weird between us."

"Honestly?"

"Always," I answered.

"I've been dreading having to talk to you about something."

I jerked my head back, my attention locked on him as he laid on his back. "What do you want to talk about?"

He sat up from his recline on the mat and rested his forearms over his hiked-up knees. "You think we can speak privately? In your office or something?"

That didn't sound good.

"Yeah. Sure." I pushed myself up on my feet, using my hands. "Let's go."

The open-planned area was empty, mainly because I'd booked out the space to train Everett privately. There weren't any clients in this part of the gym, so Everett's request to be alone was a little concerning.

Still, I led the way. When we got near my office door, he stepped forward to open it for me, waiting for me to step in before following me inside and closing the door behind us.

"What's up?" I asked the second he faced me.

His eyes gave my office a once over. Not much to see besides a desk, a chair, and the shower room to our far right.

"My ex stopped by my condo yesterday afternoon."

"Shut up," I exclaimed, briefly raising my hand to cover my mouth. "How'd that go?"

"She wants to get back together."

I couldn't help the pinched expression I felt on my face.

"I know." He chuckled softly, reading my reaction. "She's on some bullshit, but I'm gonna give her the rope."

My expression deepened. I was still confused. Even more so after his comment.

"What do you mean by giving her the rope?"

"I'm moving back to L.A." He ran his hand down his low-trimmed beard. "I'm flying out there next week to get everything back in order for my arrival on the first day of August. I plan to fly back to New York a few days before my community center appearance in July, and that will be my last visit to the city."

"Wh-what?" was all I could get out. I certainly didn't want him to repeat himself, but I was confused. "You're moving back for *her*?"

"I always planned to move back home after the community center's appearance." He shook his head. "I sublet my L.A. condo instead of opting to sell. I was only supposed to be in New York for the opening."

"Everett, you were just suggesting we move in together."

"I know."

"So, *what* are you telling me right now?"

Air was becoming harder to pull in.

"I would've changed my plans for you." He lifted and dropped his shoulders. "I would've stayed."

"And now you're moving back for *her*?" I spat with disgust.

Because his decision disgusted me.

All the progress he made, the happiness he's found here and now when he's all patched up and better again, here she is to scoop him back up?

I was so livid inside I could scream.

"No." He shook his head. "I'm moving back for closure."

"Closure?" I raised my hand to my face and ran my palms down my cheeks to keep myself together. "What's that look like for you?"

"She wants another chance."

"And you're actually going to give it to her?!" my voice echoed around us. "Why would you give her such a privilege, Everett? Why would you offer her an opportunity like that when she did a piss-poor job with the one you gave her the first time? All in the name of closure? Really? Come on! Be fucking for real right now."

"Because I've always wanted one for myself. Because I swore that if I had another chance whenever I fucked up, I'd show I was different. I'd prove I wouldn't make the same mistake."

I blinked hard, sincerely in disbelief now.

"So, you *are* taking her back?"

"No."

"Fuck, Everett." I combed my fingers through my hair. "You're talking in circles right now."

"I'm giving her the chance I always wanted, to redeem herself, but I'm not taking her back. I'm just not cutting her off."

"Is this because I wouldn't move in with you?" I walked closer, stopping in front of him to press my hands to his chest. He was all solid muscle now. A work of art I played a part in sculpting. This was all wrong.

"Apryl—"

"Because I can't let you do that. If it *is* about the moving in thing..." I swallowed hard. "Then we can—"

"No, don't do that." He took my face in his hands and bent his legs at the knees to meet my eyes. But I closed them in response to his touch, leaning more into it. "Don't settle. Don't go back on your word to yourself, on what you want, on what you said you wanted. Apryl, don't do that for me."

And I was so ready to.

To swallow my pride and to get over myself, my plans, my wants and desires all to keep this man in this city... do the one thing I promised I wouldn't do again - tie my plans to a man so I wouldn't lose him.

But this one was worth it. I was sure of it. And his ex knew that.

I didn't know her, but I knew I wouldn't like her if I did. Everything was fine before she brought her ass back into the frame. Why was she here? To disrupt his new life, that's why. She had to sense he was doing better without her. Because there was no way she had changed in this short time and she knew that.

Why was she doing this?

A knock came at the door.

"Apryl?" our receptionist, Michelle, interrupted on the other side of my office door. "Your next appointment has just arrived."

"Shit," I hissed, shaking my head. "I'll push the appointment back."

"What? No?" he told me. "Go, it's cool."

"Okay, so." I looked up at him. "We can talk about it later—"

"Talking won't change anything for me."

I sagged my shoulders in defeat.

"Apryl?" Michelle knocked once more.

"The timing ain't good right now, Apryl." His voice was serious, but the look in his eyes even more. "You know that."

I did.

"And if we force it, it won't feel the same."

"You're taking her back?" I whispered.

He shook his head.

"Then what are you doing? Why go back? What closure do you need in L.A. that you can't get from here in New York?"

"I need you to do something really crazy right now." He stroked my cheek with the pad of his thumb. "I need you to trust me on this."

I wrinkled my brows.

"Apryl?" Michelle called again. "You in there?"

"It may not make sense to you right now, but I need you to trust me. Trust that I know what I'm saying right now. What I'm doing."

I couldn't stop the tears from welling in my eyes.

"Apryl?"

"Baby, answer her," he ordered, gently. "Please."

I didn't bother breaking eye contact when I told Michelle, "Let them know I'll be there in five minutes."

"Okay, will do," she confirmed, presumably leaving her post at my door.

Everett and I held our stares for a few beats. I wanted to say so much, but the same pride I looked on at him while he aced his workout was the same pride keeping me from begging him not to go this time.

I shook my head and looked away to keep the tears in, because why the hell did I want to cry?

This sucked so much. The situation, how things had changed between Everett and me in the short time we'd known each other.

It sucked, this sucked, but I shouldn't want to cry because something that wasn't supposed to be anything was ending unless... I was falling in love.

I was open to putting myself out there to find companionship. I only thought as far as dating, though. I was so unprepared to fall in love again.

Fuck.

I fell in love with him.

I shouldn't have done that.

"I gotta go," he told me, pulling me out of my thoughts and back in the now.

Everett stepped into my space and pulled me close by my lower back to place a soft kiss on my forehead, then my cheek, lingering there a second longer.

He slipped past me and exited my office next, and I couldn't decide which emotion to give agency to - regret or disappointment.

"Oh my God," I exhaled, dropping my face into my hand. "Did I fuck that up?"

TWENTY-NINE

I should've called first.

Should've called at least once this week before just showing up.

I stood at the bottom of Apryl's townhouse staircase, looking up at her front door. The lights were off at every window except for the one in her bedroom.

My flight to California was the next morning. I was leaving with the lone designer keepall bag I flew into New York with. When I arrived in New York City, I came to escape a love that turned to hurt. Now I was returning to Los Angeles with a love that hurt to leave.

It seemed right, though. To not rush into something permanent with Apryl. I mean, I wanted more with her and her hesitation was a little surprising, but it was responsible. It was honest. It was right. We were right, just at the wrong time.

"This day came around so fast," my mother said. *She walked two steaming mugs of coffee over to me and sat one down in front of me. "Too fast, if you ask me. I can't believe I have less than a week left with you."*

I was still trying to process Brielle's visit a few hours prior, get my head right, as I sat at the wooden kitchen table in the Brooklyn brownstone where I grew up. Brielle was the plot twist I didn't see coming. The catalyst to turn my day upside down. Out of all the things I knew I had to do today, including visiting my mother on her free day - one week before I was to leave New York for a brief trip back to L.A. - seeing and speaking with Brielle wasn't one of them.

"A minor part of me knew your stay in New York would be temporary, but I guess deep down I wished it wouldn't be."

I stared down into my cup of coffee. "Brielle popped up at my condo today, ma."

I lifted my gaze in time to see my mother press her hand to her chest and lift her slacked jaw to shut her mouth.

"Not what I was expecting you to say," she started. "But, I've heard stranger things?"

"I didn't kick her out."

"Well, why would you kick her out?"

I dropped my head. "Because she broke my heart," I exhaled in a whisper.

"Mm-hmm," she replied lowly. "That's definitely a reason."

I looked up at her again. "I should've kicked her out, right? I shouldn't have invited her up to begin with. That was so stupid."

My mother parted her lips to speak but stopped when I said, "Because maybe if I had kicked her out, I wouldn't have agreed to give her another chance."

My mother blinked hard, then blinked a few times more. "Are you two back together?"

"Absolutely not." I ran my hand down my beard.

"Are you thinking *about getting back together?"*

"I have no intentions of taking that woman back any day, in any week, in any month, in any year."

"Then, Everett, my love, another chance for what, exactly?"

"To prove to myself, I made the right decision, breaking up with her and moving to New York for three months."

My mother sat silent.

"To prove to me that the new love I may have found here is legit, and not a rebound from Brielle."

Her brows piqued this time. "As ideal of a thought as that might sound, you can't depend on Brielle to prove that to you. That's something you should know for yourself. Nothing outside of you can prove that to you."

"I know, that's all the more reason to do things like this and to give Brielle another shot." I bit at my bottom lip. "And to consider her father's offer."

My mother straightened her back in her seat. "Her father's offer? What is he offering? You didn't tell me about an offer."

"Because it's a heavy one." I pinched the space between my eyes. "Mr. Chadwick, Brielle's dad, is offering me close to one million dollars an episode to host a show on his network. And not any show. An award-winning show. But only if." I held up a finger. "I marry his daughter."

"Goodness gracious, Everett," she exclaimed. "That is not an offer, my love. That is a bribe."

"A lucrative bribe." I dropped my head into my hands, then ran my palm down over my lips. "And I'm trying to decide what to prioritize here. Love or money."

The confused look on my mother's face hadn't changed.

"Her name is Apryl." Saying her name made my lips twitch into a smile. "The woman I think I might love. Her name is Apryl Wilde."

A matching smile appeared on my mother's face.

"She's incredible. Like..." I ran my hand down my mouth again. "The incredible that makes me want to be perfect, to make everything around us perfect, for her."

My mother parted her lips again to say something.

"And I know, perfection impedes improvement or whatever wise, clever thing you always say."

"That's it," she confirmed.

"But Apryl makes me want to strive for that, even knowing it may not be possible, but still aiming for perfection, anyway." I nodded. "I don't want to leave anything unfinished when I approach Apryl again. I don't want an ex who thinks she can pop up where I live, her father, who thinks *he can raise the price to lower my dignity, a condo in another state I may or may not return to, to live permanently. I don't even want to doubt if these feelings I have for Apryl are real or a reaction to having my heart ripped out of my chest. I need clarity. I need to know for sure that my decision to end things with Brielle and everything attached to the life I had with her was for the best. Not because of her slip up but because she wasn't supposed to be my wife from the start. I want no questions. I know the signs were always there. She was never the one for me. The signs had to be there. But I now have to recognize those signs for myself and I can only do that if I give Brielle a solid chance to prove me right. And that might sound insane—"*

"It sounds like a brilliant plan, Everett. A very mature, thorough, highly eclectic, but a grown-up plan. It's delayed gratification."

I lowered my mug of coffee from my lips and tilted my head to one side, curious. "What do you mean?"

"Delayed gratification is something I feel you've struggled with since you were a child. No patience and a desire to consume anything without pause from food and drinks to people and experiences. You never consumed with discipline. But this, *what you just detailed? Taking the time to create order out of chaos is discipline. A discipline with no immediate reward. All in exchange for something more rewarding, but at a later time. If that time will still exist. It's the unknown. It's a gamble. Putting off your heart's desire until you are prepared to receive and maintain a love you've transformed from being what you wanted to what you have. You're delaying gratification. And what you detailed is not only a plan, it's a testament of your growth." She smiled proudly. "Good for you."*

As solid of an idea as it was, the point from where I was to where I wanted to be was a distance that seemed so far. I wasn't sure if Apryl would wait while I journeyed.

Nor was I willing to ask.

I would never do that. Ask her to put herself in line with my plans.

As cliche as it sounds, if we are to be a couple, then we'll be.

I was confident I knew what I was doing with all this, but I had to bid a proper goodbye in case I was wrong about everything.

I climbed the staircase two steps at a time and rang the bell when I arrived at her door. My intentions were to tell her I was leaving in the morning, to thank her for all she had done for me and with me to help get me back in shape. All the praying I did before arriving, hoping I'd know what to say to her when she arrived at her door, went in vain.

It was the simplicity in her appearance that did it for me. Loose top bun with strands of hair sticking out everywhere. She wore a gym shirt that, due to wear and tear, had a collar that slouched off one shoulder. The faded blue varsity shorts that clung to her toned hips and thighs seemed like something she just threw on to sit around her house.

Just fine for no reason.

She said nothing when we locked eyes, though.

"Hey," I greeted her with a smile.

A smile she didn't return. Instead, she leaned on the doorframe, waiting for me to continue.

"I... uh." I swallowed hard. "My flight to L.A. is in the morning."

She tucked her lips into her mouth and rubbed her lips together, still saying nothing.

"I'll be back in a few weeks, for the community center opening or whatever, but I, um." Her silence was deafening. "I wanted to stop by to let you know."

She only blinked in response.

"I could've called," I added. "Probably should've called instead of popping up like this." I chuckled softly.

She gave me not even so much as a smirk.

"Shit, Apryl..." I inhaled a deep breath and released the air through my lips. "Baby, look, I—"

She closed the distance between us, balanced herself on the arch of her feet, never breaking eye contact. Until she fisted my tee to pull me close and onto her lips.

I exhaled all the tension in me, along with the need to talk.

Her mouth opened against mine and she searched for my tongue with hers. I walked her backwards and out of the doorway and against the nearest wall.

Her lips were pillowy and soft as always, but her kiss was more eager, more urgent. I would've had her right there at the door, but for what I had planned that night, I needed the rest right after.

So, I lifted her into my arms and carried Apryl to her room, broke our kiss long enough for us both to get undressed in silence and to reconnect beneath her sheets.

Sex that night was more than penetration. I slid inside her slowly, only thrusting once, maybe twice, until we became distracted with kissing and caressing. Her hands never left me. Running her fingers up and down my back or palming the back of my head. Grabbing my backside when she wanted me to pump a little deeper before searching for my lips with hers.

And I gave them to her. Gave her whatever she wanted that night. Hoped like hell this wouldn't be the last time we'd lie like this, but still reminding her why she should save my spot. I left my lip and fingerprints on every part of her. Sucked her nipple into my mouth and started the first series of consistent strokes when she circled her hips beneath me, letting me know she wanted more.

We spoke in heavy breaths and stuttered exhales. She whispered God's name so often in my ear she convinced me I was a god that night.

Her first warm release spilled from between her thighs, wetting the sheet beneath us and triggering something in me.

I turned her on her stomach, slid in with my knees astride her hips, and encouraged her with deep strokes to come twice more. Her walls sucked and released my erection repeatedly, challenging my resolve with each contraction. Her walls quivered and her body shivered at the feel of my lips, and I wanted to give her more.

To make her feel what I couldn't say.

As I repositioned myself to spoon her, sliding in once more from behind, depleted and defeated, no longer able to hold my release any longer, I tunneled in her slowly, found her clit with my finger and circled her ball of nerves with my fingertip.

She felt so right in my space, so perfect against me, like God made this spot for her and me. We were like puzzle pieces, uniquely made for each other. How we found each other was a testament to that. I sucked her neck while picking up speed behind her, circling her clit and pumping my hips in one targeted motion. Her walls fluttered again and her cries grew louder. My grunts and groans increased in volume and soon the sounds of our bodies meeting and us losing ourselves in the feeling of it all filled the room.

"Everett," she moaned.

"I'm right there too, baby."

She reached her hand behind herself to grab the back of my head and I gradually picked up speed to send us both rocketing toward a release simultaneously.

She dug her fingertips into my scalp and screamed.

Her orgasm was so intense it made her walls convulse, providing the sensation of her milking my dick. I shuddered behind her, thrusting my hips forward, losing control for only a moment. And I let myself go, burying my face into her hair and whispering, *I love you* against the back of her neck.

We fell asleep, still joined beneath the waist, and I didn't awake until right before daybreak. She was still asleep when I dressed to leave. Right before exiting her room, I left a kiss on her forehead. And as I stepped out of her bedroom, headed to her front door, I prayed the night before was proof enough for why she should save my spot with her.

———

"Stas," I said to my sister's back. "You ever had breakup sex?"

I sat on her island stool, finally ready to make sense of what had happened the night before with Everett. On my own, I'd spent the last few hours sorting out what had occurred. From the moment I found him at my door to when I woke the next morning to an empty bed.

Everything felt like a dream, like it had never happened. If it hadn't been for the wet spots on my bed, I probably would've convinced myself it didn't.

"Breakup sex?" She asked, back still turned to me. "Why on earth would I do such a backward ass thing like that?"

I rolled my eyes closed and pinched the space between them.

"If we're breaking up, we're breaking up," she added, turning to face me. "Keep your hands and your dick off me—"

She stopped the second she got eyes on me. Stas asked me several times since I'd been at her house if everything was okay, and I told her everything was fine. I wasn't ready to discuss what was really in my heart.

More like who.

Everett.

If my feelings for Everett weren't confusing before, last night sure did the trick.

"Aww Apryl." Her shoulders sagged. She pressed her hand to her mouth and whispered into it, "I thought you were asking a random question."

I lifted, then dropped my shoulders. "Nope. Based on a true story."

Stas let her hand fall to her side. "What happened?"

"Where to even begin?" I laughed sardonically.

"At the beginning," she whispered.

So, I caught her up. Told her everything that happened after therapy. His asking for me to move in, to stay the night and me inevitably telling him we needed a break. Then about what he told me about his ex and moving back to L.A.

"And then he shows up at my house last night and..." I ran my fingers through my hair and tugged at the strands near the middle. "I'm pissed. I am absolutely pissed he's at my door after I haven't even gotten a call from him after his last session on Monday. And then I'm livid when he tells me he's leaving in the fucking morning."

I check over my shoulder toward the living room where my niece Luna's cartoons are keeping her engaged.

"Any reasonable person would close their door in his face, right?"

I paused for a response, not exactly expecting a response.

"Not me though." I closed my eyes and dropped my head into my hands. "I walked up to him and I kissed him. Leaned my entire *being* onto him and just... kissed him. And he should've rejected me, because he's getting back with his ex—"

"He's getting back with his ex?!"

"Well, he says he isn't. He's just giving her another chance." I shook my head. "Don't ask me what that means. I do not know what it means. And I don't care at that moment because I'm with him, at my front door, in his embrace, absolutely lost there, not wanting to be anywhere else, even though I'm so confused."

Stas pulled out the stool and took a seat.

"The man is incredible in bed." I drooped my shoulders, remembering at that moment how he felt the night before. "Sex with him is always amazing, but last night, the shit was a getaway I did not want to return from."

Stas blushed. "Jesus."

"And Mary, and Joseph," I added.

She giggled and I couldn't help but to giggle myself.

"He sexed me like he didn't have a flight in the morning. Like... time wasn't a factor and I just couldn't wrap my mind around how we were breaking up - even though we were never together - but the sex felt like a prelude to something else."

"Did you guys talk?"

"No, not at all. The occasional whisper of something sexy maybe while in the act but actually discussing the situation, what we were or what we were becoming or whatever... no discussion."

"Kwamé and I broke up for like a week after college."

"Really?" I folded my arms. "You never told me that."

She fanned her hand in the air. "I didn't think the breakup was anything serious, and I figured we'd get everything sorted out, which we did. Anyway, we'd started new jobs after graduation and while I was damn near losing my mind trying to get adjusted to life after school, his ass was living his best life. Drinks with coworkers after work, phone calls with his too friendly assistant manager Trina at late hours that seemed inappropriate to me but just fine to him. The shit was ridiculous and I couldn't take it, so I told him we needed to take a damn break and he told me, let's just end it."

I arched both brows.

"He pissed me off. And I decided we were through. We'd obviously outgrown each other and us ending things would probably be for the best. But then." She blushed. "He came to pick up his stuff from my place one night and we hooked up. He apologized profusely, telling me how much he loved and missed me. We ended up mending the relationship, and he proposed a month later."

I smiled, remembering vividly him asking to marry her in front of us all.

"It wasn't breakup sex, but it sounds a lot like what you and Everett did last night."

I scoffed. "The only difference is, we didn't have a relationship and I can't tell you what we have now."

"Apryl."

"But we both experienced fucked up relationships with people who weren't shit who we thought were. We gave our hearts to them in different time zones and now our prize is the situation we're in now." I gritted my teeth. "I'm so angry he's giving this woman the time of day after what she did to him. She doesn't deserve to get him on the phone, much less get him to give her a second chance... whatever the hell this second chance is, according to him. I am just so tired."

My sister took my hand.

"I'm tired of helping to build these men back up, doing what I think is best and them going and choosing women who bring the worse out of them once they're back at their best. I'm tired of doing the right thing and getting punished for it. When is it going to be my turn?"

"It will be."

"When?" I posed, genuinely hoping she'd know. "When I'm mom's age and all I have to show for it is my children's father, who finally wants me now after the new car smell is long gone off him?"

"Don't say that."

I rolled my eyes. "I want what I want. If I can decide I want to be a millionaire by 30, why can't I decide when I want a relationship and for it to happen in *my* time? Why does my love life have the same energy as a box of jigsaw puzzles?"

The mention of love reminded me of something that happened last night. I dropped my head back between my shoulders in response.

"I think he told me he loved me last night, Stas."

"You *think*?"

I leveled my head to meet her eyes. "I can't be too sure. He said it while I was in the middle of... you know. And I black out a little when he gets me in that state."

She snickered.

"So, I don't really *know*, but I *think* that's what he said."

"And if he said that?" she started. "How would you feel about it?"

"The same way he does." I pressed my fingers to my temples.

"Oh, my goodness, Apryl." My sister slapped her hand to her mouth. "Shit."

"Yeah." I bobbed my head up and down slowly. "I know." My head was in my hand again when I said, "I didn't want a relationship, but somehow *I* fell in love with a man I'm not with. Ridiculous." I pressed my fingertips to my eyelids next. "My life is a tragic romance novel."

My sister stuck her bottom lip out in a pout and I laughed at the sight.

"Love finds you everywhere you go, Apryl. Nothing wrong with that."

"Yeah, but now I miss him. I've been missing him all week and when I finally got used to not seeing him, he pops up unexpectedly, blows my mind beyond comprehension, and leaves before we can discuss what happened or even what's *going* to happen between us."

I exhaled a sigh in defeat. "And I'm trying to decide what's worse - having my heart broken or making the wrong choice to pass up a good thing when it was right in front of me."

Stas stared at me with puppy dog eyes and I couldn't blame her for not knowing what to say to me.

"I don't know what to call this junction in Everett and my thing, but whatever it is, whatever *it* is I'm feeling? I don't love it like I love him."

THIRTY
SIX WEEKS LATER...

"Try this French toast," Brielle insisted with her mouth half full of food. "It's to die for, I swear."

We were back in New York City seated at Bella Bella, an upscale restaurant in a Manhattan high rise that overlooked the East River.

Brielle insisted she fly in with me the day before, although I didn't formally invite her. She somehow figured out how to get a first-class seat on my flight so she could arrive in New York at the same time I did. I almost fell for her, convincing me to book a room together, but my common sense prevailed.

Thank God.

My lease was up on the New York condo I rented earlier in the year, so it wasn't an option for me to stay anymore. I hadn't told Brielle where I was staying for my one-day visit in New York for the community center opening, and that was probably for the best.

She'd been working overtime to be in my face every minute of every day. Calling and texting, only to say she was thinking of me. Popping up at my Los Angeles condo at least twice upon my return. I was actually looking forward to taking this trip to New York, believing I'd leave her in Cali, but to my surprise, here she was.

It had been six weeks since I'd left New York for California. My return to California has been uneventful. Brielle tried her damndest to take up most of my time while I was back west, but I did well at keeping my distance.

Plus, my sister Eryn helped with that.

"Tell Brielle if I catch her anywhere with you while out and about," Eryn threatened. *"It's gonna be me, her, and my fists. God forgives, I don't."*

With venom and reason to hate Brielle, Eryn has simply been waiting for space and opportunity to do what she's always wanted to do to my ex.

I used the side of my sterling silver fork to cut out a piece of my egg white omelette. "I think I'm gonna stick with my eggs and toast, thanks."

"It's so boring though." Brielle lifted her glass of mimosa to her lips and gulped down a good amount. "Bella, Bella is world famous for their French toast. You'd have to be a fool not to order your own." She giggled. "But because I love you so much, I'm willing to share some of mine."

"Hmph," I huffed, reaching for my glass of grapefruit juice. "I appreciate it, but no thanks. I want to feel light when I get into that pool. It'll allow me to remain agile in the water and avoid cramping up."

The day had finally arrived for the community center opening. I needed to arrive two hours before they cut the red ribbon and let the kids in. My early arrival at the facility would afford me time to take pictures and to converse with some reporters from local stations. My agent, Daquan, was already at the community center in Brooklyn. And once I finished eating my breakfast, I'd be there as well.

"At least try it for the orange marmalade sauce." She poked her fork into a piece of French toast, swirled the brioche bread around the sticky sauce, then held the French toast inches away from my lips for me to take a bite.

Just the sweet scent of the marmalade sauce wafting up my nose made my mouth water.

Brielle and I would order the whole damn menu in our day as a couple. Run up a tab at the bar and stumble out of the restaurant hours later with full bellies and drunk out our minds before noon. It was our thing.

Our thing was just as unhealthy as the relationship was.

I still hadn't found what I was looking for from her, the reason to support my decision to cut her off completely. Obviously, the sex tapes were a damn good reason, but I had to be the thorough I told my mother I was aiming to be.

"I'm good," I reiterated. "Thanks."

She shrugged her petite shoulders and turned the fork to her mouth, sliding the French toast off her fork with her teeth. She moaned as she chewed and instantly, like a flash, her gratified sound reminded me of the sex sounds she made while having sex with those two guys on that sex tape.

I squeezed the body of the glass in my hand.

"I think you're putting too much emphasis on this community center opening," she droned, eyes down on her plate. "It's just a spot in the hood."

"It's *my* hood," I fired back as calmly as possible. "And what I'll be doing for the opening is what's important to me."

"I don't know why. What's so great about teaching kids how to swim, anyway?" she mumbled, peeking up at me and smiling sweetly.

I sneered at her.

I've told Brielle about Chase several times and how his death changed my life and was the reason I developed a love for swimming. This was the reason I've been so vocal my entire boxing career. To advocate for children who looked like me and their need to know how to swim. I'm not a professional swimmer, and yet everyone knew that about me. And I've told her that more times than I can count.

"I mean," she continued. "I think it's so cool what you're doing, charity work and everything, but maybe we should focus our time a little more on bigger things next, you know?"

"*We?*" I questioned. "That French toast got you speaking French now or something?"

She snorted. "Silly."

I took a breath to hide my annoyance because I wasn't joking in the least.

"Daddy says he thinks you'd do well securing an endorsement with a sportswear company, *and...*" She cleared her throat. "Finally accepting his offer to host Neutral Corner on his network."

I clenched my teeth. "He told you about that, huh?"

"Of course." She shrugged. "Daddy tells me everything and I tell him everything."

I pushed the tip of my tongue into my cheek and nodded slowly. I was unsure why the revelation of her knowing surprised me, or even bothered me, but it did. It felt like I was being played.

"He's made the people who work for him millionaires. Many *multi-*millionaires." She forked another piece of French toast into her mouth and moaned again, turning my stomach. "I suggest you take the offer, Everett."

"Do you, now?"

My pressure was rising, my temper brewing inside. I wanted to clear this table with a swoop of one hand and snatch that fork out of her hand, just because.

"Despite my misstep, I'd make an excellent wife."

"How so?"

"I know what to do now in bed, to satisfy you, which you've seen."

The fuck?

I clenched my jaw so tight I thought I'd shatter my back teeth.

"I'm beautiful, exciting, persuasive and best of all, I bring opportunity to earn *a lot* of money." She smiled condescendingly. "Safe to say, I'm a prize."

I stared at her for a moment. Brielle was all of those things, a catch in the eyes of many men.

But this man was seeing through her bullshit facade.

I lifted my napkin off the table to clean my mouth instead of furthering the conversation.

She'd shown her hand.

"I have to get going or I'll be late."

She nodded her understanding. "I'd tag along too, but Brooklyn isn't my scene. You have fun, though, and get plenty of pictures taken. I'll find something to do on Fifth Ave or something while you're away. And if we miss each other, I'm sure we'll catch up when you're back home in Cali."

I stood, and she stood too, walking close to me to press her lips to mine. I casually offered her my cheek and a forced smile.

"Later, handsome." She winked.

With luck, I wouldn't have to see her until I was back in L.A. and, if blessed, not even then.

THIRTY-ONE

"But auntie," my niece Luna whined beside me. "I already know how to swim."

"I know LuLu, but do your auntie a huge favor today." I crouched down to be at eye level with her. "Don't tell anyone that inside, okay?"

She rolled her pretty brown eyes. "Okay."

I kissed her forehead and stood upright again.

We stood outside of the Community Recreational Center of Brooklyn amongst a large crowd of people. Varying faces of brown complexions made up one part of the crowd while camera crews and reporters with microphones donning news station logos composed the other. News vans lined the curbs of two city blocks.

This was a big deal, and it showed.

The neighborhood of Bedford Stuyvesant was alive with activity on a hot and sunny Saturday afternoon, and I was a part of the organized chaos.

Besides the community center opening, the crowd gathered outside to gain first access to the new indoor pool and to lay eyes on the star of the event, Everett.

Just the prospect of seeing him again after six weeks of not seeing him at all made me feel a little giddy inside, but I had to keep it together.

It's amazing how I could go a lifetime without seeing or even knowing him, but a few months of his company was enough to make me mourn his absence, unable to kick the strange feeling of losing a piece of myself when he left.

That was crazy for me.

Insane.

Despite that, I didn't reject the feeling.

To get on the list of first access attendees to the community center, I used my niece's name, without the permission of my sister. I asked Stas if Luna could accompany me to the opening, though, and Stas agreed. Not that I gave Stas much of an option to say no.

"I need to borrow your kid next Saturday," I told her the week prior.

She folded her arms over her chest. "Should I stamp her forehead with the preferred return date?"

I laughed, and she did, too.

"Borrow her for what?"

I twirled a strand of hair around one finger. "The opening for the community center Everett had been training with me to prepare for his appearance is happening next Saturday."

Stas arched a brow.

"To gain access to the pool while he's there, parents have to sign their children up before a certain date. I signed Luna up for lessons and now I have to show up with her or I'll look like a creep showing up there without a kid."

"And using your six-year-old niece to reel in a man isn't creepy enough, huh?"

I pursed my lips together. "I'm not trying to reel in a man. I just need a reason to be in the same room as him."

"But Luna knows how to swim. She's been swimming since she was a toddler, so how are you going to pull off her needing lessons when she gets into the water and shows Everett she knows what to do?"

"Let's just get her in the building and I'll figure all that other stuff out."

My sister stared at me, sporting a knowing grin.

"I just need to get my fix seeing him."

"And what happens when you see him and you realize you need more than a visual fix?"

I twisted my lips to one side.

"Because this is looking a lot like a drug withdrawal right now."

I fought back my smile. "I'll handle that just like I'll handle Luna already knowing how to swim."

The complex was massive, taking up an entire city block. There were three levels in the building that consisted of kitchen facilities and two large meeting rooms - one planned to be used for their after-school program and the other for various events like community meetings, birthday parties, wedding receptions, or swap meets to benefit the community. There was a youth lounge outfitted with a mounted flatscreen, a pool table, and a black leather sectional. A room served as an indoor arcade, and a tiny suite filled with books served as the facility's library. At ground level was a massive basketball court without bleachers. Through the basketball court's doors led to the outdoor playground, one section for big kids, the other for the smaller ones. And at the far end of the building, housed in a dome-style structure with a retractable ceiling, was the pool.

We all filed in as a group into the space.

I didn't have to search far to find Everett. Although I hadn't physically seen him, I knew where in the crowd he stood. Reporters swarmed the area near the lifeguard's station. The camera flashes and clicks of their shutters lit up the pool area as photographers had to be blinding that man with an onslaught of photos.

The pool was Olympic size, spanning from one side of the area to the next. There were water level markings and floating deep end dividers. A station built for pool noodles, water wings, swim vests, and aquatic exercise dumbbells sat feet away from the pool.

The entire community center looked amazing, but the pool was the star, much like the man debuting it.

"I love it!" Luna bounced on the balls of her feet. "When can we go in? I wanna go in, auntie?"

"You can go in right now," his orotund voice echoed from up ahead of us.

I followed his voice, and our eyes slammed right into each other. But that was brief. As he closed the distance between us, my attention went south of his neck immediately. Seeing Everett was definitely a highlight in my week and thrilled me, but seeing the proof he'd stuck with the workout routine I designed specifically for him, along with the eating plan I advised him to stick to, months ago, made my heart sing.

His arms were hillier, his abs far more ripped, his shoulders stronger and broader. Even his thigh and calf muscles appeared more defined. I paused at the bulge in his swim trunks, blissfully distracted.

Everett was in the best shape ever, and I played a part in that.

It was a bittersweet realization.

I could have said anything, but, "Your abs look like a tatted Hershey's chocolate bar," was the first few words out of my mouth to him.

He slid a hand and then his arm around my waist, holding me at my lower back to pull me close enough so he could whisper in my ear, "Want a bite?"

I shivered, forcing myself to get a damn grip.

He kissed me where he whispered his invite, then gave me another kiss on the cheek.

Everyone in attendance pointed their eyes our way, and I couldn't help but to blush at the attention.

He lowered his gaze beside me. "And who do we have here?"

Luna couldn't contain her shy grin, and I couldn't blame the girl.

I smiled at her innocence. "This is my niece, Luna."

"Luna," he repeated, crouching down to meet her height. "I'm Everett, Luna." He offered his big hand for her to shake. "Nice to meet you."

She placed her tiny hand in his and giggled. I snickered in response.

"Ready to learn how to swim with the rest of the kids in here?"

"I already know how to swim."

I squeezed my eyes shut.

"Do you, now?" He asked her before looking up at me from his crouched position in front of her. He wore a sly grin on his lips.

I pointed down at him. "Shut up."

"Using your niece to gain access to a new facility?"

"No." I softened my eyes. "I used her to see you."

His smile deepened and my heart did somersaults in my chest.

I cleared my throat. "I know how important this day is to you."

His brows squished together.

"Well, maybe not the day itself."

I'm sounding so corny right now, ugh!

"I mean, teaching the children in the neighborhood where you grew up, especially after what happened to your friend when you were younger."

His smile gradually faded as he stood at his feet.

Now I sound like a fucking creep.

I scratched the back of my head, unsure how to read his change in expression.

"I remember you telling me about the accident your friend had when you were like, ten, I think?" I cleared my throat, suddenly regretting bringing it up. "You told me like once in our silly game of twenty-one questions."

His face was serious now, eyes darting along my face.

"Shit, I'm sorry," I said low, running my nail over my silky brow hairs. "I shouldn't have brought it up. It's such a happy day and I'm ruining it—"

"Nah, nah, nah." Everett removed my hand from my face and held it in his hand for only a moment. His touch made me warm all over.

His excited smile returned, brighter than before. "I'm just... I'm surprised you remembered..." He shook his head, then lifted my hand to kiss the back of my palm and said, "Thank you. That means more than you know."

I skipped a breath.

"Luna." He lowered his attention to my niece, who I honestly forgot for a moment was there.

I'm an awful aunt.

"Since you already know how to swim..." He peeked over at me and

I bit back my smile. "How about agreeing to work as my assistant today and helping me teach the class?"

Her face lit up. "Cool!"

"And you..." he said to me before turning toward the lifeguard station, where reporters gawked in our direction. Everett waved an arm and an army of journalist power walked in his direction, heading toward us. "... can spend some time answering some questions about how you got me in shape for my appearance today. There were journalists from Shape Magazine and Sports Illustrated who were asking for my fitness routine, and I told them you'd have all that info for them when they contacted you for a quote. But since you're here today, you can give it to them now. I told them everything. My struggles and how you got me together, one hundred percent your genius effort. So, don't be modest at all. Take all the credit. You'll disappoint me if you hold back."

My jaw slacked for a moment. I peeked over his shoulder and saw a group of them heading my way. "Oh my God, Everett."

He winked. "Tell me all about it later."

He and Luna went off to join a group of children and they all entered the lowest end of the pool with two lifeguards flanked on either side of Everett.

The reporters and journalists from local news, newspapers, national fitness magazines, you name it, were in my face a second later, fielding so many questions and taking even more pictures of me. And I was ready. So ready for this moment. I also said a silent thank you to myself for deciding to get really cute to see Everett. I would look great in the pictures they shot because of that decision.

If it wasn't clear before today, it was crystal clear now.

I'm in love.

Thirty-Two

"You are so spaced out," Eryn surmised behind me from her seat on the couch. "And it ain't even funny."

"I'm not spaced out." I stared at the view of downtown L.A. from my floor-to-ceiling window. "I'm thinking."

More like reminiscing...

About Apryl.

I'd been back in L.A. for four days now and thoughts of her had yet to let up.

After seeing her at the community center opening that Saturday, I would not leave New York without seeing her one last time.

She was always in my plans when I knew I was returning to New York for the opening. I told myself even if I just stopped by her place because I was in town, I'd do it.

But then she showed up at the opening. And she told me her reason for being there besides just to see me.

It took me aback.

I'd only told her about Chase once during one of our games of twenty-one questions. She asked me about a chapter in my life I wish I could rewrite and I shared the story of Chase's drowning and she remembered.

She did not know her saving that to memory, how much something so little wasn't little at all and meant so much to me.

So, I was at her front door by six that evening. In her bed ten minutes later. I had no intentions of sleeping with her during my brief return to New York. I didn't want her to think I'd reduced our relationship to only that. But then I saw her in her doorway and didn't think, didn't hesitate. I went with the first expression I felt a pull toward...

Kissing her.

And she kissed me back.

Hard.

She spoke to me fluently in body language. And I interpreted loud and clear. She wanted me. And I wanted her so much more. Couldn't form the words with my mouth, so I did with other parts of me. Expressed gratitude and reverence with each deep slow stroke I delivered, each thrust of my pelvis I executed. Even when I slid out of her for only a moment to write my name between her thighs with my tongue.

We stayed locked on lips the entire time after that. Somehow, finding our mouths to one another in every position, I twisted her.

"See?" my sister uttered, now at the window waving her hand in my face. "Spaced out."

Eryn showed up at my condo soon after I returned from the gym. I let her up, because unlike everything else in this town, Eryn's presence was the only thing that felt familiar since I'd been back.

My phone chimed in my pocket. When I lifted the device within sight, I recognized the phone number on the screen.

"Mr. Chadwick," I said when I answered.

Eryn jerked her head back. "What the hell?"

"*Shh,*" I shushed.

"Everett," he voiced on the other end of my device. "Good to hear your voice and even better to hear you're back in town."

I glanced at my sister to see her brows gathered over her eyes. She mouthed, "What the fuck?" before I walked away, leaving her at the window.

"Listen," he began, "As I informed you a few months ago, Kyle Leigh's contract is up for renewal, and I would love to see you in his chair with your name beneath Neutral Corner's logo on the air."

I slid a hand into my pocket.

"The offer still stands, Everett."

I seesawed my jaw from left to right.

I'll admit, I've been toying with taking Mr. Chadwick up on his offer. Rearranging the scenario into so many outcomes, coming up with ways where I could take the job, officially end things with Brielle, and be with Apryl, but all roads kept leading to a situation where I walked away the loser of something.

"Brielle told me about your trip back to New York together."

"Brielle and I only flew out together, Mr. Chadwick, and that was all her effort," I clarified. "We haven't seen each other since the day we had breakfast or since I've returned to L.A."

He laughed lowly. "You're still upset with her."

"Upset is the least I am with her... sir."

Done with her is more like it.

"Okay, I'll tell you what." He cleared his throat. "Let's meet up at the station next Friday at seven in the evening."

I blew out my cheeks, then released the air slowly through my lips.

"I have to fly out for a meeting in Chicago tonight and won't be back in L.A. until next week. This will give you more than enough time to make up with Brielle and to consider my offer. When I return, I'll show you around the Neutral Corner studio, give you something to visualize."

"Mr. Chadwick—"

"I've been in talks with the board and they're willing to grant that million an episode sooner than we discussed."

I brushed my hand down my mouth slowly. "And does this deal still include Brielle as the caveat?"

"The caveat?" He had the nerve to sound offended. "Last time I checked, you and my daughter were madly in love."

"*Were* being the operative word in your comprehension... sir."

"Look, Everett, she messed up, I get it," he reasoned. "But she's been remorseful about it. She regrets her actions. You've got to give her credit for that."

"*Hmph.*"

"Take the meeting with me next Friday," he insisted. "We'll sort everything out there."

"I'll have to think about it."

"You've been thinking for months now," he grumbled. "Now *please,* let's act. I'll have my assistant put you on my calendar. No confirmation is necessary. Just show up."

I shook my head.

"You're a smart man, so I know you'll make the wise choice. To walk away from an offer that's promising you one million an episode and you have not an ounce of on-air experience? Everyone would view you as insane if this ever got out," he jeered.

I didn't share his logic.

"See you then," he bid, ending the call soon after.

I stared at my phone screen after, unsure of what had happened during the last few seconds of the call.

"Mr. Chadwick? As in Brielle's *father*, Julian Chadwick?"

"Yes, Eryn."

"What the *hell* is Brielle's father doing calling you?"

"To talk business."

"What kind of business could you possibly have with that hoe's father?"

"Eryn, chill."

"Don't you dare defend Brielle *the bitch* after what she did to you!"

I sighed. I simply didn't have the energy for this. "He's offering me a job on his network. Hosting Neutral Corner."

She rolled her eyes and turned away.

"One million an episode."

Eryn whipped her head so fast in my direction I could have sworn I heard the bone behind her neck crack. "*Ex*cuse me?"

"You heard correct.

She folded her arms. "What's the catch? Because I know there has to be one if your ex's father wants you to work for him."

"That I marry Brielle."

"Nigga." She busted into a loud laugh and I closed my eyes again, shaking my head too, this time.

"I know the fuck you aren't actually considering this extortion."

"It isn't extortion," I reasoned. "Bribery, maybe."

"Tomatoes, potatoes, Everett!" she yelled. "Whatever you call the shit, I *know* you will not agree with it, right?"

I swallowed hard.

"Because I *know* my big brother ain't stupid or a damn fool."

"I mean." I lifted and held my shoulders up in the air before letting them drop. "She fucked up, but I've fucked up too in the past."

"With other women, Everett!"

"I could learn to get over it," I said with my mouth, shocked I actually voiced it out loud. "For one million an episode on a popular ass network, I could—"

"Lose your fucking dignity? Tie yourself to a woman who ain't shit and who, at least to me, has never really loved you from the start?"

She had a point.

"You're not hurting for money, Ev. You're not!" Eryn threw her hands up. "You could think of a million other ways to make one million dollars post-retirement. This ain't it, bro. It's not." She shook her head. "That's why you came back, huh?"

"I came back because my sister looked like someone stole her life savings the day I left."

"But you were happier in New York."

I stared at her.

"You found whatever you lost here over there."

I turned away from her, placing my hands on top of my head.

"If this is what you came back to Cali for? To get whored out by your ex's father? Please take your black ass back to the East Coast."

I shook my head. "Nah."

"Nah, what?"

"I'mma take the meeting with him."

"What?!" Her jaw dropped. "Did Brielle take your balls while y'all were in New York?"

"I wanna see what I can work out with him."

She wagged her finger in my face. "See, that's exactly why I broke into that bitch's place the other day."

I couldn't have heard her correctly.

"Broke into *whose* place?"

"Brielle's co-op." She placed both hands at her waist. "Well, technically, I didn't break in, per se. I let myself in with the key to her place you kept on the same key ring as the condo keys you left with me so I could let the movers from the storage facility into your condo when you had to fly back to New York for the community center opening. Since Brielle flew there with you, I thought it would be the perfect time to stop by her co-op."

My lips were in the position to help me question my sister, but I was very much in shock.

"Her building didn't have a doorman. That surprised me. What surprised me more was discovering you kept her key in your key ring and she didn't change her locks. I was only trying my luck. I didn't think I'd actually get into her place."

I slacked my jaw. "Are you crazy?"

"I can be." She bounced her head up and down. "Yup. I let myself in and went into her closet, the same place you said you found her box of DVDs the last time. I was prepared to spend all day looking for those DVDs in her place, but the dummy put the box right back in the same spot behind her shoes. So... I took like five of the DVDs, as insurance."

I gasped. "Yo, you buggin'."

"No, I don't play about you, is what I am." She clapped her hands with each word spoken. "Let her daddy know I got her DVDs and will leak them shits if he doesn't give you the job without tying her ass into the deal."

"Eryn, I ain't doing that."

"Why not?"

"'Cause I ain't trying to get arrested for extortion, that's why."

She sucked her teeth. "But he's extorting you."

"What that man is doing isn't extortion, Eryn, but this shit you're suggesting is. Are you kidding me?! It ain't worth it." I pointed at her. "And you're gonna put those DVDs back."

"I'm not."

I inhaled a deep breath to stay calm. "Where are they?"

"Since I see you don't want to use 'em." She shrugged a shoulder. "None of your business."

"You know what? Fuck it." I backed away from her. "I can't deal with this right now. You didn't just tell me that. I'm going to pretend you didn't tell me that."

"Smart."

"You just be careful and do nothing stupid with them."

She batted her lashes and warned, "And they better not give me a reason to. Cause I'll do something real stupid with them."

I grunted. "You're so frustrating sometimes."

"And so are you," she sniped back. "You should go back to New York."

I bit at my bottom lip. "Nah."

But deep down, I knew Eryn was right.

Eryn was right in more ways than she knew.

Because I was here and Apryl was there. It was only day four, and I was missing her terribly.

"I'm good here," I said, hoping that maybe by tomorrow, my feelings would catch up to my words.

Thirty-Three

APRYL

I created a visor by pressing the side of my hand against my forehead to see through the sun's glare. I just had to get a good look at them. Giggling and necking.

Didn't even know necking was an actual thing until I watched it being done for nearly an hour right in front of me.

I sat beside my sister, her baby boy, Raphael - who she cradled in her arms - and Stas's husband, Kwamé. We were all relaxing on a park picnic table in Brooklyn's Prospect Park, and I was dividing my attention between my niece playing with a child she met in the park and those two lovebirds necking across from me.

And no, it wasn't my sister and her husband finding it hard to keep their hands off each other on this hot August day. It wasn't a teenage couple, either.

It was my parents.

We were barbecuing, taking full advantage of the summer heat on a Sunday afternoon.

I wanted to spend the day in bed comfortably watching anything from the 90s I've watched over a thousand times, but my sister begged me to come out and play.

She didn't tell me our parents would join us.

"Y'all ain't tired yet?" I asked across from them. "Kissing and doing all this stuff? It ain't too hot for all that?"

My parents glanced at me, then looked at each other before bursting into a fit of giggles.

"I'm still not quite over that infamous day, so if you two could calm down, I'd appreciate it."

The hate was strong in me, and everybody at the table knew it.

I pinched the bridge of my nose, annoyed with myself.

Ever since the last night I spent with Everett, hours after the community center opening, I've been in a mood.

Cynical, fussy, borderline bitch. That's why I stayed to myself most days. I went to work and returned home. I would spend an hour and a half every night pounding my feet in some Nikes running against the belt of my treadmill as I turned the machine up at high speed. To stop thinking about him, I needed to feel like my heart would explode in my chest.

"Babygirl, you all right?" My dad asked, draping an arm over my mother's shoulder.

Any person in their right mind would be so thrilled to see this picture in living color. My parents were back together, and they looked so in love. But I was too much of a sourpuss to celebrate.

"Yeah, girl." My sister nudged me with her shoulder. "Why are you being so blah today?"

I glanced her way, then rolled my eyes away, refocusing on my parents. "Why now?"

I had everyone's attention with that one question.

"You've married every other woman but her."

Kwamé cleared his throat, and my sister shifted in her seat, repositioning Raphael to rest his tiny head over her shoulder. I noted the discomfort, but ignored it.

"It's been over thirty years since you two had any semblance of a relationship."

"Apryl," Stas said through her teeth. "Can you *please* chill?"

"Why are you now interested in pursuing anything with my mom? And why now?"

The table fell silent.

My mother smiled and simply looked over at my dad, and he did the same for her.

"Well, damn, Babygirl," my father started. "You're acting like you're not my daughter, too."

Everyone laughed. He even got a slight chuckle out of me.

"I guess now is as good a time to address this, huh?" he stated, looking at each of us.

I blinked, waiting for him to continue.

"Okay." He removed his arm from my mom's shoulder and straightened his back in his seat. "When your mother and I met and fell in love, we fell hard and at an inopportune time. I was building my career as a guitarist playing in bands, booking gigs at bars and lounges, and your mother had just started her career as an EMS dispatcher. We misaligned our time. When she was awake, I was asleep. We only had time to do one thing, which was to get physical. Very little talking, which meant we weren't getting to know each other on a meaningful level. We were both young when we started dating. And right when we were getting the hang of the dating thing, we got pregnant with your sister."

"We?" my mother challenged. "I don't remember you carrying and pushing out that enormous head over there."

Everyone laughed some more. I snickered to myself.

"Your sister's arrival emphasized the obvious flaws and lacks in your mother and my relationship. And instead of addressing it, we — well, really I — walked on eggshells, refusing to get to the root of our issues, creating more problems on top of the other ones that existed by not dealing with any of them. Now, your mother has always been clear on what she's always wanted out of a relationship." He glanced her way. "She wanted a partnership. One that defied gender roles before you kids made it a thing in this generation, and someone who truly supported her. I knew nothing about any of that. To me, a man was a man, and a woman was a woman. She did what her mama did and what women before her did as well, and I had to do the same as my father and the men before him. I didn't consider the changing times and how much of a burden I was creating with my thinking. Until it was too late."

He sighed.

"Your mother ended things when you two kids were still young. She put my ass out, and I always believed it was her who was the problem. So, I went looking for her replacement. Women I believed fit who I wanted to be. The vision of what a man was. And that vision attracted women who suited that vision. The relationships kept failing because the vision they suited wasn't really my vision, so I wasn't happy and neither were they. This resulted in three failed marriages. With each iteration - before I came to my realization that society's vision of a man wasn't what I wanted to uphold - I thought about trying again with your mother. I did. But she had demands I couldn't meet. Demands I thought I couldn't meet, so I went and settled down. Three times. Which brings me to the point of answering your question of why now?"

He looked at her again and wrapped an arm around her. "Because I grew tired of trying to find your mama in other women. She just wasn't there, and trust me, I looked."

I twisted my mouth to one side to bite the inside of my lip.

"I used to tell myself there wasn't anything special about your mother. That I could find any woman and mold her to what I wanted her to be, no problem. Take the good parts I loved about your mother. Encouraging it in other women while not having to deal with the extra work your mother required. So I formed relationships with women who reminded me of your mother on the surface, but I quickly learned they didn't have the values or qualities inside that attracted me to your mother. That's because people are the sum of their experiences and how they respond to them. And the thing that made me love your mama wasn't something I could duplicate in other women, because those qualities were unique to her and her alone. They were based on what she'd gone through and those experiences, both good and bad, shaping her to be the person I'd fallen in love with."

"That's a long way of saying I am the original," my mother joked. "And the others were photocopies."

My father chuckled. "Your mother has always been clear on what she wanted, a partner. She never wavered on that, never compromised or skimped on what she knew she deserved, so I knew I had to come correct to truly be happy and for her to give me another shot. So I took my ass to a cooking class to learn how to help in her kitchen, joined a group of brothers to form an accountability group to work on being a better listener, communicator and to learn how to take accountability for my mistakes to be a more empathetic spouse. I put the effort forth to be a decent individual, which was all she was asking me to do. All that my ex-wives expected from me also, but that I was too selfish to provide."

I smiled.

"And you're right, Camille. You are the original," he told my mother. "Can't replicate or duplicate because the results of such actions would be disappointing, always. Camille, I have loved you from the moment I saw you step into Sam's Jazz Hall in Harlem, wearing daisy dukes, sipping hard lemonade through a red and white straw."

We all found that comical, including my mother.

"I have looked and looked, and looked again and have determined there is no one else like you. You are the win. You are the prize."

"I know that's right!" My sister shouted beside me, making me giggle.

"I want to stop wasting my damn time and finally live out the rest of my days in your love and embrace, where I belong." He stood from his seat and kicked one leg at a time over the picnic table's bench, got down on one knee behind my mother.

"Oh my God," I whispered.

She twisted in her seat to sit facing him.

"I was planning to do this when we were back at your house later, but now is the right time, out here, under this beautiful sun, our daughters and our son-in-law bearing witness." He took her hand again while dipping his other hand into his pant pocket. My father pulled out a black velvet ring box, flipping open the lid to reveal an emerald-shaped diamond ring tucked in the slit.

My sister and I gasped.

"Camille Loretta Frasier," he started, "Will you do me the honor of being my wife?"

"Absolutely, Martin," she told him and we were all up on our feet celebrating. Families from neighboring tables joined in on the celebration, clapping, hooting, and hollering.

I couldn't help but to hold back tears at the moment, watching my parents hug and kiss.

The change in our day instantly brightened my mood and sparked a new flame in my resolve.

My mother had never wavered. She also never obsessed over being attached to any man. She lived her life, loved herself, and gave herself all the things she expected others to give her.

As I watched my father handle her like precious china, I realized what my mother's secret to attracting exactly what she wanted was. She didn't expect people to know how to love her. My mother showed them how to love her, whether or not they wanted to see it. She gave them no choice. By pouring into herself, knowing what she wanted, never going back on what she expected for herself, which was the best. She set the standard, the bar, at which a man would need to meet her for him to have the privilege of being with her. It's brave to know what you want and to refuse to settle for less than your expectations, and I wanted to be that through and through.

I wanted the very best, and I had to know in my heart of hearts I would get it no matter what.

So, as I watched on as my mother gracefully accepted her happily ever after, I decided I'd finally listen to her and take her advice.

I'd get into a relationship... with myself, and I'd see what life would match that energy with.

"You all right?" Stas asked when all the excitement was slowly settling down.

I smiled proudly while staring ahead at my parents, who were now engaged. "I've never been better."

Thirty-Four

EVERETT

"I have spent the entire day looking at wedding dresses," Brielle gushed. She lifted the rim of her champagne glass to her lips. "My assistant gave me a stack of wedding magazines this morning. Apparently, daddy insisted she plant them in my office for inspiration."

I inhaled a deep breath and focused my attention elsewhere, anywhere, but there at our table.

We were in DTLA Grill in downtown L.A. having an early dinner, something Brielle suggested we do. I had a meeting with her father at one of his studios in an hour, specifically the one where they recorded his Emmy-winning sports show, Neutral Corner.

I've entertained the idea of taking Mr. Chadwick up on his offer for days, weeks, months even, and I still wasn't sure what I wanted to do. My bodily reaction to it was repulsion. The offer left me disgusted after considering it for this long. Eryn was right, agreeing to take him up on his offer, which included marrying his daughter, was like me whoring myself out.

But one million an episode was a lot of money and a gig as a host was an excellent career move post-retirement. With the promise of fifteen episodes a season, I would be so set. Possibly for life.

I sighed, raising my glass of water to my lips to sip.

"Gosh, are you a fish now?" Brielle asked across from me, pouring herself yet another glass of champagne. Her third since we arrived. "Ever since you've been back, whenever we go out, you drink water."

"I don't care to drink as much as I did before."

"You don't care to eat either," she admonished. "This place has the best steak in the city and you order a Cobb salad?!" Brielle said, as if I was eating a plate of shit. "What the hell happened to you in New York?"

The mention of New York brought back a rush of memories all centered on Apryl. Since my return to California, I haven't spoken to her. I called her once and got no answer, and I didn't bother calling again. I figured it was probably for the best. I didn't quite know what decision I would make about this deal with Brielle's father and I didn't want to go back and forth with Apryl, settling with one part of her when I knew we could be so much more.

She deserved more than that.

She deserved certainty.

"Here, have a bite." Brielle held her fork inches from my lips. On the prongs was a piece of steak, A1 sauce dripping off the seared flesh and landing on the crisp white tablecloth, staining it.

My stomach growled.

My mouth watered.

I swallowed hard to contain it all.

"Come on, babe," she whined, bringing the fork closer. "Take a bite for me."

"I'm not interested, Brielle," I told her. "I told you all about the food program I'm on that I want to stick with."

"And you look better than you've ever looked. A little bite of steak will not change that."

"But that one bite will only open my appetite for more and I'm not trying to go down that road right now, especially from where I'm coming from. Maybe at some point I can have a little something, but not soon. Not until I get my head right." I shook my head. "It's more than how I look, anyway. I feel fucking amazing. I have the energy of a twenty-year-old and the stamina to match it. My thoughts are clearer. I feel good."

"Oh, Everett, take a damn bite!" She rolled her eyes. "You're acting like I'm asking you to swallow a cyanide pill."

"I wish you would ask me to do that," I sniped back. "Because I'd much rather swallow poison than to continue sitting here with you."

She jerked her head back.

I scoffed a laugh. "I've really been going through my mind, honestly considering taking your father up on his offer. But the thought of marrying a woman who doesn't respect me helps make money look only like paper at this point."

She dropped her fork on her plate, the silver clashing with the ceramic loudly.

"You are *not* good for me, Brielle."

"Oh, please."

"You don't listen to anything I say. I tell you I don't want something. You push for me to have it."

"Everett, stop it," she spat. "We have gone out to restaurants many times and ordered off the entire menu while washing it down with every color of liquor. You and I have always done us and had a great time together. We're in love."

"We're in love? How can that be when, throughout our entire relationship, you were fucking other people behind my back?"

"Hey!" she hissed, checking around us to make sure we didn't have other ears in our conversation. "I told you my reason behind that, and I've apologized profusely."

"Oh, for sure. Your ass was so remorseful you went on an island getaway with some guy shortly after I ended things with you."

Her jaw dropped.

"Yeah." I forced a smile. "I saw the photo before you deleted it."

She fixed her lips to say something but stopped herself.

"Is he on one of those DVDs?" I quizzed. "Or, what? Daddy didn't like him, huh? Realized how close he was to marrying off his only daughter until she fucked things up for herself, so what did he do? Offer me an obscene amount of money in the guise of me working for him, but really, that fool's bribing me to marry you. 'Cause he knows you ain't shit."

"Fuck you." She tossed her hair off her shoulder. "You don't have a clue what you're talking about."

"He's been bailing your ass out of everything since you were a child, but he can't bail you out of this, Brielle."

I licked my lips slowly, a genuine smile appearing on them shortly after. "I met someone while I was out in New York."

She sat up in her seat. "What?"

"A real good woman," I disclosed. "So good, I didn't want to start anything serious with her when I knew I had baggage I needed to sort through. You're that baggage. And I'm just about done sorting through you."

Brielle looked away, gathering her breath to remain calm, I assume.

"As fucked up as it was what you did," I continued. "You were one of the best things to happen to me, Bri."

I leaned forward in my seat to take her hand. "Though you weren't honest in our relationship, I was. You were the first relationship I put an effort into being faithful and being honest. I didn't think I was capable of it in this town. I knew how to turn on the discipline for fights, but I couldn't figure out how to do it in my relationships. You taught me I could, so thank you."

She closed her hand around mine. "Then let's work it out. You've made mistakes, so you know how this goes. I've learned from mine. Let's just repair it."

I shook my head. "You don't love me, though."

"Of course I do—"

"No, you love the idea of us." I pulled my hand free. "Brielle, I'm getting up there in age. I can't eat and drink like we used to. After the breakup." I shook my head. "I was consuming shit at a rate that was far from normal. Drinking every day, eating my feelings to the point of getting sick in public and still going back for more crap. It took a toll on me. And I told you that when we linked back up in June, and you refused to see how serious shit got for me. How can you want to be with me forever if you're helping me do things to cut my life short? I've told you several times I've changed my diet and you've been trying to make me break my commitment to myself ever since. You don't support me, you don't respect me, you don't love me, Brielle, so let's stop forcing whatever this has become between you and me."

Her chest rose and fell hard before she slammed a fist on the table.

That garnered us some attention.

"You will *never* find the deal my father and I are offering you anywhere else in this town."

"I'm sorry?" I tilted my head to one side. "Your father and... *you*?"

"I told daddy to call you with the offer. He didn't think you could carry an entire show on your own. He thought you were just a boxer from the ghetto who got lucky and figured out how to hold on to most of your money instead of filing for bankruptcy." She held her hand out in front of herself, checking her nails. "You shocked him by having something to show for your career besides an undefeated title. He just couldn't understand how you could avoid squandering your money and not living beyond your means like the rest of your kind. Your financial intelligence impressed him. But I see there's still time to be a fuckup." She shrugged. "Because you sure are showing signs right now that you won't last post-retirement."

I scoffed.

"Everett, sweetheart, you were worried about what you'd do after retirement to maintain your lifestyle, and I thought up something for you. You're very welcome. I've been telling daddy to up the offer since the start."

"The fuck?!"

"I want children and I want marriage. I'm thirty-two. I've had my fun, and I was this close to getting everything I wanted until you found those *fucking* DVDs." She threw her hands up as if she were giving up on the thought. "I knew I should've thrown them out."

She ran her hand through her hair. "Neither one of us is perfect. You need me and I need you. We've already invested five years in this thing between us. Let's patch things up and get on with it."

"I just told you I met someone else while in New York."

"Yeah, well." She folded her arms. "Safe to say, Everett, whoever she is? She could never and will never be me."

"And that's one thing I love the *very* most about her."

Brielle pressed her hand to her chest and slacked her jaw. She blinked repeatedly while sitting back in her seat.

I dipped my hand into my back pocket to retrieve my wallet, singling out a one-hundred-dollar bill, placing the bill on the table. Brielle could afford to buy this entire restaurant with her father's money, but I refused for her to pay for my meal... however meager it was that night.

"Tell your father thanks, but no thanks." I pushed my chair back. "I don't want to *get on with it* with you, not after getting a preview of what real love feels like from someone who means it."

I was up and out of my seat and beside hers, leaning over just enough to leave a kiss on her forehead. "I wish you well, Brielle, I sincerely do. But do not call me ever again and tell your simp ass daddy the same."

I made my way out of that restaurant feeling lighter after shedding the last weight I had to lose - the dead weight known as my ex.

———

"I'm headed back to New York..." I announced. "For good this time."

My sister stopped hiking up the dirt-dusted path and turned to face me.

I insisted she go hiking with me on a Sunday morning right before daybreak.

We were in Ascot Hills Park, the view of the sun rising to our far left. Trees everywhere. Us being there reminded me a lot of the park Apryl and I visited in Upstate New York. Just the memories of our time out there made me all warm inside.

"Moving to New York for good," Eryn repeated. "Figuratively and literally, huh?"

I nodded. "Definitely a double entendre."

She began walking again and so did I. The temperature outside was perfect, something I'd miss the most about sunny California when I left for New York yet again.

"The end of one chapter and the start of the other," she said low. "I am *so* happy you left Brielle in the last chapter."

"*Hmph.*"

"I wish I could've seen her face when you left her sitting in that restaurant." She smiled with glee. "I would've paid to see that, actually."

When I retold the story of what happened that evening, about how I ended things with Brielle officially, literally, an hour before I was to meet with her father, my sister was so happy. She was happier than I've ever seen her before.

"I'm so proud," she exulted that day. "I could cry."

Eryn inhaled a deep breath, placing a hand at her waist against the waistband of her designer leggings. "When I told you I wanted to leave New York all those years ago, you told me you'd leave with me, no questions asked. New York was more your home than it was mine and you left. Just to be here with me."

"More my home? Eryn." I laughed. "You grew up in New York like I did. That's *our* home."

She shoved me. "You know what I mean."

Eryn stretched her arms out at her sides, dropping her head back between her shoulders. "I'm a Cali girl through and through. Have been from the time I was born. Before I even knew what it was like to live out here. I breathe this place."

And she was right. Carefree, beach bum, optimistic life of the party, and a complete fitness freak. Los Angeles was in Eryn's DNA. California culture suited my sister more than New York ever did and probably ever will.

"Go on back to dirty ass, cold ass, boring ass New York." She stared out in front of us. "You somehow could find your happiness over there in that concrete jungle of broken dreams. I sure can't relate."

I kicked a pebble on the ground up ahead of us.

"You gonna link back up with your new boo out there?"

I chuckled.

"Oh, you thought I didn't realize the love bug bit you and part of the reason you are trying to transplant back east is for some pussy?"

I paused my steps to glare at her.

She cackled, slapping her hand to her mouth. "I'm only kidding. I know it's more than pussy."

"Can you please stop saying pussy?"

Eryn laughed even harder, and I shook my head in response.

"She's a good one?"

"She's a great one," I answered without missing a beat.

"Y'all left things on good terms?"

I inhaled a deep breath and exhaled through my mouth, shrugging at it. "Good enough, I guess."

With Brielle finally out of the picture and with no way back in after our last interaction, I could look at my situation with a clearer focus. I wanted to be with Apryl, but I wasn't sure how fixed in her decision she was about not having a relationship these days.

I had a plan for that. Because if there was anything I wanted with Apryl, it was to be with her and nothing less.

"When do you leave? And what are you going to do with your condo this time?"

"Put it up for sale," I said with certainty. "And I'm out by next Friday. The place I rented for the summer is available again. I have already wired the down payment to the company that manages the property to buy it. I'll pay the balance when I get there."

"Damn," Eryn whispered, eyes down on the ground beneath us. "You got it all figured out."

"You gonna be all right out here all by yourself?"

"Oh, of course." She looked up at me with her big babydoll eyes. "I got Cali and Cali got me."

"You ain't alone either." I peeked down at her. "Simeon is only a few hours away—"

"Now, why would you bring that nigga's name up?" She screwed up her face. "It's a beautiful damn day. Why would you do that?"

I scratched the back of my head. "I'm reminding you he's right there in Oakland..."

"His ass could be right here in front of me, and I still wouldn't speak to him."

I sucked my teeth. "Dammit Eryn, will you tell me what happened between y'all?"

She pointed up ahead of us at the incline in our path. "I'll race you up that hill."

"Are you trying to avoid the question right now?"

She rolled her head around her neck and shook out her arms. "On your mark..."

"Eryn—"

"Go!" she shouted and took off. She yelled over her shoulder, "The loser pays for lunch."

I bust up laughing, taking off behind her.

Even though she drove me crazy every day in this city, I sure was going to miss my sister and all her bullshit.

THIRTY-FIVE

APRYL

"Your shrimp Fra Diavolo should be out shortly," my server informed as she grabbed the plate of crumbs that originally held my fried zucchini and marinara dipping sauce appetizer. "Let me know if there is anything else I can get for you before then."

I smiled up at her. "I'm all good for now, thank you."

She smiled back and walked off, leaving me alone again at my table.

The restaurant Al Dente was just off Fifth Avenue and bigger than I remembered. I'd dined there with Everett when I was trying to pile on the weight. We have actually come here a few times since it was only blocks away from my townhouse.

Maybe that's why I remembered it being smaller. I was in good company back then when he and I visited and probably didn't survey the space much while we were there. With only me at the white cloth table, with a bouquet lying on its side to my right, a wineglass of water over my plate, and a single long-stem candle directly in front of me, the restaurant might as well be as big as a block in Times Square.

Every so often I would scan the surrounding faces, reading them for judgement. I already told myself I shouldn't care what anyone says, because I was doing this for myself.

Taking myself out on a date.

I raised my glass of water to my lips to sip.

Tonight was the night I'd been preparing myself for. I started the evening with a spiritual bath to clear my mind and to get in the mood. Filled my tub with fresh water, Epsom salt, Florida water, and essential oils before decorating the water with herbs and petals from red roses. I'd had the two dozen long-stem roses delivered to my townhouse, along with a card that I had sent with a handwritten personal message from myself.

Love finds me in all ways, and this is one way it has found me.

I used the petals from one of the dozen roses to fill my bath water and I read the message repeatedly as I soaked in the tub, doing my very best to get out of my head, thinking the whole thing was silly, and to get in alignment with my words so I could unapologetically love on me.

I was delivering on my promise to myself. To love me the way I would love to be loved. And I started that journey by giving myself the best that I got. A luxurious bath, a personal gift of roses, and a night dining at one of my new favorite restaurants.

To say I wasn't uncomfortable would be a lie. I'd never eaten out alone, so the feeling of sitting at a table on my lonesome honestly felt incomplete.

Which is why I started my plan of dating myself this way. Rip the bandage off and to do the one thing I've dreaded, but that would be something nice for me.

My sister Stas was excited for me, telling me she thought this was much better than any dating app. And my mother was kind enough to give me tips and suggestions to make the most of my plan. I listened this time. My mother was the reason I did this, having seen her do it many times in the past. I used to judge her for it, but it was quite clear she was on to something.

For the night, I got all dolled up. Sprayed on some expensive perfume, dusted on light makeup, slipped into a form fitting candy apple red dress.

I peeked down at my outfit and smiled to myself, kind of wanting to laugh a little for being so over the top.

I needed this, though, to feel special for no one but myself. For my gaze to be paramount and to matter the very most. The feeling I got from it was different, but it felt so right.

I glanced up again to survey the restaurant, taking in the surrounding faces. When I saw a familiar one headed my way, I did a double take.

I almost didn't recognize him. Consistently dressed down in athletic leisure clothes, he traded in his workout clothes for something sexy and casual.

I blinked repeatedly as my heart rate increased at the sight of him closing the distance between us.

He wore a blue linen dress shirt with the top two buttons undone beneath his neck, sleeves rolled up over his elbows, exposing the ink on both his forearms. Everett paired his shirt with black knit denim shorts and white low-top lace-up sneakers. He swaggered to the table with so much big dick energy; I had to cross my legs to calm the purring happening between them. Because just the sight of him made me feel he was inside of me already.

We kept our eyes on each other the whole time until he arrived in front of me.

"Well, this is a surprise," I said when he stood at the back of the empty chair across from me.

"Maybe for you." Everett smirked. "But I knew you'd be here." He gestured at the chair in front of me. "Mind if I crash your date?"

"Oh, my God, will you please?" is what I wanted to say.

I kept my composure together enough to tell him instead, "I don't know. It's going well."

He licked his lips, tipped his head to one side, then arched his brow, waiting for me to oblige. So I gestured at the seat, giving him the permission he didn't need because, my God, he looked good.

His cologne filled my space as he joined my table. I inhaled the air deeply to get a nose full of the decadent fragrance, moaning to myself.

"Saw your photo update in your social stories of a plate of deep-fried zucchini strips and marinara sauce and knew exactly where you were. Thought I'd drop by to say, hey."

"Stalking me?" I teased.

"*Mm-hmm.*" He nodded.

I looked away to hide my blushing. "I didn't know you were in New York." I turned to face him again. "I thought you were in L.A. giving your cheating ex the chance she didn't deserve."

"Well, now you know where I'm at and who I'm really with, someone who's much more deserving."

"Is that so?"

"Very much so." He nodded. "And I wasn't giving her another chance to be with me. I was giving her a chance to prove me wrong when I realized she *wasn't* the woman for me. It's always been you, though, from the moment we locked eyes from across the gym. And that's the truth." Everett's eyes fell on my bouquet of roses and he made an impressed expression using the corners of his lips. "These are nice."

"I think so."

I couldn't take my eyes off him. Didn't want to. I was doing somersaults inside, seeing him sit in front of me, backflips after hearing him say what he said a moment ago so easily and casual, like speaking from the heart was second nature to him. I was about to lose my cool for sure.

He's here and I can't believe it.

"So." He pinched his chin. "I know you said your date is going well, but how well is it going? I'm trying to see how I can compete."

"Compete?" I smiled. "Well, for one, my date lives in the greatest city on the planet, so I don't have to worry about dealing with anything long distance."

"All right," he confirmed with a nod. "So far so good, 'cause I'm back in New York permanently. Closed the deal and purchased my condo I rented for the summer. I own it now."

My eyes widened, and I had to blink them free.

"What?" I whispered next.

"What else you got?"

I could jump out of my seat and into his lap. That's how ecstatic I was inside. I couldn't recover.

"You still on the 'no relationship' thing?" He asked next. "Is your date understanding of that?"

Oh, I liked this Everett. He was coming in hot!

I fought back my smile. "They're very understanding of it."

"Okay." He rubbed his hands together. "And they're willing to give you everything you like?"

"Every single thing."

"Cool, because I am more than prepared to do so too, so what's up?"

Why fight my smile after that?

"You are?"

"Hell yeah."

My server returned to my table with my plate of shrimp Fra Diavolo.

"Oh!" she shrilled. "I didn't realize you had someone join you. Would you like me to bring an extra plate?"

I raised my gaze to her. "I'm likely about to take this to go." I glanced over at Everett. "I'm just waiting for a good reason."

He chuckled sexily and my server grinned at us.

"I'll be around," she assured, blushing. "Just let me know."

My attention returned to Everett.

He leaned forward in his seat. "Let me keep it real with you."

"Please do."

"I want a relationship with you and I know you've been a little uneasy about having one, so tell me what I gotta do to ease your worries."

"How do you want me to answer that?"

"Truthfully." His top lip curled when he smiled. "Meet me halfway. Tell me what you want, tell me what you like. Tell me all the things you need to feel comfortable in a relationship with me and I'll do it. That's my word."

I twisted my lips to one side to keep from smiling harder than before.

"Look, Apryl." He licked his lips, scooting forward more on his chair. "I know the thought of a relationship makes you uncomfortable. It does for me too. We had really terrible experiences that had the power to break us, but it didn't. So, I'm confident we got this. I have genuine feelings for you and I have every intention of doing right by you. That's gotta be a start, right?"

The only thing keeping me from believing I wasn't dreaming was that I remembered everything before that moment.

"So check it - you know how kids have build-a-bear." He tapped his broad chest twice. "I'm offering you build-a-bae."

I hollered a laugh.

"Build me, baby." He winked. "And let's do this."

I stroked my chin with my manicured nails. "Where do we even start with *this*?"

"Let's start with this date you got set up here." He leaned back in his seat and gestured at the roses. "You like getting flowers?"

"I do."

"You like getting them just because or on special occasions."

"Both."

"All right then, bet." He pointed around himself. "This restaurant, is this your scene?"

"I prefer the memories made here with my present company more than anything else."

"Good to know," he acknowledged.

Everett and I stayed in the restaurant for almost an hour and a half. Our conversation flowed effortlessly, like always, and time didn't seem to exist in his company. I ended up eating my meal there in the restaurant, not because Everett didn't give me a good reason to go. He gave me a better reason to stay. He ordered his own plate of pasta and continued his quest to get to know my likes and dislikes. When it was time for a change of scenery, he offered to cover the bill. Only if I approved, of course. So I did, and we were on our way.

The walk to my townhouse was pleasant, filled with playful banter and light conversation.

Night had fallen in the city. The streetlamps, crosswalk signals, lights gleaming through storefront windows, and, of course, the various traffic lights directing traffic lit up the night.

"I don't want to ask this," I confessed, at the bottom of my townhouse's staircase, "but if I don't, I won't be able to stop thinking about it."

"Ask me anything," he asserted.

"Was it worth it? You going back to your ex? Was it worth it?"

"First, let's get something clear. I didn't go back to her," he insisted. "I gave her a chance, an opportunity to show me she learned from her mistake. The same opportunity I wanted when I used to cheat that I didn't deserve, and she proved not to deserve one either." Everett turned me by my shoulders to face him. "Second, and most important to note, my decision to go back to L.A. had more to do with me finally closing doors on an old life than with me choosing my ex over you. Which I would never do. She doesn't compare, therefore she isn't competition and I'm not saying that just to say it, I'm saying it because it's true. And let that be the last time we discuss her, because none of this is about her."

I couldn't argue with that.

He circled his arm around my waist to bring me close. "You didn't want a relationship."

"I didn't."

"And neither did I, So I thought. Turns out the relationship was what I wanted. I just didn't want the gambling feeling of being the only one all in while completely unaware that the other person had one foot out."

"See, I understand that feeling completely," I admitted. "It doesn't feel good to be the only one all in. I've been there, and I believed that the imbalance in my relationship with my ex was normal. Worse than that, I accepted it, thinking what I had with my ex was the best I could do."

I pressed a hand to his chest.

"Sometimes we don't know how good things can be when we settle." I ran a finger down the side of his jaw. "I'm really glad we didn't settle."

Everett glanced up the stairs at my front door, then lowered his view to me again.

"Oh." I smirked. "Are you trying to tell me something?"

"I mean..." He tightened his grip around my waist, bringing me even closer. So close, I could feel a little something that wasn't so little pressed against me. "I kind of am trying to tell *you* something."

I giggled, lifting my arms to twine around the back of his neck. "Would you *like* to come up?"

"Would *you like* for me to come up?"

I couldn't help but to smile at how his teeth gleamed when he smiled. The man was handsome, with royal motherland features and a heart I had every intention of doing right by.

Dating myself was fun... for the few hours it lasted.

But Everett was back, and I would not miss the opportunity again to have him all to myself.

"For over an hour, we've been talking all about what I like."

"'Cause it's your world, baby," he insisted. "I'm just—"

I pressed my hand to his lips to get him to stop speaking. "Another thing I like, out of all the many things we discussed tonight, is a man who lets his woman please him just as much as he pleases her."

"*Mmmm*, his woman," he repeated. "I love how that sounds right there."

He held me tighter.

"Is that what you are to me?" He bit his bottom lip. "Are you my woman now, Apryl?"

"Yes," I asserted. "Because I'd be a fool not to be. But you should do your due diligence and come upstairs to confirm if that's really true. Because actions are louder than words."

"Oh, I should *come* upstairs."

I balanced myself on the arches of my sandals to press my lips to his neck. He dropped his head back between his shoulders, giving me full access.

I whispered, "I think we should *both come* upstairs."

We couldn't make it past the front door before we were all over each other. The short time away from one another made us practically savages. Things moved fast after I unlocked my house door. Everett guided me to the closest wall when we passed beneath the arching entry-way. Held my face in his hands as he pressed his lips to mine and his body against me. Kissing led to touching, and that touching soon got intense. By the time we were pulling and tugging at our clothing, I knew we wouldn't make it to the bedroom. We changed positions on the wall. Did it enough times we'd somehow ended up at the entrance of my living room. We mutually decided without words that this would be our spot for the night.

Everett and I moaned on each other's lips. Fussed with buttons and zippers until we resorted to ripping. The popped-off buttons on Everett's shirt made soft thuds as they fell to the floor, when I pulled the shirt apart.

He peeked down at himself, then looked up at me with a smirk. "I just got that shirt tailored."

I ran my hand up his torso, my fingertips trailing over firm muscle and taut, inked skin. "It was a great shirt, but I like what's underneath better."

I shoved him back until he fell against my couch, and I quickly straddled him in his seated position.

He hiked up my dress, and I lifted it high enough for him to do it.

His lips were on my neck when I slung my head back between my shoulders. He hardened against me, and that realization excited me. I leveled my head to get him in my sight to watch him as I rolled my hips atop him.

"*Mmm,*" he groaned, lowering his gaze to watch my movements.

A sexy smile spread across his lips when he met his eyes with mine again. Bit his bottom lip when he reached between us. While moving the seat of my panties to the side, I wiggled free from his hold, shaking my head.

He groaned, reaching for me.

"Woman, if you don't get over here," he warned.

I didn't listen. Instead, I kept lowering myself until I was on my knees in front of him.

He chortled low as I undid the belt, then the button on his denim shorts and, without another word spoken, pulled out his dick and flicked my tongue over the thick head slowly.

He moaned, dropping his head back against my couch's neck.

Everett did that a lot when he wasn't watching me bob up and down the length of him. He bit at his bottom lip when he wasn't doing either of the above and mumbled expletives whenever I covered him to the root with my mouth.

After a few minutes, he slid me off him, using his grip around my hair.

"You in trouble with me," was the last thing he said before lifting me off my knees and planting me on the couch where he originally sat.

The process of him ridding me of my underwear and him burying his face between my legs was a quick one, but not the action of him licking me to a trembling orgasm.

That couch saw a lot that night, me face down on it, ass high in the air and Everett behind me pummeling me repeatedly to a secret rhythm only he could hear.

We colored the night in moans and groans loud enough to bounce off my walls and ceilings. We left parts of ourselves, mostly me, on my seat cushion.

My living room floor was the landing spot for something soft and sensual. Exhausted but still yearning for each other, Everett and I slowed it down. He delivered strokes so slow and so deep; I swore I could feel what he felt. I did not know how long we'd been at it, but I was quite content that I wouldn't have to count the minutes, fearing when it would end because it wouldn't.

He was mine, and I was his, and that fact turned me on more.

My walls between my thighs quivered, the sensation growing more intense each time he thrusted forward. But on the fifth thrust, I was arching my back, angling my hips, and moaning as a warming sensation swallowed me whole, blissfully losing my breath in a room with plenty of air to breathe.

On an exhale, "God, I love you," spilled from my lips as my warm wet release pushed through between us. Everett increased the pace, grabbing both of my wrists and using them to raise my arms above my head to hold them down together with one hand.

He grunted with each thrust. Pressed his lips against mine and inhaled my exhales as we caught our breaths together.

"I love you too," he whispered to me.

I opened my eyes to his, smiled, and whispered, "You better."

"Physical touch," Apryl whispered softly in my ear. She lingered in my space, kissing me from my ear to my neck, while her fingers slid beneath the sheets. She made her intentions clear when she wrapped her warm hand around my relaxed dick.

I closed my eyes slowly and groaned.

"You do not know how in trouble you are with me now that I'm equipped with that kind of knowledge about you, Everett."

I smiled, eyes still closed, wanting to get lost in this moment indefinitely. "Be careful now."

She giggled, burying her face in my neck.

The following day, we lazed in bed all up under each other with no plans to change that.

When we returned from the restaurant the night before, we sexed in her living room and eventually made our way up to her room, only to get an hour's worth of sleep, if that. Our plan to head up to Apryl's room for rest was useless the second we got into bed together. I was all over her before her head could hit her pillow.

"If I recall the results clearly," I started. "Physical touch is right up there under acts of service for you, too."

I ran a finger down the cleavage of her ass, palming a cheek soon after. She shivered and squirmed under my touch.

I smirked, pleased with her reaction. "So it seems like we're never getting off this bed."

When she and I awoke from our short slumber, we freshened up and ordered a breakfast of egg white village omelettes, wheat toast, and a small side of garden salad from a local restaurant and bakery. We took a few bites until satisfied, then we were all over each other once again.

With no limitations between us, no unfinished business, or reason to hesitate on acting on what we both wanted to do, we'd been damn near inseparable for almost twenty-four hours and I loved it.

She hiked her knee beneath the sheets and moved in closer than before, sending a rush of blood to my dick.

Yeah, we're never leaving this bed, for real.

"I know physical touch is not all about sexual acts and all, but..." Apryl ran her finger up my chest, making my dick jump again. "I really like that's important to you. There's some security in knowing you like what I like and I can deliver on something you enjoy, because I enjoy it too."

We'd taken a love language quiz when we could come up for air. All in the spirit of being our best to one another. It did not surprise me to see acts of service and physical touch as being her most significant love languages. Receiving confirmation reassured me.

"I agree," I said, lowering my lips to kiss her forehead, holding her closer to me. "The test helped confirm a lot of things I already knew about you, and I'm beyond thrilled about putting all that shit into practice."

She looked up at me. "Oh, yeah?"

"Hell yeah."

I turned over, moving her beneath me. She spread her legs wide under me, making room for me to take my place.

Apryl stared up at me with the softest eyes I'd ever seen her have with me. This side of her was so beautiful, vulnerable. Only a fool would want to take advantage and not preserve it. I had every intention and goal to do exactly that. To preserve her light. I'd make her a believer in genuine love with her as my woman.

"Did you mean what you said last night?"

I wouldn't even front like I didn't know what she was talking about.

"When you said—"

"That I loved you too?" I finished. "I meant every word."

A bashful smile brightened her eyes more than before.

"When you said it..." I grabbed the side of one of her legs so I could get in position. "Did you mean it? Or were you just coming really hard?"

"Absolutely." She reached between us to take hold of me. "Every word, even when I was coming really hard."

I chuckled.

She rubbed the head of my erection against her opening, closing her eyes and whining her hips, running wetness up and down her clit. I let her use me like a toy because the shit was so sexy to watch her do.

"Twenty-one questions."

She cracked up. "Right now?!"

"*Mm-hmm.*" I nodded. "Right now."

Apryl rolled her eyes playfully. "Shoot."

I lowered myself onto my forearms and moved in close to her ear. "Since we're talking about relationships and everything... if you could only choose one goal for us, what we should aim for? What would it be?"

She opened her eyes and looked up at me, then said, "For us to be happy."

I shook my head. "That's too plain, baby." I pecked her once.

"Aht, aht! Don't judge my goal."

"I'm not judging." I smirked. "I want you to go deeper with it. Think harder. I'm counting on you here. You're good at goals and planning. Give us a good one, and I'll make it happen."

"*Mmm.*" She slowly circled her hips beneath me. "I got some place you can go hard and real deep, to make something happen."

I sighed. "Apryl."

She let out a breathy laugh and stopped whining her hips.

"Okay, fine. *Hmmm...*" She twisted her lips to one side, attention focused up on her ceiling, eyes moving along the surface as if the answers were up there. When she locked eyes with me again, she smiled and pledged, "I want the goal to be for us to make each other feel like we're the lucky ones in our relationship. Meaning, I feel like I'm the luckiest one, and you feel you're the luckiest one, too. I'd like that to be the only argument between us; who got it better?"

I chuckled.

"I know that's unrealistic. I'm sure we'll butt heads on other stuff, but I sure would like to strive for that kind of love, you know?" She nodded. "Yeah. If I had to choose one goal, one aim. It would be that."

"Then, done." I bit my bottom lip. "And I can definitely do that."

She arched her brows. "Yeah?"

Life is fascinating like that. Love was the last thing I wanted when I left California for New York. I wanted to escape my problems, clear my head, and to get back right and to do right by myself. I got all those things, and an incredible woman who does not know how much I'm going to spoil her.

Whoever said it, said it right. Not all storms come to ruin things. Most storms come to clear the path for something new, something better.

My heartbreak in Cali was also proof that some gifts come wrapped in sandpaper.

"For sure. Baby, consider that goal met, because I already feel real lucky." I angled myself and tunneled my way in between Apryl's wet lips, feeling as her walls held me tight. I told her, "And I'mma make damn sure you always feel luckier than me. Promise."

Epilogue
Saturday, May 26, 2022
– 9 months later...

APRYL

I couldn't stop blushing.

Standing at the altar, eyes locked on Everett, completely distracted by him as he stared back at me.

My sister nudged me on my back. "Can you focus, please?"

The pastor ahead of us was in the middle of talking about the patience of love and how there was no control over when love happens... or that love happens in God's time.

Honestly, I don't know what the man was saying because someone distracted me.

That damn Everett.

He winked at me, and I balled my lips to keep from smiling.

"I'm gonna pop you on the back of your head," Stas stage whispered behind me, adjusting the strap on my white dress. "Pay attention or you're going to miss your part."

I leaned a little to my right to whisper back at her, "Everett looks good in white, huh?"

She snickered to herself. "You are so damn sprung. Oh my God."

The sun was high and bright, but far from harsh. The day was a perfect one for a wedding on the beach. We were worried that morning when we saw gray clouds move in over the sun. Panicked when a few drops of rain threatened to ruin a day we all have been waiting for. Me more than anyone, if you let me tell it.

Coney Island beach was the ideal setting to witness a love that was always meant to be from the very start.

My eyes wandered to Everett again, a brilliant white smile taking up residence on his lips. He watched on, hanging onto the pastor's every word like I planned to quiz him on it later.

That was a good sign.

It was a great one.

"The rings?" I heard the pastor beckon. I couldn't be too sure, though. Distracted, remember?

Everett moved his attention off the pastor and onto me.

"The rings?" The pastor repeated.

Stas nudged me again, this time harder. "Girl, the rings."

"Oh... oh!" I transferred the bouquet onto one hand and stepped forward to hand my mother's wedding band to my father and my father's band to my mother.

Their wedding party was small. Just me and Stas as maid of honor and matron of honor for our mom, respectively. Stas and I also stood as a man of honor and the best man for our dad. I handled the rings.

Our parents smiled back at me, accepting their rings. My mother pressed her palm to the side of my face. "Thank you, baby."

"You're welcome, mama."

They were really doing it. My parents were finally tying the knot in this lifetime and the day was absolutely perfect.

"Told you to pay attention," Stas whispered behind me. "So damn distracted, flirting with your boyfriend like y'all ain't together."

I tightened my lips to keep my laugh to myself, knowing she was telling the truth.

It had only been nine months, but it was the best nine months ever. Everett and I went full force into our relationship. He was great, almost too great. I found myself most days fighting off negative thoughts that our relationship was too good to be true. But he said something to me one night when I expressed to him the silly worry of waking up from this dream that is our life together and realizing none of this was real.

"If life has a way of removing someone you never thought you'd lose, life can replace that someone with a person better. A person you never dreamt you could fall in love with." He ran his finger down the fullest part of my lips while we laid in bed. "Both must exist."

He was amazing like that. I had never thought I could trust a person as much as I do Everett. With him, I set no limits to my imagination. I wanted it all with him, which still shocked the shit out of me, but it was true. Marriage, children, a life together until our last breaths. *I* actually wanted that permanent stuff with a man now.

But not any man, a good one. Who looked damn good in white.

While we all wore white at my mother's wedding, she and my father wore red to signify their true love for each other. One that was everlasting.

Those two were my inspiration, the reason I considered giving love another try.

"By the powers vested in me by the State of New York," the pastor arrived. "I now pronounce you husband and wife. Sir," he addressed my father, "you may kiss your bride."

My parents were married. Never thought I'd say those words, see it ever happen in front of me, in a million years. Life was interesting like that.

Everett not only improved my outlook on life, he helped skyrocket my career. The interviews I took part in during the community center opening last summer garnered me new recognition. I went from training only celebrities to athletes damn near begging to be placed on the waitlist to be trained by me. When mentioned in online articles and magazines, I was no longer referred to as Chloe Rae's personal trainer. I was just a celebrity trainer named Apryl Wilde.

Everett helped do that, sending over those reporters that day. Something so simple freed me from the shackles of my past. On top of giving me a love I never imagined, he was immensely supportive and a great boyfriend.

"Now you know you look fine," he said in my ear as he approached me from behind, wrapping his arms around me.

We'd moved the wedding festivities to a designated part of the beach where we planned to have the reception. The setup was really simple. A long line of tables, the chairs beneath them. The wedding planners positioned the setup in such a way for us to view the water.

String lights hung over us, held up by metal postings. Two tents, one for the DJ booth and another for the caterers to work from. It was simple, but beautiful.

I placed my arms on his and leaned my head back against his chest. "You were distracting."

He buried his nose in my neck. "You're the distracting one."

"I can see who'll be next," Stas surmised, approaching us from behind. "You had my sister completely smitten at that altar. I sure hope you can take a hint."

I widened my eyes at her.

Everett snorted. "No pressure, right?"

She laughed, and I did too.

Talks of marriage weren't something we'd had. He and I were enjoying our time together, but I would be lying if I said I wouldn't love to walk down an aisle, headed toward him.

"Anyway," Stas went on, gesturing toward the setup. "I came this way to let you two know it's time to start the dinner."

"Thanks, Stas." I turned in Everett's arms to wrap my arms around the back of his neck. "You look *so* good in white."

He wrapped his arms around my waist. "And you look so good, period."

I tossed my head back in an irrepressible laugh. When I leveled my head to meet my eyes with his, he looked at me with a softness in his eyes that melted me all over.

"What?" I asked softly.

He licked his lips slowly and said, "I can't help but to think that the only thing missing at this moment is a ring."

My face warmed instantly, and a delighted smile pulled at my lips a second later. I could burst from the rush of feelings that one statement caused. I had to lean my head against his chest to keep from exploding from pure elation.

He chuckled softly at my reaction. "I love getting you like this."

Everett reduced me to a blushing, giddy mess in his presence these days. Sometimes I annoyed myself, but I gave myself permission to feel. To be loved beyond measure. To enjoy the decadence of being in love, like really in love, with a man who was worthy of receiving love from me and who gave it just the same.

He'd been delivering on his promise because I for sure felt like I was the luckier one in our relationship.

I'd never felt so full with a man, so fulfilled, and not wanting anything until Everett. My relationship before him starved me of the basic amenities of a relationship that I honestly believed would've been privileges had I received them. Everett made things so sweet with him. I barely thought of my ex and his betrayal. I was sincerely happy, satisfied, and fed. Everett was a dream in a fantasy, one I never wanted to wake up from.

"Come on." I took his hand. "Let's eat."

EVERETT

Apryl and I burst through my condo's door together, my lips on her neck and her hand holding my head in place.

I could ravish her right now.

Her parents' wedding had awakened something in me I couldn't make sense of.

Well, I could make sense of it. Marriage had been on my mind after heartbreak. It was only a year ago that I wanted to ask my ex, Brielle, to marry me before the monkey wrench that was the sex tapes changed all that.

Brielle tried one last time to make a reappearance into my life during the autumn of last year. She got wind of Apryl and my relationship and threatened to go to the press with the lie that Apryl had broken up

Brielle and my engagement. Eryn threatened Brielle with the sex tapes she had in her possession after I told Eryn about Brielle's threat. I totally didn't condone Eryn's threat. I wasn't mad at it either. It seemed to work, because I hadn't heard from Brielle since.

"I'm in the mood for a snack," Apryl announced, peeling herself away from me and headed to my fridge.

I rounded the island, headed her way. "I'm in the mood for some of you."

She turned and pressed her back to my fridge. "Well, now, I'm always in the mood for some of you."

Apryl and I divided our time between my condo and her townhouse. I never broached the subject of moving in with each other again, although it would make more sense to do it now than it made sense to do it then, but I had bigger plans.

Her parents' wedding had lit a flame under my desire to make this thing between Apryl and I a forever thing, and I knew she was as ready as I was.

My tablet on my island chimed with a video call. Apryl and I glanced that way to see it was Eryn calling.

"Why hello there," Eryn greeted, smiling on screen when I pressed the green circle. "I see you got your boo in the house. Hey Apryl, girl."

"Hey girl."

Unlike with Brielle, Apryl and Eryn clicked instantly. When I flew back to L.A. with Apryl, and they met in person, it was as if they'd been friends forever. It was a new feeling watching my sister get along perfectly with my girlfriend after years of there being tension with my ex.

"How was the wedding?" Eryn queried.

"Perfect," Apryl answered.

"It was real dope," I added. "On Coney Island beach, beneath the sunset."

"It was everything," Apryl reported, locking eyes with me.

"*Ugh*!" Eryn whined. "I miss Coney Island."

"Girl, you need to come out here and see how good it looks now," Apryl insisted. "The improvements they've made all around will amaze you."

"Uh-uh," Eryn voiced, wagging her finger. "If you ever see me in New York, know things are not good with me."

Apryl snorted a laugh, and I shook my head.

"So damn dramatic," I mumbled.

"Anyway." Eryn rolled her eyes. "I was just calling to check in on my big brother and his boo thang."

Apryl giggled.

"Oh!" Eryn pointed. "Ev, do you have an opening date for that boxing gym in Brooklyn? Remember, I still got you on the press release."

"I'm aiming for autumn," I answered. "We gutted the place. Equipment comes next month. It looks good."

"Great!"

The boxing gym was Apryl's idea, a genius one. I'd been thinking of ways to capitalize on my retirement and she suggested opening a boxing gym for all ages. Obviously, Gleason's was the standard in New York, but I wanted something small and accessible to the same kids who frequented the community center. Since being back in New York, I volunteered my time at the center, teaching the kids how to swim. Every other day, there was press in the building. It was good for getting the center's name out there and attracting new donors. It was good for the community, and it kept me busy.

Things were *genuinely* good.

Especially with Apryl.

I walked up to her and wrapped my arms around her from behind, burying my nose in her neck.

She shivered then attempted to bump me away, likely because my sister could see us, but I definitely didn't care. This woman of mine made me want to express love in every way for her, regardless of who was watching.

Apryl was my sanctuary. An endless vacation. My new home. She was actually good to my mind, body, and soul. I couldn't get enough of her even if I tried. Bliss felt good to me.

"Oop," Eryn teased. "Did the wedding start something? Am I going to go back on my word on flying into New York to attend to something special?"

Apryl pointed at the screen. "Don't even start, Eryn."

Eryn covered her mouth to hold back a laugh.

Apryl leaned her head back and against me to peek up at me from in front of me. "We're just enjoying life together, no pressure. If things move in that direction, I wouldn't oppose it, though."

"I definitely wouldn't oppose it either," I confirmed. "In fact, I can't wait."

"Aww, a couple who are not here for the games," Eryn acknowledged. "I see y'all!"

"To answer your question, though, baby sis? I think the wedding started something."

Apryl turned her head to glance at me over her shoulder.

"Because for real, for real, if I had a ring this evening, we would've had a totally different conversation tonight." I turned Apryl to face me, wrapping my arms around her waist to hold her close. "Because I can't think of anything better than to be married to you, baby."

"Awww," she whispered. "Everett."

I lowered my lips to hers and she welcomed me in, parting her lips to meet my tongue, drawing me into a kiss so deep. For a few seconds, I forgot all about the video call with Eryn.

"Y'all make a girl want a relationship," Eryn said from the tablet behind us. "But I ain't crazy."

Apryl and I broke our kiss to laugh against each other's lips.

I glanced over Apryl's shoulder and reminded Eryn, "Simeon is still one phone call away."

Apryl tilted her head to one side. "Who's Simeon?"

"A nobody," Eryn shouted. "See, now, Everett, why would you ruin a perfectly good video call by mentioning that nigga's name?"

"I'm just saying."

"And now I'm saying goodbye. I can't stand your ass sometimes, *ugh*." Eryn sucked her teeth. "Later Apryl. Go to hell, Everett."

Apryl gasped, then snorted.

"Love you, too, Eryn."

"Yeah, whatever," she responded before ending the video call.

"Whoever Simeon is, you weren't supposed to bring him up," Apryl remarked.

"And you aren't supposed to still have clothes on right now, but…" I shrugged a shoulder. "Here we are doing what we're not supposed to be doing."

She laughed.

I ran my hands down her sides, then dug my fingers into her hips. "Apryl, I'm hungry, baby."

"Me too," she echoed. "Let me get this snack going—"

"Uh-uh." I placed my hands on the island on either side of her, caging her in. "See, what I want to *eat* isn't on any shelf in that fridge."

A sly grin slowly appeared on her lips. "Is that right?"

"Very much so."

I grabbed her by the waist, lifting her off her feet and placed her on the island's counter behind her.

She licked her lips when I walked between her legs, sliding my hands up her thighs and under her white dress in search of her panties side wings.

"You got me on this?"

She nodded. "I always got you."

"Is what I want ready for me to eat?"

"*Mm-hmm.*" Apryl moaned. "It's hot and ready."

"Good." I grabbed a stool and pulled it directly in front of her. I took my seat and slid her closer to me, spreading her legs wide opened. "Then feed me, baby."

The End.

FINAL WORDS

Dear reader,

Thank you for reading *Gluttony*! I hope it was as much of an enjoyment reading Apryl and Everett's story as it was for me creating it. This slow burn romance was one of the first in my catalog. When I started writing Everett and Apryl's story, I realized quickly that it would take time to get this couple together. I worried if readers would be patient enough to see their romance blossom organically. And as hard as I tried to make this story my usual brief novella length, it just would not compromise!

Gluttony was so much more than just a book about a "sinner" who liked to eat lol. It was about seeing heartbreak and emotional turmoil from a male perspective, living vicariously through a woman, discovering intimacy through acceptance, highlighting the importance of love starting with the individual and that energy having no choice but to be matched accordingly. It was also about love not needing to be forced and allowing it to just happen in its time.

Gluttony is a layered tale, and I hope I could bring forth all the elements for you to have seen that for yourself. The journey to "the end" wasn't an easy one, but I sure enjoyed it from start to finish.

If you liked these two, you'll get to read a little more about them in the future.

Eryn, Everett's sister, is one of the main characters in *Sloth*.

Sloth will be book seven and the last book in the series. All the series characters will make appearances, even characters from the *Forbidden* series in *Sloth*. It'll be like a series family reunion and I can't wait to attend.

The worlds are colliding, and everything will come full circle!

There were a few characters from my previously published stories that made appearances or were mentioned in *Gluttony*. Check the Character Cameo list to see which ones appear in other books or have books of their own.

Thank you again for reading.

If this is your first book by me, I'd like to think you're a Brookelynite now. So, welcome!

To my readers who have been reading from a book or several books ago, I thank you so much for your continued support. This one was different, right? Longer than my usual ones, too, huh? But thank you for still sticking with it and with me to the end! As of this writing, we're going on 8-years of this. 8-years! So many lessons, so many "The Ends," and I'm still growing. They don't call it a journey for nothing.

As always, I'll see you at the end of the next book!

Love,

Brookelyn.

BOOK CLUB QUESTIONS

1. What was your first impression of Everett Peters?

2. What was your first impression of Apryl Wilde?

3. What did you think about Apryl and Everett's first actual interaction at Everett's training session?

4. What did you think about Apryl and Everett's dynamic?

5. What are your thoughts on both of their parents?

6. Did you agree with Apryl's choice to go with Everett for therapy?

7. Did you agree with Everett's decision to return to California?

7. What did you like most about Everett? What did you like the least about him?

8. What did you like most about Apryl? What did you like the least about her?

9. How do you feel about the ending?

10. Who grew the most between Apryl and Everett in this book?

CHARACTER CAMEOS

In the order they appeared or were mentioned in Gluttony...

Chloe Rae

- Mr & Mrs Jones
- Home for Christmas
- Meant to Be

Liz Peters

- Last Comes Love
- Ebb & Flow
- Meant to Be
- Lust
- Envy

Meki & Cadence Knight

- Unsilent Knight
- A Love Deferred

Simeon King

- So This is Love

Eva and Jaleel Gordon

- Home for Christmas
- Home Before Midnight

ABOUT BROOKELYN MOSLEY

Brookelyn wrote her first short story when she was a sophomore in high school. Back then she discovered how using her experience as a teen living in Brooklyn to create romantic shorts was just as exciting to her as retail shopping and going on dates. After starting her first semester of college two years later, Brookelyn's creative writing became more of a hobby and something to escape the stress of midterms and finals.

Now in her 30s as a freelance writer, penning short stories and novellas is her everything. While her experience with writing has evolved for the better, her undying love for creating fiction remains unchanged. Brookelyn's focus is on creating contemporary women's fiction with characters based in urban settings. Her stories chronicle the emotional journeys and erotic experiences of women today through her characters and the scenarios they're thrown into.

The motivation behind her brand of writing has a lot to do with what she discovered storytelling provided for her - an escape. Her goal with her work is to create characters and urban worlds that offer a great escape for fiction readers looking for a break from the daily grind of adulting and who prefer to relax with good books and short stories. When she's not freelance copywriting, doing yoga, or showing her husband, son, and daughter lots of love, she can be found sitting at her computer desk, with her legs folded, and a cup of coffee (or a glass of wine) at arm's reach as she types or edits her latest short or novella.

Connect With Me Online!

Twitter: @brookelynmosley
Facebook: http://facebook.com/brookelynmosley

Facebook Reading Group: Brookelynites Book Lounge
Instagram: @Brookelynmosley
My Website: BrookelynMosley.com (*FREE short stories!*)
My Readers Website: BKBookLounge.com
My Mailing List: BK Insiders (*Join via BrookelynMosley.com and receive 4 complimentary shorts in your email inbox when you sign up as a new subscriber!*)

www.ingramcontent.com/pod-product-compliance
Lightning Source LLC
Chambersburg PA
CBHW030922300726
48970CB00001B/276